Readers love the Bonfires series by Amy Lane

Bonfires

"...I just adored this story. There is such warmth and love here between these men that you can't help but want everything good for them."

—Joyfully Jay

"I can't recommend this enough. It was sweet, exciting, romantic, touching, and also really, really relevant and thought provoking."

—Open Skye Book Reviews

"This is Amy Lane at her finest."

—Paranormal Romance Guild

Crocus

"It's everything I expect and want from an Amy Lane novel, plus the chance to revisit a favorite couple and their family. Very much recommended."

—Jessie G Books

"Crocus is a story of family and love and acceptance. It's about overcoming obstacles and keeping what's important at the forefront. It's about love. So, so much love."

—Diverse Reader

"Amy Lane does real life like no other author I know. Gritty, messy and hectic does not begin to describe the life these two men live with their kids."

—The Novel Approach

By Amy Lane

An Amy Lane Christmas
Behind the Curtain
Bewitched by Bella's Brother
Bolt-hole
Christmas Kitsch
Christmas with Danny Fit
Clear Water
Do-over
Food for Thought
Freckles
Gambling Men
Going Up
Hammer & Air
Homebird
If I Must
Immortal
It's Not Shakespeare
Late for Christmas
Left on St. Truth-be-Well
The Locker Room
Mourning Heaven
Phonebook
Puppy, Car, and Snow
Racing for the Sun • Hiding the Moon
Raising the Stakes
Regret Me Not
Shiny!
Shirt
Sidecar
Slow Pitch
String Boys
A Solid Core of Alpha
Three Fates
Truth in the Dark
Turkey in the Snow
The Twelve Kittens of Christmas
Under the Rushes
Weirdos
Wishing on a Blue Star

BENEATH THE STAIN
Beneath the Stain • Paint It Black

BONFIRES
Bonfires • Crocus • Sunset

CANDY MAN
Candy Man • Bitter Taffy
Lollipop • Tart and Sweet

COVERT
Under Cover

DREAMSPUN BEYOND
HEDGE WITCHES LONELY
HEARTS CLUB
Shortbread and Shadows
Portals and Puppy Dogs
Pentacles and Pelting Plants
Heartbeats in a Haunted House

Published by Dreamspinner Press
www.dreamspinnerpress.com

By Amy Lane (cont)

DREAMSPUN DESIRES
THE MANNIES
The Virgin Manny
Manny Get Your Guy
Stand by Your Manny
A Fool and His Manny
SEARCH AND RESCUE
Warm Heart
Silent Heart
Safe Heart
Hidden Heart

FAMILIAR LOVE
Familiar Angel • Familiar Demon

FISH OUT OF WATER
Fish Out of Water
Red Fish, Dead Fish
A Few Good Fish • Hiding the Moon
Fish on a Bicycle • School of Fish
Fish in a Barrel

FLOPHOUSE
Shades of Henry • Constantly Cotton
Sean's Sunshine

GRANBY KNITTING
The Winter Courtship Rituals of
Fur-Bearing Critters
How to Raise an Honest Rabbit
Knitter in His Natural Habitat
Blackbird Knitting in a Bunny's Lair
Weddings, Christmas, and Such
The Granby Knitting Menagerie
Anthology

JOHNNIES
Chase in Shadow • Dex in Blue
Ethan in Gold • Black John
Bobby Green • Super Sock Man

KEEPING PROMISE ROCK
Keeping Promise Rock
Making Promises
Living Promises • Forever Promised

LONG CON ADVENTURES
The Mastermind • The Muscle
The Driver • The Suit
The Tech • The Face Man

LUCK MECHANICS
The Rising Tide • A Salt Bitter Sea

TALKER
Talker • Talker's Redemption
Talker's Graduation
The Talker Collection Anthology

WINTER BALL
Winter Ball • Summer Lessons
Fall Through Spring

Published by Dreamspinner Press
www.dreamspinnerpress.com

By Amy Lane (cont)

Published by DSP Publications

ALL THAT HEAVEN WILL ALLOW
All the Rules of Heaven

GREEN'S HILL
The Green's Hill Novellas

LITTLE GODDESS
Vulnerable
Wounded, Vol. 1 • Wounded, Vol. 2
Bound, Vol. 1 • Bound, Vol. 2
Rampant, Vol. 1 • Rampant, Vol. 2
Quickening, Vol. 1 • Quickening, Vol. 2
Green's Hill Werewolves, Vol. 1
Green's Hill Werewolves, Vol. 2

Published by Harmony Ink Press

BITTER MOON SAGA
Triane's Son Rising
Triane's Son Learning
Triane's Son Fighting
Triane's Son Reigning

Published by Dreamspinner Press
www.dreamspinnerpress.com

SUNSET

AMY LANE

Published by
DREAMSPINNER PRESS

8219 Woodville Hwy #1245
Woodville, FL 32362 USA
www.dreamspinnerpress.com

Trade Paperback ISBN: 978-1-64108-728-5
Digital ISBN: 978-1-64108-727-8
Trade Paperback published February 2024
v. 1.0

Printed in the United States of America
∞
This paper meets the requirements of
ANSI/NISO Z39.48-1992 (Permanence of Paper).

To Mate, who has been my sunset for more than thirty-four years. And to the kids, who save us from premature irrelevancy every day.

Author's Note

ALL FICTION. Also: My oldest son—age 30—is getting married this year. It's a huge to-do, and everybody's worried about seating charts and RSVPs and what to wear and corking fees and… *mind explodes.* My husband and I had the equivalent of a kegger in the park, with food my family and I prepped the evening before the wedding. I know more about weddings and what they're *supposed* to be now, but I also know more about what comes after. What comes after is more important. Wedding vows are promises. The *marriage* is how to keep the promise. I always hesitate to write weddings because, hopefully, the lover's vows have already been seen, and the relationship has shown us how the people will keep those vows. Larx and Aaron know this. My son… well, I'm pretty sure he and his lovely wife will learn. It's a hard lesson for everybody. Don't expect Larx and Aaron to go away just because this is *their* last book. I fully expect them to be involved in the lives of many other couples to come.

Graduations and Other Disasters

"AND SO," boomed the slender, midsized man at the podium, "without any further ado, I present to you your graduating class. May God have mercy on our souls."

And with that benediction, Principal Larkin, second love of Aaron George's life and his son's science teacher, started the round of applause that signaled the end of the ceremony.

With a burst of laughter and whoops of joy, the hundred and fifty students sweltering on the football field stood up and flung their caps in the air, while their parents guzzled water in the red-dust-scented morning and cheered.

Aaron George, deputy sheriff of Colton County, California, turned to his very pregnant stepdaughter and said, "Are you going to have that baby *now*?"

Olivia gave a strained cackle and accepted the cool cloth that her husband had been keeping in the ice chest at his feet while she balanced the shade umbrella that Elton—aka Wombat Willie, as the family had named him—held over her head. "Sorry, Aaron, no can do. I may be done, but I'm afraid our little tadpole is still cooking. Besides, don't you have kids to go greet?"

Aaron grinned and scanned the football field, where his son Kirby and his and Larx's foster-son-of-sorts, Kellan, were currently getting patted on the back and hugged and adored by their fellow classmates in the chaos that followed most graduations, even small ones in tiny towns in the shadow of the tall pines of the Sierra Mountains.

Over the milling black-robed graduates, a reedy, sprightly figure in a white sundress trimmed in blue bounced up and down, madly waving a matching straw bonnet in an attempt to get Aaron's attention.

"And there's your sister now," he said dryly, just before the loudspeaker crackled and Larx said, "Christi-lu-lu-belle, they see you. You can stop doing that now."

Christiana turned toward the graduation podium in honest surprise. “Daddy!” she cried, and Larx, looking legitimately horrified, put his hand over his mouth.

Aaron’s own laughter boomed over the field, and Larx looked at his youngest with honest contrition. “Sorry, honey,” he murmured into the microphone before his best friend—and vice principal—turned the damned thing off. From Aaron’s position across the football field, he could see Yoshi Nakamoto—black-bird’s-nest hair water combed neatly for once, broad face shaved clean, soft, compact body as neatly dressed as Larx in a suit he probably brought out once a year—bitching at Larx in an epic harangue that no student would ever hear but that teachers would be repeating on memory loop for *years*.

Olivia’s low laughter resonated in Aaron’s stomach. Larx’s oldest daughter was lovely—she had her father’s dark hair and eyes a slightly lighter shade of hazel than Larx’s, and Larx’s sharp chin and cheekbones with a rounded, feminine flare—but the thing she had that was most like her father was her sharp, sometimes caustic sense of humor.

Her year—dominated by an unplanned pregnancy and a bitter, daunting battle with bipolar depression—hadn’t been an easy one, but the fact that she pulled herself out here to her stepbrothers’ graduation said loads about her character.

Olivia had it in her to be very much like the man who had just blessed an entire graduating class with a funny, heartfelt speech and a comic gaffe all in the same ceremony.

And she’d made the effort, which Aaron couldn’t claim for his own two daughters, a fact he was determined not to dwell on in the bright June sunshine.

“Go, Aaron,” Olivia told him, giving him a little shove on the shoulder. “I know you’re dying to hug Kirby. I saw Maureen sneak in at the last moment—I’ll be here when everyone’s ready to go.”

And like her father, Olivia was a master of what Aaron was starting to think of as “big group engineering.” Who needed a ride? A hug? Dinner? How do we get that ride, that hug, that dinner, to those people who need it most, all at the same time? Who is best suited to *give* the ride? The hug? The dinner? How do we help all the people around us balance in harmony and not deplete ourselves of our own strength until we have no more spoons to give? Olivia’s living situation—herself and Elton, along with two brothers who were also currently renting the house

Aaron used to live in before he'd moved in with Larx—was proof that Olivia had inherited Larx's ability to create families out of chaos.

And sometimes to create chaos out of her family, witness Larx and the little mishap with the microphone.

"Maureen?" Aaron said, looking around for his middle daughter. "She's here?"

"Go find Kirby," Olivia repeated. "He'll be looking for you."

Aaron shot her a look, and she wrinkled her nose at him, sending him on his way. As he waded through the throng of students and parents, he was frequently waylaid by both—people who wanted to shake his hand and thank him or offer words of encouragement for him and Larx. When the two of them had come out that autumn, Aaron had been expecting a long rough haul battling prejudice in their small, often backward, little town. But while things hadn't always been wine and roses—there were some parents who were giving him a disgusted side-eye that he returned with bland indifference—for the most part he and Larx had been pleasantly surprised.

Not everybody was awful. Some people really *did* see that the lawman and the educator, working so hard to keep their small town safe, were simply folks like themselves, doing their best and raising their children.

Life presented so many other challenges—Aaron was glad he didn't have to make fighting to have a second chance at love, at family, with the entire goddamned town one of them.

Finally, after shaking so many hands in the bright sunshine that he was pretty sure he was sweating through his suit jacket, Aaron found his way to the middle of the madness to where the three teenagers were standing in a knot chattering excitedly, and got a look at his youngest child, his baby, the boy who reminded him most of his late wife but who seemed to have taken the most easily to their new living situation.

"Hey, Dad!" Kirby grinned, his almost perpetually arched eyebrow taking a rest today and joining its fellow in a look of wide-eyed innocence and excitement. "How'd you like the speech?"

Kirby had been salutatorian of his class, and instead of syrupy sentimentality and a sniffly "These are the best years of our lives" kind of speech, Kirby had given a brief, funny exhortation to his peers to get off their behinds and find a way to do things when the world told them they couldn't. He'd used Larx and Aaron as examples, and while sometimes they'd been a little embarrassed to find their family so fully on display, mostly the speech had given them hope that as Kirby and his peers ventured off into the world, they'd show the same resourcefulness at life as Kirby claimed his parents showed turning random refrigerator artifacts into dinner.

"It was embarrassing," Aaron said, but with a grin so his son would know how proud he was. "Did the entire school really need to know Larx and I color-coded our boxer-briefs?"

Kirby's laughter had a diabolical edge. "Once we realized that's what you were doing, there was no stopping me," he cackled, and Aaron had to hug his sarcastic, brilliant son or his heart would have exploded right there.

"So proud of you," Aaron said into his son's ear, realizing that Kirby—who had a couple inches of growing yet to do—was nearly as tall as he was, if ganglier.

"Back atcha, Dad," Kirby said, surprising him and making it damned hard not to cry. Kirby had been his and Larx's biggest cheerleader from the moment he'd realized that not only was his father bi, but Aaron was dating Kirby's science teacher. From embracing the relationship to helping to move into Larx's house in record time, Kirby had more than enjoyed becoming a part of a larger, more chaotic family unit—he'd *thrived.*

And speaking of family unit, Aaron had more hugs to deliver.

He and Kirby released each other almost like it was choreographed, and Aaron snagged Kellan Corker, Larx's unofficial foster kid and the son he probably would have had if he'd chosen one, by the shoulder. Kellan even looked a little like Larx—smallish, compact, with straight dark hair and brown eyes. He'd fit right into Larx's household so smoothly Olivia had been calling him little brother pretty much since they'd met that Christmas. But she'd called Kirby the same thing, which really did make her Larx's daughter.

"Hey, you," Aaron said, pulling Kellan into a tight hug, "did you think you were going to escape?"

Kellan gave him a shy smile. Kellan's family life had *never* been optimum—his parents were well-known in town for being drunk or high and always violent. Toward themselves, toward each other—it didn't matter. General consensus was Kellan had been lucky. His ADHD was *legendary*, but that had drawn the attention of counselors and teachers from a relatively young age. Kellan couldn't come to school bruised or battered because *somebody* would have noticed and reported, but that didn't mean the verbal battery wasn't horrific.

And Kellan had lucked out there too. He'd attracted the attention of Isaiah Campbell, one of the brightest, most gifted students the entire school district could ever remember having, and then, in a sort of miracle, the two boys had fallen in love.

When Isaiah had been attacked by a raging psychopathic bitch (as Larx referred to the woman), Kellan's life would have fallen completely apart if Larx hadn't stepped in and dragged him into their family. The fact that this had happened right when Aaron had made his move, decided that he needed to be with Principal Larx more than he needed to maintain his squeaky-clean reputation—or even his beloved profession—hadn't deterred Larx one bit. But then, that's why Aaron had fallen in love with Larx in the first place.

Larx put the kids first. Always. And Aaron had extended his finely honed dadness into not just being a stepdad to Larx's girls, but being a parent to Kellan Corker, a kid who needed as many good parents as he could get into his corner, as well.

Kellan clung to Aaron's shirt like a drowning kid, and Aaron cupped the back of his head and let him shudder out breaths that were a combination of laughter and tears. Aaron had been there for this kid since October, when he'd moved into Larx's house, and he'd helped with the medication and the studying and the heartbreak of having the one person he'd counted on—Isaiah—move to Sacramento to recover from his injuries. Aaron could hold this kid now in triumph.

Kellan released Aaron abruptly and looked around. "Now Larx," he said awkwardly.

Kirby slung a brotherly arm around his shoulders. "Good luck with that. I remember Olivia's graduation—it took him two hours to find Christiana, right?"

Kellan's laugh was a little bit cracked but mostly whole. "I was there! Zay and me hung out with you for part of that time. Remember, Christi?"

Christi nodded and then scowled. "Well, after shouting my nickname all over the school with the PA system, I think when it's *my* turn to be looking for my dad on the football field, I'll leave him here to rot!"

"Says the woman who named me Wombat Willie and made it stick for the *rest of my life*," said Olivia's husband, finding the George/Larkin eye of the tornado unerringly, much the way he'd found Olivia from across the state earlier that year.

There was a low chuckle from Elton's side, Aaron grinned at Jaime, Elton and Olivia's housemate and another one of Larx's kids.

"You like that name?" Aaron asked.

"Olivia's started to call him that at home!" Jaime cackled, and the rest of the kids joined in the merriment as Aaron gave Larx's son-in-law a pained glance.

"Pregnancy doesn't last forever," Aaron said kindly, and Elton just shook his head.

"But that name is gonna," he said with a sigh. "Where'd Larx go anyway? Livvy and I were going to go back to the house and get her in the AC… uhm, I mean start getting things ready for the, uhm, refreshments." He gave Kellan and Kirby a furtive glance.

"Party," Kirby said decidedly. "Dad has today off, and we're having pretty much half the senior class—"

"And Jaime," Kellan added, winking.

"And definitely Jaime," Kirby added, nodding, "over to your guys' house, and we're going to have pizza and soda, and we're going to use the pool."

Aaron chuckled. "Yes, son, yes we are."

The house Aaron had moved into when he'd come to Colton—had essentially raised his children in after his wife had passed—was about six miles from Larx's house on the main road. What made it the perfect location was that it was *two* miles from Larx's house on the well-maintained service track that the forestry service used, and Larx and Aaron had started their courtship by running together. Aaron had been mostly in love with Larx anyway—he'd seen his kid's favorite teacher and school principal running in the heat without his shirt after school, and that, along with Larx's sharp tongue and clever brain, had been that, as they say. Aaron and Kirby had moved in with Larx over the fall and winter months, and neither of them regretted it for an instant, but as June settled over their heads, it became more and more imperative that the mess of teenagers he and Larx now parented have access to the pool that Aaron hadn't made much of when he'd lived there.

The access had, in fact, been the one caveat in letting everybody—Olivia, her husband, Jaime Benitez, and his brother, Berto—live there paying just enough rent to cover the mortgage and utilities.

Berto had been kind and accommodating, which was saying a lot because part of the reason he was in that living situation was that coping with PTSD was its own special stress. Berto and Olivia had apparently formed a bond over things like medication and meditation and keeping the house uncluttered and stress free. Part of the pool deal was that Kellan, Kirby, and Christi did their best to keep the pool area clean and the noise down to a minimum. For the party, Aaron understood that they were basically going to trade houses. Berto was going to make use of Larx's TV and streaming services, as well as the family dog, Dozer, who was still his favorite in spite of his household's *own* animals, two Pomeranian mixes that were, quite possibly, the ugliest dogs Aaron had ever seen. And there would be air-conditioning and a full refrigerator and quiet for the shy Berto, and lots of loud kids and hot dogs and a swimming pool for the graduates.

Olivia would get her choice of venues—Aaron rather suspected she'd take the peace and streaming services with Berto and Elton—and Aaron, Larx, and Yoshi, were on for supervision.

Aaron liked this plan, but he could understand how Olivia would be impatient to get the ball rolling.

He turned to scan the crowd again, particularly near the podium, and that's when he saw trouble striding for Larx in a pair of overalls with a thunderous expression on its face.

"Oh shit," Aaron muttered. "Kids, could you maybe get Olivia back to the car with Elton? Christi, you can drive your dad's minivan—I'll take him back."

And with those instructions, he began running across the field in his tennis shoes and khakis, one of the most formally dressed people on the field. As he ran, he looked around for law enforcement, hoping Warren Coolidge had drawn graduation duty this year, since Aaron was watching his own kid graduate as a parent. Oh shit—there was Warren, and there was Percy Hardesty, the fucknuggeted bigot who had pulled a gun on Larx once when Larx had pretty much saved a girl's life—and his own—with some quick thinking.

But Warren and Aaron had been partnered for a number of years, and Warren looked up with that intuition that good partners showed.

With a murmur to Percy, he excused himself and zeroed in on Aaron's trajectory.

Yup, Billy MacDonald was on the loose and aimed at Aaron's busy, no-bullshit boyfriend.

"Larkin! Larkin, you little faggot, why isn't my son here?"

From across the field, Aaron could see Larx glance up from a conversation with Yoshi and then narrow his eyes in anger. Yoshi put a restraining arm on Larx's shoulder, but from what Aaron could see, Larx didn't even feel it.

With a straight back and a furious expression, Larx strode across the field to meet a guy who stood six and a half feet if he stood an inch, with dump-truck muscles and a mean streak legendary across the county.

"Ooh," Jaime said, surprising him from Aaron's side, "this is gonna be bad."

Aaron turned in agitation. "Jaime, man, you've gotta go with the others. This is going to be dangerous enough."

Jaime was fifteen, and while his growth spurt *might* have been looming sometime in the coming year, it was looking more like a medium tide than a tidal wave. The boy *may* top out at five foot seven, but right now he was five four at the outside and weighed about ninety-five pounds.

Which made it even more heartbreaking when he said, "Nobody talks to Larx that way, man. Don't worry, Deputy George, I got his back."

They drew near Larx before Billy MacDonald got there. Aaron had just enough time to ask Larx, "What's his damage?"

Billy got close enough to grab Jaime by the shoulder and hurl him out of the way with an "Outta my way, you worthless spic!" and kept advancing.

Aaron took two steps in front of Larx and snarled, "One more step and I add witness intimidation and hate crime to your list of charges, Billy. Jaime, you okay?"

"Fine-fine, Detective Aaron!" Jaime said, like this sort of thing happened to him every day. From the corner of his eye, Aaron could see the boy scrambling to his feet, and he thought that maybe in his old neighborhood, it *had* happened every day. But that didn't mean it had to happen *here*.

"Keep the little—"

Aaron knotted his hand in Billy MacDonald's shirt collar, twisting it enough that Billy had to scrabble for breath. Oh yeah, Aaron took every personal defense seminar he could find. This move was one of his favorites.

"Now you will keep your racist mouth shut, asshole, and concentrate on whatever ugly bug crawled up your sphincter, do you understand me?"

Billy gasped for breath and nodded, clawing uselessly at Aaron's arm. Well, Aaron ran almost every day with Larx and worked on his upper body during downtime at the station—he had no intention of letting heart disease or slow reflexes push him into early retirement.

"I'm going to let you down easy," Aaron said, and then, catching Warren Coolidge's eyes as the man hurried to back Aaron up, he added, "and you are going to talk to Principal Larkin with respect in your voice and no more physical force or Warren here is going to arrest you for more than assault. Do we understand each other?"

"Yemfph," Billy managed, his arms going out to his side as he lost control of his flailing.

Carefully, Aaron set him down, glad that Billy was only three or so inches taller than he was and much less skilled at combat. If the man had started throwing punches, he had enough power to clean Aaron's clock with one clumsy haymaker.

"Now," Aaron said, not moving from in front of Larx an inch, "what can we do for you, sir?"

He felt the tap on his shoulder and ignored it. "Uhm, Aaron—"

"Where's my boy?" Billy demanded, and alcohol and brutality may have shaped his voice to a perpetual yell, but there was a thread of honest fear in his tone that made Aaron cock his head. "Where's Curtis?"

"I don't know," Aaron said levelly. "Larx, do you know?"

Larx socked him in the arm hard enough to bruise and moved around his adamant body. "No," he said, sounding irritated and surly. "I do not. But I *can* tell you that he wasn't supposed to be *here*!"

"Why not?" Billy asked, and God help them all, he sounded almost hurt. "He's a graduate, same as the rest of 'em."

"No, sir, he isn't," Larx told him. "And between his teachers and myself, we have over fifteen documented phone calls, five letters home—including one sent by certified mail with a picture of the letter in the mailbox near the road—trying to tell you that Billy has been failing this entire semester and he was not going to have the courses to graduate. He needed English, history, and algebra to graduate, and he failed all three classes. And not just a little bit. He turned in maybe the first three assignments, failed *those*, and then stopped trying. Billy, I had the school psychologist calling your wife on the regular—"

"She didn't tell me none of that!" Billy snarled. "Dumb bitch didn't say nothin'!"

"Well, maybe she was afraid you'd wipe your feet on her face if she did," Larx snapped back. Billy advanced on him, lowering his face to Larx's, and Larx took an involuntary step back—right into Aaron, who would lift him bodily to get him out of the way if worse came to worst but who wasn't going to give in to this man's intimidation.

"I don't hit my wife!" he growled, and if Larx's expression was anything like Aaron's, it spoke of patented disbelief.

"I've got several domestic disturbance charges to the contrary," Aaron said, and oh, thank you Jesus, Billy stepped back to look up into Aaron's face.

"You fuckin fa—"

"Stop," Larx ordered. "Just stop. Stop calling us names, stop yelling at us about it being our fault. Tell us what you think happened to your son so we can press charges against you for assaulting poor Jaime here and get on with our day."

"No worries," Jaime said from somewhere behind Aaron. "I'm all fine-fine, Mr. Larx."

Aaron didn't need to see Larx's face to know the wry, rather sweet smile that would twist his mouth as he glanced at the boy. "You are always fine-fine, Jaime, but nobody has the right to push you around in my school." He looked back to Billy. "When was the last time you saw Curtis?"

Billy scowled. "You know damned well there was that… that senior party thing that went for three days, and then he said he'd get ready for graduation at a friend's! I told him I'd see him here!"

Larx blinked rapidly. "Grad Night?" he asked, surprised. "Billy, Grad Night was earlier this week. And only graduating students could go. They left Friday and got back Monday—they went to Disneyland." Larx and the school had fundraised all year to make sure *every* student could afford to go. Kellan had confessed to Kirby that besides his twice-monthly visits to Isaiah in Sacramento, it was the only time he'd been south of Auburn. "Billy, it's *Thursday*. Where's your kid been since then?"

It was as though a bubble of silence descended over the entire football stadium, and they could all *hear* Billy MacDonald swallow.

"Billy," Larx said softly, "Curtis knew he wasn't going to graduate. What would you have done if *you* knew?"

Billy's expression grew hard—ugly—and for a moment not a soul in the vicinity had any doubts as to what would have happened if Billy MacDonald had a moment to take his fury out on his son.

"Yeah," Larx murmured. "I thought so."

Aaron grunted. "Warren, have Percy Hardesty take Billy down to the station for charges. Then tell Eamon he's going to have to put out a missing person's notice on Curtis MacDonald."

Warren grunted and then sent Aaron a pleading look, and Aaron quailed. God, no. No. He wanted nothing more than to go celebrate his son's graduation. Hadn't his family and Larx's family earned this?

Then Warren shook his head like he was pulling up his big-boy panties. "I'll do that, Aaron," he said. "You're not even on duty. I'll report it to Eamon." His plain, wide face assumed rueful lines. "That don't mean Eamon might not call you up later this evening," he warned, "but for now, let Sheriff Mills do it."

Aaron nodded his head and then gave Billy MacDonald a level look. Billy ground his teeth together and put his hands behind his back for the cuffs. It occurred to Aaron that he might not have pressed charges—and Larx probably wouldn't have even mentioned them—if the man had shown the tiniest bit of regard for Jaime's well-being, or even some remorse for pushing the boy down.

But he hadn't, and it was clear to Aaron that Billy's son's spiral in school had been partly his own doing—and definitely predictable. Lowering his head slightly, Aaron asked, "Will Curtis be okay on his own?"

Larx grunted and shot Billy a disgusted look. "The boy was on his own more often than not as it was. He's had four days head start on us. He could be anywhere by now—Auburn, Sacramento, LA." Larx frowned. "Billy, did you give Curtis any money to go to Grad Night?"

Billy scowled. "I did. You fuckers owe me three hundred dollars!"

Larx stared at the sky and let out a breath. "Trip only cost fifty, Billy. We did fundraising. Every graduating senior got to go."

Billy opened and closed his mouth, and Aaron ignored him, nodding Warren over to listen to their convo.

"Warren, have Eamon check bus routes and train routes—and petty crimes between here and Sacramento." He frowned. "Larx, does Curtis have any friends or relatives outside of Colton?"

Larx glanced to where Billy stood, scowling, his hands cuffed behind his back—but waiting patiently. Apparently Billy MacDonald was a racist, bigoted asshole who didn't treat his family particularly well, but he was still a father who wanted to know where his son was.

Ugh. Aaron did not feel good about leaving Warren and Percy in charge.

"He does," Larx said, a troubled look on his face as he gnawed his lean lower lip. He glanced up. "Look, guys—I've got to make sure the field is squared away and then join everybody at my house. Give me two hours to check my sources, and if I get any new info, I can have Aaron phone it in." He gave Aaron an apologetic smile. "But that *does* mean I need to keep Aaron as planned, or I won't be able to talk to the people I need to. We good with that?"

Aaron raised his eyebrows, wondering what Larx had in mind.

"Can do, Larx," Warren said, and he grabbed Billy *gently* by the upper arm. "Come along, Mr. MacDonald. Let's get you booked and get your court day set so we can concentrate on finding your boy."

Billy glared at Larx as he passed by. "Why couldn't you just let him graduate?" he demanded, chin over his shoulder.

Larx took a deep breath. "He quit, Billy. He quit, and so did you. Every time we saw him, we offered help, offered tutoring. Everybody gave up *except* us, do you understand that?"

Billy turned his head and spat. "Faggot," he muttered and allowed himself to be led away.

Aaron allowed himself to relax. "Larx, *gees*," he muttered, rubbing the arm that Larx had socked. "Did you have to dig a hole in the muscle with your knuckle?"

Larx shook out his wrist. "Unlikely," he said. "Jesus, you've been working out a lot."

"Charming," said Yoshi, rolling his eyes at Billy's back as he hurried up to Larx and Aaron, Nancy Pavelle at his side. "Did you all have a nice tea party in front of the graduating seniors?"

Larx smiled grimly at his best friend. "No, because that asshole didn't bring cookies, and you know how I hate to have a tea party without cookies."

Yoshi's quick grin told Aaron all he needed to know about how much fun Yoshi and Larx had baiting each other. "I will always bring cookies to your tea parties," he vowed, then turned toward his boyfriend's sister and the other Musketeer of Larx's work clique, Nancy. Nancy was a science teacher, middle-aged, blond, chubby, and adorable looking, but between swearing and sarcasm, she, Larx, and Yoshi could put most longshoremen to shame. "Did you see what just happened?"

Nancy nodded and chewed her lower lip. "I did," she said softly. "But I didn't hear all of it. Larx, did he say Curtis was missing?"

Larx nodded. "He told his father he needed $300 for Grad Night *literally* on the day the class got back from Disneyland and then disappeared. That's not a lot of money—"

Nancy made a noise and wrinkled her brow, and Larx, Yoshi, and Aaron all stared at her.

"What?" Larx asked.

"I… look, I have no concrete knowledge, only suspicions." She sighed and shook her bangs out of her eyes. "I'll meet you at the party. Let me talk to some kids."

And with that she turned heel on the football field and strode off.

"That was odd," Larx said.

"It's only odd because usually it's you and me doing it," Yoshi scoffed. "She's a woman. She has secrets. Let her be a mystery unto herself."

Larx and Aaron shared a stare of outrage before Larx turned to his best friend with what Aaron knew was a *scathing* retort about how much his friend did *not* know about women boiling on his tongue.

Yoshi gave a feline smile and cut his eyes to the right and to the left, *daring* Larx to say what he was thinking in public, surrounded by students and parents. Larx shook his head.

"It's a damned good thing you're indispensable," he said bitterly. "I can't believe I got shot to get you back as my VP."

"It was a small price to pay," Yoshi said, smug as one of Christiana's cats, his nose in the air and his chia-beard and mustache threatening to grow back for no other purpose than to give him whiskers to flaunt.

"Next time," Larx said, "I'm trading you in for a new computer. Now let's get this place cleaned up so we can go eat all-beef franks. Did you hear that, Yoshi? All. Beef. You have to bring your own soy dogs."

Yoshi cackled. "Silly, silly man. How do you know I didn't have Olivia buy me my delicious vegan hot dogs without your permission?"

Together they all started striding toward the makeshift stage and the podium, making sure the custodian and the football coach had the wrap-up well in hand.

"Dammit," Larx muttered, obviously displeased not to have vegan hot dogs to hold over Yoshi's head.

Aaron touched his shoulder. "I'm going to make sure the kids are all on their way to Olivia's place." He glanced over to Jaime, who had been listening delightedly to Yoshi and Larx bickering. "And make sure Jaime has first crack at the sodas and cookies."

Jaime grinned happily. "You're a good man, Sheriff Aaron. A good man."

Aaron grinned back. "Thanks, kid. Anyway," He looked around, hoping nobody was watching but, in the end, not caring enough to not lean forward to drop a quick kiss on Larx's cheek. "I was going to give you a ride home, but now I'm going to get the kids and leave you to Yoshi. Be careful. We don't know where Curtis MacDonald is. I'll see everybody back at the house and we can compare notes then."

Larx nodded and then gestured with his chin to where the kids were embracing a freckled, redheaded dynamo—Aaron's middle child, Maureen.

"And you can go hug your daughter," he said quietly, the tone of his voice indicating he knew how much it mattered to him that Mau had made it.

"That too," Aaron said, feeling the comfort seeping in whether he'd intended it to or not.

"See you at home, Deputy." Larx winked and then moved off to be a responsible adult, and Aaron indulged himself in getting to hug his little girl.

The Dark Side

"ALL RIGHT," Yoshi said as they trotted over the football field toward Coach Jones. "What aren't we telling him and why is it so much hotter *on* the grass than it is on the track?"

Larx grimaced. "Because the heat on the grass is a wet heat, and the track has a noticeable drop in humidity." What he *really* wanted was a good stiff breeze to dry the sweat under his arms right then. God, that had been close. Billy MacDonald had been wanting to take a crack at him for the last two years, and today had been the perfect opportunity. Larx was pretty sure he could have dodged the hit, but Aaron, standing in front of him like a Roman Centurion, had scared the crap out of him. He hoped he'd left a bruise, dammit. Aaron should know better than that; MacDonald was ten years younger and fifty pounds heavier and *meaner*, for God's sake, and Aaron could have gotten hurt!

Bless his protective Neanderthal heart.

"And that other thing?" Yoshi prodded. "I saw your face when Nancy spoke up. What is she looking at?"

Larx sighed. "*Think* about it, Yosh. What did we think was going on with Curtis all year, but we couldn't pin his parents down to talk about it?"

Yoshi wrinkled his nose. "Drugs," he said without a doubt. "We all saw what happened to the boy after football season. It was like as soon as he stopped doing push-ups, he started tweaking. Lost forty pounds, skin turned yellow, teeth got brown—it's why you were so desperate to get hold of his parents."

"Well, yeah," Larx said, wanting to spit in disgust. "But it's not like Billy and Angie MacDonald are going to put a stop to it. I mean, we tried…."

Yoshi nodded, and Larx felt a little better. They both knew what it was like to teach at a larger school. You almost expected to lose a few kids every year. Kids dropped off the map, no forwarding addresses. Sometimes you would spot them out in public. If you lived in your district, interacted with your community, it was inevitable. And sometimes it wouldn't be such a bad thing. He'd met a few girls who had dropped out of sight to have their babies. A few guys who had seen they weren't going to graduate and who had started working the family business after taking the GED. Kids didn't always respect paperwork, and sometimes the paper trail would be left in the dust while the student moved on to their own life. But that was sometimes.

A lot of the time, the kid dropped out of school and became a ghost. A wraith. Usually drug dependent, often coasting on prostitution or petty crime for their next fix. Larx had seen those kids literally fade from society, only to be whispered about in the hallway, a name in the yearbook without a picture, a "whatever happened to" before anything happened to anybody in high school. The student had simply disappeared.

He'd tried hard not to let it happen to Curtis MacDonald, and he hadn't been alone.

"Was that Billy MacDonald who just got hauled off to jail for pushing the little Benitez kid?" Coach Kenny Jones asked as Larx and Yoshi drew near.

"Yeah," Larx said, appreciating the beefy younger man's insistence that he do all the heavy lifting involved in dismantling the stage. Larx was feeling the crankiness of no sleep that usually came this time of year, and the thought of squatting down to help Kenny do the physical work made the small of his back ache preemptively. "Seems to be surprised that Curtis isn't graduating."

Kenny straightened up and scowled. "First of all, where does that guy get off pushing Jaime? Seriously. What. An. Asshole."

Larx hid a smile. Kenny Jones had a good heart, but it often took him some heavy thinking and solid boots to walk the path of reason.

"Yeah, Billy's an asshole," Larx agreed. "But the more concerning thing is that Curtis scammed him out of money Monday morning and disappeared. *We* knew he wasn't here because there was no point. The last week is all about signing yearbooks, talking about the good times, and saying goodbye, and Curtis said goodbye sometime in March. He just didn't tell his folks. His dad thought he was at Disneyland."

"How much money?" Kenny asked, giving Larx a sideways look.

"Three hundred dollars."

Kenny let out a low whistle. "Well, Jesus. That either gets him down to Sacramento to snort a little bit of meth or down to that house off

Juniper Street or the one on Dropoff Drive to get enough to make him stroke out."

Larx and Yoshi both sucked air through their teeth, because while they'd obviously both been *thinking* it, it really sucked to have it stated out loud. Then Kenny said the other silent part out loud, and Larx wanted to kick him, which wasn't fair because it was an honest question.

"Where are we about caring about that, by the way? 'Cause, I mean, the kid turned eighteen in January, and we've been trying to tell his folks he was heading down a bad path for *months*. And now he's… you know. Set free. School's out for summer, man, and he's got no class and no principals and nobody to blame but himself."

Yoshi let out a breath. "Fair question, Larx. I get Aaron's gotta worry about this, but can't you go to your house and party with your kids?"

Larx grunted. "I *have* to go to my house and party with my kids," he said. "Because sure as shit stinks, one of the AP kids Kirby invited is going to try to sneak booze into the whole thing, and that could cost me my job, and it's dangerous to boot."

"My money's on Cassie Clemson," Yoshi said, nodding sagely. "She hasn't done anything yet, but she's got sneaky party girl written all over her."

Larx shot him a dirty look. "Wait until she gets to the college dorms to make that assessment. For all you know she's got library rat written all over her."

"I'm not buying it," Yoshi told him, "but moving on…."

Larx needed to answer the question.

"It matters," he said after a moment. "We care. If Curtis is found dead that's… that's gonna leave a hole in all our stomachs. I know we can't control him, and he's technically a grown-up, but…." He gestured to all of the young graduates moving excitedly toward the parking lot. "Look at them. They're still kids. We hold Grad Night parties and trips so they don't get drunk and wrap themselves around trees because it *hurts* when that happens. We don't stop caring about this kid because it's Thursday."

Kenny nodded his head slowly. "I hear you," he said. "I'll ask around. He's still tight with some of the football team—or he was before he dropped off completely. I'll see what I can dig up."

"Great, Kenny." Larx gave him a huge smile. "Call me. I've got to go check on the PA system and make sure the school itself is locked down."

"By the way," the coach said, "can I thank you some more about making us get all our grades in *before* graduation. God, my sister doesn't get any time to do it until the kids leave, and she says coming back in three days after school's out *sucks*."

Larx chuckled, pleased. "Well, you know. I was a teacher too. It *does* suck. But don't forget we've got the schedule meeting on Monday morning, before it gets hot, so we're all clear what we're teaching when we come back."

Kenny regarded him blankly. "PE, right?" he asked. "'Cause I know it says history on my credentials, but—"

Larx held out his hands, calming the big man down. "Don't worry," he said. "Nobody's going to make you teach history, Kenny."

"Oh thank God. See you Monday!"

Larx waved, and then he and Yoshi turned back toward the main school building, which was a little bit of a hike, and Larx fully expected Yoshi to whine all the way. When he was uncharacteristically quiet, Larx said, "What?"

"Two things," Yoshi said. "The first is, do you really have next year's master schedule all written?"

Larx grunted. "No, and you know that because if I did you would have looked it over already. But it's close. And no, he doesn't have to teach history. The kids adore him, but I understand that when he's in the classroom he has gas that can kill a deer in an enclosed space. There were quiet complaints. It's really best if we keep him in the gym."

Yoshi stared at him. "Are you telling me that all I have to do to get out of teaching a class is to fart on command?"

"No," Larx said patiently, "I'm telling you that all you have to do is"—his voice dropped because he hated this—"ask. That's what I'm having problems with, Yosh. You and me still teaching while we do this fuckin' job. Ask."

Yoshi made an unhappy sound. "I've started to train Kopecky on how to teach AP. She's not bad, but…." He sighed.

"What?"

"I really want to teach your daughter Shakespeare, Larx. I mean, I *really* want Christiana in my class when I do *Hamlet* and *Macbeth* and *Midsummer's Night's Dream*. Christiana Larkin has been the carrot to the VP stick since you gave me this fuckin' job. Don't make me give her up."

Larx didn't have the heart to tell him that Olivia had already brought home all Yoshi's materials to share with her sister. Christi's foreknowledge would just make her more of a delight.

Besides. "That's all I wanted to know," he said softly. "Let me know when it gets too much. I need you as my right-hand guy, Hamilton. Don't let me overwork you."

Yoshi gave a "*pfft*" and waved his hand. "What about you? Christi already took AP Physics this year. You keeping your hand in?"

Larx nodded. "I am. But I have an idea—sort of like you training Nicole Kopecky up. I was thinking I'd split the class with—"

"Please don't say Rich Peterson," Yoshi chanted, closing his eyes and crossing his fingers. "Please don't say Peterson."

"Christ no," Larx told him in disgust. Peterson was sort of the worst. He was dry. He was pedantic. He made science boring and sad and depressing, and he didn't get the students' papers back until the end of the semester. They *never* knew how they were doing. "Corbin Barker."

"The new guy?" Yoshi said, opening his eyes so he could maybe not trip on the stairs that led up to the quad. "The new guy you just hired as a sub?"

"That new guy," Larx said in confirmation. "He's got the background. I saw him interact with the kids over Amber's maternity leave. He's, you know, young. Exciting. And if he watches me present one day and takes questions and sets up labs the next…."

"Yeah, I get it. You'll train him up, and… and what?"

Larx yawned. "Have options, Yoshi. I might not give up teaching a single class, but basic chemistry is a lot easier, and I can have a TA do all the correcting. I'm saying it's something to think about."

Yoshi grunted. "Think about it during the weekend, Larx. We're always exhausted this time of year. You're not…." His voice deepened with suspicion. "You're not *dying*, are you?"

"No!" Larx protested. "No, I'm fine! I just…." He tried to keep his smile from getting too goofy. "Did you see him stand in front of me, Yosh? Did you see him protect me?"

"Oh God," Yoshi groaned.

"I mean, he's a superhero, right? I'm living with a superhero."

"You should be *married* to a superhero," Yoshi protested. "Weren't you going to let me and Nancy take care of that? When are you green-lighting the wedding, moron?"

"I don't know!" Larx threw his hands in the air. "We're always so damned busy. That's what I'm trying to say! He's going to be running for sheriff in the fall, and I just thought that maybe, now that I've got a superhero who has my six, wouldn't it be great if we had a night a week to eat dinner in Tahoe or go swimming without the kids or see a movie or whatever it is couples do. Frankly, we've forgotten a little, which really sucks because we only got together in October."

"Get married," Yoshi said firmly. "Couples get married in mid-August, a week before school starts, so the principal can go on vacation and get laid before his job turns into a flock of homicidal ducks."

Larx blinked. "Ducks?"

"Can you imagine being pecked to death by ducks, Larx? Slow, painful, irritating? Remind you of anything?"

Ooh… this was ringing a bell. "The first staff meeting of the year?" he asked. "The one where everybody is pissing on their books and marking their territory?"

"I've wanted to turn it into a reality game for *years*," Yoshi confirmed savagely. "Like the Hunger Games, where we put the book sets for the classes everybody wants in the middle and the victors get AP classes and the losers get pre-algebra and remedial reading and are never heard from again."

Larx grunted. "Give it up, Yoshi. The special ed department would sit back, sharpen their knives, and feast on the blood of the victors, then use their books as bedding and sleep like the blessed. I've observed those people—they're fucking fierce and they know how to fight dirty." Well, campaigning for the most vulnerable population in the school would do that for a platoon.

"Ooh… I forgot about SPED," Yoshi murmured. "Good point, Larx. I have to rethink my game plan now. I mean, if that one teacher at the middle school could survive wasps, a physical assault, and the school trip to the cabins in the woods in her first year, that's some Titan Class teaching balls there. Are they all built that tough?"

Larx nodded. "The tinier female ones can cut you with a shiv fashioned from a giant crayon. Don't fuck with special ed."

At that point they reached their offices, and both of them took keys and walkie-talkies and went from room to room to room, making sure everybody had left, everything was locked, all the lights were down, and even the computers were powered off. There were a few teachers finishing packing their rooms up for summer, and Larx and Yoshi both went in and loaned a hand, but for the most part, the school was closing down. The master schedule meeting would be on Monday, and people would be allowed in their rooms then for a couple of hours, but then the school would be vacant for two weeks for deep cleaning and computer updates before summer school started. Larx was turning his keys over to a student in the administration program then, getting her MA so she could be a principal in her own district. A friend at the state college had asked Larx, and Larx had agreed. He could keep an eye on things, but he could also, well, father. Help Kirby and Kellan decide on their next course of action. Help Olivia get ready for the baby. Make sure Christiana had applied for every scholarship known to man. The prospect of having so much time to simply *be* with his family was strange and hedonistic, but it also felt necessary.

Which was why he'd been wondering about keeping his AP course. When he'd been a single dad, everything about it had made sense. He was keeping his identity in spite of The Man, dammit! The school district could force him to be principal, but he didn't have to like it! He'd *make* them let him still teach!

Which was awesome; it had worked well for the past year. But he'd proved that it could. And he wasn't a single dad anymore. He had an adult he wanted to spend time with when all the kids were off learning and growing and flying.

It would be great if he had some time to spend.

But, well, Aaron *was* going to be sheriff in the fall. Did Larx really want to risk being bored while his hus—erm, partner—was off being big and important and busy?

Dilemmas. He needed to talk to Aaron. But then that would lead to the "When are we getting married?" question again, and Larx didn't want to push.

He had no problem with Yoshi and Nancy pushing, though. Fact was, he couldn't be married to Deputy Aaron George soon enough.

He recalled again Aaron's broad shoulders, his biceps bulging under his suit jacket, the furious expression on his face when he realized Billy had been planning to pick Larx up and shake him like a puppy—and he had the bulk to do it.

Nobody hurt Larx on Aaron's watch, and while Larx had been on his own for going on nine years, the very *idea* that Aaron loved him like that was enough to warm him from balls to teeth.

And all the places in between.

All he needed was a little bit of time to talk about the wedding.

But then, maybe taking the summer session off would be all he needed.

"Are you still chewing on the wedding?" Yoshi asked as Larx got into the passenger seat of Yoshi's tiny economy car. Larx assumed Aaron and Kirby had gotten everybody else back home to change and then to Aaron's house, but that meant Larx's minivan was nowhere near the high school. "The seat scoots back, you know. You don't have to sit there with your knees around your ears like some sort of giant bird of prey."

"I'm five nine, Yoshi. I'm hardly a giant. Doesn't Tane ride in this thing?"

Yoshi's boyfriend—erm, husband—Tane, was tall and angular. Larx could swear he was taller than five nine.

"Tane's five seven," Yoshi said, his voice an arid wasteland. "I'm five five. He looks taller because you *see him next to me*."

Larx felt his eyes widen, and he turned his head to stare at his, uhm, little friend. "Really?" he asked.

"We are a small but hardy people, Larx. You and your Neanderthal boyfriend have already passed along your giant Nordic genes."

"I could swear my genes were midsized and Mediterranean, but whatever."

Yoshi gave him a disdainful side-eye before he put engaged the clutch and put the car into reverse. "You're Mediterranean like I'm Californian. Your people may have visited Greece before they came to America, but you're all European white people. And I'm mostly Japanese born in California."

"Mostly?"

Yoshi shrugged. "It's a guess. My porcelain complexion suggests someone who doesn't tan got busy in my bloodline. And as diverting as all of this is, it's overlooking the fact that we're supposed to be planning your wedding. Aren't we? Don't you have a ring on your dresser that says there's a commitment? I could swear there was a whole proposal and a dinner and a ring and—"

"Fine," Larx said. "This August. That gives us two months. I'll tell Aaron today." The words filled him with an amazing satisfaction. There *had* been a proposal and a family dinner and a ring. All of the sloppy romantic things that Larx had never really put much stock in had happened, and suddenly they'd meant the world. There'd been a *promise*, and after Larx's first marriage and the betrayal and anger that had ended it, having someone Larx *really* loved promise to be there, to work as a partner, that had meant something.

Particularly because it was Aaron, and Aaron didn't break promises.

Larx's happy musings—and they *were* happy, which was new for Larx—were interrupted by the sight of something alarming at the edge of the parking lot.

"Yoshi," Larx said, hoping he was suffering some sort of heat stroke. "Stop for a second."

Yoshi hit the brake with undue force, probably because he saw it too. "No," he said. "No. No, Larx. God, please. Aaron's place. I've got swimming trunks and a matching shirt in the back. Celebrating with kids—we absolutely positively can't—"

Larx let out a sigh. "Look, just pull up even with it and let me get out and look inside."

Look inside the giant bruiser of a Chevy half-ton pickup truck that Curtis's father had given him to drive to and from school. Their discussion on the football field had been so hurried, so slapdash, it hadn't occurred to any of them to hunt down Curtis's truck.

Larx climbed awkwardly out of Yoshi's Toyota and ventured toward the vehicle. The dented body was covered in a combination of electric teal paint and primer red spots to keep the dings from rusting. Even that harlequin quilt of colors was coated thickly in red dust and yellow pine-tree pollen, which was par for the course this time of year, but Larx figured it would have taken a couple of days for this level of accretion to build.

Say, maybe, four days. Monday morning, when Curtis had driven it to school after getting the money from his father to today, Thursday, when his father realized that all his dreams for his son to graduate from high school were crashing around his feet.

Hesitantly Larx cleared the dust and pollen from the passenger window, cupped his hands to ward off the fierce glare of the late morning sun, and peered inside.

His knees went wobbly with relief when he saw that Curtis wasn't in there, because if Curtis *had* been in there, it wouldn't have been the boy, it would have been the boy's body, and there was such a level of awfulness to that. Larx was so damned glad they didn't have to go there today—not today, when they were celebrating Kellan and Kirby and all Larx's AP kids after an emotionally brutal roller-coaster of a year.

Larx let his anxiety seep down his spine and peered into the truck again, hoping for clues. What he saw made his heart hurt.

Empty dime bags littered the passenger side of the bench seat, what looked like vomit coated the floorboards, and several layers of filthy clothes were piled on the back of the seats and the dashboard.

Curtis had been living here, Larx thought painfully. God. They'd all seen it. They'd had interventions with the counselor. They'd tried *desperately* to get hold of his father, but Curtis had curled into himself like a pill bug. They couldn't even get him to admit he *took* drugs, much less had a problem.

But they'd known. They'd known, and they'd tried to help, and—

Larx stepped back and took several deep breaths before turning to Yoshi and shaking his head no.

He climbed back into the Toyota, grateful that the air-conditioning was finally working, and leaned his head back against the seat. "He's not in there, but a bunch of drug paraphernalia is. Let me call Eamon, and they can have their forensics team come check the truck out. We'll talk to the kids, and Aaron can tell us what they found later."

"Oh thank God," Yoshi muttered, gunning the motor to get them out of the parking lot. "I…. God, that kid was a pain in the ass. He was racist. He was bigoted. He was mean. He was angry. But I really didn't want to have to see him ambulanced out of here in a body bag, you know what I mean?"

Larx pulled his phone out of his pocket and dialed Eamon's phone number with shaking fingers. "Yes, Yoshi, I really, really do."

Larx took one more deep breath and pressed the green Connect button, relieved when Aaron's boss picked up in two rings.

"Aren't you two having a party? I could swear you were having a party at Aaron's pool. I know because I was going to drop in, have a dog and a soda, and put the fear of the law into those kids in case anybody was trying to sneak in booze."

"You're a good friend," Larx said sincerely. "But you heard about the MacDonald boy?"

"Yeah. I heard Billy MacDonald caused trouble at the graduation about Curtis but he hasn't shown up yet." Eamon Mills was in his late sixties, Black, with a tight buzz of graying hair under his Colton County Sheriff ballcap. He was, Larx knew, the closest thing to a father Aaron could claim since his own father had passed away more than twenty years ago, and he'd been one of Larx and Aaron's biggest cheerleaders when they'd first come out and started dating. Eamon had *wanted* them out and proud and running the school and the county with all the discipline they could muster.

Larx and Aaron had done their best, and Eamon was getting excited about backing Aaron in the fall election while Eamon retired. Larx had no doubt that Eamon would still keep his hand in—Aaron would be asking his old friend and mentor questions every day—but Eamon could answer them from his front porch or while taking dancing lessons with his wife or out on the lake fishing, and it was Larx and Aaron's turn to root for Eamon having as much happiness as he could manage.

The man had done his time—over thirty years in the sheriff's office, working his way from rank deputy. He'd more than earned his rest.

And today he was giving *Aaron* a much-deserved break, and Larx was more than grateful.

"Well," Larx said, pulling himself back to the present, "we just spotted Curtis MacDonald's pickup truck on school grounds, back in the corner under the trees—"

"Where nobody parks because of the pine pollen?" Eamon guessed.

"It's like you were here," Larx said dryly. "I took a look inside"—and had gotten yellow pollen all over his suit jacket—"and there's a lot for your forensics folks to look at, but nothing I want to touch personally. And most importantly—" He let Eamon fill in the blank.

"No Curtis," Eamon said.

"Much to my relief," Larx confirmed. "And with that I'm going to go change into my board shorts and my madras shirt and have some hot dogs, chips, and watermelon."

"Give me a few hours and I'll see you there."

"Thanks, Eamon. See you there." He pocketed his phone, and Yoshi sent him a glance.

"God, Larx, it sounds like you're opening Aaron's house up to the entire county. You sure you've got enough supplies?"

Larx gave a semihysterical laugh. "Eamon contributed a hundred dollars with the caveat that we carry his brand of soda and the hot dogs he likes. Nancy is bringing pretty much a pallet of chips because her oldest works at a big-box store, and my kids collected ten dollars per kid and then helped us shop so everybody would get their favorite cookies and such. Christiana is such a little capitalist. She was, like, 'Dad, if people put in their own money, they'll value their time there. Trust me. We'll keep them from trashing Olivia's house, I swear.'"

"She's a smart kid," Yoshi said, his voice full of avuncular pride. Well, he got to be proud, Larx thought sourly. Odds were she was going to be a literature major, and Uncle Yoshi would make sure she never ever held a job that would earn her a secure living.

But then, Uncle Yoshi loved his job and his subject, and Larx couldn't bring himself to shit on that either.

He tried to let himself relax into family conversation—dammit, if there was a time for it, *today* was that time. He was so damned proud of Kirby. He'd loved that kid before he and Aaron had become a couple, but after having him in his household for the better part of a year, Larx couldn't love him more if Kirby had been flesh and blood. Sarcastic, verbally playful, with an optimism that was, as far as Larx could see, an act of will, Kirby was everything Larx loved in a student—and everything he loved in a human being as well. When Aaron's wife had died suddenly in a car accident, his entire family had been devastated, not least Kirby, who had been a little kid, waiting in the rain for the mother who would never come get him from school.

Kirby had pulled his emotional health up by his bootstraps. His older sisters had cared for him, yes, and Aaron was a wonderful father, but Kirby had made an active decision to be hopeful. When he'd realized his father was in love with another man, he'd been *surprised*, but he'd also been happy, and not just for Aaron. He'd been happy for them *both* because he missed his sisters who had gone off to school, missed having a family unit, missed having a group of people who were both support and, in Kirby's case, amusement.

Nothing made Kirby happier than other people.

And Kellan? Kellan *could* have been Curtis MacDonald; his parents were certainly from the same stock. But his kindness, his hope to do good, and his efforts to keep his pinball-bouncing brain working *with* his goals instead of *against them*—his work effort was so pure, as was his heart. Larx *needed* to celebrate with those boys. They needed to see him there. It was absolutely imperative.

And besides—they both liked science. Christi was *great* at science, but she didn't *love* it like Kellan and Kirby. Larx felt like Kellan and Kirby were his reward for daughters whose troths were already pledged to the humanities.

"All my kids are smart," Larx said, bragging and not ashamed of it. "And thank God, or Aaron and I would be going crazier than we already are."

Yoshi let out a breath. "Is it just me, or are young adults getting dumber?"

Larx made a pained noise. "I try not to go there, Yosh."

"I mean, I swear to God, that last student teacher we had? I felt like I had to remind her to breathe out. She was going to pass out at the white board, completely unconscious, because she was so full of TikTok videos and Twitter scandals that she forgot how to breathe."

Larx shook his head. "I'm not going there."

"But Larx, I swear to God—"

"No, Yoshi, because the minute you go there, the minute you say the upcoming generation is too stupid to provide for us in our dotage, *that's* the moment we're *in* our dotage. There's not a specific age to dodder—it happens as soon as you say, 'These young whippersnappers are too stupid to live!' Scientific fact, Yoshi. Don't force me to get you an 'Old Man Shakes Fist at Cloud' T-shirt, because I'll do it."

Yoshi whinged and continued to pilot his little yellow Toyota around the curves of the mountain roads that made up their home. The dry red dust of the area formed a kind of photo filter, and through it the sky looked bluer and the trees darker green, the contrast of the bright sun and the deep shadows enough to hurt the heart with dark and light and the azure, ochre, and forest green in between.

A comforting silence fell between them, and then just as Yoshi took the split in the road that no longer led to Larx's little house on one side of the forestry track and instead led to Aaron's old house on the other, Yoshi said, "August sixth. I'm telling Nancy. We'll work on invitations tonight."

Larx swallowed, surprised. School got out on the first week of June. "Two weeks before school?" he asked. Then, "Isn't Olivia due on August twelfth?"

"I understand the first baby is often late," Yoshi said with dignity. "Besides, Larx, it's not like we're going to expect her to help a lot. We'll buy her a gauzy white dress, give her a flower crown, make her a pregnant woman's throne, and let Christiana and Kirby carry off attendant duties."

"Not you and Nancy?" Larx asked, feeling bad because hey, they were *planning* the damned thing.

Yoshi was an able driver, so he did *not* shoot Larx a glare while he was steering the vehicle around a series of curves. It didn't matter. His look of horror said it all.

"Nancy and I will be sitting in the front row with your other kids. Except Aaron's oldest. Is she still a bitch?"

Larx grunted. "We've tried," he said. "We thought she might have been coming around when he got shot this winter, but all she sent back when she got Kirby's graduation announcement was a cashier's check for a hundred dollars and an airplane ticket to their grandparents' town."

Yoshi's sound was pure horror. "Yeah. So Nancy, Tane, and I will be making sure Aaron's oldest daughter stays the hell away from the wedding. Tane plays dirty, but don't worry. She'll be able to feel her fingers again eventually. That nerve never stays pinched forever."

"Yoshi!" Larx laughed, but Yoshi apparently wasn't fucking around.

"No. Our town needs this, Principal Larkin. It needs its principal and its sheriff's deputy to be happily married. And then people can say, 'Yeah, they're gay, but they keep the town from falling apart, so who cares.'"

"I swear to you," Larx said dryly, "nobody is going to say that."

"Yeah, they will." Yoshi blew out a frustrated breath. "If politics has taught us nothing else over the last few years, it's that feudalism existed for a reason. People need a shining example to follow or they end up like Billy MacDonald. You and Aaron are that shining example."

"Ugh. Yoshi, I'd just as soon be Aaron's husband. You get that's all I want out of this wedding thing, right? I don't want to be a figurehead. I don't want to be a shining example. I want our kids to be able to say,

'Our dads,' in public and either of us to be able to visit the other's kids in case of an emergency."

"And you want to ride off into the sunset with your cowboy and know you've got happily ever after waiting for you."

Larx felt a blush coming on involuntarily. "Is that too much to ask?"

"We'll work on it," Yoshi reassured him, and then pulled into the driveway leading to Aaron's old house.

The kids had done a good job of marking territory. The living room was a go. Jaime's room was the changing room, and the downstairs bathroom could be used for the same thing, but Berto's room was marked with red "Keep Out" tape and probably locked besides.

There was a string of the tape at the base of the stairs, keeping anybody *not* part of the family from going upstairs into Elton and Olivia's part of the house, but the garage was open and the extra refreshments were stacked within easy sight of the door.

The pool was actually good-sized, although Kirby and Aaron had kept it empty for the past three years, partly in deference to the drought-ridden Sierras and partly because Maureen and Tiffany had been the ones who'd used it the most, and they'd been away at school. Larx and Aaron invested in cleaning it up and filling it and balancing the chlorine in early May, and Olivia's gratitude had been profound. For that matter, the other members of the household seemed absolutely delighted—Jaime and Berto spent a lot of time out there, and Berto did more than his share of the upkeep. Berto was working so hard on himself, finding ways to overcome the PTSD that had resulted from a horrific beating down in Sacramento, that watching him quietly blossom, becoming a retiring member of an extroverted family, had been almost miraculous.

Olivia and Elton had apparently told him that he was welcome to be their housemate as long as he needed to be, and Berto had replied that he wanted to stay until Jaime, at least, was out of junior college, if not longer. Apparently he wasn't daunted by the advent of the baby. The two boys had been used to a big rowdy family unit until the changing political climate had made much of their extended family go back to Mexico. Jaime and Berto had stayed—and almost not survived. Moving to the Sierras had been Berto's last, most desperate act to recover their lives from the poverty and violence that had followed trying to make it on their own.

To them, the baby, the living situation, the family dinners—all of it meant hope, and they were desperate to embrace the hope.

Larx couldn't have asked for better extended family.

Which was why he and Aaron were so absolutely serious about making sure their house was treated nicely during this party. But then, so were the rest of the kids.

"Hello," Christiana burbled as they walked in. "Welcome to the Larkin/George pool party. The changing rooms are marked with blue tape. Feel free to use the bathroom if you need it, but no going upstairs—that's private. The kitchen has cool drinks and fruit, the barbecue is going on the back porch, and there's a table to put your side dishes or chips." She narrowed her eyes at them. "You do *have* side dishes or chips, don't you?"

Larx regarded his youngest with an amused arch of his eyebrow. "We paid for the rest of the banquet, sweetie. I think that's a free pass out of the side dishes or chips duty."

"I know, Daddy," Christiana told him, breaking her flight attendant persona. "But I'm practicing my schtick. We've all agreed to take living room duty for an hour at a time to make sure nobody wrecks the house."

"And you got first shift?" Larx asked, curious as to how that happened.

"Nobody important shows up in the first hour," she told him with a straight face, and then she managed a sheepish look. "And I got really hot at the graduation. I figured I'd chill out, read a book—" She gestured to the paperback romance she'd left on the coffee table. "—and lower my core temperature a little before going out into the water."

"How very responsible," Larx said dryly.

Christiana grinned. "Besides, Schuyler and Jessica are coming *together* toward the beginning, and I wanted to make sure there was still something left when they arrived."

Schuyler was Christiana's *ex*-girlfriend, and Jessica was her very best friend in the entire world. Christi had announced her intention of making them both good friends so she could have a trio to replace the one that had just graduated, and this was her first step.

"Well, good luck on that front," Larx said diplomatically. He didn't remind her that the whole reason Schuyler and Christiana had broken up was because Schuyler had been jealous of Christi's friendship with Jessica. That seemed like too much meddling, even for a concerned father. “Yoshi and I are going to go get changed, and I’ll join Aaron at the grill.” He thought sourly of the increasing heat of the day. “Or in the pool and then at the grill.”

She grinned and ran up to kiss his cheek. “It’ll be fine, Daddy. Nobody’s going to wreck Olivia and Wombat Willie’s house, I swear.”

“Well, thanks for making sure that doesn’t happen,” Larx said, before giving her a quick two-armed hug. “Now I’ve got to hurry up—I’ve got some news for Aaron he’s going to want to hear.”

Christi stopped him with a hand on his arm. “Daddy, you’re not going to ruin the party by leaving to go look for Curtis MacDonald, are you?”

Larx grimaced. “Well, no. We’re going to let the police do their jobs. But that doesn’t mean we can’t, you know, brainstorm a little to help.”

She made a face. “Ugh. Moral dilemmas. On the one hand, he’s a kid, but on the other hand… what an asshole.”

“Right now we’re going to remember that he’s a kid who needs help,” Larx told her gently. “And ask the other kids who made it through high school if they remember anything to help him.”

“You’re a good person, Daddy,” she said decisively, and he wondered what Curtis MacDonald had done to her, personally, that would make her not want to even look for the kid.

“We’ll talk later,” he said, and she looked away, two spots of color confirming his initial suspicion that MacDonald had been messing with her in some way. “Right now, let me go change so your entire AP class can see me in my board shorts and Hawaiian shirt, thus proclaiming me the dorkiest teacher in history.”

“An award I shall win by a mile,” Yoshi said with an air of superiority that made Larx wonder exactly what his barbecue-by-the-pool outfit looked like. He stared as Yoshi marched into the bathroom to change, and Christiana snickered.

“I can’t wait,” she said, her voice high and thready with suppressed laughter. Then she gestured to Jaime’s room with an imperious finger. “Go change. Go have fun. Stop fretting over Curtis MacDonald.” She sobered. “C’mon, Dad. Kirby and Kellan are so excited, which is funny because they’re both hanging around the house for at least another two years.”

Larx smiled at her. “Do you mind?” he asked.

She shook her head. "I'm even glad Livvy's close by. It's dangerous, you know. Who says you'll get rid of me when it's my turn to graduate?"

He chest gave a little throb. "You have all this light, Christi-lu-lu-belle. I think I owe it to the world to share."

The laugh she gave was an evil promise of what was to come, and it was enough to encourage him to run away and get busy.

One graduation at a time.

BY THE time he got to the barbecue, flip-flops, straw hat, zinc oxide and all, he had to concede Yoshi won in the swimwear department. Larx's shorts were loud, Santa Fe patterned, and obnoxious, and his purple Hawaiian shirt clashed terribly, but Yoshi? Yoshi was wearing pink Pusheen board shorts, with the chubby, iconic cartoon feline engaged in every pursuit from skateboarding to eating birthday cake, and his violet shirt had the same pattern.

Larx spent a full thirty seconds staring at his best friend and vice principal in disbelief.

"Your boyfriend let you out of the house? Knowing you'd be wearing that?" he asked in horror.

Yoshi gave an almost kittenish shrug. "You got shot so I could wear this outfit. Get over it." And then he walked toward the pool, showing off his Pusheen threads and doing a little dance while a small crowd of arrivals called out, "What? No Hello Kitty?"

"I did not get shot so he could wear that outfit," he grumbled, looking over Aaron's shoulder and resting his hand on his hip briefly. He wanted a full-body hug, but as much as they claimed to be "out," *knowing* your principal was living with the deputy was not the same as seeing them necking by the pool.

"You sort of did," Aaron teased. His own board shorts were pale blue, and his shirt was white with little blue dots. He looked like he could be in a menswear catalog, and Larx wanted to flip through his pages and drool. Possibly because it had been a good long week since they'd been able to have sex, but also because Aaron George was six feet, three inches of broad-shouldered, blond, blue-eyed perfection, and Larx had discovered he definitely had a type.

"I don't have any idea what you're talking about," Larx said loftily. "You need to turn the burgers—they're going to get burned."

"Not everybody likes them rare, Larx," Aaron returned patiently, but he turned a couple anyway because Larx obviously did. "And Yoshi came out and got removed from his job, and then you got shot and went on television all fainting and heroic and told people that you didn't want a medal, you wanted your vice principal back, and you got him back. So yes. You *did* get shot so he could be your out and proud vice principal and wear that…." Aaron couldn't do it. He looked over to where Yoshi was doing the cannonball from the small diving board at the end of the pool and shuddered. "My God. It's your fault. I know it shouldn't be, but I blame you."

Larx cackled, and together they turned to watch Kellan and Kirby, surrounded by a small number of their friends, exclaim over the refreshment table. There would be more coming, everybody knew, but the boys were like Christiana—aware of their duties as hosts. Both boys were wearing board shorts, and they were tan from having used the pool before, and beautiful too, in the way that healthy young men are.

And they were smiling and excited, and their entire world stretched in front of them.

"I know I've said this," Aaron murmured, "but I'm sort of glad Kirby's staying for another two years."

"Kellan too," Larx said. "I love my haiku poem, you know?" Kellan, Kirby, and Christi—Yoshi had insisted it wasn't *really* haiku, but Larx didn't know what else to call it.

"Yeah," Aaron said. As they watched, Kellan excused himself and ran toward them, his cell phone in his hand.

"Hey, guys," he said brightly, "smile for Zay, okay? I know he can't make it, but I promised him as many pictures as I could."

"I took some of the ceremony," Aaron said, after they posed and he clicked. He handed Larx his grill fork and reached into his back pocket, pulling out his camera and finding the pictures of Kellan and Kirby crossing the stage.

"Kirby's speech too," Larx said. "It was really good."

"Buffering…." Aaron mumbled, probably waiting for the speech to load. "And… there. Pass them on."

Kellan's grin held a tinge of sadness in it for the first boy he'd ever loved, who had nearly been taken from all of them. Isaiah's parents had moved to a small apartment in Sacramento so they could be near their son as he underwent several operations and physical rehabilitation. He'd be graduating this year, yes—but through independent study, and Larx's heart ached for the boy, who probably would have been valedictorian if a vengeful woman hadn't stabbed him for rejecting her daughter's advances in favor of Kellan's. The boys were officially broken up—Larx and Aaron had been there to pick up the pieces of Kellan's shattered heart when it had happened—but Larx had hopes that once Isaiah regained his mobility and he and Kellan had a chance to reconnect, their romance might continue. Both boys had shown a constancy and a devotion to each other as friends that a lot of adults didn't have over a long separation.

"Are he and his folks coming home soon?" Larx asked softly, and Kellan's shrug wasn't promising.

"His dad's looking for work. They all miss Colton, but it's hard. They might have to sell their property and just start over."

Larx grimaced. "I'm sorry, Kell. But you two have stayed friends all this time. It's not going away now."

Kellan gave him a smile that he obviously had to work hard for, but that didn't make it any less valuable. "I razzed him a little, said it's a good thing he wasn't here, or Arial Cho might have been salutatorian, and we never would have gotten to hear Kirby's speech."

"Not true!" Kirby called, moving into their little circle as his classmates went to town on the refreshments. "I would have worked just hard enough to *beat* Arial in order to give that speech." He winked at Kellan. "Isaiah was way ahead of both of us, so there was no catching up with that much greatness. But Arial? Yeah. Totally."

"In your *dreams*, George!" Arial called from the refreshment table, and Kirby turned to grin at her. Then he turned back to Larx and his dad and nodded in complete sincerity.

"It was a lock," he assured them, sotto voce. "I had the extra credit projects all lined up."

"To be salutatorian and not valedictorian," Aaron asked, sounding baffled. Larx grimaced and looked at Kirby in frustration.

"Ooh! Did I forget to tell Dad my grand plan?" Kirby asked, and Larx nodded.

"You did," he said. He'd been privy to it because he'd heard Kirby waxing rhapsodic during AP Physics, a class that was pretty much kick back and party after the test had been given in early May.

"See," Kirby told Aaron earnestly, "the thing is, the valedictorian had to give a *really* serious speech. That's, like, tradition. And I wanted to give a happy, perky speech about family and you guys. I didn't want to *give* the valedictorian speech, so I found out what Arial's GPA was probably going to be, and Colby Brunel told me straight up what he thought he was dead-center perfect, and I calculated *my* GPA to the last fu… er, frickin' fraction, with extra credit waiting in the sidelines if I had to weight and balance it." He nodded, looking insufferably pleased with himself. "So if Zay had been here, I still would have been salutatorian, and Zay would have been responsible for the big, heavy, 'we have a moral obligation to succeed' sort of speech."

Aaron was staring at his son with the same sort of disbelief that Larx had shown about Yoshi's swimming costume. It was a good thing Larx had the grill implements, because some of the hamburgers would have been burned crispy, given how long it took him to recover.

"I…," Aaron said, dumbfounded, still staring. "I… I got nothin'." He shook his head and came back to himself. "Let me get the plate there, Larx. If you flip those one more time they're going to fall apart."

He disappeared for a moment, and Larx said, "Good timing. I think you missed a lecture on not doing the bare minimum by about as much as you missed watching Colby Brunel get to give your speech."

Kirby chuckled. "No way. I told you—extra credit lined up in every class." He sobered. "But the lecture, though. You were right. Wait until it all fell out and he couldn't get mad at me."

Larx stared at him. "That's not what I said." Dear lord, he *hoped* that wasn't what he said.

Kirby shrugged. "It was close. You said 'You might want to pick your moment to tell your father. He's been stressed this spring.'"

"So the rest of that you made up," Larx told him, relief coursing through his body. He did *not* want to be responsible for Aaron's reaction to his son's cheerful disregard for the "be all you can be" school of parenting rules.

"Pretty much," Kirby said, and Kellan socked him in the arm playfully.

"You're being an asshole."

Kirby pretended to think about it. "You're right. Must be the heat. Let's go swim."

Kellan set his phone down on the picnic table, and together they headed for the pool—two boys, one tall and slender and golden and the other shorter, stockier, and dark haired, but more like brothers than any two kids Larx had ever met.

He shook his head and went back to the grill, taking the plate Aaron had returned to offer him.

"Did you know?" Aaron asked, still sounding a little shocked.

"He bragged about it to his entire AP class," Larx said. He shook his head. "I told him he should tell *you* about the plan, and he said he would." Larx grunted and struggled to get most of a hamburger on the plate. "I had no idea he'd do it *now*, but you gotta admit, it *did* happen."

Aaron shook his head in disbelief and then did that Aaron thing that Larx loved so much and took a deep breath and let it go. It was how Kirby had dealt with learning his father was dating a man, and apparently it was how Aaron dealt with realizing his bright-and-shining son had the soul of a true grifter. "That kid," he said, "has a very… *distinct* destiny. I don't know what it's going to be. He could be an FBI Agent, or he could be a mysterious millionaire with an unidentified source of income, but it's going to be *very* unique."

Larx chuckled and bumped arms with Aaron, wanting to hold him very badly. "I look forward to seeing it unfold."

He handed Aaron the plate of meat and rotated what was left on the grill while Aaron went to fetch another plate of uncooked food, including some giant marinated portobella mushrooms they'd found that would make excellent vegan patties.

Kids had trickled through the kitchen door in ones and twos, each kid bearing a contribution to the potluck and a towel—and a smile—and Larx had that very real fear hosts get that there wouldn't be enough food.

"Relax," Aaron murmured into his ear. "So far we've got the perfect balance of food and voracious eaters. I see no surreptitious glances, no drinking from a paper bag, and Kellan and Kirby look—"

"Grown-up and happy," Larx said with satisfaction. "But still willing to be totally under our wing for another two years."

"Mm…." Aaron's voice had a sort of whine in it—like he knew something Larx didn't and didn't want Larx to get mad.

"What?" Larx shot him a sharp glance.

"Uhm, Kellan was… well, he was asking me about sponsorship through the academy," Aaron said apologetically. "He's planning on taking criminal justice classes at the junior college for two years, but you know. He, uh, is sort of thinking about an endgame."

Larx swallowed, his throat suddenly tight, torn between pride and worry. "He wants to be a cop?" he asked, his voice squeaking.

"Sorry, Larx." Aaron's expression was sympathetic, and Larx gave him a watery smile.

"That's fine," he said. "Kirby gets to be a bad boy, and Kellan gets to be a cop. It's very fitting."

"For our family," Aaron agreed, "it certainly is."

Larx had been a "bad boy." Not so much on the legal side of things, but he'd been a broody, motorcycle-riding, sleep-with-anything, Byronic hero in his day. His day had ended when he'd knocked up his girlfriend, but Aaron liked to remind him in the best of ways that bad boys could be sexy—particularly after they were reformed fathers and sterling members of the community whose only concession to a shady past was a sharp tongue and a refusal to let bureaucracy take over their lives.

"Well," Larx said, swallowing the lump and engaging securely with the relief that Kellan had found a goal, a niche in the world that he felt he could fill, "your news is a lot more positive than mine."

And with that he filled Aaron in on Curtis MacDonald's abandoned truck and the state of things inside.

"OH GOD," Aaron murmured. "How did it get so bad?"

Larx shook his head. "We knew, Aaron—how could we not? But I'm not running my school like a prison. No drug-sniffing dogs, no shakedowns. We must have had a zillion meetings with the kid, but until his parents showed up, our hands were tied."

Aaron looked at him unhappily because they both knew there was one more thing he could have done, but it would have put Curtis in a juvenile detention center instead of a rehabilitation facility. "You could have asked us to come search his vehicle," Aaron said softly, just to get it out in the open.

Larx grunted and looked away. "God, Aaron, I didn't sign up here to put kids in jail."

"I know," Aaron told him, getting it but also hoping Larx got it too. "But you can't save every kid. I wish you could. I mean, *you* can save more than most, but this kid—he was angry and mean. We both know he missed college scouts because he couldn't keep his racist mouth shut during football games and you suspended him. You should have. You made the kid respect the rules because you weren't afraid of him *or* his father. But Curtis made bad decisions, and he's old enough to have to pay for them."

Larx groaned. "God. Truth and reason. You gotta hit me with that now?"

Aaron resisted the urge to pull him close and kiss the top of his head. It was something he would have done if they were in private, but not here, in front of all their kids' friends. Not because he was ashamed or embarrassed or uncomfortable, but because he and Larx, when it came down to it, were private people. Larx was hurting, but comforting would show the rest of the world he was hurting, and Aaron didn't want him exposed like that.

"You did your best by the kid," Aaron said. "And you're right. Arresting him and getting him in the system isn't going to do him or his parents any favors. But right now they'd probably rather he be in juvenile or state detention, getting weaned off the meth, than out there in the world with three hundred dollars to inject, snort, or blow."

Larx gave him a dirty look. "Thanks. That image—" He kissed his fingertips in the classic chef's-kiss gesture, but Aaron knew that was because it had hit home.

"But even if you'd turned him in," Aaron said with a sigh, "there's no guarantee the charges would have stuck or he wouldn't have been released on his own recognizance because juvenile detention is full. Don't second-guess yourself. Like I said, you did your best."

"Just maybe trust you guys a little more," Larx said on a sigh. "I get it."

"Get what?" Eamon said, striding across the patio toward them. He paused and took a detour toward the food table, then drew near balancing a cold soda and a plate full of hamburgers, potato salad, and these little quiche things that somebody's mom had made and Aaron thought were really delicious.

"Larx here was just saying that next time he had a kid like this, he might call us a little sooner," Aaron told him. "He's also going to—"

But he couldn't go on because Eamon was laughing so hard Aaron had to hold his hand out for his boss's plate of food.

Aaron watched as Eamon bent double, rested his hands on his knees, and whooped, while Larx studiously ignored them both and continued on with the grill.

Finally, as Eamon was straightening and holding his hands out for his plate again, Aaron gave Larx a droll look. “I feel as though I’ve been had.”

Larx’s mouth, pursed in a grim, flat line of disapproval, cracked into a smile. “There was no collusion, officer, I swear.”

“Thanks for that,” Eamon said, taking a bite of his hamburger and chewing. He swallowed. “Could be the best laugh I’ll have all day.”

And that thawed Larx completely, because he chuckled. “We aim to please. Now did you get anything off the truck?”

Eamon grimaced. “Well, yes and no.”

“That would be my least favorite answer to any question,” Larx told him ruminatively while Eamon took another bite of burger. Suddenly Yoshi was at his elbow, his improbably bright outfit drying in the sun and a triumphant look on his face.

“Did you get all those nasty honors students with the big squirt gun, Yosh?” Larx asked, and Aaron chuckled because after the cannonball in the pool, that had been Mr. Nakamoto’s next trick. The kids had helped him fill up the giant squirt guns, too, so he could get all willing participants in a furious blast of comeuppance—and chill off the kids who hadn’t been taking advantage of the pool before they got too hot.

“It was glorious,” Yoshi told him a little maniacally. “Ten out of ten. We need to do this *every* year!”

“Then what are you—hey, give me that back—doing over here!” While he talked, Yoshi very competently took the grill tongs from Larx just as he’d swiped them from Aaron.

“Go eat, Principal Larkin,” Yoshi told him sententiously. “Jump in the pool for a minute. Talk to Eamon about scary real things and then play with the kids.” He gave an intentionally shifty look from side to side. “I may or may not have promised them all a chance to gang up on you and totally wipe you out after you’ve eaten, so, you know. Be ready to have fun whether you want to or not.”

Larx gave him a flat look. “Traitor.”

“All day every day,” Yoshi returned cheerfully. Then he turned to Eamon with a slightly more serious look on his face. “Sheriff Mills, good to see you. If you tear these guys away from this party, I swear I won't vote for you."

"You won't be voting for me," Eamon said indignantly. "You'll be voting for Aaron! And I hear you." He took another bite of burger. "Besides, I get at least one more of these before I go anywhere, so come on, guys, let's sit down and talk. George, could you get my soda there? I was looking forward to finishing that."

The kids managed to flee the three serious-looking adults without being too obvious about it, and Larx had to laugh as he realized that two of the people they were displacing were Jessica and Schuyler, who apparently *had* made peace at Christiana's insistence. Well, his daughter really *was* a dollop of sunshine. Jaime had made himself unofficial houseboy and was busy conducting people in and out of the house and directing them to the bathroom, or to the living room in case they got too hot or too tired. Aaron could see through the kitchen door that a small group of kids had gathered around the TV to watch a kid's show that had been popular when these young adults *had* been children, and they were all watching the cartoons breathlessly, like they'd never have a chance to see them again.

Well, maybe not as children, he realized, and wondered when teenagers had gotten so wise.

They had just gotten settled when there was a rustle from the kitchen and then Kellan came out yelling, "Stay there, man with a suit. We don't know you!"

Larx and Aaron turned around to stare, and Aaron recognized the tall bald man wearing short sleeves and a tie as somebody both important and, well, surprising. Larx called, "Kellan! That's Superintendent Hassbender! You sort of have to let him in—he's my boss!"

Kellan wrinkled his nose. "But you're the *principal*," he said, sounding indignant. "You don't *have* a boss!"

"Were you not paying attention to the people speaking today?" Larx asked, laughing in exasperation. "He *spoke at your graduation*!"

Kellan cocked his head. "Dude, there were adults going blah blah blah, some girl sang, and then Kirby gave his speech and you told us all it was over. Do you really think I know what was going on during the blah blah blah?"

Larx stared at him and started massaging his temples.

"Here," Aaron said, slipping a root beer into his hand. "It's the caffeinated kind. You need it."

"Police academy?" Larx asked him bitterly.

"Sorry, baby. With that attitude he's already halfway there."

Larx grunted and then called to the superintendent. "Harvey! Come sit—but grab some food first. The parents helped us put on quite a spread."

"I know," Harvey Hassbender said, smiling as he surveyed the table. "My wife donated a casserole, which I see has been appreciated! Right on. She'll be so proud."

"I did not know that," Larx said. "Yoshi, did you know that?"

"Maybe," Yoshi said, putting his evil soy dogs on the grill as Aaron watched. "It's vegan, Larx. Vegan casserole. I bet you ate it and loved it."

"I don't hate vegan food," Larx retorted, which was totally true. Aaron's kids frequently accused him of trying to poison them with fresh vegetables. "I just don't think it belongs in my hot dogs," he grumbled to himself.

Hassbender chuckled and joined them at the table, his plate piled satisfyingly high. "Do you know I saw a whole other round of food in the kitchen? Nobody's parents are going to be cooking for a week—their kids are going to go home sunburned and round as whales."

"Our final graduation gift to the students of Colton High," Larx said with satisfaction. "They're welcome."

"Well," Hassbender said, surveying the busy pool area and listening to the happy chatter with the occasional shriek of laughter, "You've done a good job here. There was a kid keeping a list of who showed up when I walked in. That young man, right? Kellan Corker?"

"Yessir," Aaron said. "He's sort of a, erm, fosterling."

"I know," Hassbender said, surprising him. "Larx has kept me apprised. I'm just impressed. You managed to throw a nice shindig here with your young people. I've seen official school functions that didn't look this wholesome."

Aaron and Larx both grimaced. "We're hoping nobody gets pregnant tonight," Larx said earnestly. "Seriously, they've come this far, right?"

Hassbender laughed. "Yes, they have." There was a moment of quiet as everybody took advantage of the lull to eat, and then Harvey Hassbender left the meat of the lunch table for the meat of the conversation.

"So," he said with his mouth full, "about the MacDonald kid?"

Eamon sighed and wiped his mouth. "I've got dibs on the frosted brownies for dessert," he told them all soberly before proceeding to business. "So thanks to Larx, we found the kid's truck and we established a timeline. We know the kid had a substance-abuse problem, and the truck had evidence of meth. Now we know that there are two condemned houses in the area that house addicts, and one of them is about five miles from Colton High."

"The one just off Dropoff Drive?" Aaron asked. He was familiar with both of them, but Dropoff Drive was particularly problematic because it was backed by a canyon that had barely managed to lay out a road in a valley of loose shale. They'd lost a couple of people off the unfenced back of the drive. Most of them, it was widely believed, had been under the influence. It did not bode well for Curtis MacDonald if he was inside that house; even if he hadn't run through three-hundred-dollars' worth of meth in the last four days, the danger of falling into the canyon was very real. Not to mention the weapons and poor judgment that invariably came from a place where people's only goal was to blow their minds out with chemicals. Unless police had a warrant or probable cause, there was no reason to raid the house.

"Did you get Clancy to sign off on probable cause?" Aaron asked, talking about Clancy Yarborough, the county judge.

"I did," Eamon said. "But it was a hard, hard pitch. I had to threaten to call in the county DEA, and he was *not* pleased with me. Apparently the MacDonalds are distant relations of his wife, and he was full of the 'young men will go off and party' bullshit. Don't even get me started. I swear to Christ the good ole boys network around here is so incestuous you have to have walleyes and a clubfoot to get elected."

Aaron managed to keep a straight face, but next to him, Larx snorted up casserole and had to be pounded on the back while he coughed.

"Thanks for that," Larx rasped, swallowing the last of his root beer. "Sincerely, Eamon, I'll never forgive you."

"*You*?" Hassbender asked, wiping up his own spills. "I have to beg these people for money every year. How am I going to look them in the walleyes after that?"

Eamon gave a very real chuckle. "Welcome to my world, people." He wiped his mouth with a sigh and eyed the brownies longingly. "Anyway, I get to come here and eat with you nice people because we're waiting for a task force from Sacramento to come up and help us. Detectives, SWAT team, and all. We suspect lots of guns, lots of crazy trigger fingers here, and we want backup with Kevlar and lots of beanbag guns."

Aaron made a sound of complaint—and resignation—and Eamon glared at him severely. "No. No, you can't. You and Larx have taken a third to a half of the senior class off our minds just by letting your kids have them over to swim. The rest of Colton is cleared out—kids going down to Sacramento to celebrate, or up to Reno. When were you closing this little shindig down, by the way?"

"Eight or nine," Aaron said, glancing at Larx. "We've got lights out here, but once it gets too cold to swim, the kids get tired."

"Perfect. I'll let you know if you need to brief any parents, but Dropoff Drive is a ways off the beaten path—most of the houses that lined it have been deserted since the canyon started to eat their backyards." The houses themselves were built on the first granite table in from the edge, but the backyards, such as they were, grew smaller and less safe every year.

They all nodded, and Aaron felt marginally better about his place in the scheme of things—he was keeping kids safe just by giving them a place to enjoy themselves. It was the philosophy that made Larx such an outstanding administrator.

"But how do we stop this from happening again?" Hassbender asked apprehensively.

Eamon grimaced. "Well, from what I can see, Larx did his best. Two certified letters? Isn't that what you texted me?"

Larx grimaced and nodded. "Yes. We tried *so* hard to connect with the parents."

"But you didn't want to turn him over to law enforcement because that would have ruined his life," Eamon said with a grimace. "And it might have. We don't have any of our own facilities, so he would have either been placed in juvenile detention, or he would have been set free almost before the withdrawal shakes subsided. So we'll work on that. It would be great if *our* community had a protocol that could take care of our own. I realize we can't save everybody—" He shook his head. "—and this MacDonald kid was probably not where we should start. I've had run-ins with him before, and he's a piece of work, like his father. But we still do need a better alternative than to ruin his life before he's out of high school."

"I'll put it on the list of world problems to address," Larx said dryly. "Harvey?"

"Right at the top," Hassbender said with a grim smile. "But in the meantime, I agree with Eamon. Keep kids here, keep them safe, keep them sober." He glanced around. "It looks like a fun day. Keep it that way and we'll stay out of Eamon's hair."

"What's left of it," Eamon said, rubbing his graying buzz cut with a smile. Heaving himself to his feet, he said, "Now about those frosted brownies…," before wandering off to the table.

"Is that why you stopped by?" Larx asked Harvey once Eamon was immersed in dessert heaven.

Harvey shrugged and smiled sheepishly. "The student council has been talking about nothing but this party at the admin building. I just, you know, wanted to see the kids happy one more time before they weren't ours anymore."

Aaron smiled widely. Larx had told him that the superintendent was a pretty awesome guy, but this was his first real meeting with him. Suddenly that whole "takes a village" thing didn't sound like sanctimonious bullshit.

They talked desultorily then about plans for next year, Aaron's campaign, and how Harvey Hassbender planned to fully support him.

"Who's your competition going to be?" Hassbender asked irritably. "Please God not Percy Hardesty!"

Aaron grimaced. "He's made noises about running on the heterosexuality platform. That's got a bigger following than I care to admit."

"Oh please," Hassbender muttered. "That's like saying he should win because he's right-handed. Yay Percy! You're in the sociogenetic majority! Go you!"

Larx and Aaron sputtered with laughter, and Larx said, "And what *are* his contributions to heterosexuality? Is he married? Seeing someone? Has he met a potential mate who *doesn't* experience nausea, vomiting, and compulsive regret in his presence?"

Harvey laughed so hard he choked, and Yoshi had to leave the grill to come over and bang on his back. Finally, after a few more sips of soda and some bread, Harvey could breathe again, and Aaron went to rescue Yoshi's soy dogs. While the moment had been happy, and this entire day was happy, he couldn't help but brood just a little bit about his fellow deputy, the problem Eamon couldn't get rid of for Aaron before the fall election.

And Eamon had tried; Aaron had seen the paperwork. Eamon had recorded every incident, every time Percy Hardesty had drawn his weapon in anger and not necessity, every time he'd tried to use his job as a platform for his outdated, bigoted, and racist beliefs, every harassment complaint, every potential lawsuit, but Percy was (in Larx's words) waxing every knob at the county seat because the people Eamon looked to wouldn't let Percy go.

"I swear if Eamon breaks wind in his office, somebody from the mayor's office is visiting to check on his health," Aaron had complained to Larx. "I hate that this good ole straight white boy thing is that powerful!"

But Larx had worked at an inner-city school. He'd seen a contractor finish a wealthy white school site in six months while they spent four years on an identical site in a diverse area so he could milk the school for everything they had—and because he hadn't needed to fear the repercussions from "those people." Larx had heard kids whose parents had been born and raised in the Sacramento valley told to "go home," and he'd seen white-power signs exchanged among the kids who never seemed to get in trouble from other teachers.

Larx had believed it and had warned Aaron to be careful about Percy Hardesty. "He doesn't have your back," he'd said soberly, and Aaron stabbed a soy dog with unnecessary force, thinking that he probably didn't have Eamon's either.

The thought made him shudder, especially in light of the raid Eamon had hinted about when he'd sat and eaten with them. Aaron suddenly wanted very badly to beg his children's forgiveness and run off to suit up. The only thing that kept him from doing exactly that was the thought that Eamon had the good sense to wait for the units from Sacramento.

That and Warren Coolidge, who may not have been the sharpest knife in the drawer, but Aaron had always counted on Warren to have his back.

Still, Aaron was well on his way to a good brood when Christiana came up and nudged him to look at what was happening by the pool. Larx was standing and talking to Yoshi, who kept maneuvering him, it seemed, a little to the left, a little to the left, until he was right on the pool's edge, staring at Yoshi in irritation. Well, he should have been—he was about to fall in, flip-flops and all.

Christi suppressed a giggle, and Aaron looked wider and realized that while Yoshi was keeping Larx entertained by telling a story that apparently needed a *lot* of hand gestures, the rest of the AP kids were getting quietly in position. Armed with small but powerful squirt guns—a purchase the kids had made with their *own* money, Aaron remembered—Larx's entire AP class was gathered around the pool, hiding their little plastic toys in the backs of their shorts, in bathing suit covers, and the more bosomy girls were even concealing them in their cleavage. Larx glanced up and caught Aaron's eyes, concealing a tiny smirk of awareness.

He knew what was coming, all right, but far be it from Mr. Larkin, everybody's favorite AP teacher, to squelch creativity or initiative.

The noise on the pool patio got quieter and quieter, almost like an old western movie, and just when Larx was biting his lip—presumably to keep from telling the whole class to get on with it—Yoshi yelled, "Now!"

Oh, the carnage! Oh, the chaos! Oh, the humanity! Every kid at the party, including Jaime and Christiana, turned on Larx with their squirt guns, and then, because he should have known better, they started taking out Mr. Nakamoto as well. Yoshi cried out, "Traitors!" and Larx gave his best cartoon western impersonation.

"You dirty varmints, ya got me!" he called, clutching his chest. "What a world, what a world…." And with that—and a quick look behind him to reassure himself the pool was clear—he toppled over backward into the cool water.

Yoshi, who had no such illusions of dignity, screamed, "You'll never take me alive, coppers!" before doing his second cannonball of the day into the depths.

And that was it. Every kid with a squirt gun screamed and jumped into the pool in a frenzy of splashing and squirting and general mayhem, including Christiana, who had gotten her father with the biggest squirt gun they owned.

BY THE time the mayhem was sorted out, the sun was actually back behind the trees, casting long shadows. The kids all helped to put what was left of the decimated food away, storing it neatly in Elton and Olivia's refrigerator.

"This way," one girl said happily, "it can be sort of a thank you for letting us use their house."

Aaron took his own dip in the pool as Kirby and Kellan, along with the help of their friends and using an inexhaustible store of energy Aaron envied, swept the pool patio and picked up any trash. Other friends gathered trash bags to put in the big bin in the garage, and the kids not doing that were straightening and vacuuming the living room. The consideration of the kids humbled him, and he pulled Kirby aside to tell him so.

"You know, one of the reasons your sister showed up was to clean up after the party tomorrow," he said. Maureen, after hugging Kirby until his head nearly popped off, had opted to hang with Olivia, Elton, and Berto in Larx's living room that night. She'd be there all week, she told Aaron, and he was looking forward to spending some time with her. She'd had plans to go into the Peace Corps that year after her own graduation, but a problem with credits had arisen, and she'd had to put off her plans until the next year. He'd spent hours on the phone with her, but he knew his daughter still needed her daddy to help make the boo-boo a little better.

He was also starting to sense that the break was giving her time to rethink the Peace Corps plan entirely. She'd majored in science, but she had enough classes in upper division biology and anatomy to qualify as a premed student, and she'd taken the MCAT that February. Her results had come in, and he could tell from her suppressed excitement that she'd qualified for a couple of places that he couldn't possibly afford. That wouldn't stop his Mau-Mau, though. Kirby was irrepressible, but Maureen was *unstoppable*. He just needed to talk it through with her so she could decide on a course of action.

"I know," Kirby said now in response to Maureen's good intentions. "But this way, all we have to do tomorrow is sleep and veg and eat leftovers. I know you'll probably have to work, and Larx is going to want to help with the Curtis MacDonald situation, but we claim absolute broccoli tomorrow. The most energy any of us plan to spend is arguing over which movie to watch."

Aaron chuckled. "That's totally fair," he said. The last two weeks had been hellishly busy for the seniors—finals, the graduation trip, school checkout—and he figured they all had sleep coming their way. And they weren't sitting still over the summer, either. Aaron had unashamedly used his pull to get Kirby and Kellan part-time jobs at the station, Kellan in dispatch and Kirby as unskilled labor in the tiny forensics office. They'd be starting in a week because Aaron suspected they'd need more than one day in which to be broccoli, but look at the kids! They worked hard and played hard, and as far as Aaron could see, deserved the time off.

"Dad?" Kirby murmured, pausing in the work and moving close to Aaron, who was scraping the grill off in anticipation of powering it down before taking the racks to be washed.

"Yeah?" Aaron could hear the seriousness in Kirby's voice, and in the melancholy hour of the late afternoon, he suspected they were going to get to the throat-tightening, hug-thumping part of what was admittedly an emotional day. Tiffany had been self-contained and stoic on her graduation day, which had been celebrated with a few friends who had mostly ignored the grown-ups and hidden in Tiff's room, plotting world domination. Maureen had happily cried all the way through a kid-planned picnic in a park in Auburn while pretty much the entire senior class signed her annual. Kirby was neither stoic and self-contained nor weepy, but he did have a healthy respect for the big moments. He'd always worked hard to make Christmas as special for his big sisters and for Aaron as they'd worked for him.

"I wanted to say thank you for all of this. You and Larx, doing the house swap, going all out for the party. I mean, even though you know we're going to be leeching off you for at least two more years, this was pretty awesome."

Aaron smiled happily, because the appreciation went both ways. "It's easy to throw a party for people who work so hard for it," he said, but then something about the inflection Kirby had given the words, "at least two more years" caught his attention.

"So, uhm, *at least* two years?"

Kirby grinned. "You caught that, did you? So, uhm, I was thinking…. Junior college, *yes*, but also EMT training, because a new class opens up in July. I can take classes after work, get my certification, and work the job and go to school. And, uhm…." He sort of wiggled his shoulders in apology. "Dad, I… I get school. I get why you worked so hard for us to be able to go. But Dad, I'm *tired* of school. If I can get some training, work a worthwhile job for a couple of years, and then move on to something different, I just… you know. Think it'll be easier."

Aaron nodded, suddenly knowing how Larx felt about Kellan's decision to start in the academy. "Uhm, son," he said, "EMTs are first responders. It's, you know, not always easy. In fact, uhm, it's gory and heartbreaking and hard and—"

"And grown-up," Kirby said, like a, uhm, grown-up. "It's not for little kids. I get it, Dad. And I looked at the pay. I'm going to want to do something that makes a little more after a while—unless they have sort of a teacher/first responder renaissance and billionaires start paying their taxes and stuff."

Aaron twisted his upper lip. "I, uh, wouldn't count on that, son."

Kirby nodded with the same expression. "I am *not*," he agreed, then sobered. "But I *am* serious. I'll still take the job in the tech office—it's only three days a week. Don't worry, Dad. I got it, well, not handled, but you know…." He bit his lip, and Aaron could see not only that this meant a lot to him, but also that he wasn't as sure as he was trying to make out.

And a part of Aaron wanted to take advantage of that. God, being the first medical technician on a scene was such a hard job. Kirby was so capable, so competent, but Aaron didn't want his *baby* out there on the front lines.

But his baby wasn't a baby anymore. He wasn't fully ready to launch—he'd made that clear—but he *was* fully ready to explore the world on his own terms.

Aaron's job here was not to keep him in the nest, bound by fear and trepidation. It was to give him the confidence to try the things he might really love. Kirby *loved* helping people. He was *good* at it. And he had a unique ability—not to shrug things off, but to put them in perspective. Aaron would be doing his son a disservice if he didn't give him props for the things he could do well.

"I think you could do a good job," Aaron said softly, meaning it but afraid. "I think… I mean, you've been worrying about me all your life. This could be a good way to pay me back, but I don't think that should hold you back."

Kirby's grin hit Aaron right in the solar plexus, and he realized he'd been bracing for this blow all day. It didn't matter. There was nothing to prepare him for the knowledge that his youngest really wasn't his youngest anymore. He was an adult and more than capable of making plans for his future.

"It'll be fine," Kirby said with a careless wave. "No worries. I mean, how bad could it—"

Aaron held his hands out in panic. "The first thing you have to learn about first-responder world," he said, "is not to ask that question. Ever. *Ever*. Yes, we're superstitious—have you not learned that over the last eighteen years?"

Kirby nodded and managed to smother his smile. "It'll be awful. I'll hate it. Probably barf all over the place on my first call. Probably won't even last the first week of training. You'll be fine."

"That's my kind of plan," Aaron agreed, and then before Kirby was too old, too wise, to back out of his reach, he reached out and pulled his kid in close for a tight, shameless hug. "You're so grown-up," he whispered. "Just remember you'll always be my baby boy, okay?"

"Oh, Dad." Kirby didn't struggle out of the hug—he stepped back, like an adult. "I'm going to be freeloading off you guys for a good long time."

And then he hurried off to finish the cleanup as the temperature dropped a little more and the sun dipped toward that magic space on the horizon where it could knife through the trees.

THE PARTY quieted down after that, with kids drifting home a few at a time. Aaron broke out the firepit, and the dropping temperature by the pool was soon countered by a cozy blaze. At one point Kirby went inside and came back with a guitar in a case that looked very familiar—probably because it lived under Kirby's bed in the other house. Aaron stared at it, wondering if Olivia could play, when his son offered it to Larx, who was sitting at the picnic table with Nancy and Yoshi, back from the kids a little, but still part of the crowd.

Larx stared at it, then gave Christiana an embarrassed look. "Christi-lu-lu-belle…." He whined.

"I know you still play it sometimes," she said, laughing.

"He does?" Aaron asked, legitimately surprised.

"Usually when you're working late nights," Kellan said. "He'll sneak it out and go on the back porch."

"He's good," Jaime said loyally, but then, Jaime thought they were *all* good at *everything*, and while Aaron didn't mind that kind of confidence, he was pretty sure it was not to be trusted.

"C'mon, Daddy," Christi wheedled. "If you're good, it'll increase your cachet. If you suck, I'll spread it all around the school and humiliate you in public. Win/win!" She gave two thumbs-up.

Aaron could read Larx's arched eyebrows and wide eyes like a book. He was both impressed with the kids and dismayed at being put on the spot—and a little bit pleased, too, at the opportunity to perform.

"Green Day!" Aaron called, remembering the posters Larx kept on his bedroom walls. His misspent youth, he liked to say, but Aaron wasn't surprised by the guitar because he knew, from those posters alone, that this music was part of Larx's identity.

Larx gave Aaron an unfriendly look as he whistled and applauded, a one-man cheering section, but still Aaron's beloved and best friend reached out for the guitar.

Larx took it and tuned it, playing with the strings in a way that sounded familiar. "So," he said, "something sad and sloppy?"

There were a few, "Sures!" and a host of groans from the remaining students, and Larx smiled, the light from the firepit making him look a little diabolical and a lot fun—a grown-up Peter Pan, a lean-lipped, tanned, and weathered adult Cupid.

"Maybe not," he conceded, and the tune emerging from under his fingers became a little more real. "I've got one, but I think… I think I'm going to need help." And then he hit it, exactly, that perfect combination of notes, the one everybody recognized, one of the most famous songs in the world, and suddenly they were coming out of their cage, and they were doing just fine—and singing about jealousy at the top of their lungs as Larx surprised everybody with exactly how "not bad" he was.

He played a few more after that—Green Day, Pearl Jam, Springsteen, Collective Soul, and he finally finished with Foo Fighters' "Home."

His voice ached with love, with the need for peace, with joy to have the one thing he'd ever wanted just waiting for him to make it real. The last notes faded, along with Larx's surprisingly sweet tenor, and Yoshi said, "That's a hint if I ever heard one."

The party broke up, and Aaron looked around and realized that Olivia, Elton, Maureen, and Berto had come back to the house for the impromptu concert and it was time for him and Larx to go home.

He checked his phone surreptitiously—he would remember that—to see if there was any news about what had gone down at the meth house. Nothing. Which bothered him because Eamon would have normally texted him to at least say nothing had happened. But Aaron didn't want to bother his boss, and besides, as he and Larx headed for the minivan, the last vehicle to leave that night, he realized that the other kids had elected to sleep in the living room here at Olivia's, where pillows and blankets had been spread out to keep the party going.

And Olivia had brought her two stupidly cute dogs home with her, after Berto had taken them to Larx's house during the party, and there was a lot of excitement about petting them.

And Larx and Aaron got to go home alone.

Sweet Summer Skies

LARX CLOSED his eyes during the short drive home, grateful that Aaron had chosen the longer paved way, rather than the bumpier offroad-service-track way. The temperature had dropped, so Larx put pause on the AC, and they both rolled down their windows and let the mild night air flow through the car. It smelled like sun-warmed red dust and sugar pine trees, the nearby lakes and the river that fed them, and asphalt still baking from the day's heat. The trees stretched above their heads like greedy supplicants, glorying in the faint light from the stars and the waxing moon.

Aaron had turned the SUV's radio to a classic rock station, and Larx chuckled as Green Day's "Holiday" played.

"I should learn this one," he said, pulling his hand inside the car. He'd been playing with wind currents, but it was getting a wee bit chilly for that.

"I'm super impressed by how many you *do* know," Aaron said. "I had no idea you played that thing."

Larx smiled to himself, pleased. "It's good to pull out a few surprises," he said. The look on Aaron's face as he'd played was everything Larx had ever wanted from an adoring fan but wouldn't have known what to do with when he'd been twenty years old. Now, nearly thirty years after Larx had taken a random guitar class and had just kept on teaching himself, he was finally reaping the reward.

Like everything else good in his life—his kids, his job, his relationship with Aaron—it had taken its sweet time, but it was so, so worth it.

"I hope you're not too disappointed when it turns out I've got nothin'," Aaron said seriously, and Larx was pulled to him like a magnet, totally in the moment.

"You surprised *me* today, Deputy," he said soberly.

"Yeah?" Aaron asked, his lips twitching at the corners. "What did I do?"

"Chose family," Larx said promptly.

Aaron frowned. "You thought I'd be out at the raid?"

Larx shook his head. "No—I know you wouldn't be. You keep your promises. But you didn't just elect to *stay* with your family, you were *here* for them. Connected with the boys, played with the kids, chatted with the grown-ups. Only a little bit of brooding—"

"You caught that, did you?" Aaron asked, but his lips were twitching again.

"I did. You're worried about Eamon."

"Still am," Aaron told him seriously. "But yeah. I did brood a little."

"But you came back to us," Larx said simply. "You… you made a determination that today was absolutely your day with your family, and then you stuck to it. I… I always *thought* you would be that guy, but today you really lived up to it. It was impressive."

Aaron preened. "Impressive, yeah?"

"Yeah." Larx smiled to himself, knowing what was to come. Aaron didn't grab his knee or anything physical—this part of the road was winding, and that would be too risky—but the electricity, the physical tension in the car, was potent enough to raise the fine hairs on the back of Larx's neck.

He leaned into his seat and let the want roll through him, thick and rich and heady, a delicious counterpoint to the sensuality of the mild summer night.

"Stop that," Aaron purred.

"Stop what?" Larx asked, not even trying to hide his smile.

"You're thinking about sex," Aaron told him.

"Oh God, am I."

Aaron's chuckle went low and filthy. "Good."

WHEN THEY got home to Larx's low-slung little house, they behaved like grown-ups. Aaron parked carefully on the driveway in front of the lawn, pulling up to the garage door in such a way that would let another car park next to it and two more park behind those.

They made their way through the front door—locked, because Larx didn't raise fools—and greeted Dozer, short for Bulldozer, their big blond dog—as they came through.

The dog was ecstatic to see them but also had been fed and loved and made much of for the afternoon, as well as having a chance to play with the tiny twins, as Olivia called her household dogs. Dozer wagged and woofed and took his nighttime treat (of which Larx suspected there had been many, judging by the half-full bag) and then curled up with a woof on his giant beanbag in the living room. His tail thumped tiredly as Larx and Aaron moved about making sure things were locked and the extra food was put away, their keys were in the bowl by the door, and the windows were open and the air-conditioning off to capitalize on the cool breezes flowing through the house.

"Must shower," Larx murmured on their way up the stairs. He smelled like sweat and sunscreen and BBQ smoke and chlorine, and he didn't want to make love all sticky.

They didn't get time alone in the house that often. He wanted to savor.

"Same," Aaron said, leaning in to kiss his cheek. "I'll take the hall shower, you take the bedroom. Meet back when we're clean?"

Larx grinned at him. "Like you read my mind."

Which Aaron seemed to do frequently, Larx pondered as he let the hot water beat some of the day out of him. It had been a big one—and a good one—and Larx wanted to crawl into bed, clean and soft and sweet so he and his lover could touch each other in the pine-dust-scented night.

He slid into their bedroom in nothing more than a towel to find Aaron already there, wearing the same thing. He was sitting on the bed, texting on his phone quickly, but he set it on the charger as Larx walked in.

For a moment Larx considered giving him a hard time about "being there," but Aaron *had* been there, and Larx knew he was worried about his friends and fellow officers.

"Any word?" he asked.

Aaron shook his head. "No, but that's probably good." He gave Larx a shy smile. "I mean, us, alone, in the house? This is like a blue moon event, right?"

Larx grinned wickedly. He'd been thinking about this all week, and while his fantasies tended to get elaborate—bells, whistles, tricks, and toys—seeing Aaron there, in the flesh, pale skin painted a faint gold from his time in the sun, was the headiest aphrodisiac of them all.

He sat down next to Aaron, his towel loosening as he leaned over and kissed a bare shoulder. Ooh… underrated erotic potential in a shoulder—this should be explored!

He kissed upward, moving toward Aaron's neck, and Aaron tilted his head sideways, giving Larx his way.

"You have a plan?" Aaron murmured, and Larx chuckled into his ear, biting the lobe gently.

"I tease, you top," he said, earning a warm chuckle.

"You've got this covered?" Aaron asked, leaning back so Larx could nibble under his jaw, along his Adam's apple, down his chest.

"God yeah," Larx admitted.

Aaron turned his head and kissed Larx teasingly on the lips, pulling back right when Larx was ready to completely surrender, to lay back on the bed and let Aaron take charge.

"Turns out," Aaron murmured, moving from Larx's lips, where he was absolutely panting for more kissing, and down his jaw, his neck, and toward his nipples, "I thought I would *both* tease *and* top!"

Larx groaned. "Where's the fun in—oh God! Yes! The nipples, Aaron—*right there*!"

Aaron's chuckle vibrated through Larx's flesh, and he bucked his hips, suddenly *very* needy and not teasing or playful at *all*.

"Larx?" Aaron purred, moving to the other nipple.

"Yeah?" Larx whimpered.

"How about if we put the teasing off until round two?"

"Yes!" Larx begged just as Aaron's lips closed around the nipple and his hand found Larx's cock, rapidly growing hard along his thigh.

Aaron stroked him, soft at first and then harder as Larx grew harder, and Larx dragged his fingers through Aaron's hair and tried to breathe. He *wanted* foreplay, had *craved* foreplay all throughout this frenetic week, but now his body was *done* with foreplay, and he wanted *fucking*, raw and dirty, even though he wasn't quite… couldn't quite….

"Shh…," Aaron murmured, taking his mouth again. Larx fell into the kiss this time, no teasing, just mouth to mouth while Aaron continued that firm, necessary stroking.

Some of Larx's frantic urgency dissipated into Aaron's warmth, his strength, his seemingly never-ending patience, and he grasped Aaron's biceps and poured himself into the kiss, using Aaron as a focus for his often bouncing brain.

Aaron kept kissing, kept stroking, leaning on one elbow and moving his hand from Larx's cock to his hip, his flank, his chest, his shoulder.

Larx melted, still needy, still wanting to be possessed, but not as manic.

"Aaron?" he breathed, pleading, and Aaron kissed him again.

Aaron's wandering hand, however, nudged between Larx's thighs, and Larx answered the request by pushing back on the mattress, propping his feet up on the bed, and spreading himself, making himself vulnerable. Aaron caressed his thighs then, his balls, that wicked, wayward hand finding its way between Larx's cleft, his fingers teasing, penetrating gently, and Larx shuddered.

But he stayed in the kiss, stayed right with Aaron as Aaron reached across his body for the lubricant under the pillow and began the seductive dance at Larx's opening for real.

One finger, two—Larx had goose bumps already, and Aaron swallowed his cries of need.

"Now," Larx finally begged, shaking from arousal, as firmly in the moment as Aaron had been, his body crying out for possession at a height no other lover had ever driven him.

"Yes," Aaron murmured. He took a moment to oil his own cock before positioning himself at Larx's entrance and thrusting in.

Bliss! Larx shuddered at the first ache of possession, relishing it, and then wrapped his legs around Aaron's hips and settled in for the ride.

Aaron George was never anything but direct. Thrust after thrust shook Larx's body, shook his desire, destroyed his inhibitions, leaving him incoherent, trembling, consumed by Aaron's cock in his asshole. And by the tenderness of their skin on skin.

His climax, when it came, took him by surprise, swept him into its surf without warning, leaving him gasping, his entire body convulsing, his nerve endings *screaming* with pleasure, as he was rocked with wave after wave of orgasm, spurting between them as Aaron continued his sensual ravishment of Larx's senses.

But Larx's climax, his grip on Aaron's cock, must have sent Aaron over. Within heartbeats he cried out and thrust one more time, his hips stuttering as their driving purpose faded because Aaron was already there.

Larx felt the burst of him inside, and much like Aaron's kisses, his come served to focus Larx's fevered brain. With one last cry, one last shaking spasm, he was done, replete, falling limp into the mattress as Aaron tightened one more time and followed him, the two of them disintegrating and reforming in each other's arms.

Their panted breaths filled the silence of the nearly empty house for long moments before either one of them tried speaking.

"Goddammit," Aaron mumbled.

"What?"

"I'm falling asleep."

Larx squeezed his eyes shut. "God, so am I."

"Not that what we just did wasn't wonderful—"

"So amazing," Larx agreed.

"But I wanted more."

Larx smiled and nuzzled his temple. Aaron was still lying on top of him, their bodies still joined, and Larx was content to be like that for a few minutes.

He chuckled weakly. "Two things," he said finally.

"Go."

"There is no rule that says we can't fall asleep now, and then one of us wakes the other one up when one of us has to pee in the middle of the night."

"Oooh," Aaron mumbled. "That's a plan. What's the other thing?"

"I'm lying on top of the towel," Larx told him, almost gleeful. "When we finally decide to move, we can just throw the wet spot in the hamper."

Aaron's broken chuckle was what finally drove him out of Larx's body, and with minimal fuss and cleanup, they both put on clean briefs, crawled under their summer comforter, and fell asleep.

Larx thought dreamily that falling asleep mostly naked in Aaron George's bed had been worth the wait.

AARON TURNED out to be the first one to go to the bathroom, and his mouth on Larx's cock was every dream Larx had ever had as a growing boy, coupled with the man's body and man's experience to know what to do with it. Aaron had cleaned himself off and round two was a giggly, sloppy sixty-nine that somehow turned into a sensual, tender experiment to see who was the most easily aroused in the most places.

As scientific data went, the experiment was pretty sketchy, but as results went, they both came fitfully in the other's mouth and then pulled up their briefs and aligned so they could give each other sloppy, come-flavored kisses, and it was damned near the most decadent thing Larx had ever done as an adult, and *definitely* the most dirty-sweet-fun thing he'd done after he'd achieved fatherhood in his midtwenties.

This time when they fell asleep, Larx thought they'd pretty much reached a ten out of ten on the two-adults-in-the-house scale, and he was content to fall into dreamland in his lover's arms.

He awoke when Aaron's phone went off by the bed, the strident ringtone Aaron reserved for emergency contact from work.

"Eamon?" Aaron mumbled after crawling over Larx to get his phone. Whatever the answer on the other end, it made Aaron scramble upright and reach for the light. "Warren? The hell?"

Larx heard him take a deep breath, like he was steadying himself. "He's alive?"

That made Larx scramble up to his own sitting position. Eamon had been hurt? Why hadn't Aaron known about it sooner?

"Oh he *does*, does he?" Aaron snarled into the phone. "Does he know you called me?"

Larx was already scrambling for his jeans and a button-down, but he watched Aaron's face for the answer to this one.

A grim little smile told Larx that Warren—stolid and plodding, but with a good heart—still had Aaron's back.

"Where's everybody meeting?" he asked. "The hospital?"

Larx went for his sturdy walking boots for footwear, although tomorrow he would wish he'd gone for something lighter, he was sure. As Aaron was talking, he was doing his own dressing, pulling on his uniform, his boots, his ballcap, and his sturdy gun belt after he visited the gun safe in the top of the closet.

"Okay, good. Are they going to be there in, say, twenty minutes?"

Aaron let out a low chuckle. "Don't worry about it, Warren. We'll be there in fifteen." He paused for a second, and the look he sent Larx let him know that Warren's last comment had pertained to him. "Yes, I'm bringing him. For one thing, from what you said, Curtis MacDonald is *not* absolutely the shooter—it could have been any number of people. For another, he's Eamon's friend, and he's going to want to be there at the hospital with him. Why?"

Aaron's eyes narrowed. "If he wants to make it a big deal, Warren, let him make a big, bigoted deal in front of all the Sacramento SWAT people, in front of their detectives, and in front of the entire staff of the hospital. I can assure you, the hospital people are fans of *ours*, and they're *not* of Percy Hardesty. Nossir, we'll need him, but it's fine if you want to back out of what's coming." His jaw hardened. "It's not gonna be pretty."

Politics on the Job

"So…," Larx said after they'd loaded into Aaron's department-issue SUV. Aaron hadn't driven it all day because he had made a big deal about being *off the job*, but boy, he was on the job now, wasn't he!

"So?" Aaron asked, his mind racing. He started up the vehicle and hauled it into the pine-scented darkness, grateful for the ultrastrong LED lights that would let him go faster than was probably safe.

"What did Percy say about us that pissed you off so bad?"

Aaron grunted, feeling copicidal. "That the reason I wasn't at the raid was because I was afraid. You know, people like me get scared."

Larx laughed, his cackle scraping Aaron's back right up before he remembered who he was talking to. "You?" Larx asked, incredulous.

"It was a shitty thing to say while they didn't know if Eamon was going to live or die," Aaron muttered.

"It was a shitty thing to say in any circumstance," Larx confirmed. "But you told me you're Eamon's second-in-command, right? Undersheriff? That's an official thing, right?"

"Comes with a rank and a paygrade," Aaron confirmed.

"So you walk in, go, 'I'm Undersheriff Aaron George, I'm second-in-command now that Eamon's out of commission. Please brief me on the situation.'"

Aaron's lips twitched. "Listen to you, being all political and shit."

He felt rather than saw Larx roll his eyes. "I've spent a long time watching teachers piss on their corners for status, Aaron. Pathetic and sad? Yes. But I know what little people leading little lives look like when they're trying to make themselves bigger."

Aaron frowned. "But… but they're *teachers*!" he protested.

Larx shrugged. "Yes. And most of them are in it for the right reasons. But I watched an entire department of female English teachers *stop talking* once, in the middle of a meeting. Every time one of them opened their mouths, the tiny little men leading the meeting interrupted and belittled them. In the end they went to the principal and said, 'Here are our recommendations. No, the department heads didn't sign off on them, but here you go.' And they walked away. The next year, one of *them* was in charge. Because they knew that winning *that* battle didn't matter. What mattered was they were there for the kids—the tiny little carpet pissers would go away eventually. Just remember, Percy's a carpet pisser, but he's got a gun."

Aaron grunted. "Can't forget the gun," he said. He didn't have the particulars on the gunfight that had resulted from the raid that night, but he'd heard the entire story of how Percy had drawn down on *Larx* when Larx had disarmed a suspect in defense of a child. That story—more than any of the others Eamon had hit the mayor's office with—had come the closest to getting Percy Hardesty thrown off the force.

"Don't you dare," Larx said grimly. "Percy's a threat, but he's a stupid threat. Which means if you go in with a cool head you've already won. At least on the hill you plan to fight on tonight."

Aaron kept his eyes on the road, but his attention sharpened. "What do you mean?"

"You plan to go in there, assume authority, and find out what went wrong and how Eamon got shot, am I right?"

"Yes," Aaron said. "And then address it with a cool head. Warren made it sound like they were arming for Iwo Jima and then summoning the winged monkeys and sending them after Curtis MacDonald. I asked him if MacDonald had been the one to shoot, and Warren didn't even *see* the kid. In fact, he out and out swears nobody in the meth house was armed, but they're detoxing in their cells right now, so all we have is Percy, shouting at them to stop puking, I guess."

Larx sucked in a breath. "Oh Jesus. Aaron, where's Billy MacDonald?"

Aaron grunted. He hadn't even thought of that. "Fuck," he said succinctly. "Okay. Tell me more about this calm-and-powerful thing you're selling. I may need to buy me some of that."

Larx let out a humorless laugh. "You know damned well what it is. I take lessons in it from *you*, remember? Just… don't forget about it tonight. By the way, I texted the kids."

"Were they—"

"Still awake talking about the good times at three in the morning? Yes, they were," Larx told him, and this time his laugh held some warmth.

"But Olivia said she and Elton would be by at nine, and then the others could meet them at twelve to help sit with Eamon's wife."

Rosie Mills was Eamon's long-suffering spouse. She was known for being kind, for adopting as many stray cats as the house could hold, and for baking the most gawdawful cookies and coffee cake in probably the entire state of California. But she was such a sweetheart, nobody had the heart to tell her that her baking could be classified as a weapon.

"Good," Aaron said grimly. "I hope Percy wasn't the one to tell her—but mostly, I hope there's good news."

As it turned out, *nobody* had called her, which made Aaron one step closer to losing his temper entirely.

When they got to the hospital, he found the OR waiting room full of policemen that he did not know, with a handful of the ones he *did* know in the back corner, staring balefully at Percy Hardesty as he held court in the middle of his new friends.

"I tell you, that's the way I see it," he said, hand on his gun belt. "That kid opened fire on one of our own, and God love him, if Eamon can't go back and fight for himself, it's our job to go do it for him!"

"A sentiment Eamon would appreciate if he knew who shot him for real, Percy," Aaron said, striding to the middle of the circle of SWAT officers and what appeared to be two detectives who were looking at Percy like they would a dead mouse. Pick it up with their fingers? Sweep it away? What if it jumps?

Aaron had seen Larx's cats with that exact same expression.

"Nice of you to finally join us, George," Percy sneered, and Aaron ignored him.

"I'm Undersheriff Aaron George," he said, extending his hand to the dark-haired, dark-eyed fortyish man in the suit. Usually he simply said, "Deputy" or "Sheriff's Deputy." Undersheriff was, in a town their size, a formality, one that Eamon had made official when Aaron had come back on duty after getting shot that February. He'd seen then that he couldn't get rid of Percy Hardesty, and he'd wanted Aaron to have as much armor as possible. "And you are…?"

"Detective Christopher Castro," he said, taking Aaron's hand and giving it a hard shake. "SAC PD. We thought you were off at a—" Castro gave Percy a distasteful look, "—a kid's party?" he said, like he couldn't see how that would be enough to keep Aaron out of the field of what would probably be one of the biggest police actions to happen that year if Aaron hadn't been wounded in another one of those.

"My family was hosting a graduation party for about a third of the senior class," Aaron said. "Eamon told me to stay where I was. The more kids at that party—"

"The more kids aren't wrapping their cars around trees," said the younger man next to Castro. In his late twenties/early thirties, he had red-tinted hair, a square jaw, and really lovely green eyes. "I'm Detective Tad Hawkins. We're both from Special Investigations. And that makes more sense," he said with some exasperation. "This yo-yo made it sound like you were hosting babies in bounce houses. We were…." He grimaced.

"Confused," Aaron said. "As am I. First of all, I see a nice presence here for Eamon, but where's his wife? Has anybody filled her in?"

Both men glared at Percy. "We assumed Sheriff Mills's second-in-command would do that," Castro said, and Percy scowled at them.

"We were waiting on his status," he said, puffing his chest out. Aaron heard Larx's words about him being a "carpet pisser with a gun" and managed not to backhand him.

"What *is* his status?" Larx asked the two detectives. "I can make the call, Aaron. If you give me your keys, I can go get her."

Aaron nodded gratefully. "Have Gracie take you," he said, nodding at Gracie Rodriquez, one of their forensic investigators. "I may need the unit." She'd suited up tonight, probably to see what was in the house after the raid had wrapped up. Aaron wondered if SAC PD had brought their own forensics team and figured Larx could get that out of her as they drove.

"He's in surgery," Castro said, "but it… it looked bad. He was shot twice—once in the shoulder and once in the side." He and his partner exchanged the sort of look that told Aaron that not only were these two men partners who had worked together for a while, but they were both keeping their counsel on Eamon's wounds.

"From where?" Aaron asked, and they looked at each other again.

"We had the place surrounded," Castro said. "And trust me, when I say SWAT coordinates, they coordinate. Nobody shoots who isn't supposed to be shooting, and nobody goes in who isn't supposed to be in. Eamon was on the megaphone because we figured he was the voice of reason in this town—"

"He is," Aaron said, eyes going from one detective to another. "Nobody in the town messes with Eamon."

Castro nodded. "We figured that. So he was talking to the people in the house, and the whole situation was… you know. Tense."

Aaron cocked his head. "Huh. Tense. Go figure."

The other man had the decency to flush. "I know you people think we do that sort of thing daily in the big city, but no, running raids on meth houses in the pitch-black surrounded by trees is sort of a new one on us. Yes. We were jumpy as fuck. There was… was it a gust of wind?" He turned to his companion.

Tad Hawkins gnawed his lower lip. "You know, I've been playing it back in my mind. It was the wind or a twig snapping or a dog barking—it was a natural sound. Not… not a man-made sound. And then two rounds in quick succession, but I can't tell you where they came from."

"Your man went down," Castro continued, nodding, "and somebody…. It wasn't our SWAT Commander—she's getting coffee. Somebody called out either 'Fire' or 'We're taking fire,' and…."

"Bang, bang," Aaron muttered. He sighed. "Do we know how long he'll be in surgery?"

They shook their heads. "I'm suspecting at least an hour. Just…."

"You've been in this room before," Aaron said softly to Castro, who'd spoken.

"Yeah."

"Aaron was in the other room," Larx said, bumping Aaron's shoulder. "Not a picnic either way." He turned toward Gracie, who nodded because like everybody else in the room she'd been listening. "Gracie and I will go get Rosie. You…." He gave a sideways glance to Percy, who was pouting, shoulders slumped, with his cronies in the Colton side of the room. "You do what you gotta. Let me know where you end up."

"Thanks," Aaron murmured, and then, suddenly not caring about the new guys or his own force or the Percy Hardestys of the world, he kissed Larx's cheek. "Drive safe, Principal."

"Backatcha, *Undersheriff*."

Aaron let a smile crack, acknowledging the fact that he'd used that instead of "Deputy," Larx's usual endearment.

"Understood." With that he turned back to the detectives and prepared himself at their quizzical looks.

"He's the principal of… the high school?" Hawkins hazarded.

Aaron nodded. "Yes. And before you ask, two of our kids graduated to—erm, yesterday, I guess."

Castro nodded like he got it. "And the pool party makes more sense. Gotcha." He sent a disgusted look Percy's way, and Aaron took a deep breath.

"I do not even want to know what that man told you about me," he said grimly. "We've got real business to do. I hope you don't mind, but since I *wasn't* there, I'm going to conduct a *very discreet* inquiry about what happened as we wait here. Nothing that will stand up in court, but I can tell by the way you two are looking at each other you smell something bad. You got called up from Sacramento to do what you thought was a simple raid, and you are not excited the actual sheriff got hurt on your watch—have I read that right?"

"Yessir," Castro said crisply, and Hawkins gave a short nod to indicate he was on board.

"Good," Aaron said. "Now before I go about riling people up, I need to ask. The purpose of this entire clusterfuck was to find a lost kid—Curtis MacDonald—who went missing on Monday but who lied to his father and wasn't noted as missing until today."

They both nodded. "There was no sign of the kid," Hawkins said with relief. "When we went in, there were several occupants." He grimaced. "Two had been deceased prior, due, we believe, to ODs, and the rest were incapacitated."

"Were any wounded?" Aaron asked, and he allowed some arctic frost to crackle in his voice. He suspected the answer to this—it was written in the shoulder set of the two detectives and in their story of the shooting.

"No, sir," Hawkins answered after a moment, and this time his furious glance at Percy could not be contained. "They are all being held in the jail at this time."

Aaron frowned. "Have any of them been questioned?"

They both shook their heads. "We understand there's one person at the jail supervising all of them—"

"We've got one person at the jail with how many recovering junkies?" Aaron's voice squeaked, and his "nothing but the facts" voice completely disintegrated.

"Six, sir," Castro said.

"Can I borrow some SWAT guys?" Aaron asked, knowing he sounded like Larx and unable to stop himself. "Please?"

The SWAT lieutenant had come into the waiting room as they'd been talking and was now listening shamelessly.

"I'm Lieutenant Janine Johnson," she said, offering her hand. "I was just coming to ask you about that. I couldn't believe nobody had addressed that situation yet."

Aaron grunted. "Well, ma'am, I am Eamon's undersheriff, and I got here as soon as I was notified."

She grunted. "Who *did* notify you? I assume it wasn't *that* asshole." Percy had damned near grown horns as Janine entered. Aaron hoped she'd ordered his ass to hell and back during the op.

"I have my sources," Aaron said dryly. "And now I need to talk to my troops. Lieutenant, if you could assign some men to go with mine to the jail—we need a debrief now. Detectives…?"

"I'll go," Hawkins volunteered.

"He's got a way with people on the comedown," Castro said. "He can help them out."

"I'll ask if the hospital can spare some med staff," Aaron said, feeling grim. "God, I don't even want to know what our one guy is doing right now. It's got to be a nightmare."

"I can ask someone," Hawkins said. "If you can direct me to—"

"Go to the same nurse's station you passed to get here," Aaron said. "Use my name but…." He knew his face heated. "Uhm, call me Deputy George. I really *am* the undersheriff but—"

"Small town, no formality," Castro deduced. "We gotcha." He nodded and gave a sigh of relief. "I've got to tell you, we're relieved to have you here. Sheriff Mills seems okay—we've worked with him before—but some of his staff…."

Aaron felt his face shut down. "Eamon has a paper trail of dealing with that," he said. "City council has declined to act."

"Why?" Lieutenant Simpson asked sharply. She was a medium-height Black woman with her midnight hair tightly braided back into a regulation french braid.

"Exactly why you're thinking," he told her. "He's well-liked and well-respected by the townspeople here, but *somebody* is related by blood or blackmail to half the council. You can draw your own conclusions."

He gave one of those kinds of sighs that was also a signal for "girding one's loins." "I've got to go deal with my people. I'll have a contingent to join your people and the med staff in about ten minutes. We can reconvene then."

"Looking forward to it," Castro said, and he turned to his people while Aaron went to his.

"Oh, so look who finally decided to show up—"

"Percy, you're on leave pending an investigation," Aaron bit out. "You will surrender your piece and your badge to me *right now* before you leave this place, or you will be considered a fugitive from justice, and *you'll* be the first on the roster for SWAT to track down and arrest."

He stopped and glared at Percy Hardesty, aware suddenly that the eyes of both his department and the resources borrowed from Sacramento were staring at him.

"You can't—" Percy stammered, and he stared at Aaron as though he might cry.

"I just did," Aaron said. "You lied, repeatedly, to commanding officers, and you failed to alert *your* superior when your sheriff was injured."

"You didn't even know where Eamon *was* tonight!" Percy snarled, voice low and venomous.

"He told me when he stopped by my house before he left," Aaron snapped back, gratified at the look of surprise on Percy's face. "And I have as my witnesses—"

"Your faggoty little boyfriend?"

Oh, all the poison was coming out now. "The district superintendent, Harvey Hassbender, who was there at the party too," Aaron said. "Along with Principal Larkin and Vice Principal Nakamoto and more than a few parents who stopped for some chow. Yes, it was a party thrown by our kids, Percy, but it was also a community event, and Eamon came by to wish us well and to tell us what was going down." He swallowed, his worry for Eamon battering at the layer of protocol and necessity he'd erected. "I was worried about him all night," he admitted. "I was worried about all of you. I *thought* you'd be okay because you had each other's backs, but apparently you didn't have anybody's but your own, right, Percy?"

Percy glared at him. "Wasn't my fault he got himself shot—"

"Do you think we won't compare ballistics to every gun that fired tonight?" Aaron asked quietly—loud enough for Percy but not loud enough for anybody else in the room. Percy turned white, which just confirmed Aaron's suspicions and made him wish he had enough for an arrest warrant *now*. "Now surrender your piece, and remember, there's more than your buddies here in the hospital who are armed."

Percy reached for his gun slowly and then threw it—and his badge—at Aaron's feet. "I'll be back for those, faggot," he snapped. "You'd better shine 'em up real nice."

"Providing they don't match the ballistics pulled from Eamon, that might happen," Aaron said evenly, and all his people gasped and stared at him. He'd been listening. He'd been reading between the lines. Castro and Hawkins hadn't wanted to say it. Neither had Lieutenant Simpson. But Aaron could almost smell the air as both units converged on the little house, which sat back from the road and only about fifty yards from a drop-off into a canyon. It was quiet, it was dark, and Eamon's voice spoke into the bullhorn about dropping all weapons and surrendering to a search.

And then a dog barked, or the wind brushed the branches of a tree together, or somebody, maybe even Percy himself, stepped on a twig, and Percy, jumpy as hell and afraid—always so afraid—had squeezed off a round into the ether.

And Eamon had gone down.

And hell had broken loose.

And all that was left was for Percy to do what he did best—panic and shoot into the house, where a bunch of unarmed drug addicts were probably pissing themselves if they hadn't already.

But all that needed to be proven later.

What could be proved *now* was that Percy had failed to contact his second-in-command in a reasonable amount of time and many, *many* mistakes had followed that decision.

"The raid was scheduled for ten o'clock, Percy. Eamon's been in surgery for at least four hours. You let—who? Who is at the jail right now?"

"Alex Conrad," somebody said from behind Aaron.

"Oh holy Jesus," Aaron snapped, angry all over again. Alex Conrad was a rookie, had been promoted to the department while Aaron had been on injury leave in February. "You let *Alex Conrad* ride herd, by himself, over a jail cell full of recovering drug addicts? That's not just incompetent, Percy, that's *cruel*. If we had any room over there, I'd send you to clean up the puke."

"You can't make me—"

"Oh, I can," Aaron said. "But mostly I want you out of my sight. As of this moment, you're on unpaid leave pending an investigation, and you need to not be anywhere fucking *near* the rest of us as we try to do our jobs."

"This ain't the last you've heard of me," Percy spat, turning to stalk out of the waiting room. "You'll see. This department'll fall apart without me. It'll just be the ni—"

"Do you really want to say those words?" Lieutenant Simpson asked, her voice ringing from the door where she'd paused to watch the show. "Because my team would take exception to them, down to a man."

Percy glared impotently, and Aaron used the reprieve to ask a question he should have asked first.

"Before you leave, Percy, I need to know."

"You don't need to know *shi*—"

"Did you leave Billy MacDonald in a cell, or did you cut him loose?"

Percy stopped and licked his lips, looking to both sides. "I, uhm… I mean, it was a bullshit charge—"

"He came onto school grounds and pushed a kid down. It was assault. Was he booked and released, or did you leave him there when you shoved all of the recovering addicts into the jail?"

"I, uhm… I don't rightly recall," Percy hedged.

"He never got booked," Warren said, surprising Aaron. "Eamon was organizing tonight's takedown, and Percy let MacDonald go before we got to the jail."

Aaron nodded. "Percy, I know you and Billy MacDonald are buddies. I need you to keep this in mind. I'm sending out a warrant for Billy MacDonald tonight, and if you two decide to get together, tie one on, and find all of Billy's guns, *you* are under investigation, and *Billy* has a warrant out for his arrest. If I were either of you, I'd stay home, get sober, and hope my past actions haven't caught up with me, do you understand?"

Percy sent Aaron a look of pure hatred. "Nobody wants to hear what *you'd* do, faggot!"

"Which is why I don't plan on getting arrested anytime soon," Aaron said. "Now leave. We are sitting vigil in this room, and you have forced me to violate that enough as it is."

With that, he turned his back on Percy, knowing it was a calculated gamble. Percy was angry—angry enough to attack Aaron as he stood.

But Aaron was surrounded. Aaron knew there were enough men in his own department who might feel some loyalty to Percy—who might even agree with his hateful ideals—to make this an iffy strategy at best. But he also knew that SAC PD and SWAT were pretty disgusted with Percy Hardesty at the moment. At best they felt him a small-town hick, and at worst they suspected him of the same things Aaron suspected him of. They felt no loyalty and no pity for the man, and if he jumped Aaron's shit, Lieutenant Simpson at the *very* least would take him down and probably give him a front row seat to the terrible havoc Percy had arranged at their little station's jail.

Aaron put his foot on Percy's badge and gun and gathered the eyes of every one of the men in his department while he waited for Percy to leave.

He *felt* the sigh of relief when Percy left the room.

"Amanda?" he asked their other forensic tech, who was staring at him with big eyes. "You got some evidence bags on you?"

She pulled them out of a pocket of her cargo pants. "Right here, Aaron—er, Chief."

He smiled slightly. "Aaron's fine. I need his gun collected and fired. Where's Tommy?"

"He's at the station, processing prints and IDs for the detainees."

Aaron took a breath. They had lots of junior techs but only three techs who could supervise. Gracie was one, and he'd just sent her with Larx. Amanda was another, and judging by her exhaustion, she was near the end of her shift. and Tommy was a third. Still, it appeared Tommy's placement was priority.

"As soon as he's done with that, he needs to start this. We need to see if there's a ballistics match. We need to address this matter immediately if Percy's going to get reinstated."

"You, uh, want to do that?" Warren asked uncertainly. He shifted as he stood and gave a couple of Percy's cronies a baleful look, but Aaron was grateful.

"I do not," Aaron said. "But if he's *not* the one who shot Eamon from behind, we need to rule him out. And if he *is*, we need evidence. One way or another, he would have ended up on this end of the investigation. In fact, *everybody* who fired a weapon will need to have it checked out, and someone will do that before you leave the station. But Percy did enough bad shit tonight for us to need him just gone while we proceed in this matter." Oh God—now he really *was* channeling Larx. "I mean, he violated too many protocols to simply ignore his actions. Warren, I need you to take Roberts, Deitz, and Palmer to the station with Lieutenant Simpson and her people. We need the people in the holding cells interviewed, if they're in any state to be interviewed, and we need them taken to Auburn."

He looked at Paul Roberts, Jimmy Deitz and Evan Palmer, figuring Jimmy was the most competent *and* the most compassionate. "Jimmy, I need you to make contact with the rehab facility in Auburn. Explain the circumstances and that the patients have probably been traumatized by Percy's actions and are having a *really* bad night. See if you can't get *them* to send a couple of ambulances, at Colton's expense, to come give some of these folks a ride, okay? The entire reason we haven't raided these two houses *a year ago* is that we flat out don't have the resources. *Nobody* has the resources—that's why it's a goddamned epidemic!"

"Hey, Aaron," Jimmy said, holding his hands out in front of him. "I'm the choir, remember?"

Aaron smiled a little, letting his face and his forehead relax. Jimmy was an able deputy in his midthirties with two kids in middle school. Plain as a potato—average hair, average eyes, average nose—Jimmy was also the deputy most likely to rescue kittens from trees or dogs from storms. In fact, he and his wife had many rescues from the local shelter for things like that. Jimmy also had a brother who had been in dire straits some years back, frequenting houses like the one on Dropoff Drive as often as he frequented rehab. Jimmy's brother hadn't made it—he'd died of an overdose just when the family had been hopeful—but Jimmy hadn't lost the perspective that addicts started out as human beings first.

"Sorry, Jimmy," Aaron said. "I'll get off my soapbox now and back to the job."

"You're doing fine," Jimmy told him. His homely face lapsed into lines of worry, and his hazel eyes showed depths of empathy that probably made him the most handsome man in the world as far as his wife was concerned. "We're all worried about Eamon. Thanks for coming in and taking over like a boss."

That made Aaron grin—and helped him keep his temper *and* his perspective. "I can only do my best. Okay, so Jimmy, you need to get on the horn, and the rest of you need to head off to the station. Warren, get a debrief from Alex before you send him home, okay? Jesus, that poor kid."

"Yeah," spoke up a guy from the back—Carey Brooks, one of Percy's usual cronies, Aaron noted, surprised. "That… that was no good."

"Well, let's make it right. Someone will be here repping our department at all times. You'll all be kept in the loop about Eamon. Keep him in your thoughts and prayers, guys. He's one of the best."

There was general assent then, and Aaron breathed a sigh of relief. It would be great if he could keep his whole department from self-destructing before Eamon got out of surgery.

THE JAIL contingent left, and as the door shut behind them, a nurse came out of the OR to give them the news that there was no news. Eamon still had an hour of surgery at the very least, and that's when they'd get the two bullets for forensics and not before. In the meantime they needed blood and plasma, all donors welcome. The hospital could only accommodate about two donors at a time, so Aaron had the people closest to off-shift go first.

For everybody else, he had plans.

He texted Larx. Eamon lived about half an hour away from the hospital, so if nothing else, he could give Larx and Rosie some breathing room in what was sure to be a panicked commute.

We're just ready to leave now—thank you for the update. Hang in there, Deputy.

We'll be at the house on Dropoff Drive. It's going to be light soon, and I want to take a look at the backyard with SWAT. I don't think SAC PD realizes the extent of the wilderness back there.

There was a moment of thought bubbles, and Aaron realized he was confiding in Larx as though Larx was another police officer. It was a habit he'd gotten into since they'd first gotten together, and he wondered for a moment if it was appropriate, given Aaron's new position.

Then he realized he did not actually care. Larx had a good mind for this sort of thing—Eamon had depended on it many times, particularly when the school had been involved. Aaron wasn't going to break something that worked fine, not when they needed it most.

Good idea. Be careful. Maybe send a car out to Daffodil Canyon if you don't see anything at the house.

Daffodil Canyon wasn't actually on the map. Locals called the place that because it turned yellow from the pine pollen in the spring and summer, which was funny, because the place was as far from a soft, fat flower kind of place as it could get. The houses on Dropoff Drive backed up against woodland that then *dropped off* into the man-made canyon below. There was a service road, much like the one that connected Larx and Aaron's houses, that ran a half circle along the side of the canyon and then spanned the dry creek bottom before rising up to half circle the other side and join with the main road. The land between was covered in scrawny pine trees—lots of them—and scree and rock rubble. The place had been hydraulically mined back in the day; water had been pumped against the sides of the mountain until the earth had ground to a slurry and washed through the creek bed to be sifted for ore. Rockslides had halted the mining, as well as restoring a semblance of natural topography to the canyon, and the softened soil had allowed the trees to try to find purchase in the denuded rubble of the canyon's sloped sides. The result was a mess of dangerous terrain and potential rockslides, with most of the perils half hidden by the trees that had managed to find purchase and grow over the last hundred and twenty or so years.

Daffodil Canyon was *not* the kind of place you sent nonlocals, and you *definitely* didn't go there without alerting everyone from the forestry service to the Marines that you were going.

I'll need to see who can back me up, he returned. *I won't go before I see you.* Larx was, after all, a *science* teacher—he'd have some idea, at the very least, of the hazards that sort of terrain could pose.

Good. Till then.... And he'd texted a heart.

Aaron sent him a heart back and then looked up, surprised to find Castro at his shoulder.

"What next?" he asked, and Aaron gave the man an amused smile.

"What makes you think anything comes next?" he asked.

"For one thing, you walked in here and pretty much took over, which was fine because this is your local guy's rodeo and we're just along for the ride. But you also knew *how* to take over, which makes me think you've got a plan."

Aaron smiled grimly. "First, wait until Hawkins gets back to us with whether or not any of the detainees have a story to tell. Then, pending his info—or lack of it—we go check out the Dropoff house as soon as it gets light."

"What do you think we'll find there?" Castro asked. "Either place?"

"This whole thing started because we were looking for a kid," Aaron said. "This entire clusterfuck. Raiding the house, calling you, Eamon getting hurt. You know what we haven't seen yet?"

Castro grimaced. "The kid?"

"Yeah. And I don't think that's because Eamon had bad intel. Either someone tipped Curtis MacDonald off to get him out of there or…."

"Someone helped him go," Castro said.

"Bingo." Aaron nodded grimly. "And at this point, we've got Billy, who wasn't detained when he was supposed to be—"

"And Percy, the loudmouthed deputy who fishes with Billy," Castro finished.

"You heard that?" Aaron hadn't been sure how much Castro and Hawkins had caught when Aaron had addressed the Colton department.

"We were just watching you in awe, buddy boy," Castro said, laughing slightly. "It was like watching Tommy Lee Jones in *The Fugitive*—a goddamned thing of beauty."

Aaron laughed humorlessly. "Let's see if you still feel this way after we have to go check out the house and the back area. You're going to *wish* we were in that movie, because I gotta tell you, the terrain was a whole lot friendlier."

Castro sucked air in through his teeth. "So," he said, looking down at his slick and shiny shoes, now covered in red dust and pollen, and his rumpled suit in pretty much the same condition. "Are you saying I should find some boots and some jeans?"

"And get Hawkins some too," Aaron told him, not kidding around. "There's a hunting and fishing outfitter across from the local Starbucks that might be able to help you out."

Castro nodded and then indicated the few remaining SWAT team members. "Do you mind if I send this half of the unit home? I can see how you'd still need some reinforcements, but…."

"But if we're going to take down another drug operation, we'll let you know," Aaron said dryly, before mumbling to himself. "Except… except there wasn't really a drug operation at Dropoff Drive, was there?"

Castro paused. "Huh?"

"There were *drugs*," Aaron said, "but we busted a pot farm a while back, when it was still mostly illegal, and before the DEA got there and hip-checked us out, we got a look at it. There was… you know. Processing, packaging, inventory, revenue. It's a business like anything else, and the one thing I haven't heard from anybody was that the business was *there*. Was it?"

"No," Castro said, surprised. "But there were junkies. And I understand there's another house in town—"

"Junkies," Aaron confirmed. "But it's closer to town, in the little neighborhood behind the main drag. We've raided it a couple of times, mostly to get the people to help. So far no weapons and no big operations. Just people making really shitty life choices. Dropoff Drive was different because it was farther away and because the canyon behind it is dangerous." He grimaced. "We've had a couple of addicts slide down the canyon, and they weren't found until much later. That's why we need to get a look at the yard in the daylight. We've got a dog. Among other things, we need to see if maybe the MacDonald kid went over the embankment and into the canyon."

Castro blew out a breath. "A thing that Percy guy did not mention." He muttered to himself and shook his head, and Aaron grunted.

"But I bet you know a whole lot about my sex life you never wanted to know," he said dryly.

Castro gave an embarrassed smile. "Frankly, the way he was talking about you, we were starting to wonder if you were a drag performer—which, you know, enjoy the shows myself, the wife has the rainbow flag in the window, but it would be an unusual choice for law enforcement."

Aaron snorted. "I will leave that barrier for others to break," he said with a grunt. "Mostly Larx and I want to keep our community safe and get back home to run with the dog and talk to the kids in the evening."

"Your guy, Principal Larkin?" Castro was looking for confirmation, and Aaron nodded.

"You saw him. Same guy."

"Yeah, Sheriff Mills told us to trust him and that he was a good source of community information. It was just such a… a contrast, what one man said to what the other said. Believe me, after being forced to listen to Percy for half the night, it's good to see that Mills was right on target."

Aaron felt something in his chest unfurl a little. An ally—and hopefully a good officer—had put himself at Aaron's disposal. It was a load off his mind.

"So we have a plan?" Aaron asked, making sure.

"Yeah. I'll go get some decent gear for me and Hawkins—"

"And I'll go check on the jail," Aaron said, as his phone buzzed in his pocket.

Alex knocked unconscious, it said. *All the recovering addicts escaped. Percy needs to clean up the puke.*

Aaron stared at the text and groaned. "Fuck *me*," he muttered. "Meet me at the jail around six."

He turned toward the people who were waiting to give blood and then finish out their shifts. "You guys, give blood and then go home, but after eight hours and a meal, we're going to need you back at the station. Alex was knocked unconscious, and the detainees are out in the wild—if we want an accurate accounting of what happened and some sort of report on where Curtis MacDonald went, I'm going to need your help."

There were several pained grunts as they all recognized that *this* was why Aaron had sent Percy on leave.

"And I need to go see to things there. Can I have two people who are willing to get their nap and their meal here so we can have a presence for Eamon's wife?"

Amanda raised her hand, and so did Buddy Garrett, one of the older deputies.

"Thank you," Aaron told them. "Larx is going to be here with her shortly, and after sunrise he's going to employ our army of miscreant teenagers to take care of you. Feel free to abuse them—just a little. No coffee is too far to fetch, no sandwich is too outrageous a request, understand?" There were some amused head nods, and he continued. "And everybody else due off soon, I'd be happy if you stayed until your turn to give blood is over. Those of you who can't for whatever reasons, go home now and get your sleep—we're going to need all hands on deck soon enough."

The waiting room cleared out a little more, and Aaron was sure the hospital breathed a sigh of relief. He approached Amanda and Buddy and said softly, "I know Larx is going to tell Rosie this, but please, you guys tell her that the department's prayers are with her. She's been a cop's wife long enough to know that the manhunt that started this and the investigation into *who* shot Eamon is going to take precedence, but her husband has served this community for a good long time, and she needs to know he's loved. Amanda, get her anything she wants and bill the department for it. Spoil that woman the way she spoils us, okay?"

"I hear you, boss," Amanda murmured. "My sister's already baking her coffee cake and getting ready to order a traveler of coffee from Starbucks. We've got Eamon's back."

Aaron grinned. "Knew I could count on you. And, uhm—" He winked. "—have your sister save me some coffee cake, okay?"

"Will do."

"Update us with anything. I mean *anything*. If Eamon breaks wind, we want to razz him about it, understand?"

Amanda was a middle-aged single woman who loved her cats and her romance books more than any man and who ran the lab with absolute proficiency. Her eyes grew bright and shiny because she knew what this request *really* was. They wanted to be there for Eamon—they *all* wanted to be there for Eamon—but they couldn't be, and if the worst happened, they wanted their chance to mourn.

"Completely, Aaron. We'll keep our eye out."

"Roger that."

And with that, Aaron had put off leaving long enough. It was absolutely time to go check in at the jail before he went to the house on Dropoff Drive. And somewhere in there, he and one of his fellow officers was going to have to go interview Percy Hardesty for real.

Aaron had an ugly feeling in the pit of his stomach about Percy, and he was afraid Eamon's many attempts to get rid of the man had not gone unaddressed.

Cookies for Breakfast

LARX WAS sure to call Rosie before Gracie's department-issue vehicle made it onto the winding driveway that led to Eamon's cabin. Like a lot of the property out there, the plot of land had been woodland to begin with, and the trees had to be razed and the services piped in and the whole enchilada before anything close to livable was erected where rubble used to be.

Most residents had stories of the time the plumbing failed, or the septic tank exploded or something, and life was reduced to five-gallon bottles of water, camp showers, and porta-johns not too far from the house.

But having a visitor in the wee hours of the night could be scary, and Larx was pretty sure Rosie could use a shotgun. Her law enforcement husband wouldn't have left her alone in the middle of nowhere if she wasn't protected.

Her light was on, and she was waiting outside on the front porch swing as they pulled up, their middle-aged black lab next to her. Her hair—gray now and usually worn scraped back from her temples in a bun—was up in a scarf, and she was dressed in faded jeans and a tatty cardigan. Her skin was the color of pale earth, many shades lighter than her husband's, and tonight it was showing every rumple, every wrinkle, from their forty plus years together.

As the SUV slowed, she called the dog to her and hurried for the automobile, and Larx got out so he could sit in back. He was grateful the vehicle was for the forensics team—it meant the back seat wasn't outfitted for prisoners.

He was unprepared for Rosie to throw herself into Larx's arms.

She wasn't a small woman—Larx's height, with the soft, squishy form that came from a happy retirement baking cookies and fundraising for the children's charities around town—and she held him so tight, for a moment he was afraid he wasn't up to consoling her.

But he held her back just as tight, remembering this had been him in February. Aaron had been shot, his ribs had punctured his lung, and he'd been in the OR for an eternity. Maybe two, but who counted.

He held her even tighter and she let out a shuddery breath. "Thanks, Larx," she said softly. "Needed that. Tell me I'm not stupid for taking the dog."

Larx grinned. "Not stupid. You're Eamon's wife, Rosie. His department will build a doghouse for Captain here, don't worry. If worse comes to worse, my kids are showing up in shifts and they can take ol' Cap to go play with Dozer. We got your back, honey. Now climb in front."

"I'll take the back with the dog," she said. She took in a shuddering breath. "And you can tell me in person what you couldn't tell me on the phone."

That was fair; Larx just wished he knew more.

He told Rosie what he had—that the force had been all suited up and surrounding the house on Dropoff Drive when two shots in quick succession hit Eamon, and then someone called for everybody else to open fire.

"SAC PD SWAT seemed to be pretty disciplined," he added. "I don't think they did. It was mostly our guys who opened fire into the house, and the two detectives from Sac calmed things down. They had ambulances on standby, so Eamon got bussed to the hospital ASAP, and after that…." He sighed.

"Aaron wasn't there," she said as though she'd known this. "Eamon brought my casserole and cookies to the event you two were supervising. Said they were appreciated, and he told you to stay with your kids."

"Yes," Larx said, grateful she'd known. "Eamon had been in surgery for an hour before somebody thought to call Aaron." He checked his phone for the time. It was less than an hour from the time he and Aaron had arrived in the hospital. "By the time we got there, other people—"

"Percy fucking Hardesty," she supplied, voice giving no quarter.

"Yeah. Percy Hardesty had pretty much made a hash of everything, including shoving all the detainees in the jail without much supervision. Aaron relieved him of duty and took over. You were his first priority."

She let out a sigh. "Of course, because Aaron knows what the hell he's doing. Let me guess, the waiting room was full of people making a show of things, and nobody was doing their jobs?"

Larx turned to smile at her fondly. "It's like you were there," he said softly. "Aaron texted me when we were on our way out. Eamon's still in surgery, but they might have some news when we get back. I think Aaron has to go check on the situation in the jail—it, uhm, wasn't good."

She scrubbed her face with her hands. "Do we know who shot my husband?" she asked, her voice frail again.

"Aaron has suspicions," Larx said diplomatically. "But he's testing everybody's weapon. I think as soon as we get back, we're turning Gracie loose to get that done."

"Good," Gracie said. "What about you, Principal Larkin? What will you be doing?"

"The hardest thing," he said, those terrible moments from February flooding back to him, and he turned to Rosie. "Waiting for news with my friend until Aaron and I go meet at the Dropoff house to look for the young man who set this in motion."

"Thanks, baby," Rosie mumbled. He saw her wipe her hand across her eyes, then, and let her have her moment to herself.

THE WAITING room was much less claustrophobic as they walked in, Captain at Rosie's heels. The hospital staff hadn't said a thing, and Larx helped Rosie sit down, with Captain beside her, and went to fetch her coffee while Gracie hurried to talk to Amanda and find out what Aaron's orders were.

Larx asked one of the men still waiting what the situation was and was told that Aaron and much of the SAC PD force had left already, but Larx checked his phone again and caught Aaron's last text.

So. Much. Vomit. Goddammit, I sent Percy on leave too soon—I would have used him as a mop.

Larx chuckled weakly to himself. *If you can authorize payment, I'll contact the janitorial staff at the high school to help.*

Make it double, Aaron texted back. *We need this mess cleaned up stat.*

Larx got busy calling people, knowing that the job was bad but the pay was good and hoping a couple of people got to go on vacations this summer as a result.

I told Rosie I'd be here until the kids are, he told Aaron dispiritedly. *How soon will you be at Dropoff Drive?*

I was hoping for sunrise, Aaron texted, reminding him of how close that was, *but given the mess here, I think 9:00 a.m. at the earliest. I'm asking their SWAT Lt. if she wants her remaining guys to suit up and assist our forensics team. Gracie's off-shift, Amanda is on duty there, and Tommy Cortez can only do so much by himself.*

Good idea, Larx texted. *Is SAC PD playing nice?*

So nice. Someone got shot on their watch, and they feel played. They want accountability stat, and I seem to be leading them in the right direction.

That's my boy. Larx was incredibly proud of him. God, he'd been so good at walking into that waiting room crammed with anxious, fidgety people and restoring order.

So if the kids are there by ten, come to the house. I want your opinion. If nothing else you can help canvass the neighborhood.

Larx chuffed out a breath. *How I spent my summer vacation....*

Please. Larx had been kidding, but Aaron's text took the humor out of the situation and reminded Larx of what was at stake. *I don't know what happened last night, but somehow it's all wrapped up in Curtis MacDonald, and you're our one link to him.*

What about his father? Shouldn't he be back in vomit central?

Percy never booked him.

Larx gaped. *Never what?*

Yeah. Something is really foul here, and I'm going to need help sniffing it out. But first, I need to find some way to round up the detainees—they're going to be jonesing and desperate and dangerous.

Roger that. I'll keep Rosie company until the kids come. You try to keep the force from falling apart.

Roger that. Love you, Principal.

Love you back, Undersheriff.

Larx smiled as he imagined Aaron's snort and then turned to Rosie, who had been talking to Amanda and Gracie. "Aaron sends his love," he said quietly, and Gracie yawned.

"I'm off-shift. I'm going to go see if I can give blood before I leave, and I'll be back to pick up where Tommy left off after a couple hours of shut-eye."

"Fair," Amanda said. She looked apologetically at Larx. "Larx, I feel like I should be out in the field. Aaron was making assignments on the fly, but is there any way I can go help Tommy? Especially if Aaron's crew is busy getting the junkies back in the bottle."

Larx gnawed his lower lip. Aaron had texted almost the same thing, but Rosie—

"Tell him, Larx," Rosie murmured. "They're shorthanded as it is. I don't need a watch crew—except for maybe your children." She smiled tiredly, and Larx thought that the offer of the young people to keep her company had meant a lot more to her than she'd let on at first.

Larx nodded and texted, getting the affirmation from Aaron. Then he caught a text from Olivia, who had woken up early and was bringing Wombat Willie—dammit, *Elton*—to the hospital so the teenagers could sleep in. Larx relayed that information, finishing up with "They've been warned to bring lots of coffee and hot chocolate," he said soberly. "And the teenagers will be here to give Livvy a break when she's ready for her nap." This was all predicated on Eamon being all right, he knew, and he crossed his figurative fingers. *Please, higher power whom I only call on when shit gets dire, let Eamon be all right.*

Rosie asked, "Did the youngsters have a good time?" and Larx loved that, as worried as she probably was, she remembered.

"The best," Larx said, shrugging. "I like the fact that they all felt like they *could*, even surrounded by old farts and authority figures." He shook his head. "In my day, we could not *wait* to shake the olds and go out and get laid."

She cackled. "Well, giving them a place to be safe probably makes that getting laid thing not quite as urgent." Larx grimaced, thinking about Olivia and her headlong rush into motherhood, and Rosie chuckled. "I didn't say not urgent at all…."

"Witness pending grandfather-hood," Larx acknowledged dryly. He and Aaron had been dealing very nicely with the mechanics of *how* to be grandfathers and dodging the entire reality of how that made them *feel*. It had been a tough gig to swim in the waters of De Nial, particularly with Olivia at their house every other day growing rounder by the second. But Larx and Aaron had done a *stellar* job of pretending they were like any other couple starting out in the world, because *dammit*, it *felt* like they were brand-new and perfect.

Rosie chuckled again and then grew sad. "I wish I could tell you," she said softly, "what it felt like. How to deal. But Eamon and I never did have children. They just…." Her chin crumpled, and Larx seized her hand because while he knew—Eamon had told Aaron long ago in a fit of confidence—this was hard for someone to say. "They just never took. Not for any length of time, that is," she finished, choked. "And I had to content myself with making cookies for Eamon's entire department." She sniffled. "I'm not even any good at it. My cookies are terrible."

Larx wrapped his arm around her shoulders and pulled her in, grateful that he didn't have to deny the fact because this wasn't about her cookies anyway.

"We love getting your cookies," he whispered.

"I never got the secret to them," she mumbled. "I kept trying and trying—"

"Butter, sugar, and baking soda," he said softly. "Margarine makes terrible cookies, honey. That's all it is."

"Oh." And with that she cried quietly on his shoulder for the next twenty minutes while he rocked her back and forth and the small contingent of Aaron's officers not giving blood or out in the field sat there with them, showing support the best way they knew how, while Captain rested his head loyally in his mistress's lap.

They dozed for a little while—Larx really *had* needed his vacation. When the sun started cracking through the shaded windows, Larx checked his watch and saw it was about six thirty. He yawned and looked at his phone; no updates from Aaron, but then, Aaron wasn't in a place to update him on his every move.

About the time he got oriented to who he was and what was happening, the all-important door from the OR opened, and a doctor Larx recognized from when Isaiah had been stabbed appeared, wearing a fresh lab coat over blood-spattered scrubs.

He saw Rosie and smiled, eyes rimmed with exhaustion. "Mrs. Mills?" he asked, and Larx helped her up, both of them moving stiffly from their weepy little doze in the hospital chairs over the last two hours.

"He's okay?" she asked, and the doctor's tired smile deepened.

"Yes, ma'am. For the moment, he's in recovery. We can take you in when he's awakened slightly, but he's going to be *very* loopy. He caught two slugs—one in his shoulder. It missed his vest on the way in and tore up a lot of flesh bouncing off the inside of the thing because it couldn't get out. There is going to be a *lot* of work reconstructing that shoulder and building the muscle back up after our repairs, so be aware the work isn't over yet."

"Good thing he's retiring," Rosie said, her voice laced with grim determination. "He'll have lots of time to take care of himself, won't he?"

"He will," Larx soothed. "You said two slugs?"

The doctor nodded. "The other one caught him in the vest, right over the kidneys." The doctor moved his hand to his back, over his right side. "Whoever shot him from there, he was close enough to rupture one of the organs. We spent a lot of time stitching it back together and hoping it doesn't leak like a sieve when it's done. The good news is, he's got another one if we have to take out the damaged one, but we'd rather not because—"

"He might need the spare," Rosie deduced. "Because that's what getting old means."

The doctor nodded. "It does indeed," he said. "So he's not out of the woods entirely, but right now he can breathe, hopefully we've caught all the bleeding things in his body and tied them off, and he can start to heal."

Rosie let out a breath she probably didn't know she was holding and wiped her eyes on her sleeve like a child.

"How long until she can see him?" Larx asked quietly.

"Half an hour, minimum," the doctor said softly. "The nurses had to clean him up for you. He was a mess."

"I appreciate that," Rosie said. She wiped her face on her shoulder, and Larx grabbed a box of Kleenex from the nurse's station to offer her one. She took it with a nod of thanks, and Larx felt compelled to ask things she might have forgotten.

"Will she be allowed to stay with him in recovery?" Sometimes it was a yes, sometimes it was a no, depending on how injured the person was.

This time the doctor shook his head. "A short visit for now," he said. "Once we've determined Eamon's stable, we'll bring him to the ICU, and then she can some sit with him." The doctor glanced down at Captain, who stood patiently by Rosie's side, and sighed. "The dog can visit for a moment," he said, "because we know sometimes animals offer comfort, but you may want to find another place for him. Dogs get awfully restless when they're cooped up here too long."

"My kids are coming," Larx said. "One of us can take him to our house and Rosie won't have to worry."

"Thank you." The doctor pulled in a sustaining breath. "Sit down, rest a little. Someone will be out in a bit."

With that he turned around and went back through the double doors, and Rosie managed to wobble her way to the seats.

"He's going to be fine," Larx soothed, but he knew what was coming. He knew what *he'd* been doing when Aaron had been shot. He watched as Rosie's lower lip wobbled and then crumpled, and he was there to hold her in his arms as she came apart and sobbed.

"HE'S ASKING for both of you."

The nurse shook Larx lightly by the shoulder about an hour after they'd spoken with the doctor. Larx smiled at the young man, wondering where he'd come from. He usually knew the high school graduates of this age, and this wasn't one of them.

"Both of us?" he asked groggily, patting Rosie on the arm.

"Yes, sir." The nurse nodded. "Asked for Deputy George first, and when I told him he'd been and left, he asked for you. Seemed to know you'd be here."

Rosie let out a gruff laugh. "Because he knows their family, son. Now show me to my husband so I can yell at him and he can deal with it like the saint he is."

"Absolutely, ma'am," the kid said. His name tag read Jed Williams.

"You seem like a sweet boy," Rosie told him as the young man in peach scrubs escorted them through the hospital corridors, Captain padding by their side. "Why don't I know you?"

"I was born in Baltimore," the nurse told her. "I went to school there, and the school paid for my degree as long as I traveled somewhere on their list. Colton was in California, and I thought that would be cool, so here I am."

Larx blinked, his brain exploding a little. "I'm sorry. You must feel like you were robbed."

The young man—Black, with a pale brown complexion, tiny dreads, and a wide smile—laughed outright. "No, sir. I'm an hour away from Lake Tahoe, five hours away from the ocean, and a day's worth of driving from the Oregon Coast. For a cheap plane ticket, I can be in Disneyland, and in the meantime, I get to smell pine trees in the morning. The ones that smell like vanilla."

Larx grinned. "Sugar pine," he said. "With the picture-puzzle bark. That's a nice tree."

"Right?" The guy shrugged. "It's a good place. Not as many Black people as I'm used to—" He winked at Rosie. "—but lots of nice people, so that's okay too."

Rosie was holding on to the man's arm, which he'd offered in an old-fashioned courtesy, and she patted it now. "It's good to meet you too, Nurse Jed. If my husband survives this, we'll be sure to ask you to dinner to welcome you right."

Nurse Williams smiled at her. "That would be kind," he said, before leading Rosie into the room where Eamon sat, propped up on pillows and smiling at his wife like a weary man greeted the dawn.

Larx stayed back for a minute and let her approach him, haranguing him, it sounded like, within an inch of his life.

"You old jackass," she said, taking his hand and holding it to her cheek. "Are you too old for this fucking job *now*? Can we retire *now*? You've gotten shot—*again*. Can we quit this foolishness and retire? I want to travel to the ocean, goddammit, and you get *shot*?"

Larx heard Nurse Williams snicker, and the two of them stepped back even farther, letting Eamon's low tones soothe his wife as she let loose her worry and exasperation on the man who'd caused it, however unintentionally.

"She's something," Williams muttered. "Damn. My grandmother could flay grandpa with the side of her tongue, but that was something special."

"It's rough being a law enforcement spouse," Larx said with a sigh.

"Your wife…?"

"Boyfriend," Larx told him, hoping it wouldn't wreck the camaraderie.

Jed Williams grinned at him. "Good for you." Then he frowned. "But bad that you know that. I take it that's why her husband wants to speak to you?"

Larx grimaced. "Yeah. Aaron and I tend to share the same brain sometimes. I think Eamon might need to pick it to settle this whole mess."

"Larx, get in here," Rosie demanded. "He seems to think he's still got something to say on this matter."

Larx patted the young nurse on the shoulder. "If Rosie doesn't invite you for dinner, our family will," he said decisively. "God knows, we've spent enough time in here, we should get to know the staff better." And with that he ventured into the room to talk to Eamon, hoping Eamon would have answers that would help keep Aaron safe.

Rosie stalked away, wiping her eyes with her hand and burying her hands in Captain's fur, and Larx met eyes with the young nurse, glad to see him leading Rosie away, hopefully to the cafeteria for some coffee or hot chocolate.

"Hurry, Eamon," Larx joked weakly. "If you move now, I can sneak you away before she comes back."

Eamon gave a wan smile. "It's too late for me, boy. Save yourself!"

Larx sobered. "Too late for me too," he said softly. "I'm sort of doomed to take her place. What can you tell me that'll help keep Aaron out of here?"

Eamon grew grim. "Besides the fact that I'm pretty sure my own deputy shot me in the back?"

Larx grimaced. He'd seen the way Aaron had dealt with Percy and had seen Percy's face after Aaron had relieved him of duty. He'd known this was coming, but it was still hard to hear.

"You sure that's what happened? Aaron already confiscated his gun and is running ballistics. As soon as they get the slugs they pulled out of you and off your body armor, they'll have some news."

Eamon sighed. "It's not always easy to get ballistics off slugs that have hit body armor, but there's something else. Tell Aaron that I think there was more than one shooter. I can't be certain—not of anything—but I caught one slug in the back and one in the shoulder at the side, and…." He shook his head.

"You haven't seen that happen before?"

"I tell you, son, it literally *feels* off. But there's more." He took a deep breath, and Larx knew his ribs wouldn't let him do this much longer. "Percy was acting awfully strange. He let Billy MacDonald go, which I didn't know until we got close to the raid. I kept him on, thinking it was better than being a man down, but he was… obstructive. Said repeatedly we should stay away from the house on Dropoff Drive, that it wouldn't do anybody any good to go. It was… it was damned odd the way he said it too. Like he was warning us for our own good. I don't know what was going on, but he knew something about it, I guarantee you that."

Larx nodded. "Aaron relieved him of duty first thing," he said.

"On what grounds?"

"Failure to report to a senior officer, I think." Larx shrugged. "And general dumbfuckery. He didn't call us, Eamon. You'd been in surgery for hours before Warren thought to call Aaron, in case Percy hadn't let him know what happened. Isn't that enough? Percy had assumed authority outside the chain of command."

Eamon gave a sort of fierce scowl. "Good for Undersheriff George," he murmured. "Good. Make sure he doesn't forget about those ballistics, but have him look under the layers. I… I could swear there's more going on than Percy shooting me in a blind panic, and if he wanted me dead, the headshot was right there."

Larx shuddered. "God, Eamon, you are *not* filling me with confidence right now."

Eamon closed his eyes, obviously done. "George is smart," he murmured. "He'll figure out what's doin'. Send Rosie back when she's done being mad, okay?" His voice took on a wistful quality, and Larx patted his hand gently.

"I can do that. Get better, Eamon. I'll tell Aaron what you said. He's smart. He'll put shit together."

"Thanks, Larx." He paused and breathed carefully. "Did the kids have a good time?" he asked, and Larx's eyes burned.

"They had the best time," Larx said gruffly. "But they're still going to come and take care of Rosie when I'm gone helping Aaron."

Eamon nodded. "Future's in good hands," he mumbled, and then his breath evened out in sleep.

Jed brought Rosie back a few minutes later, and she sank into the seat next to the bed and sighed, nursing her coffee while her body sagged in exhaustion. Captain puffed out a breath and flopped by her feet, and just when Larx was wondering about the patient animal, Jed leaned over and murmured, "We took him out to do his business. I don't think we have anything to worry about there."

"Good." He checked his phone by reflex and saw Olivia's *On our way, Daddy!* text, complete with a picture of her living room, which featured sleeping teenagers on the couch, the recliners, and the floor. "My daughter and her husband are going to come sit with Rosie in about half an hour. If the dog needs to go, they can take him when the younger kids come to join them. They know their way around the hospital, but—"

"I'll help them out," Jed told him. "Just started my shift, and Sheriff Mills here is my priority patient."

"That's reassuring," Larx said, shaking his hand. "And I meant it—you're about to be eyeballs deep in dinner invitations. Don't let it freak you out."

Jed chuckled. "Beats eating alone by a mile."

"You say that, but—" He cast Rosie a glance and dropped his voice. "—don't eat her baking. She never did get the hang of it."

Jed snorted as though caught by surprise, and Larx excused himself from the unit to talk on his phone. He had to catch folks up.

"WE'RE STOPPING for two-dozen doughnuts," Olivia told him, sounding perky over the phone. "And Elton said I could drink real coffee because he doesn't want to be a homicide victim."

Ah, compromise—the basis of any good relationship. "Just remember," he said, willing to be the bad guy, "not too much—"

"Sugar," she said, the long-suffering note in her voice very understandable. If somebody had been telling *Larx* to cut back on sugar at this moment, he'd probably be found guilty of assault with a deadly doughnut. "I hear you. It makes me puke. But *a* doughnut and *a* coffee are all moderation."

He smiled; he could practically see her self-administered halo.

"Thanks, honey," he said. "I appreciate it. She's sitting with Eamon now, and I've got some information I need to give Aaron. When are the sleeping giants coming to relieve you, by the way?"

"Christi promised me three hours," Olivia said. "It's probably the longest time I'll be able to stand hospital chairs. Why?"

"Because Aaron and I are going to meet at the scene and look for any trace of the MacDonald boy at ten, and oddly enough, I don't seem to have a vehicle."

She grunted. "Fine. There's a coffee shop across the street, and—"

"And Rosie brought Captain, so he'll need to be walked."

"Captain?" His daughter, grown—mostly—and soon to be a mother herself, could still sound like a little girl when presented with a beloved animal to care for.

"Yes, sweetie," he said, voice dripping with patronization, "there's gonna be a dog."

"Well, okay, then," she agreed cheerily. "If there's gonna be a dog, you can take our vehicle."

Larx, as the grandfather-to-be, wasn't sure Elton's Kia Sportage actually *qualified* as a vehicle, but since Olivia's even tinier Toyota *also* didn't qualify as a vehicle, Larx would have to be grateful for boxes of metal with functional engines and leave it at that.

And then Larx tried to call Aaron—and failed. The call didn't go through, and Larx frowned.

Their cell reception *wasn't* great in the mountains. It frequently went out when someone was driving, traveling around hills, that sort of thing. But the town had their own tower, badly disguised as a pine tree, right in front of the Starbucks, and Larx should have been able to call Aaron, who was not two miles away at the sheriff's office. Larx checked the time—getting near nine—and frowned. Aaron said to meet him at Dropoff Drive at ten, but that didn't mean Aaron hadn't gotten there earlier. In fact, he'd been planning to.

Larx tried one more time, almost throwing the phone across the room when it went to voicemail again.

He started to gather himself, standing up and stretching, excusing himself to use the facilities, stocking up on the coffee Amanda's sister had left in the waiting room.

The minute Olivia and Elton toddled into the waiting room with a giant box of doughnuts and Larx's travel mug of more coffee, Larx was on his feet, hugging a fitfully sleeping Rosie, and heading for the door.

"Daddy?" Olivia said, after he gave her a perfunctory hug and a kiss on the cheek. "You're off already?"

Larx had never lied to his daughters. "I'm itchy," he said frankly. He glanced up at Buddy and made sure the older deputy was listening. "I can't get in contact with Aaron, and he and the two detectives were supposed to be at Dropoff Lane with a few SAC PD officers to check things out. I haven't heard anything, have you?"

He looked to Buddy, who shook his head. "All I'm getting," he said through a grateful mouthful of doughnut, "is a ration of shit about how I don't have to clean up the jail and really stupid suggestions for how to get those people back."

Larx grunted. "Any suggestions for how to go after Billy MacDonald or suggestions for where Percy Hardesty might be?"

Buddy grimaced. "Not so much," he murmured. "Should I call somebody?"

"Call Warren and give me the phone," Larx said, aware that his own phone had Eamon's number in it and a few of the deputies' wives.

"Warren?" he asked as the line clicked live. "This is Larx. Where's Aaron?"

"He took a few of the SAC PD people to the house," Warren replied, sounding puzzled. "Why?"

"I can't get hold of him. Is one of the other detectives there?"

"Yeah—uhm, Chris?" he called. "This is Chris Castro—he elected to stay behind since the other guy was more prepared for rough terrain."

Fair. "Detective Castro?" Larx said. He hadn't wanted to correct Warren on protocol, but yikes! "This is—"

"Principal Larkin?" came the voice of the first detective Aaron had spoken to when he'd arrived. "What can I do for you?"

"Can you get in contact with your guy at the Dropoff site?" Larx asked, and the puzzled silence on the other line did nothing for his confidence.

"Hold on a sec," Castro murmured, probably getting his own phone out of his pocket. Larx waited patiently as he muttered, "C'mon, Hawkins, pick up. C'mon…."

Larx knew exactly the moment Castro entered the same land of worry Larx had.

"Not getting a thing," he said. "Your boy and Hawkins went in together to take a look around. We sent part of SWAT home, but the rest were staying here to track down the detainees who escaped."

"Do you have many?" Larx asked.

"Almost all of them, partly thanks to you for getting someone here to clean up since all the law enforcement was wandering around with their thumbs up their asses saying things like, 'I think they have Lysol somewhere.'"

Larx choked back a snort.

"And partly," Castro continued, "due to George and Hawkins, who told them to go look behind the bakery and the two coffee shops to see if they were hanging around looking for food and warmth. We're missing two guys, and as soon as the hospital staff gets to these guys and gives them something to keep the DTs from starting for real, we'll start on interviews."

Fair enough. "Okay, then, keep me posted. I was going to meet Aaron at the Dropoff house at ten, but I'm… itchy," he repeated helplessly. "I was going to go check again."

"I'll join you," Castro said. "It's not like Hawkins not to check in or go MIA. Wait for me before you get out of the vehicle," he finished.

Larx glanced at Elton, who was watching him with interest, and grimaced. "It'll be an electric-blue Kia," he said. "Don't ask."

Castro snorted. "Oh, I will—but at the site. I'm itchy too, dammit. I'll see you there."

Larx grunted and handed the phone back to Olivia. "I'll call you when I get a bead on Aaron," he soothed when he saw her concern. "No worries. Just gonna go scratch an itch, okay?"

She launched herself at him and hugged him hard this time. "Careful, Daddy," she said gruffly. "Remember, me and Elton need you. His parents are pretty fucking useless."

Larx grimaced. "Livvy…."

"No, sir," Elton said, his good-natured expression unruffled. "She's right. We're going to need you and Mr. George, so, you know, be careful."

Larx blew out a breath and nodded. "Yeah, I will. You guys take care of Rosie. She's resting now. Livvy—"

"Going," she said, saluting him crisply. His daughter was so beautiful—dark hair, big hazel eyes, piquant little face, even with the rounding from pregnancy. He winked at her and hurried away before he wrapped his arms around them both and sheltered them from absolutely everything in the world he could think of and some things he couldn't.

They were adults, he reminded himself. They'd be in charge of a whole other human being soon, and they were already running a household on their own, including an adult with PTSD and a needy teenager who had lost so much stability in his life he clung to every adult within reach.

They'd be fine.

But Aaron needed him *now*, and that's what his job needed to be. Without another look behind him, he hustled off to the parking lot to find Elton's obnoxiously colored vehicle.

Unexpected Companions

AARON GRUNTED, staring out over the property on Dropoff Drive with a practiced, jaundiced eye. Once upon a time, the place had sported a paved walkway from the badly leveled road to the door and a lawn that had probably been carefully nurtured sod that had sat in a carefully measured square around the house. Aaron could see rotted fence posts and some horizontal splinter piles that testified to the memory of a split-rail fence. But those days had been long ago—probably before Aaron and his kids had come to Colton more than ten years earlier. What remained was an oddly square mat of forest floor—red dirt with patches of crabgrass springing up in the remains of the sod, and lots of pine needles and pine cones to boot.

Aaron was almost afraid to look around the back of the house—the canyon had a tendency to creep outward, looking for more soil to erode and pull into its sloped sides, and what had probably been a good fifty yards of leeway between the back porch and the drop-off had probably decreased by at least ten yards in the last twenty years.

The house itself was a good half-mile from its nearest neighbor and surrounded by thick stands of sugar pine and scrub oak, taking advantage of the plateau that had been leveled when the canyon had been formed. The ground was flat enough to make visibility a problem. At least with hills you could see somebody *on* the hill, but this was… perilous.

This was a damned good place for an ambush is what it was.

And that didn't include the house itself, which was sagging from roof to walls, the stucco flaking off, the once-painted siding sliding off to expose rotting drywall. If the cops hadn't raided it the night before, it might have collapsed or caught fire before the end of the summer.

The catching fire was the nightmare part—they lived in fire country. More than one person had lost their home in the wildfires from three years prior, and while this last year had been *wetter*, that also meant *more growth*. This fire season was threatening to put the last one to shame, and this house on the edge of the wilderness had been a concern to more than just the sheriff's department this year.

"I thought that would look less creepy in the daylight," Hawkins muttered. "Sadly, not the case."

Aaron grinned at the young detective, who winked back. Aaron had been impressed with both Hawkins and Castro—partly because they'd both been respectful of Eamon, and partly because they'd both freely admitted that this wasn't their party. As soon as Aaron had come in and started directing resources, they'd been more than happy to help. Organizing the jail had been a nightmare, and Aaron might have given up and quit if Larx's janitorial staff hadn't come in to give them a hand. Tad and Jimmy had been the ones to suggest looking in the trash areas of the coffee shops for the escapees, so that had been a huge help to recovery. Alex, the poor kid clocked on the head and left on the floor, had still been muzzy before he'd been taken to the hospital to be checked out, but the one thing he'd said that had given everybody pause was that he'd just finished checking the door to the jail when he'd been knocked out.

Castro suggested that maybe the poor kid had been overwhelmed, but Aaron didn't think so. He'd been found in front of the first cell by the door—the one he'd be standing by if what he said had really happened—and that begged the question of who had knocked him on the head if he hadn't been overpowered by the prisoners.

Aaron had a couple of guesses, but it couldn't be his priority.

The whole time he'd been cleaning up the mess, Aaron had heard Curtis MacDonald's heartbeat in the back of his mind. There was a ticking clock here—Aaron could *feel* it. And somehow, all trails of time led back to this house. Curtis had, in all likelihood, disappeared here. Eamon had been shot here, probably in order to obscure what was going on in this house. Billy MacDonald had been missing, Percy had been *lying*, and they'd both covered for each other when things had first started to go down.

Aaron had managed to talk to two of the people rounded up from the Dropoff house, one of them a girl, heartbreakingly young, who'd told him that she'd given a boy like the one in the picture a blowjob for part of his stash. Her eyes shifted left, and Aaron could guess the rest.

"Part," he asked without judgment, "or all?"

She shrugged. "He was out if it," she said defensively. "He wasn't going to use it." She shuddered, and a touch of humanity passed over her meth-ravaged features. “He was so sad,” she said softly. “I told him to take it easy on the meth, and he said….” Her voice broke. “He said he was hoping to die, but it just wouldn’t happen. He wasn’t that far gone, Sheriff—why’d he want to die?”

Aaron thought sadly of Larx’s insistence that this kid get second chances. And third. And that they not give up on him when he disappeared. Apparently the only person who hadn’t given up on him had been Larx, because Aaron was pretty sure Billy MacDonald wasn’t looking for his son to give him a hug.

“I don’t know, honey,” he said after a moment and then looked at her—maybe nineteen, with sores on her face, wrinkles, her collarbones showing through her tattered T-shirt. “I don’t know why any of you want to die. I… I wish I could give you the thing you needed.”

She started shivering then, and apparently cursed with self-awareness for a moment more, said, “Nobody wants to hug a junkie. Too late for me now.”

Aaron let out a sigh. “Honey, we’re going to ship you to rehab, on the state’s dime, no arrest for possession.” He pulled out his card. “The minute they start talking about turning you loose from the facility, you call me. Someone will be waiting for you when you get out. *Someone* will have a plan for you. Tuck that in your pocket. Hold it, okay?”

She nodded and clutched the card, looking skeptical. She was covered in vomit, scabs, and lice, and he had no time and only one set of clothes. Tad was hovering near the door to the freshly cleaned cell with a pile of emergency blankets, waiting for the woman to be unlocked so he could wrap one around her shoulders. Aaron stood and grabbed one, wrapped it around the girl. and pulled her into a one-armed hug. She sobbed, and he tried not to gag, but as she crumpled onto the small jail cell cot, he heard her mumbling, “Thank you. Thank you so much. Thank you.”

He’d sighed and backed out of the cell, not proud of how he checked to make sure no part of his skin had touched hers.

“Here,” Hawkins said, handing him a small pocket bacterial wipe. Aaron squeezed some out and got his hands, his shoulder, even his cheek, which may have brushed her hair.

“I feel like an asshole,” he muttered, but his sense of being unclean had faded.

"Forgive yourself," Hawkins said softly. "It's not a sin to want to be clean. She was a mess. But maybe you gave her some hope today, so thank you."

Aaron had looked at him quickly, wanting to know why he'd thought that—and how someone who looked barely thirty could sound so wise—but Chris Castro had arrived with gear, and Aaron had to put his tactical brain on and decide who was coming with him to the house and who was going to stay and round up the rest of the detainees, making sure they got to the rehab facility in Auburn.

In the end, he'd chosen Hawkins to come with him and Castro to stay at the station with some of Lieutenant Johnson's men to take care of things there. Castro was the senior detective, Johnson had more command experience, and Aaron was going out into the field. He needed to leave his department in good hands, and after the debacle of Percy's de facto takeover, he wasn't too excited about leaving his own guys there.

But it was more than that. Something about Tad Hawkins's compassion and common sense with the detainees in withdrawal told Aaron that Hawkins would be a handy guy to have around if they actually found who they were looking for.

So now they sat in Aaron's unit in front of the house, waiting for Lieutenant Johnson herself, as well as a forensic tech she'd called from Sacramento on the woman's day off to come fill in for the thin spots in Aaron's personnel. Aaron was trying to connect with Larx to see if he was leaving the hospital soon, and the lack of cell coverage was really pissing him off.

He tried for a second time and barely refrained from chucking his phone across the car.

"Easy there, Chief," Tad murmured, taking the phone from Aaron's hand and giving it back to him nicely. "Don't you have, like, a radio?"

Aaron grunted. "Yeah, but…." Blargh! Some of his irritation deflated from his shoulders. "But the dispatch lady is Percy's ex, and I don't trust her to put me through to Larx or to relay a message."

"Larx—oh!" Hawkins's voice went up almost comically. "Your uh, partner?"

Well, that was diplomatic. "See?" Aaron muttered. "Why couldn't we ever get the hang of saying *that*? Instead we keep saying 'boyfriend,' and you know what?"

"What?" Hawkins sounded like it was a loaded question and Aaron might be the gun, which made Aaron realize he was probably acting a little crazy, but damn, he was tired and he was pissed off and he wanted to talk to Larx!

"We're too damned old to have boyfriends! I was going to try for 'husband,' but shit kept getting in the way. Kids and jobs and meetings and… holy crap, adulting *sucks*!"

Tad's deep laughter made Aaron look at the guy—*really* look at the guy—and he saw someone else who'd had an awfully long night, but who was putting up with Aaron's loose-lipped bullshit just the same.

"Have I thanked you and Castro yet?" he asked, smiling slightly. "For stepping up and helping out? This can*not* be what you signed up for."

Tad shrugged. "Chris is Eamon's friend, but I have to admit, once we got up here and shit went south, we sort of… you know, those eye-to-eye meetings partners have?"

Aaron nodded. Even Warren had learned to read eyeball semaphore. "Oh yeah."

"We just wanted to help," he said with a shrug. "It's… it's nice working for people—you, Eamon—who are looking to do the right thing and don't step on dicks or whine about egos or bureaucracy while you're doing it. We've got some cops at SAC PD who are like that. It's why we do our jobs."

Aaron nodded and let out a breath. "So, uhm… I couldn't help notice how—"

"Gay I am?" Hawkins asked, laughing, and Aaron sputtered.

"That was *not* what I was going to say!" he protested. "Not even a little bit!" He chuckled some more. "But God, the fact that I had no idea pretty much tells you why it took years for me to move on Larx, doesn't it!"

Hawkins colored prettily, looking twenty-five again instead of thirty, which Aaron thought he might be. "Well if it took you years to hit on *that*," he said, "you're dumber than you look, Undersheriff, and that's all I'll say on the subject. You really didn't know?"

Aaron shook his head. "No. It didn't even occur to me. I thought you were going to say you had a girl waiting for you at home. Heteronormative—I'm a poster child, I guess."

Hawkins snorted, obviously still amused. "No girl. No boy either," he said, grimacing. "But… a hope."

"A hope?" Aaron was suddenly interested in the kid's personal life. Was it easier being LGBTQ in law enforcement now than it had been when Aaron had gone in? He didn't regret his first marriage or his children—would never regret falling in love with a woman and building a life. But would he have made different choices if he knew falling in love with a man was a possibility when he could still keep his job?

Hawkins lifted his shoulder and held up his phone. "We've been texting," he said with dignity. "He seems a bit… snakebit, I guess. Skittish. I barely got his phone number, but he's been texting back."

Aaron nodded. Well, the younger generation had its ways. "How long?"

Hawkins grimaced. "A few weeks. We had… well, a night. I was hoping I'd get to see him play last weekend—he's a musician—but we caught a case, and I caught overtime. He understood. I think. I was going to be there last night, but this came up—he says he understands, but just once, I'd like a chance to see him when I say."

"What's he play?"

"Drums, guitar, and vocals," Hawkins said promptly, making Aaron wonder how long he'd been studying. "But seriously. he's got the sweetest voice. Uses it mostly for heartbreak songs, but it's still sweet."

Aaron chuckled tiredly, wishing the best for Hawkins and his snakebit guitar player, and then remembered his original question. "So," he said, "what I was going to ask you before…."

"This scintillating conversation about my personal life?" Hawkins said dryly.

"Yeah, that." Aaron dropped his voice because this subject could be, if anything, more delicate than the personal life one. "That girl in the jail. You… you seemed to know a lot about her—or folks like her. Have you volunteered?"

Hawkins grunted, and for a moment there was silence in the vehicle. Aaron had rolled down the windows and killed the engine, because they were in the shade and it didn't hit ninety until later in the afternoon, and for a moment, they could hear the whisper of trees and the hum of a far-off vehicle.

"My sister," Hawkins said softly. "For a while—a year or so—it got really bad. I… I had to go into one of these houses and haul her out one night. I…." He let out a breath. "I sedated her against her will, which is more than illegal, and then I bathed her and shaved her head because seriously, I can't even…." He shuddered. "And then I kept her sedated and hooked up to an IV bag for a week while she bled out the shakes and puked and cried and fought and cursed my name." He shook his head. "And when she'd overcome the *physical* part of the addiction, that's when the hard part started."

Aaron was staring at him by this time—not in horror, but in sympathy and admiration. "Brother," he said after a moment, "that is a hard road to walk. That took some dedication."

Hawkins shook his head. "She did six months in rehab and a halfway house. Not twenty-eight days. Not two months. Six months. She told me that after everything *I'd* been through, she wasn't going out on her own until she was sure it was going to stick." He shrugged. "I… our mother died, and April just… lost her way. And I couldn't do it. I couldn't lose her like that without trying. But…." He shuddered again. "It's hard. To let her go. I visit her twice a month, and sometimes she still can't look at me. I overstepped *so* many boundaries. So many things I shouldn't have done. But drugs are so fucking bad. I…." He shivered again, and the face he turned toward Aaron showed the ravages of grief and the consequences of making hard choices. "If any experience I have can make it easier on someone else, I feel like I owe it to the world, you know? Because I got her back, but I might have accidentally killed her, and I'm just lucky it didn't work out that way."

Aaron nodded soberly. "Wow," he said, not sure he had anything to come back to that.

"Wow," Hawkins said with a shrug. "See? Easier to tell you I'm gay."

Aaron chuckled. "Larx's oldest daughter," he said, feeling like he was sharing a secret that wasn't his, but also feeling like he owed Hawkins something. "She's struggling with bipolar—and she's pregnant. She… she's doing okay now, but this winter it was touch and go for a while. Larx apparently charged into her room and dragged her out to run with him, yelling at her the whole time. They went running for five miles. She was in her jeans and shitty shoes and was bitching back at him—and he said about halfway around the track, she actually started to run. She ran track in high school, you know. And I know how hard that was for him. He's all about peace and love and kindness and 'make good choices!' But 'make good choices' wasn't working for Livvy. He had to drag her by the hair into the land of the living, and it was hard. He probably *still* doesn't know if he did the right thing. But there's not always a right thing. Sometimes you do what you *have* to because the alternative is…."

"Unthinkable," Hawkins murmured. "Yeah. Yeah. That." He yawned. "Anyway, so that's probably why Chris and I stayed here to help. The alternative—"

"Was unthinkable."

A silence fell between them, and Aaron laughed a little to shake it off. "Look, you close your eyes and catch some shut-eye. We've got maybe forty-five minutes before Johnson gets here. I'll keep watch and wake you if I need you. Yeah?"

"Thanks," Hawkins said softly, leaning his head against his window. "'Preciate it."

He closed his eyes and dropped off in a matter of breaths, and Aaron was left staring into the sunshine and the shade, thinking about Larx and how he hadn't just turned MacDonald over to the forces that be, and how he still thought everybody deserved a second chance.

People thought people like that—like Larx, like Tad Hawkins—were pushovers. That giving someone a second chance was a cop-out. Aaron knew different. It took courage to do it, to face hurt, to face rejection, to face having a loved one *hate* you because you were taking away their autonomy and refusing to leave them to self-destruct.

For the millionth time it hit him how lucky he was that a man like Larx loved *him*. Aaron really *did* need to find another word besides boyfriends. When were they getting married again?

He pulled out his phone—which was still charging, thank God—and checked it for the umpteenth time. Nope. No service.

With a sigh, he pulled open a book that he'd been reading and settled down to a C.J. Box western, hoping it would be enough to keep him from falling asleep.

Johnson arrived at ten fifteen, shamefaced and embarrassed about having gotten lost on a backroad and having to turn around and come back the way she'd come.

"I'm sorry!" Aaron told her. "I've been there. You should have hit me up on the radio."

He'd gotten out of the vehicle and was leaning against the door, waiting for the tech to pull out her kit. The good news was, Hawkins had gotten in a solid hour of sleep, and as he made his way around the unit to join the conference, he looked a lot less ragged for it.

"Stupid pride," Johnson grumbled. "Worse than a man."

"Tired and out of your element," Aaron said gently. "But I'm glad you're here. My plan was, you two look through the house again. You're looking for signs of some sort of business going on. Not just a sold dime bag, but—"

"Product, cash, distribution," said Mary Lee, the tech, a fiftyish woman with short gray hair and eyes that were warm and sharp at once. "I hear you. Are there basements around here? Sometimes the water table won't let you, sometimes the soil—"

Aaron held his hand up and tilted it back and forth. "Yes and no. I don't know if you can see, but back behind those trees—" He pointed to a dense stand of trees and scrub about a football field beyond the road. "—is a drop-off into Daffodil Canyon. The soil there was pretty much destroyed by placer mining, and it's a nightmare of loose shale and new growth. Even the service road is an iffy proposition. And the earth that isn't held to the cliffside by trees gets sucked into the canyon every time it rains. *But* back when these houses were built, in the fifties, there was a good half-mile between Daffodil Canyon and Dropoff Drive. Each lot is individual—so owner's choice."

"Gotcha," said Mary Lee. She raked her eyes up and down the structure, cocking her head when she spotted something on the side. "I'm thinking there's a fruit cellar in there that nobody checked out. You say this raid was done in the dark. That rise and fall in the earth toward the back there—do you see it?"

Aaron could, but it was subtle.

"Yeah," Mary Lee continued. "That's not something your men probably spotted in the middle of the night. Janine and I will take a look there, and you, Undersheriff?"

"Me and Hawkins here are going to be looking to see if somebody went running along the back rim of the yards, or…." He grimaced, but Mary Lee Clemmons and Janine Johnson were apparently unflappable.

"Or if they fell in," Janine said grimly. "Gotcha. Okay, then, are we waiting on anybody else?"

"Larx is on his way," Aaron said, checking the road in frustration. "I don't know if you noticed, but—"

"No cell service out here," Janine said dryly. "I had to have dispatch tell my wife I'm not going to be home until tomorrow at the earliest. What was your partner going to do?"

Partner. Aaron really *should* get used to the word, right?

"For one thing," Aaron said grimly, "he's got an MA in physics and biology—"

Mary Lee sucked in a breath. "So help me? You're saying I'm not alone?"

Aaron gave a weak chuckle. "He has zero experience in chain of command or procedure, but yes, he can be a good eye." He sighed. "Also he's wickedly smart, and he knows the kid we're looking for. Knows kids in general."

"Well, let's get started here," Janine said. "You fed us this morning, but I saw a burger joint as we came over, and I love a small-town frosty cone and grease burger."

Aaron nodded. "Yeah, we'll take a look at the perimeter and give you two a chance to search the house more thoroughly. I really want to make sure that kid didn't go over the cliff."

There were grave nods all around, and Aaron and Tad made their way to the fringe of trees Aaron had pointed out earlier. Aaron stopped and turned toward the house, drawing a mental straight line from the back door—which was a mass of peeling paint and bullet holes now—down the splintered porch stairs and to the tree line, which masked the edge of the canyon.

In the daylight, the muddle of tracks told a very definite story.

A line of red dirt marked where feet had shuffled front to back, from the road where Aaron had parked, back behind undergrowth, and into the hidden pockets of shadow around the house.

That had been SWAT.

The front of the house, which faced the road, was particularly torn up: feet, wheel marks, stretcher marks. All of it created a mishmash of sign that was hard to figure out. There were even wrappers and bits of gauze in the area that was probably behind the ambulance. Aaron had trouble looking at that part—the thought of Eamon, bleeding, in pain, and probably pissed off and confused, hurt him.

But that was the front of the house.

Aaron and Detective Hawkins were interested in the back of the house, and together, careful not to disturb the sign that was already there and obvious, the two of them broke out their Maglites, the better to overcome the shadows that dappled the ground in profusion, much like scattered leaves—and began to study the ground to see what they could see.

Aaron had hoped they'd have a dog to help them, but the dog handlers had assured him that unless he had something from Curtis MacDonald that was personal, the dog wouldn't be able to find anything but people sign, and all of the handlers were justifiably worried about the edge of the damned cliff.

The going was slow, but after about twenty minutes, Hawkins called Aaron over to a spot about thirty feet from the other side of the house.

They both paused for a moment, taking a sip from the water bottles they each carried in a cargo pocket, and then Hawkins used his flashlight as a pointer. "See that?" he said, indicating an almost black drop of something liquid on top of a patch of pine needles. The drop was teardrop shaped, indicating whatever had left it had been traveling away from the house and toward the tree line at an angle.

"Look like blood to you?" Hawkins asked, and Aaron nodded.

"Mary Lee!" he called, and their new tech popped her head out of the hole in the ground covered by an old piece of plywood that she'd correctly deduced had been a root cellar under the house.

"I'm here. I've got some good shit for you, too, Chief."

"Can you tell me about it while you test to see if this is blood?"

"Roger that."

She—like all of them—was wearing Tyvek booties, but she was wearing the whole bunny suit to go with it. As she approached, she shooed Aaron and Hawkins away before pulling the ventilator hood off her head.

"Water?" Aaron offered courteously, and she shook her head and indicated a straw she had in her bunny suit.

"Even with this, it's going to be too hot for the suit in about an hour," she said. "But that's okay. I've got lots to begin with. I've taken samples for days. If I can use your lab, I think we're going to have ourselves an arraignment party. It'll be fun. We can bring beer, dogs—the works."

Aaron stared at her, trying not to laugh. "Uhm, whom are we arraigning?"

"The assholes who bagged and tagged all the meth downstairs. And stacked the cash. There's a lot of fingerprints on the cellophane in there—nobody was worried about evidence. It's the business you were looking for, and while a lot of the product and cash has been moved elsewhere, probably through the tunnel under the house, there's plenty down there to test."

"You… you didn't think to tell us about tha—wait? Did you say tunnels?"

She stared back. "You said your priority was the kid. Did you find his trail?"

Aaron shook his head, hard. "Yeah. Uhm, could you test that and see if it's blood, and Hawkins and I will try to find some more droplets?"

"Can do," she said, pulling a test kit from her pocket. "Janine's still in the basement but not for long. God, it's hot in there. Like I said, we've got maybe an hour before we have to call it on account of choosing life."

"More than fair," Aaron said. "Call it a little earlier, mark it with some tape, and let's see if we can come back tomorrow."

She shook her head. "It's a damned good thing we came back today, Sheriff. The tracks of people coming and going from this basement happened *after* the ruckus last night. I'm pretty sure this was done *after* everybody cleared out and went to the hospital for your friend who got shot."

Aaron gaped and then swore viciously. "I will fuck that man through his earhole with my *gun*," he snarled. "I *knew* it!"

Mary Lee's eyes widened, but Hawkins was right there with him. "He did that on purpose," he muttered. "It's why he didn't shoot Eamon in the head. He had to be alive so there'd be EMTs and chaos, and then he'd get everybody to come to the hospital."

"*That's* why he didn't call me," Aaron muttered. "He saw you guys taking their cues from Eamon. He wasn't trying to kill him, he was trying to distract *us*."

They let out twin growls of frustration, and then Aaron focused on Mary Lee, taking the sample from the ground and shaking it up in the bottle. The bottle turned blue, and Aaron knew what that meant.

Blood.

"And Curtis MacDonald is still missing," Aaron said. "C'mon, Hawkins. Let's keep looking." He paused and looked over his shoulder at Mary Lee, who was trudging resolutely back to the house that was more than it seemed. "But I want to hear about the damned tunnel later!" he called.

"Sure. It's long, it's dark, and it's full of spiders. Knock yourself out. Go play."

He and Hawkins looked at each other and grinned.

"I like her," Hawkins said decisively.

"I second that," Aaron agreed.

Now that they'd found the spatter, it was easy. Hawkins had grabbed some markers for Mary Lee and was setting them down at every drop. The drops were close together—the person bleeding wasn't bleeding heavily, but he wasn't moving quickly either. It didn't matter. In minutes, Aaron and Hawkins were at the edge of the ravine, looking at a bloody handprint on one of the trees.

Then looking at each other.

At their feet, they could see where the edge of the canyon was starting to disintegrate, and walking even two steps nearer would be inviting disaster.

"Here," Hawkins said. "I'll get down—"

His voice was cut off by a gunshot. He grunted and threw his weight against the blood-marked tree while Aaron looked around wildly for the shooter—it was somebody coming from Dropoff Drive, not the roadway leading to the house, but before Aaron could spot them, he saw Mary Lee go down, grunting hard as she fell.

He went for his gun, fumbling with the snap, and called, "Janine! Shooter!"

The piece of plywood Mary Lee had laid back down over the hole rose just enough to give Janine visibility, and he tried to help Hawkins sit down so he could check out the wound—which appeared to be in the back of his thigh—and pull his gun at the same time.

It was only luck and the grace of the gods that kept his piece holstered when the tree they were clutching to help give them cover and leverage themselves began to tilt slowly, so slowly, into the canyon.

Hawkins dropped abruptly to the ground, howling breathlessly when he hit bottom and then the bottom dropped out. Aaron stopped messing around with his gun and wrapped his arms around Hawkins's shoulders, stretching them both out backward in preparation for what was to…

Cooooomeeeeeee….

It was not a smooth ride down. Both of them fought with shale and rocks, tree roots and pebbles, as the scree and the earth, layered loosely together, lost cohesion and formed the world's worst bobsled, throwing them down the side of the canyon with abandon.

Together they careened, without direction or rudder, until Aaron saw another stand of trees in front of a drop-off that had no slope—just a sheer cliff going down fifty feet or more. In an act of desperation, he threw himself sideways, keeping hold of Hawkins with his legs and clutching one of the slenderer trees with his arms.

The bark shredded through his uniform, his T-shirt, his skin, but his grip held, and he heard Hawkins grunt solidly as the young man found another tree with his foot and kicked hard against it. Their headlong descent into the canyon stopped abruptly, and Aaron took a moment to pant and try to ignore his injury.

"Hawkins?" he called, keeping his knees locked around the younger man's shoulders. "You alive?"

"No," Hawkins replied. "I've been shot."

"Liar," Aaron muttered. "You are *too* alive."

"Did I mention the shot?" Hawkins snapped back, his voice breaking.

Aaron heard that in his bones—he'd been there. But their problems were far from over, and he couldn't let Hawkins descend into invalid mode yet. "Oh please," he panted, swinging his hips so he could release his knees and Hawkins would simply slide into a two-tree cradle. "Everyone's been shot in Colton. Eamon, me. Hell, even Larx got shot. It's a great place to live. Bring your boyfriend. Raise children. Just watch out for getting shot, that's all."

Hawkins let out a laugh that was also a sob. "You're an awful man, and if you hadn't just saved my life, I'd be glad you weren't my boss."

"Tough," Aaron panted. "I'm recruiting you. You'll live here forever." He glanced around their location and wanted to groan. The stand of trees had deep roots, but the earth was still not stable. "How badly are we fucked?"

"There is a drop-off here that is scaring the shit out of me," Hawkins replied soberly. "And did I mention the shot?"

Aaron's abrasions—including a laceration on his calf and shin that was starting to sting like a motherfucker—began to give him hell, but he laughed anyway, and then shut himself up and tried to take stock.

That was when he realized the shooting had stopped up top. Carefully, without giving up his death grip on the tree in front of him, he twisted his body to look up.

He could see the root structures dangling from the canyon overhang, the earth fresh and a little wet from where the dirt had disappeared. Down the canyon and about thirty feet to his right he saw where their friend, the tree with the bloody handprint, had ended up, its precipitous descent a little less mindful than theirs.

As he gulped air and tried to think, he wondered what was happening above them. Mary Lee—was she okay? Was Lieutenant Johnson? What about—

His blood ran cold.

Oh God. What about Larx? He was about to drive into an ambush, and Aaron was out of commission.

Oh shit.

Larx.

And then he heard more gunshots, echoing from the plateau above into the canyon, and Aaron was left hoping for a miracle.

As Miracles Go

LARX SWORE to himself as he rounded the last corner onto the side road of the house on Dropoff Drive. Elton's damned Kia had been running on fumes, and getting gas had cost him twenty minutes. He was *late*, and he still hadn't heard from Aaron. He'd managed to get hold of Detective Castro as he left the gas station and was told that Lieutenant Johnson had called in to dispatch to have them deliver a message to her family because cell reception was crap. That helped him feel just a little better, but still.

Something was wrong.

Off.

It twisted his stomach, and he couldn't get a handle on it because he was only twenty minutes late, right? Only—he saw the house through the level rain of trees in the distance, far from its neighbors, looking small and alone and tattered. One breath of wind, one more crumble of earth into the canyon behind it, and the house would disintegrate like wet toilet paper, and it would only be remembered in the fever dreams of the addicts who propped it up.

Dropoff Drive ran in front of the house—this *was* a neighborhood of sorts, even though the houses were sometimes a mile or so apart. To the side was a small road that bisected the neighborhood and turned into the service track that descended into the canyon. Here—a *healthy* distance from the canyon—was where Larx found Aaron's SUV and another police unit, marked SAC PD SWAT. Larx pulled up on the other side of the service track road, Elton's Kia facing the other direction.

He scanned the house and its surroundings, eyes growing wide as he saw a crumpled form in white Tyvek in the back area behind the house.

Oh shit! And then, as he watched, a figure in body armor and a black helmet pushed furtively past a piece of plywood lying on the ground, indicating a room of some sort underneath the house, and aimed a *gun* somewhere in front of Larx and to his right. There were two quick gunshots, and then the figure pushed out of the plywood door and into the open. A woman, Larx thought faintly, before recognizing the SWAT team leader who had come up from Sacramento to help Eamon.

He watched her speak quickly into the radio on her shoulder and then, as Larx opened his door to go see what in the hell was going on, another shot rang out.

Lieutenant Johnson—Larx remembered her name now—dropped to one knee, gun out, and fired two more shots in the same direction as before. This time, when she was done, she shouted, "*Eat that, motherfucker*!" and then ran to the crumpled figure in the Tyvek.

Larx waited a moment, then two—he didn't have any body armor—before reaching into his glove compartment for the extensive first-aid kit he made *all* the kids drag around with them. Mylar blanket, enough gauze to act as a pillow, the works: Larx's kids had it with them.

With one more fearful look around, Larx sprinted across the pine-needle and leaf-mold strewn dirt that made up the yard.

"Lieutenant," he panted as he drew near, "are they—"

Johnson looked up, panicked for a moment, and then her eyes closed as she took a deep breath and calmed down.

"You wore your vest underneath that plastic, didn't you, Mary Lee?" she asked, like she was addressing an old friend.

"Hot… as… fuck…," the woman—Larx could see she'd taken off her Tyvek hood—replied. "Fuckin' Jesus… wha' wazzat?"

Gingerly, Johnson helped her friend sit up and took another look off in the direction she'd been aiming. "Don't know who," she said, breathing hard. "I winged him good, though. He's going to be leaving a blood trail back to whatever stone he crawled out from under."

Larx peered in that direction, handing Johnson a bottle of water and the mylar blanket.

"It's hot as fuck," Johnson muttered. "The hell is this for?"

"It also shields from the sun," Larx replied patiently. "Heat stroke is as bad as shock." He turned to Mary Lee. "Honey, you've got your vest?"

The woman nodded, still gasping. "If you can," he said, speaking quietly, "I need you to slow it down. That's right. Slooooow your breathing down." She whimpered, and he took her hand, shucking the gloves quickly so they could make skin-to-skin contact. "Here. Feel my hand?"

She nodded, and Janine pillowed her friend's head on her lap.

"Good. You cling to that but slow it down. You took one in the chest." Dead center mass, but he didn't want to point that out, looking at the hole in the Tyvek. "That's a lot of pressure, but it was from a distance. You might have just bruised some ribs and not busted them. But we need you to be still as possible until the ambulance gets here. You hear me?"

She nodded, scowling. "Not stupid," she muttered.

"No, you're not," he said with a small smile. "But we forget basic stuff when we're hurt. I got shot last year—just a graze. Told the whole world I was fine. Went home right after, spent the next four days with a fever, irritated as fuck. So listen to me here and listen to your doctors later. You may *think* you're in your right mind, but it's a shock, and you're not. It hurts to admit, but we all get super crazy when something violent happens to us, okay?"

She nodded again, her lips curling up wryly, and Larx was relieved to see there was no blood on her lips.

"Janine here is going to give you some water, okay?"

"Got my own," Mary Lee nodded to a small straw sticking up from her suit. "Electrolytes."

"You are awesome," Larx said, feeling it. He wasn't sure if that was a feature of the Tyvek or if this sturdy, obviously smart woman had rigged her own suit because she knew it was going to get bloody hot that day, even in the mountains. "You take small sips of that, okay?"

"Yeah," the woman panted, sounding in better shape than she had. "What…? Janine, what was that sound?"

Janine grunted. "Shit," she said, looking over her shoulder, and Larx was confused for a moment.

"The gunshots?" he asked.

"No." Mary Lee shook her head, looking concerned. "Not… it was a tree sound. A cracking and a crash."

Janine nodded her head to get Larx's attention.

"You're Larx, right?" she asked. "Aaron's man?"

"Yeah," Larx said, glad she knew that at least. "What's wrong?"

"Undersheriff George and Detective Hawkins were over there, looking at something near the drop-off, when the shooting started." She looked over her shoulder again, and Larx took a few steps toward the area, not sure where she was gesturing.

"Where?" he asked, puzzled. He didn't see them—no bodies, no blood, no… no *them*.

"That's that thing," she said, her voice breaking. "That's what Mary Lee heard. There was a small group of trees and a patch of earth in that direction that *aren't there* anymore. Hawkins went down, the trees just… just pitched forward, and that whole section of dirt fell into the canyon. I…. Be careful!"

Because Larx was running—*sprinting*—toward what he could now recognize as a big gaping wound in the foliage and the earth on the edge of Daffodil Canyon.

He remembered to slow down as he neared the edge—something old and primal, a voice that had been born the first time he'd held a tiny Olivia in his arms, spoke up and screamed in his ear that he needed to be mindful of his own well-being, because he was in charge of the tiny creature in his arms. He skidded to a halt about five yards from two big leaning trees that marked the new beginning of the ledge, and dropped to an army crawl, disregarding the needles and the red dirt that stuck to his clothes as he wormed his way to the place where the horizon ended and a big hole in the ground opened in its place.

He peered over the ledge and caught his breath.

Trees, three or four of them, lay strewn, massive root systems displayed almost obscenely, parts that were meant to be hidden now out in the air for all to see. Two of them were broken like matchsticks—some mighty force, probably gravity, had shattered them—and a raw, exposed patch of earth, uncluttered by rocks, shale, or the sparse manzanita ground cover that grew in the canyon, marked the path where the trees had torn a rip in the fabric of the ecosystem.

Larx squinted past the spots dancing in front of his eyes and remembered to breathe.

Aaron had been standing *right where this hole in the earth was now*. He took deep breaths, slow and even, just like he'd told Mary Lee, and then peered over the edge again, this time tracking the descent of the trees, looking for something moving a little more deliberately, something that was sentient and could control its chaotic descent into the middle ring of the canyon.

He saw a shoe first, a generic climbing boot, and then, a few feet farther down, he saw a long, painful smear of blood against a rock.

He winced and continued tracking until he came to a stand of trees and scrub, marking Mother Nature's determined attempt to help the loose shale and other rocks of the scarred, bleeding patch of land heal itself.

It seemed to be a million miles away, a thousand feet down, an indescribable distance from where he hovered, head barely clearing the drop-off as he envisioned being dumped into the canyon from a fragile shelf of earth just for peeking over to see.

But from that terrifying distance he saw movement, two figures—wait, three? Did he see three people moving carefully, two of them belly crawling through the copse of trees, probably looking for stable ground?

Larx could have told them there was none, but as he tracked the rip in the earth that marked the passage of those gingerly moving figures, he noted a khaki-and-green baseball hat scattered among the shale and scree, and recognized it as Colton County Sheriff department issue.

That had to be Aaron, he thought, heart in his mouth. He didn't want to call out. He was afraid too much noise might start a rumble throughout the canyon again, and then he'd be just as lost as the people he saw trying to take stock.

Reluctantly—he wanted to check, to be sure, to get out field glasses and *guarantee* that it was Aaron he saw moving down there—he wriggled backward until he felt safe standing up.

He turned and headed back to Lieutenant Johnson, who was talking softly with her injured forensic tech friend, relieved when he heard them razzing each other gently.

"Did you kill someone else?" Mary Lee muttered. "I swear, I have run tests on more of your bodies than anything else in this job."

"You lie, woman," Johnson retorted. "They're not *my* bodies if *my* boys hit them. They're fugitives halted in their tracks."

"Bloodthirsty maniac," Mary Lee muttered.

"Bookworm."

"I'm gonna tell your wife this is all your fault," Mary Lee finished peevishly, and Johnson snorted.

"As long as I get her sister home alive, she'll be fine with it."

"God, she's a pushover. Good thing she's got you."

Lieutenant Johnson laughed softly, and in the lapsed silence, Larx could hear the faraway wail of an ambulance.

"Lieutenant Johnson?" he said softly, dropping to a crouch again, so they didn't have to shout. "I've got good news and bad news."

The face she turned toward him had tear streaks marking the red dust that had covered the woman's ebony cheeks, but her gaze was steady and sharp.

If the two women were sisters-in-law—sisters of the heart it sounded like—he figured Lieutenant Johnson was doing better than he would have.

"What's doing, Principal Larkin?" she said, and he gave her a faint smile. They hadn't been introduced—they'd both been paying attention.

"Call me Larx," he said softly. "Even the kids call me Larx." She nodded, indicating she was listening, and he took a breath, sending relief coursing through his body. Now that he wasn't hanging off a deadly ledge, looking into a wasteland of unstable earth and rickety trees, he could give some thanks for the hope at least.

But he wasn't going to be okay until he had Aaron out of that damned canyon and in his arms again.

"Okay, then, Larx," she said. "What's doin'?"

"They're alive," he said, and she nodded like she would have expected something very different from him if he thought otherwise. "They're alive, but they're down there in some rough terrain, and it might not be possible to get them from the service road. I'm going to drive down there and try—if nothing else, I can relay what they need—but they're going to need some search and rescue helicopters out here to bail them out. I'm seeing three figures down there. Do you know who they are?"

Johnson looked surprised. "Undersheriff George, for one," she said. "Detective Hawkins was the other. I can't think of anybody else unless…." She shrugged. "Unless it was the kid they were looking for when they came out here in the first place." She grimaced. "Which would make your guy the luckiest and *un*luckiest sonovabitch on the planet, you know that, right?"

Larx chuckled humorlessly. "That about fits," he said grimly. "Okay. I'm going to drive down the service road and see what we've got—"

"Can you take George's service vehicle?" she asked anxiously. "I don't like the thought of you going down there without a radio. We all know cell service is fucking doomed."

Maybe. Larx didn't tell her that down in the bottom of the pit, without the sides obscuring a signal, there might actually be a cell-service oasis. It was a *long* way down, wasn't it? Especially for a *might be*.

"I don't have keys," he said. "And I know you'll need your own unit."

"At least take your first-aid kit," she said. "And grab a flat of water from my car—"

"I've got an extra," he said, "although I *will* take what's intact there." He started rounding up the things from the kit they hadn't needed for Mary Lee. "I've got mylar blankets for days in the car. It's my daughter's," he said apologetically. "And she's seven-and-a-half-months pregnant."

She chuckled. "You tried to pack an entire hospital room, but it wouldn't fit?"

He shot her a harried grin as he fastened the kit—a soft-sided box with a handle that went over his shoulder—and zipped up the top. "If you don't know how to be a grandparent, you overcompensate as a parent. Isn't that a rule?"

"I'll let you know in six months," she said, smiling tiredly at what was apparently her *own* prospect of impending grandparenthood. "But first, Mary Lee—"

"Wha—?"

"I need to make sure Kyla's favorite aunt doesn't expire in my arms, so stay the fuck awake."

"Heifer," Mary Lee muttered.

"Twat. Stay awake."

"Fine!" Mary Lee took a deep breath to punctuate this, and Larx pulled her hair back from her forehead.

"You do what she says," Larx said. "I just watched her wing a guy at a hundred yards from the bottom of a hole under a house. Scary woman. Don't piss her off."

"Whatever," Mary Lee said. Then, without the bluster: "Janine, stay here for a bit, okay? I'm feeling woozy."

"Yeah, honey, I'll be here." Johnson said, and she gave Larx a grim look. Mary Lee's forehead had been clammy in spite of the heat. She was going to need a thorough examination for internal injuries and shock or he didn't know how to put a Band-Aid on a knee. "And you've got to go," she added. "I'll be sure to radio dispatch to tell them you'll need helicopters and search and rescue."

“Thank you,” he said gratefully. “Maybe they’ll all slide to the service road, and all I’ll have to do is turn around and come back.” Even as he said it, he knew it was bullshit. The service road *might* be stable enough to get him to back up. So far, every attempt to shore the thing up with decomposed granite or asphalt had been destroyed by the canyon’s very instability within a year.

But it was *Aaron* down there, and he’d been moving when Larx had seen him, but he might be hurt, and so might the people with him.

Larx had to try.

With grim determination he got behind the wheel of Elton’s Kia and turned it around, pausing at the gated entrance of the service road to text Olivia.

Honey, we think Aaron and the other officer have slid down into Daffodil Canyon. They’re both moving around from what I can see, but I’m going to see if the service road will reach them. Another officer has search and rescue coming in to help. I’m relying on you to keep things calm and to keep the kids from freaking out. This isn’t a tragedy, it’s a situation. It’s not dangerous, it’s unstable.

He hit Send and waited for a moment to see if it would go through.

It didn’t. He took a deep breath and added more.

We love you all. We’ll take care. Hold down the fort.

He tucked his cell phone in his pocket and checked the center console for the charger he’d made Olivia carry since she’d come home pregnant. Aha! And more than halfway full of charge. Two full phone charges left. Woohoo!

With that, he put the Kia in Park and ran to open the gate, grateful when he saw the chain wasn’t bound by a lock.

It was going to suck bad enough to do this in a vehicle; going on foot would be the worst.

At first the road held true. Decomposed granite, when packed and graded, was easy to drive on, but Larx made sure to go slow and steady. A part of him was on *fire* to just blast through the canyon. He’d *seen* Aaron, dammit, and while it had been apparent that Aaron and the other two people down in the canyon were alive, whether they could *stay* that way he had no idea. He hadn’t been able to gauge wounds or physical stability of any sort from the height he’d been, and he was *worried*, dammit!

But he couldn't help *anybody* if he roared into the canyon and took the vehicle skidding, rolling, or rock sliding to the bottom.

He drove at ten miles an hour, slowly and methodically, careful not to vary the speed too much because he didn't want the tires to spin. The road crept around the outside of the canyon, heading downward at a very easy gradient so it didn't collapse outright, and Larx stayed dead center in the middle of it. *An SUV you moron. How hard would it be to wait for an SUV?*

An SUV while Aaron bled out? Or his companion bled to death? And Larx sat on the road above and did nothing?

No.

Not Aaron. *Not* Aaron.

Larx kept going, looking to his right at the canyon side when he could to get an idea of where he was in relation to the edge. About halfway to where he thought Aaron and the detective had ended up, Larx saw a number of trees, old enough to have lost all their limbs, shored up against an outcropping of stone. They weren't piled, but lined on the bias as though they'd been sliding downward and had been guided by the harder rock edge to line up almost evenly, as though waiting their turn.

Larx filed the phenomena away, thinking it would be good to find the most stable places to walk. He also filed away the places where the loose gravel piled—that was no good. That could suck a grown man ankle deep or worse if there was nothing underneath. A part of him was absolutely positive that the old childhood myth of quicksand had started when someone had gotten their foot stuck in a pit of rounded gravel, but another part of him was *completely* positive that it had to do with the slurry created when entire cliffsides and mountains were washed away during the hydraulic mining heyday. Two hundred years ago, Daffodil "Canyon" had been a small valley between two mild mountains. One little nugget—that's all it took—and a couple of inexpert miners turned a thriving ecosystem, a place with trees and wildlife and earth and sediment, into this rocky apocalyptic wasteland that *still* hadn't grown over the scars left on the planet even 150 years later. In the spring, after the snows melted, topsoil made hopeful inroads to the destroyed sediment, and enough had settled to produce the copses of trees. The trees, however, had to extend their roots deep and deeper past the gravel, and sometimes the root systems just couldn't compete with the constant erosion.

Larx could go off on hour-long rants about the irony of one of the men—John C. Colton—being the namesake of this whole damned town.

But *now* was not the time.

Inch by inch, keeping his eyes peeled, he crept down the service track until it spiraled below where he thought he'd seen Aaron and the young detective—and the unknown quantity who might be Curtis MacDonald.

The track seemed to be holding, so he'd let his speed creep up. He was going about twenty miles an hour when his back window exploded into a pile of glass shards and he heard the sound of the shot.

His heart racing, he darted his eyes wildly from side to side, up the hill, down the hill, and through the rearview mirror and the sudden portal where the window used to be. Nothing—nothing he could be sure of, although a white dot of light, scattered as though refracted from a mirror or a gunsight, kept shifting through the Kia, over the hood, along the ground.

Unconsciously, he stepped on the gas, and in a spray of gravel, the Kia took off, faster than was safe, faster than the terrain allowed….

The car wallowed, listing sideways, before he heard the next shot.

"*Fuck*!" Sideways, sideways… he fought with the wheel and the vehicle just sort of wandered, came close to the edge of the road, leaned… leaned…

Fell limply into the canyon, rolling with a sort of comic slowness as Larx clutched the steering wheel and prayed for the carnival ride to end.

Odds and Evens

"DO YOU hear that?" Hawkins asked, his voice rusty and desperate. "I hear a vehicle."

Aaron checked on him automatically, making sure his wound hadn't started bleeding again, making sure he wasn't feverish. They were crouched against the trunk of a once outrageously wide pine tree that must have rolled into the canyon from the plateau above. The canyon didn't produce trees this robust, but Aaron was grateful for the shade it threw, even sideways, and the way it anchored them in place on this unstable nightmare underfoot.

They'd made a surprising discovery as he and Hawkins had struggled across the ground toward the sanctuary of the copse of trees that anchored the tree trunk they were using for shelter.

Lying almost under the trunk, they'd seen what first looked to be shredded clothing—white and red, Colton Bronco colors. Then the pile of rags had twitched and shuddered, and Aaron caught his breath.

Skinny to the point of emaciation, with a face that had been picked at to the point of infected sores and light brown hair that was rank and matted and down past his ears, lay the shivering, twitching form of Curtis MacDonald.

Aaron couldn't be sure if the boy was in shock or going through withdrawals or both, but he had to shake Curtis's arm *hard* to get his attention.

"Curtis!" he snapped. "Curtis, wake up. Do you know me?"

"Sheriff… George…," Curtis chattered through yellowing teeth. "What are you doing here in hell?"

Aaron blinked and tried to see the situation through Curtis's eyes. Well, he'd fallen down into a gravel pit, hadn't he? And the temperature, the sunshine at this altitude, bouncing off the shale and boulders here, it *was* hot enough.

"Not hell, Curtis," Aaron said grimly, trying to adjust himself to the stench of recovering junkie. "Not yet. You fell off the edge of the drop-off. Do you remember that?"

"Aw, fuck." With a groan, Curtis rolled slightly in his shelter until he was facing outward. His clothes—rank probably *before* his slide into the canyon—were even worse now, crusted with urine and blood and dirt—flapped from his body like filthy sails, and Aaron only wished they had the water to clean him. "Yeah. I… my dad. He came and got me. Shoved me out of the house, out the back." Curtis's voice changed. "Fucker. I thought… thought for a minute he was gonna rescue me. Save me." He squeezed his eyes tight. "Like my dad would ever save me," he finished on a sob.

Aaron glanced at Tad Hawkins, whom he'd leaned against the tree trunk and whom, Aaron could tell, was trying to keep his vision from getting lost with pain. At Curtis's words, he frowned and tilted his head.

"When?" he mouthed, and Aaron nodded.

"Curtis, when was this? Was this before the shooting started?"

"Heard gunshots," Curtis mumbled. "After Dad threw me in hell."

Aaron and Tad both grimaced, and Aaron let out a breath. "His dad came to pull him out of the house before the raid," Aaron said, and Tad nodded, following. "Whoever shot Eamon was probably trying…." He caught a long wave of stench off Curtis's body and had to pause then or vomit. His *own* body was still shocky, and he didn't have the best control right now.

"To distract," Tad finished for him. "Billy MacDonald figures out where Curtis is, shows up to haul him out, and Percy shoots Eamon in the back to start the gunfight and keep attention off Billy."

"And someone else takes a shot in the dark to try to *kill* Eamon," Aaron muttered. "Why? And why try to pull Curtis out? Billy didn't know where he was for a *week*—how'd he suddenly know Curtis was in the Dropoff house?"

"Uncle Clancy told him," Curtis mumbled. "Uncle Clancy knows everyone."

Aaron stared at him, a quiet bell in his brain ringing louder and louder. "Uncle Clancy?" he asked, hearing Eamon's crack about their incestuous city council and Billy MacDonald's connection to it. "Uncle Clancy *Yarborough*?" The judge Eamon had been hitting up for a warrant to search the Dropoff house. The one who'd been dragging his feet. Oh Lord, it made sense. But *why*?

"Yeah," Curtis said. "He's mama's special uncle. He helps us out." Curtis's voice dropped, and Aaron knew that whatever coherence he'd gotten from the boy was about to slide under the water of his current misery. "He visited me in January. He and Uncle Percy showed me the business." The hysterical crackle at the end of "business" made Aaron's stomach hurt—and that was something considering the rest of his body felt bruised, buffeted, and banged the hell up.

Business.

There had been a business inside that house. Not only junkies, but money and drugs—and employees. And bosses.

And business.

No wonder Billy MacDonald hadn't been paying attention to his son. He'd been too busy employed by "Uncle Clancy" and distributing the product that had almost killed him. And Curtis….

Aaron eyed the altogether wretched kid huddling under the corpse of a long-dead tree, mumbling to himself about not wanting to do it, Uncle Clancy, please don't make me!

He'd been a bully and a bigot and an asshole. But he'd been a kid, and kids have time to grow up.

This one might not. Aaron didn't know a whole lot about science—or addiction—but he knew the shivers ripping Curtis MacDonald's frail body apart right now couldn't be good for anybody—particularly not someone who had just had the sort of fall Aaron and Tad Hawkins had survived and then lay out in the elements for the night to boot.

Aaron eyed Hawkins again. Aaron had ripped his khaki overshirt up and bound the wound once they'd gotten to the copse of trees and out of the path of potential rockslides. They'd both sustained some bruises, cuts, and abrasions from their slide down the hill, but thankfully nothing worse than the cut on Aaron's leg. He'd used the last of his shirt and the smallest bit of water from his bottle possible to wash that off and wrap a bandage around it, and then he and Hawkins had stumbled/walked/slid to this fallen soldier, where the hillside seemed less like the world's worst carnival ride.

Hawkins eyed Curtis MacDonald with sympathy and shook his head at Aaron. Aaron could tell the young detective felt the same way about the teenager, and he blew out a breath. Oh God, this could be so not good.

And that was when he heard the sound of a vehicle somewhere in the canyon. It wasn't loud—the vehicle wasn't too big, wasn't roaring, and seemed to be well maintained. Aaron pushed himself up and scanned the edge of the canyon to find the entrance points of the service road, both the one on their side of the canyon and the one on the far side. The one on *their* side of the canyon was almost directly over their shoulder, and it wound pretty tightly to the side, intersecting somewhere below where they sat.

"There," Hawkins said, pointing. "See it? Electric-blue Kia?"

"Oh fuck *me*," Aaron muttered. "No. For fuck's sake, no."

"I'm sorry?" Tad stared at him. "You are looking that gift Kia in the mouth?"

Aaron gave him a grim smile. "That's Larx," he said, muttering. "The Kia is his son-in-law's, which is good because Larx has probably loaded it for bear, but…." He let out a grunt. "It's *Larx*."

Tad grunted like he got it. "It's your civilian boyfriend who might not know what's out here," he deduced and then sighed, the sound conveying a world of discomfort. "Much like us."

Aaron nodded and tried to make some decisions. "Okay, have we seen any signs of the guy who shot at us?"

"No," Tad replied and then grimaced. "Although…." He blew out a breath and turned around completely, leaning his back against the log and looking directly up at the place where they'd pitched into the canyon. "I… I keep seeing a flash up there. Are you seeing it?"

Aaron turned with him and stared. They were reasonably shaded by the trees around them—mostly jack pine and the occasional sugar pine—and given that the sun was coming from the other side of the canyon, it would be hard to see them in the shadow of the great fallen soldier.

But it made the glare off the rifle sight particularly easy to spot.

"Oh fuck," Aaron muttered. "Yeah, I see it. I don't think he sees *us*, but I see *him*." He could see the faint shadow of the person behind the gun—probably the same guy who'd fired at them—up on the cliff.

"Where's he aiming?" Hawkins asked tensely.

"Oh Jesus."

They could both see the angle of the reflection changing, slowly, as Larx's vehicle made progress above them, inching down along the service track, heading in a long-angled vector that would soon wind down below their position. Seeing his trajectory and the long fall should the vehicle tumble off the decomposed granite road, Aaron's body crawled with cold.

"Oh fuck," he muttered. "We have to warn him?"

"How?" Hawkins asked—not heatedly, but with cold precision. "I'm all for warning him, but how do we do it without getting picked off like birds on a fence?"

Aaron tried to think. "I'll work my way around the log," he said, "and try to find cover between here and the road."

"What do we do?"

"Got your piece?" Aaron asked.

Hawkins hand went to his gun belt, where his regulation Glock was still snapped in. "Roger that." He unhooked the piece and held it, aiming slightly at the reflection, waiting for something to happen.

"Do you want to get on the other side and use the tree as cover?" Aaron asked.

Hawkins grimaced. "Does that mean moving?" he asked, almost pitifully.

"Yeah, soldier," Aaron told him. "I can help, and then I'll try to warn Larx." His instincts were *screaming* at him to charge out into the road and order Larx to back up, out of the canyon, at all speed. But Hawkins was injured, and Curtis MacDonald wasn't making it out of the canyon without help, and the guy with the rifle and scope might *still* pick them off like birds on a wire.

"Dammit," Hawkins muttered. He snapped his gun back into the holster, and Aaron stood gingerly and made his way toward the top of the fallen soldier, which was still in the shade, as opposed to the root system, which was hanging out, naked and bleached, in the sun. He gave Curtis MacDonald a hand to the shoulder as he passed, and his heart twisted a little when the kid gave a grateful sob. Aaron would move him, but at the moment he was in the safest place in the canyon, mostly covered by the tree and almost completely invisible.

"Over here," Aaron said. "Is our tree friend stable?"

Tad stood up and, using the giant trunk as a crutch, followed Aaron to the narrow point of the thing. The trunk didn't rock—and Curtis MacDonald didn't cry out in pain—so Aaron held on to some hope that it could serve as cover. With some careful walking, sliding his body between their fallen soldier and the current living tree militia that was sheltering them, Hawkins found a pocket on the other side where he could use the tree to steady his aim and then duck behind it if he was fired upon. Fortunately, it was not near Curtis, so the odds of the kid getting shot accidentally were considerably shortened.

Aaron settled Tad on the ground and made him take a drink of his own water.

"Remember," he said softly, "only fire if he fires, and don't risk yourself any more than you need to."

Tad gave Aaron a tight, pained smile. "You're a good boss," he said. "You got any openings up here?"

Aaron's chuckle was just as tight and pained. "Well, I'm pretty sure Percy Hardesty just got fired, and since Eamon's retired, I think I'm going to need someone to replace *me*. Turn in your application if you survive this—I'll keep you in mind."

Hawkins let out a strangled laugh. "You betcha." And then he sobered. "I've got your back, Sheriff. You flag down help."

"Or keep help from being shot," Aaron agreed. He gave Tad's shoulder a squeeze much like he'd given Curtis MacDonald's and started to creep down the hill.

He was pretty sure line of sight would be in his favor until he reached the service track—the stand of trees and the boulders below them would block most of the view, and Aaron, wearing khaki pants and a white T-shirt covered in pine pollen and red dust, was all but dressed in camouflage.

As he crept down the hill, using boulders and trees to steady himself on the loose scree, he tried not to think about how miserable going back would be. Finally, after what seemed like an eternity—maybe two—he found himself crouching behind the last boulder, with a clear view of the road. Larx would see him here, but hopefully the guy up at the lip of the canyon could not. Aaron took a sip of water to reward how far he'd gotten and hoped the Kia was as full of supplies as Larx had tried to keep it, knowing that Olivia would be driving back and forth in it on the winding mountain roads.

He could really use some fucking Gatorade and a sandwich right now—or at least a protein bar. Part of the reason the T-shirt was so well and thoroughly coated in dust was that he'd sweated through it back when he'd been in the shade.

The mountains could be just as miserable with the heat as the valleys—people didn't always know that—and the altitude made the air thinner and the sun's burn sharper. Aaron's fair skin had tanned this summer, but part of that was the religious application of sunscreen. Too long out in the elements would literally fry him like bacon.

Aaron clung to the big chunk of granite in spite of the heat and blessed the shade and hoped for a breeze and prayed that Larx would get there soon.

As Larx rounded the last long switchback to bring him into sight, Aaron let out a sigh of relief. He'd just started to stand, to wave his arms, to catch Larx's attention, when the first shot hit the back of the Kia and Larx started to swerve.

Oh God. Oh God oh God oh God—Larx was still keeping the Kia on the road, and Aaron pulled his weapon and aimed behind the vehicle, cursing. The shot came from the wrong direction. Jesus, were there two shooters?

"The fuck was that?" Hawkins called.

Aaron scanned the edge of the canyon, swallowing his panic, and spotted the reflection off another rifle scope peering out from some brush in the edge about two hundred yards away. "Another goddamned shooter!" he called back. He squinted against the glare of the sun and tried to do the math. A .22 caliber rifle was accurate up to 150 meters. His police issue accuracy was 50 to 100 meters. The odds of Aaron hitting the person shooting at Larx were not good—but not impossible either.

There was another shot, this one hitting somewhere Aaron couldn't see, but judging from the way the car lumbered and drifted left, Aaron hazarded that the shot had hit the vehicle's tire. Oh God. *Hold it together, baby. Keep the show on the road.* The edge of the service track didn't drop off like a cliff; it slid down into another steep grade filled with scree. It's why the road had to wind in a long, complicated spiral instead of a series of switchbacks down one side. There were probably trees down there too, like the little cluster that was sheltering Hawkins and Curtis right now, but it was a long slide to the bottom and *Please, baby, hold it together*!

Aaron scowled and, spotting the gleam of the rifle scope again, aimed and fired a cluster of shots as accurately as he could.

He heard a scream and saw something tumble into the canyon from the edge—the gun maybe—and then the creak of metal and the clatter of rocks he hadn't known he'd feared echoed in his head like a roar.

The groan of a two-thousand-pound vehicle leaning… leaning over the edge of the service road… leaning…. Oh God. In nightmare slow motion, Aaron watched as the Kia tumbled over the edge of the track and slid down the second half of the canyon.

"Fuck!" he shouted, and Tad shouted back.

"I got mine. Did you get yours?"

"I think so!" Aaron called, trying to keep his voice steady. *But Larx….* But these two other men depended on him too. Everybody depended on him, and goddammit, he had to keep his voice steady. "But the car's over the edge."

"*Fuck*!" Tad snarled. "Go get him!"

Aaron wanted to laugh hysterically with the total weight of his panic. "There is no guarantee we will make it back up here!" he called back, hearing his voice crack at "we." There had to be a "we." That Kia had seen rogue trees and ice slicks. He had to pull his heart up, had to *not panic*. It wasn't a cliff. It wasn't a drop-off. It was the same haphazard slip and slide Aaron had just lived through, but in a steel cage with an air bag, dammit, and *Larx would be all right*.

"We'll come back and get you," he promised. "You're not there alone, you hear me?" God, he was leaving a wounded man and a sick, terrified kid alone in hell, but he had to get Larx. He *had* to get Larx!

"We'll hold the fort," Hawkins promised, but he sounded out of breath and panicked. As if to taunt Aaron, the faint sound of the car alarm drifted up through the clouds of dust choking the Kia's descent.

"I've got to get him," Aaron said, his voice quaking. "I'm sorry—"

"You'd go after him if he was a stranger, Aaron," Hawkins called, his voice dropping. "'Cause that's the kind of cop you are."

Aaron heard the compassion there, and it gave him some strength. "I am *so* poaching you from Sac," he promised, and then, checking frantically at the two places where the rifles had been aimed to make sure there were no other snipers waiting in the wings, he stood and ran across the road.

This incline was not as steep as the one he'd come down. Yeah, he had to sit down a few times, and the shale underfoot skittered out an alarming number of times, but it was less a downhill tumble and more a controlled descent. It helped that the Kia had taken some of the unstable topsoil with it, leaving the heavier, more stable packed dirt and decomposed granite for him to walk on. The cut on his leg was throbbing, his body felt like he'd spent an hour in a clothes dryer with a pillowcase full of rocks by the time he reached the Kia, and he was sweating enough to cake the dust against his chest through his shirt.

All of it ceased to matter, though, as he neared the upended vehicle. The alarm had stopped in the past fifteen minutes of his descent, but the smell of antifreeze and hot metal was still pervasive as he neared the driver's side.

For a moment—a second—he tried to prepare himself for what he might find, and his world spun. Oh God. He'd lost one love of his life; he couldn't lose Larx. He just… he couldn't. His heart threatened to stop, and he realized dimly he was gasping for breath, his vision swimming with spots. He fought to stay upright, to stay conscious, to remember his duty to the people up on the mountainside, to the children at home.

Larx!

And then a voice, weak and shaky, permeated his consciousness, and he pulled in his first deep breath in what felt like years.

"Deputy, are you hyperventilating?"

Aaron sank to his knees in the dust, peered through the hole left by the side window, and saw a pair of fine brown eyes gazing at him through a layer of airbag powder, dust, and some blood. Larx had a gash on his head, probably a concussion, and his face was red from hanging suspended, but he was conscious, and nothing appeared to be bent, broken, or permanently destroyed.

"Yeah," Aaron said, the feeling flooding back to his limbs, his chest, and his heart. "How about you?"

"I'm trying not to throw up," Larx said frankly. "But damn, I'm glad to see you."

Aaron let out a broken laugh and reached to his utility belt for the folded bowie knife he kept strapped there for things like this. "Me too. You would not be*lieve* the day I've had."

Larx's broken laughter shored him up as he started to saw at the seat belt.

Temporary Head of the Household

OLIVIA TRIED not to sigh as she shifted her awkward bulk on the uncomfortable chair. In theory, she was glad to be there. Rosie Mills was a sweet woman who had been sort of a fixture in the life of every schoolchild in Colton, whether they remembered her or not. She'd given out cupcakes to the first grade, helped organize the fourth-grade spelling bee, and was part of the club that gave out children's illustrated dictionaries to every graduating eighth grader at the middle school. What Olivia hadn't benefited from, she'd seen her sister in the middle of, and the thought of this kind woman, alone and worried in a town full of grateful generations, was absolutely not to be endured.

In theory, it was a great idea.

In practice her back ached, and she'd been up late, and she wanted her bed and a broccoli day (as Christiana had claimed) with nothing but trashy television and her tiny idiot dogs.

And Elton, she thought, giving him a fond look as he came into the ICU room bearing sausage muffin sandwiches to counteract all the sugar they'd eaten. Besides being thoughtful and responsible and patient and all the things a girl was *supposed* to look for in her husband and the father of her child, Elton was also wickedly funny, saying terrible things it felt like only she laughed at, with a totally straight face. It didn't matter. What had started out as friendship and was then consummated with an ill-advised night of pity sex had turned into—for both of them, Olivia hoped—true love. And even more than that, they had a partnership, hopefully of equals, as they both tried to run their household in the same way Livvy's father had when *she'd* been growing up.

Berto was still recovering from the beating he'd taken in order to break free of gang life in Sacramento, and both he and his little brother were still reeling from being left alone when their family had chosen to return to Mexico two years earlier. Olivia, bipolar and pregnant, and Elton, new to responsibility and trying hard to get used to small-town living, had needed to take care of the two young men as much as the young men had needed extended family to look to.

Together, she and Elton organized family dinners, worked on chore assignments, and divvied up shopping and cooking among the household, and the result? Had been lovely.

She and Elton had gotten to be adults in their own home, but they hadn't needed to be alone. And knowing that the man who'd fathered her child had that same sense of service and community as the man who'd raised her had made her feel a lot better about having a child with him.

Life was hard enough with bipolar without worrying that your partner in it wasn't dependable, and that was one worry she didn't have.

What she *wanted* was more time with the sweet guy who'd followed her up from Southern California and declared that they could *too* build a life together, even if that hadn't been part of their plan when they met. She'd really been looking forward to their day off together, she thought rather sadly, and tried not let the thought slip out where Rosie could hear it. There would be another day for her and Elton to relax. Today she was needed here.

Rosie took one of the sandwiches gratefully and then turned to Olivia, compassion in her eyes. "Why don't you take that young man home," she said, the corners of her mouth twitching. "You are not looking comfortable, and I'm sure this isn't what your father had in mind for you when he sent you here."

Olivia wanted to hug her all over again. "I'm pretty sure it is," she said dryly, "but thank you. Christiana and the boys should be here in half an hour, but you need to be warned. They're going to be groggy, and they're going to be all up in their phones and falling asleep like melted spoons all over the hospital furniture. I swear, they talked until three in the morning. It was *amazing*." And Jaime had been part of that. As Jaime's big sister/auntie, Olivia was particularly happy that the young man who had been *so* in need of a family unit had been accepted by hers.

Rosie's face split into a wide grin. "Your father said the party was a success. That sounds like the best kind of fun!"

Olivia chuckled and went for her own fun. She'd happily throw her dad under the bus if she could entertain this nice woman while they waited for the results of Eamon's latest tests.

“Want to see what Larx did at the end of the party?” she asked. “Kirby told me he still played, right? He used to play at night, when Christi and I were kids, and it was….” She smiled, the memory so good in the midst of so many other memories of her mother’s care, before Larx had gotten custody, that she’d clung to it in the worst of her depression. “It was nice,” she said inadequately. “And he apparently never told Aaron. So, like, on the nights Aaron worked late and Dad was restless, he’d take the guitar outside and practice. And Kirby had me snag the guitar and bring it to the party near the end, when Elton and I were coming home anyway, and we made Larx *play* for us. It was awesome.”

She pulled up the video on her phone—the entire magical half-hour was there—and she adjusted the volume and hit Play. Larx’s voice, more on key than anybody would suspect and firm and gentle and earnest, came out of the phone, and Rosie took it from her in awe.

“Your father,” she said, shaking her head and putting her hand over her mouth. “That man is full of surprises. And look at you all. He’s got the whole mess of you in the palm of his hand. Isn’t that something.”

Rosie held the phone like it was precious, and Olivia could see her becoming as immersed in the performance as the rest of them had been last night, even humming along to the Killers’ song, which just went to prove that Larx knew his universal music.

Elton looked over their shoulders, his hand on the back of Olivia’s neck, and he bent down and kissed her temple. “Do you sing too?” he asked hopefully.

“I did in choir in high school,” she answered, laughing. “But I’d have to practice some more to sound like this.”

“Then practice,” Elton murmured, and she turned a shy and shining glance at him.

“For you,” she said simply, “I’d sing.”

He grinned at her through his scruffy beard, and her heart did the same thing it had done the year before when they’d met and became friends during their classes at San Diego State. God, the things she hadn’t known then about this man’s character that she firmly believed in now.

Their brief moment of mooncalfing was interrupted by the young nurse Larx had turned them over to—Jed, if she remembered. He stood at the entrance to their small cubicle, gesturing urgently toward Olivia.

She and Elton met eyes, and he gave her an elbow up, a move they'd practiced so often it was almost ballet. "Excuse me, Rosie," she murmured, and together she and her husband moved to talk to Jed.

"Ma'am?" he asked. "Are you Olivia Larkin?"

"Larkin-McDaniels," she said softly, glancing to Elton so he could hear. They'd gotten married in a quiet ceremony with zero fuss and no honeymoon, back in March. Her father had wanted to wait for the baby to come and do the whole wedding enchilada, but Olivia hadn't. Her entire life—and life plan—had changed, and it was enough that she and her child's father loved each other and wanted to commit. Elton was enough, she thought—and he still was. Besides, they all knew Christiana was going to be the big-wedding whore, and Olivia couldn't wait.

Or she *could* wait, as long as *she* didn't have to be the one in the white dress picking out flower arrangements.

Jed nodded. "Okay, so you know Deputy George as well."

His eyes—and his manner—were so grave Olivia was starting to get chills.

"He's my stepdad, sort of. Why?"

Jed grimaced. "There's a woman in the OR waiting room who really needs to talk to you, and you need to prepare yourself. Something big went down involving the same incident, I think, that laid the sheriff up, and…." He shrugged. "They need to talk to you is all."

Olivia's heart stuttered. "Daddy?" she asked, twelve years old all over again.

"Come," Jed told her. "She'll tell you what's doin'."

Elton had to guide her some more, because Olivia's brain was blanking out. *Daddy?* Oh God. Aaron—where was Aaron? She needed to tell Aaron, and he needed to tell her what to do. *Larx?* Where the hell was her father?

An *exhausted*-looking woman was standing toward the back of the OR waiting room, talking urgently to a midfortyish man with some gray in his black hair and a grim expression.

"Ma'am?" Jed said. "You were asking for Larx's daughter? I told you she was here. This is Olivia Larkin-McDaniel. She's—"

The woman took a deep breath and extended her hand. "I'm so glad to meet you," she murmured. "I'm Janine Johnson, lieutenant of the SAC PD SWAT team. There's a situation with your father and Undersheriff George that you need to be apprised of."

Olivia was breathing too fast. "Larx *and* Aaron?" she squeaked. Oh fuck. Oh *fuck*. There were two households—*two*—who depended on Larx and Aaron to make their worlds go.

"What situation?" she asked, aware that she was squeezing Elton's hand until his bones ground against each other. Poor Elton—he probably thought he'd get to wait for her to go into labor before *this* happened, right?

"This morning, four of us went to revisit the scene last night where Sheriff Mills was shot," Johnson said. "My wife's sister, Mary Lee Clemmons, a forensic tech I called up from Sac, Undersheriff George, and Detective Tad Hawkins—" She nodded to the man next to her. "—Chris's partner in the force. Your father was coming, but Larx was late. Or we think he was late. It was hard to tell because there were no texts, and we didn't want to clog up dispatch."

"Aaron doesn't trust the dispatch lady," Olivia blurted, remembering conversations he and Larx had in the past, usually quiet and in code. Not the sort of thing parents wanted children to know. "She's tight with Percy Hardesty, and he's a fucking bigot."

Johnson's eyebrows went up. "Well, now he's a *wounded* fucking bigot, thanks to Undersheriff George," she said. "Aaron and Tad had tracked the kid they were looking for to the edge of the canyon from the back of the house, and Mary Lee and I were investigating the house itself. We found evidence that the place wasn't just used for *doing* drugs, but for distributing them as well—"

"It was a business?" Olivia asked, another chill going up her spine. Illegal substance businesses were *dangerous*. "Like there were drugs and cash—"

"Residue," Johnson confirmed. "Someone was keeping stash in the root cellar. Mary Lee and I found the residuals of a business that had been hastily moved—probably through a tunnel underneath the place—and Aaron and Detective Hawkins went searching for the young man who started this whole thing. They found a trail to the edge of the canyon when…."

Johnson swallowed, looking miserable and exhausted, and Olivia was suddenly wide-awake.

"Oh my God, is Aaron okay?" she squeaked. "We can't have Aaron shot again. Do you understand? He just got—my dad tried to hold it together, but he was *leveled*. Is Aaron okay?"

"Little girl," Johnson said firmly, "you need to let me get through this. If either of them were dead, I would have started with that, because I am *not* a cruel woman, but let me finish."

Olivia swallowed hard, and Elton snaked his arm around her waist, helping to bear her up like he always had.

"Go on," she squeaked, and Lieutenant Johnson gave her a grateful, albeit faint, smile of appreciation.

"Aaron and Tad were at the trees on the edge of the embankment when the shooting started. Tad was hit, but still alert and moving—firing back—and Aaron was right next to him when the embankment gave. Larx pulled up just as I stuck my head out of the goddamned basement and winged the fucker who was shooting, and he took off."

"Did you get a look at him?" Elton asked, and Olivia glanced at him, grateful he seemed to have remembered his goddamned mind because Olivia's had gone right out the window.

"I did," Johnson said, "but *he* wasn't Percy Hardesty, and this isn't my town. I need somebody at the station to walk me through the faces of the main players here, and I've got some names to start with. Whoever he was, I grazed him, and like I said, he took off, but not before…." Her voice hitched. "He got Mary Lee, who is my sister-in-law and my best bitch, and she's in surgery right now, so you gotta bear with me, okay?"

Olivia nodded. "My dad's got one of those," she said, taking Johnson's hands in hers, thinking about gentle, funny, sarcastic Uncle Yoshi, who would forever be her father's "best bitch" until they were both bitching at each other at the senile teacher's home. "I hope she's okay."

"Thank you, honey. You're a lot like your dad. I'd radioed in the shots, and there was an ambulance on the way, but your dad showed up. He helped me get her settled and gave a quick assessment, and then he went to look over the edge of the embankment. He saw at *least* two men, possibly a third, moving down below, and he positively identified one of them as the undersheriff. He took his vehicle down the service track to see if he could offer assistance to the people stuck on the side of the canyon."

Olivia remembered this feeling from the first three months of her pregnancy. "Elton," she said distinctly. "You need to help me sit down and get me an emesis bowl. I'm gonna puke, and I need to hear the rest."

In a moment she was sitting in one of the horrible chairs, and Jed had provided the bowl, just in case. Olivia looked up at Lieutenant Johnson and patted the seat next to her.

"Don't mind the puking woman," she said. "I need some protein and some fruit and some good goddamned news. Keep talking."

"Will do," Johnson told her. "So your father was driving along that canyon like he knows his terrain—"

"He used to run it," Olivia told her, remembering those days. "There was this bonkers suicidal 'fun run' where they'd run down to the bottom, splash across the stream and run back up to the top of the other service track. It's, like, ten miles total, but it's descent and ascent in the altitude and a thousand degrees because that thing is like a satellite dish collecting heat, and—"

The realization slammed into her. Not dead didn't mean not in trouble.

"Oh God. Lady, where in the fuck is my father?"

"There was another gunman," Johnson rasped. "The ambulance and my guys came to look for the shooter, and suddenly there were two rifles aimed down into the canyon. The undersheriff and Hawkins each hit one. Auburn Faith Hospital just reported a gunshot wound from one of your residents, so we've got one in the hospital who's not talking and two others off in the wild blue yonder. One guy has one of my bullets in him and the other one has Aaron's. But one of them hit the back tire of the vehicle. I-I couldn't do anything, honey. We watched it roll off the service track and slide down and out of sight. We could see Aaron go after him, but the service track was pretty weak, and now it's completely washed out, and I understand the other side is worse—it's not even a road."

Olivia took a deep breath and then another and forced her nausea back with a raw act of will.

"Let me get this straight," she said when she was pretty sure the emesis bowl wasn't going to be used. "You had care of not just *one* of my fathers, but *both* of them, and you lost them both in Daffodil Canyon?"

"Livvy…," Elton placated, but Olivia held out her hand.

"That's not what I meant," she growled. "I'm not blaming Lieutenant Johnson, but I sure would like a word with *God*, you fucking hear me?"

"I hear you," Elton agreed, and Olivia loved him for that at the same time her head was swimming.

"Okay," she said, trying to pull shit together. "I can't do any of the goddamned police work for you. Sheriff Mills might be conscious to help you with your IDs, and I'm going to keep my little college-student ass out of that bullshit. But did you call Colton County search and rescue? No vehicles can go down there, but Auburn is an hour away, and I *know* Colton County has access to their own shit plus the resources at Auburn as well as the forestry service people. I mean, we're pretty much living in Tahoe National Forest, aren't we? Did you call them?"

Johnson nodded and let out a breath. "We have," she said, "but they need authorization from somebody in Colton County. Me and my guys—we're SAC PD. Normally that would be Sheriff Mills or your father. The third in line is Percy Hardesty, but—"

"Please tell me he's one of the guys who was *shot*," she snarled.

"You're welcome," Johnson told her.

"Thank you," Olivia responded, meaning it. "Isn't there anybody else?"

"The judge," Castro spoke up. "But, uhm, he's Clancy Yarborough, and we understand he tried to obstruct last night's raid. We suspect him of being part of this, whatever it is, and he was unable to be reached for comment."

"The district attorney?" Olivia asked, although she couldn't remember who that was.

"Out of town," Castro said grimly. "As of early this morning."

"So," Olivia stared at the two of them, nonplussed. "You've got… *nobody* to get in touch with local search and rescue to get my dads out of the goddamned canyon?"

"And our detective," Castro said. "And whoever else Aaron saw down there before they slid over the edge."

Olivia was about to lose it. Open her mouth and destroy these two well-meaning law enforcement officers with her well-trained, battle-honed tongue, hardened and sharpened on the whetstone of her father's bouncy, sarcastic, brilliant mind and nurtured in the warmth of his love of humor and banter and active discussion.

And then something niggled at her. A faint memory, perhaps? She'd only dated two boys in high school—the one Aaron had caught her with when they'd been doing the dirty out by the lake and, for one disastrous date, Teddy Goddamned Harris.

And one of them had ended up at local search and rescue.

"Who's your contact at search and rescue?" she asked.

"So far we haven't been able to get past a paper pusher named Harris," Castro said in disgust. "I've tried to get our captain back in Sac to get hold of them, but—"

"It's a two-helicopter operation with an aging dog and a brand-new puppy," Olivia said. "But they can contact the rest of the forestry service." Teddy used to rhapsodize about what he'd do when he graduated and became a part of that, but he'd never gone to school, perhaps not realizing how *very* educated members of the forestry service and search and rescue had to be. "Hit the number and give me the phone."

"Babe?" Elton asked, and toward the doorway of the waiting room, she heard a general quiet rustle. She didn't have to look up to see that Christi and the boys—Jaime included—had all shown up, ready to be good kids and take care of Rosie Mills. They didn't know this had happened. They weren't aware that the two people they depended on, the rocks upon which their *entire family* depended for support and guidance and love and growing, *their* personal boulders, had just rolled down with the scree of Daffodil Fucking Canyon.

And she was the one who had to tell them.

"Colton County Search and Rescue," came the voice, nasal and a little pompous, and Olivia felt like she'd been forced through a portal of the wayback machine to that one disastrous date.

"Teddy Goddamned Harris," she snarled into the phone.

"Uhm, who's this?"

"This is Olivia Larkin—Teddy, you remember me?"

"Olivia?" She heard the wistfulness then, the yearning. The… the hopeless social backwardness that she'd tried to address by being kind and going out with him.

"Yes, Teddy. This is me. Do you remember me? *Principal Larkin's daughter*, whom you took out to a steak house in Auburn?"

"Oh God," he said, his voice dropping. Teddy had been a moon-faced kid in high school, and Olivia could practically *hear* his face turning green. "Olivia? You swore you'd never—"

"I swore I'd never talk about it," Olivia snarled. "But then I found out that when people way the fuck more important than you were *begging* you to get your ass in gear and get the search and rescue ball moving to get *my two fathers* out of goddamned Daffodil *fucking* Canyon, you decided to play power politics with them, and suddenly it's all I can think about, do you understand me?"

"I told you," Teddy's voice sank to his toes, "that perfectly heterosexual men enjoy that sort of thing, and I was trying to take the edge off before I took you out—"

"Teddy," Olivia said, not caring who heard her on this end, "I don't care about your sexual orientation. I don't care about your likes or dislikes. I don't even care that you shit an actual banana into your underwear on the trip to Auburn four years ago. I don't *care* what kinds of fruit you've had up your ass since. What I care about, *all* I care about, is that *my two fathers* are lost in the fucking canyon, and *you* are so up in your *own* ass about how important you are that you won't tell your supervisor that we need some *goddamned motherfucking help*, you useless little shit! So if you don't pass this phone to somebody more important and smarter than you in about three seconds, I'm going to hit every social media site between here and Mars, and I'm about to become an overnight internet sensation, with your name front and center, complete with your high school photo, *do you hear me*?"

"Uhm, yes, yes I do, young lady. Mr. Harris handed me the phone, and I understand you need help?"

Olivia's voice caught on a sob, and she managed, "I'm going to give the phone to somebody who knows more about this than I do, but thank you, kind forest ranger, *thank you*. Please get my dads. Please. *Please*—"

Lieutenant Johnson pulled the phone out of her hand and handed it to Detective Castro, and Elton's arm wrapped around her shoulders. Johnson got up as Olivia rested her head against Elton's chest, and Christiana took her place.

"Livvy?" she said, sounding concerned. "What about the dads? We were coming to spend time with Rosie. What… what's going on?"

"Shh…," Elton whispered against Olivia's temple. "You already rode to the rescue, honey. I'll get to organizing the troops, okay?"

"Okay," she whimpered, needing his arm around her shoulder like she needed life. "Just don't leave for a minute, okay?"

"Never," he murmured, and then he nodded to Kirby, Kellan, and Jaime to gather around the two of them while he filled them in.

Olivia tried to unscramble her brains and think, become part of the conversation, when Christiana's arm snaked under her own, and her sister laced their fingers together and squeezed her hand.

"So that was what Teddy Harris did on your date?" she asked softly, while Kellan and Kirby were peppering Elton with questions.

Olivia inhaled a sob. "Yeah," she choked.

"And you never told a soul," Christi confirmed.

"He was really embarrassed," Olivia said. "It didn't feel right."

Christi's earthy, evil chuckle seemed to feed Olivia strength through their laced hands. "I think they're probably mobilizing for D-Day at the forest service now," she confided, letting that chuckle out again. "Way to let a secret mature. I'm proud of you, Dr. Evil."

Olivia let out a broken cackle and then sobered. "Somebody's got to call Yoshi and Maureen," she said, trying to sit up.

Christi shook their joined hands. "You sit right there, Joan of Arc. You mobilized the troops, let me send the messages, okay?"

Olivia nodded and sniffled. "Thanks, Christiana." She looked at her irrepressible baby sister, who had borne with Olivia in the depths of her bipolar and done everything but tap dance with monkeys during the dark year when Larx finally got custody of them from their neglectful mother, and the three of them had been healing and building their family in this new and unfamiliar place. The reason Christiana's ebullience was so rich it made her a magic person was that she'd *worked* on it, dammit, through dark times that no child should have to live through, and she'd begged, cajoled, and teased Larx through his guilt when he'd done nothing wrong and Olivia through her moodiness when none of it had been Christi's fault, and she remained this person, this magic human, who could make Olivia feel like the world wasn't crumbling in on her head even when their fathers were lost in an apocalyptic moonscape and the powers-that-be weren't so powerful after all.

"My pleasure," Christi said, and then gave Olivia's stomach a soft little pat that not even Larx or Elton were allowed to give. "Just, you know, gestate well, mama. We're all looking forward to seeing what the human Easy-Bake is gonna put out before she goes back to being Olivia again."

"I'm still Olivia. I'm just pregnant," Olivia retorted, irritated by this entire concept and about ready to give Christi a piece of her mind after all that stupid sentiment she'd just—

Her head of steam dissipated when Christi grinned at her impishly through the sheen of tears on her face. Oh God. She was doing it again. Pulling Olivia out of her funk by her bootstraps, even when the world was crumbling on their heads.

"Christi?" she said after a moment of trying not to lose it. "If I said you were my best bitch, would you know what I meant?"

Christiana's face lit up, transported. "I'm your *Yoshi*? Oh my God! Wait until I tell *Dad*!" She sobered. "And I *will* tell Dad, Livvy. Don't give up, okay? Larx is a tough stringy little chicken man—you know that. And Aaron's built like a bear. And they're both smart—survival smart—and—"

"And Kirby and I are going to go check out the canyon," Kellan said, cutting into Christi's little pep talk. "Larx took us on the service road last September, remember? Before the rains when the soil was stable? We only went about ten yards into the canyon, but he wanted to show us the dangers of soil erosion. The AP class can help search and rescue, you think?"

"Worth a try," Kirby said while Olivia's brain scrabbled, like a cat on an ice rink, to find a way to stop that bullshit in its tracks.

And then Elton cleared his throat. "Please don't," he said softly. "I… I think you could be useful, but please. For us. You guys, we, uhm, sort of need you for a while."

Kirby and Kellan both quieted down, and even Jaime looked sober and responsible when suddenly the nurse appeared with the wheelchair.

"Ms. McDaniels?" he said politely. "Mrs. Mills insisted that we check your blood pressure and put you in a quiet room for a while before you go home in the middle of this mess. We, uhm, contacted your OB/GYN to make sure you're all good. Please let your family take care of you, and let them take care of things here, okay?"

And Olivia, who had worked so hard to be strong and useful during the pregnancy, suddenly yearned for that quiet room and a mattress and Elton or Christi's company with all of her being.

"Thanks," she said, standing up and sitting heavily in the wheelchair. "I'll take that nap now." She glanced up and realized that Elton was needed in this room to deal with the young adults who all wanted to help and to be the leader of the family while she rested.

"Christi, could you—" Her voice cracked.

"Yeah, Livvy," Christi murmured, standing up to follow. She turned, though, and addressed the boys with absolute authority. "If any of you idiots decide to leave this hospital and do something heroic without running it by Livvy and me first, you will sleep in the chicken coop for the rest of the summer. Have I made myself clear?"

All three of them stared at Olivia's sister in fear, and Olivia smiled tiredly to herself. The sisters Joan d'Arc—sometimes it was a two-person job.

She was aware that Rosie Mills had joined her as they traveled to a spare bed in the general part of the hospital, and the other woman took her hand.

"Eamon's dealing with the SAC PD people," she said softly. "And apparently they've got a cot here I can use too."

Olivia nodded, her worry for her dads not gone but somehow made bearable. Larx had given her the values of service to her community, but he'd never told her that her community would serve her back. And Larx and Aaron both served their community with their whole hearts. They'd inspired loyalty from people who had been strangers the day before. Between the two of them, there was an entire town that could rise to the occasion and help them get out of that giant hole.

Olivia needed her nap, and maybe that egg sandwich she hadn't had a chance to finish, and then she and Christiana and probably Rosie Mills would be back in the search, doing what they could to fix their world.

Nobody was out of the game yet.

The Impossible Dream

LARX ALLOWED Aaron to drag him out of the shattered window of the Kia and tried to take stock. His head hurt, and his body felt appropriately banged up. He had some bruises, he knew, that were going to blossom into enormous rage roses in the next few days, and he had a sudden yearning to be up to his chin in the cool water of Aaron's swimming pool, with a few ibuprofens and a giant bag of ice on his head.

Oh hell.

"Concussion," he muttered.

"Godblessyou," Aaron retorted, stabilizing Larx's neck and making sure his spine was straight as he settled him on the only flat spot of Daffodil Canyon, period.

"No, genius, I mean I think I have a concussion."

"Given the watermelon sprouting from your forehead, I'd say that's a safe assumption," Aaron said tightly. "Suggestions?"

Larx grunted. "Lack of movement until the world stops spinning and I don't want to vomit?" As suggestions went, it was pretty basic.

"Fair," Aaron agreed. "Lay there and look pretty, and let me check you for any other injuries."

"What about you? I mean, I don't want to brag, but at least I came down the hill in a steel cage."

"That *is* bragging and you know it," Aaron replied, but his hands felt reassuring as they traveled from Larx's ankles and up his shins, to his thighs to his—

"Seat belt bruise on abdomen," Larx grunted. "Careful of the ribs."

"Roger that," Aaron said tersely.

"And you didn't answer my question," Larx insisted.

"I've got a gash on my leg that continues to bleed, which is probably the only reason I won't die of sepsis," Aaron said heavily, his hands coming up to Larx's shoulders. Larx winced when he touched the seat belt line, no matter how gingerly, but other than that, Aaron's firm no-bullshit touch was more comforting than Larx could give voice to.

"I brought bandages," Larx said, trying for brightness but achieving only a sort of goofy dreaminess that probably worried Aaron more.

"Fabulous," Aaron said, and Larx opened his eyes to peer into Aaron's face.

There were tracks in the dust on his cheeks that told Larx that Aaron was *not* fabulous and had probably not *been* fabulous at any time in the last half-hour.

"I'm fine," Larx told him, raising his hand to cup Aaron's cheek.

Aaron captured his hand, and for a moment, the whooshing momentum spinning them both into the ground slowed.

"I saw the Kia go over, and that was it," Aaron confessed.

"I know," Larx murmured. Oh Jesus—Caroline. Aaron's wife, his first love, had died in a traffic accident. "I'm sorry, baby. I didn't mean to worry you."

"Larx, I would be absofuckinglutely worthless without you. Do you understand me?"

Larx rubbed his thumb under Aaron's cheekbone. "No," he said softly. "You would pull yourself up, and you would take care of our children, and you would be exactly who you've always been." He swallowed, and his voice broke remembering his own terrible moments of peering over the edge of the embankment, praying to a God he only seemed to talk to when someone he cared for was in jeopardy. "But your heart would be slow and sad and empty, and you'd never take a deep whole breath again." His next breath shook. "Ask me how I know."

Aaron nodded, and they both let out a shuddering breath together.

"God," he muttered. "All I want to do is hold you, but you're right. Hawkins is back up the hill, and he's wounded, and you're not going to believe this, but—"

"You found Curtis MacDonald?" Larx hazarded, because he *had* seen three people moving when he'd looked over the edge.

"You're no fun to surprise," Aaron muttered, put out.

"If you really want to surprise me, give me a good option for what to do next," Larx said. "Because right now, all I want to do is lie in the shade and close my eyes and dream about air-conditioning."

Aaron grunted. "Here," he muttered. "Foil blankets and water and shit in the back?"

"And a first-aid kit," Larx said. "In the front. Lightly used."

Aaron closed his eyes for a moment. "Johnson?" he asked. "Mary Lee?"

Oh wow. Aaron must have been so worried—he'd gone over right when things had gone down. "Johnson was okay—she winged one of the shooters." The thought made him angry, and he wanted to finish. "Mary Lee was less okay, but there were ambulances in the background when I started down the canyon. Hopefully she got medical attention before shit got real."

Aaron grunted. "Larx, don't know if you've noticed…."

Larx let out a humorless laugh and closed his eyes against the dusty glare of the overhead sun. "Plenty real," he mumbled. "I hear you."

"Hold on," Aaron told him. Creakily he rose, and using the vehicle to keep him on his feet, he went around the back of the Kia slowly. Larx didn't want to turn his head—his neck was already starting to freeze up, and while part of him wanted to pop to his feet and go hauling off into the world to fix things, he was old enough now to realize he could scramble his limited brains permanently if he did that. Let his brain rest, take some acetaminophen for the pain, wait until the sun eased up and every little thing didn't make him feel like he wanted to puke, and he might just be able to do some good.

He must have drifted off for a minute because he heard Aaron say, "Here," and in a moment the broiling glare of the sun was dimmed as Aaron used one of the foil blankets from the back as a tent by securing it to the upside-down Kia with medical tape.

The relief was so acute Larx felt tears slipping from the corners of his eyes. "My hero," he rasped.

"How's the head?" Aaron asked, his voice muffled as he continued to rummage for supplies.

Larx considered lying, but he wouldn't be any use to Aaron if his head exploded on his shoulders or his brains started to run out his ears.

"Screaming in pain," he all but whimpered.

Aaron said something that sounded like "Oolf," and then he appeared inside the magic tent with Larx, holding a bottle of water and some Tylenol. "Here," he said again, and Larx took the painkillers gratefully and the water with it. When he was done, Aaron set an ice pack on Larx's temple that should have qualified as a whole humanitarian relief effort all by its little lonesome.

"I'm pretty sure I love you," Larx teased, tears slipping from the corners of his eyes with the pain relief.

"You're just saying that to get the other ice pack," Aaron told him. With a groan, Aaron sat back on his haunches, and Larx could see the makeshift bandage on his leg.

"Don't forget to doctor yourself when you're done," Larx cautioned.

"I know," Aaron mumbled, and then he surveyed the cases of water, Gatorade, and food he'd assembled and gave a sigh.

"What?" Larx asked.

"You know who needs this? Besides us, I mean, and kudos for keeping Olivia ready to give birth at a moment's notice on the side of the road."

Larx had to work very hard not to laugh because it would have hurt his head. "A little preparation hurt nobody. Witness."

"I'm not saying it was bad," Aaron replied. He sighed again, obviously out of banter. "I'm just saying…."

"There's two people up top who need this more," Larx muttered. "I hear you." He took a deep breath, and then another, and tried to think past the oatmeal in his head. "There will be search and rescue coming for us," he said after a moment.

"How's that gonna work?" Aaron asked, and it was a good question. There was literally nowhere a helicopter could land down there, and Larx's vehicle crash had washed out the only usable part of the road.

Larx tried to envision a way in which a somebody could come fetch the lot of them, and his head gave a colossal throb. "Lowering basket?" he asked, although the throbbing in his cranium gave a miniexplosion that told him there was something wrong with that.

"Would the rotors kick up too much disturbance?" Aaron asked doubtfully. "And Curtis and Tad are in the trees. They'll need somebody to land and help load them without sliding down the shale or rolling down the hill. I mean, I might be able to get back up to the road to help, but even if I was one hundred percent, I couldn't climb up to that hillside to where they are." He'd known it when he'd come down—and so, probably, had Tad Hawkins.

"The embankment isn't stable enough to throw a rope over," Larx muttered. "They could end up dragging half of Dropoff Drive down on top of their heads if they set up rappelling equipment there."

"Unless they use a tree—" Aaron began, and Larx hated to shoot him down.

"Did you notice how narrow all the trees are?" he asked, his "science teacher" voice clicking into place without his permission. "It's because the bedrock that got turned into rubble here is too close to their taproots. If this place had been quarried, it would be one thing, but—"

"Hydraulic mining is the fucking devil," Aaron said passionately, and Larx didn't have to see the moonscape surrounding them to know that washing away half a mountain had created an alien and inhospitable environment. Much of the Nevada side of the Sierras was high desert—Daffodil Canyon was like a brutalized, pulverized section of the harshest of the Nevada side of the mountains condensed into a gravel pit. When the service tracks had been better maintained, before governmental cuts for upkeep, he used to compete in a fundraising run up and down the canyon—he'd even brought the track team down here a time or two. Every time, he and the kids had come back to his science classes and reported on the differences in temperature, humidity, and air quality that had been created by an intentionally generated man-made catastrophe over a hundred years earlier, in an effort to explain that climate change was real and human choice had an impact.

He knew from firsthand experience that this little pit of despair was nearly ten degrees hotter than the tree-shaded plateau up above, and that the air was drier and harder to breathe.

"Yeah," Larx said now, simply grateful for the foil blanket, reflecting the sun and hopefully letting people know they were alive down there, and the cooling gel pack over his eyes. "It's the fucking devil. But we've got to figure out how to get supplies up to your young detective. And water and Gatorade for Curtis MacDonald. He could die of dehydration, if nothing else."

"Larx…." Larx didn't want to hear the defeat in Aaron's voice. Not *his* Aaron, who had pulled his family together from the depths of grief to become the man Larx loved.

"Shh!" he snapped. "Give me an hour, okay? Give me an hour to not think, to just… just drift. For my brain to settle down and stop running out my ears. I… I've got an idea. I do. I just—" His voice broke with the pain and the frustration and—he could admit it—the fear. Simply *lying* there, the world seemed to spin under him, and he had to keep his eyes closed or he'd roll over and puke. Aaron needed his working brain, and Larx needed a damned second of quiet.

"Okay," Aaron murmured. "No sleeping. Sorry—"

"No sorry," Larx managed, his eyes closing. He wasn't passing out—he knew what that felt like. And he wasn't falling asleep either. His adrenaline was too up for that. His body needed the peace, the healing, even stretched out on the ground next to Elton's pulverized Kia. "A little quiet. I'll get to it. Trust me."

He reached out blindly and was rewarded with Aaron's broad-palmed, callused hand covering his own. They laced fingers, and Larx concentrated on that. Breathe in, breathe out, breathe in….

The pain faded—infinitesimally, but enough to let him breathe—and he didn't push it. Just let the thoughts swirl, let the relative coolness of the shade ease some of his discomfort, let the moisture he'd swirled in his mouth give him some ease.

Let Aaron's hand in his keep him tethered to the ground, where he was needed to help people who were in worse shape than he was.

It might have been fifteen minutes, but it might have been an hour when without conscious volition, he heard himself say, "Rope."

Aaron's painful grunt from where he sat propped up against the Kia made him smile. He hadn't been the only one to cop some rest in the middle of chaos.

"What?" he mumbled.

"Under the wheel well. There should be several coils of sturdy nylon rope. I remember having a rope moment for some reason—"

"Yeah, yeah," Aaron muttered. "I remember. You put three coils in my department issue, two in the minivan, and one in the Impala." They'd had to buy another vehicle in March because there were *four* teenagers, three with licenses to drive, all of them in afterschool activities.

"And one in Livvy's car and four or five in the Kia since they take that most anyway."

Aaron let out a little laugh. "Was someone—"

"We went down to Home Depot to get the part for the toilet, remember?" Larx asked, the memory just free-floating, like most of the important moments of his life right now. "They were having a sale."

Aaron grunted again. "Good. So we've got rope… what?"

"Shh…," Larx murmured. "More quiet."

"Sure. I'll go gather the rope."

"Put it into a bundle," Larx ordered, head pounding again. "Use the cover to the wheel well."

"What?" Aaron asked, and Larx realized he'd forgotten half of what he needed to say.

"The supplies you need to get to the people in the tree stand. Bundle them. Now shh…."

Aaron hushed.

Words were a lot—but Larx had the pictures in his head. The diagrams. The weight distributions and ratios.

"Take the rope up to the road with you," he mumbled. "Set it up down here. Rope basket. Use wheel cover as bottom. Set up pulley to transport supplies."

Aaron grunted. "I see it," he said. "Four coils of rope… let's see…. Ooh, pretty."

"Rainbow colors," Larx told him, remembering the brightly hued 550 lb. test paracord he'd thrown in the back of Elton's vehicle. "Two-hundred-foot lengths."

"Shh… I'm doing math…."

Larx didn't even need his math brain for this. "It's enough to stretch between the Kia and your boulder, doubled," he said. "And enough to stretch between the boulder and your young detective's tree."

"How do I get it up to Hawkins?" Aaron muttered.

Larx had a vision of the dog toy kept in the back of the Kia, the one with the flexible lever and the tennis ball. "Chuck it," he mumbled, and Aaron laughed.

"Hush, baby," he said. "You're not making sense."

It *would too* make sense, Larx thought, but for the moment, he let his brain go to free-floating land, and worked hard not to fall asleep.

Assembling the Genius

AARON'S WORRY was *everywhere*. It was with the guys halfway up the hill. It was with the kids who were probably worried *sick*. And it was, most especially, with Larx, whose head didn't just *hurt*, it hurt so bad Larx needed *quiet*, and it forced him to *stop talking*, and with Larx, both those states were pretty anathematic to his entire character.

Aaron was so scared for him he almost couldn't think himself.

But then Larx said, "Rope," and Aaron had a flash to what they could do with rope.

While Larx took downtime, Aaron reached into the front seat of the crushed Kia and made sure it was out of Park and the brake wasn't on. Then he stood and tested one of the wheels sticking up in the air like the feet of an unhappy turtle. Two-wheel drive had its plusses.

The wheels *still spun.*

"Whatcha doin'?" Larx asked.

"Trying to see if the wheels spin so I can set up the pulley you're trying to think up."

"So smart," Larx mumbled, gratitude in his voice. "So very smart. Are the tires still inflated?"

Aaron thumped the one nearest himself. "Oddly enough, yes," he said, thinking that the vehicle probably tilted off the road, rolled over to its back, and slid the rest of the way down the hill.

"Are they pointed in the right direction?" Larx asked, and Aaron sighted a clear path back the way the Kia had come from. On his way down, he'd depended on the fact that the dirt exposed by the Kia's descent was packed harder than the rest of the loose topsoil and scree. It would surely help him on the way up.

"They are," he said softly. "Now what do I use for a wheel up top?"

Larx was quiet for a moment, and then he said, "There is a cannister of eyebolts in the back compartment. The kids were going to suspend some exercise equipment from the ceiling in the garage."

"And where the hell are we going to suspend them now?" Aaron asked, at a complete loss. Eyebolts? Really?

"Up your keester if you don't stop yelling!" Larx retorted irritably.

Aaron tried not to snort, but then Larx did.

"Sorry," he said in a small voice.

"Brains running out your ears," Aaron returned just as mildly. "I understand."

Larx let out a cleansing breath. "Use the star jack to screw two of them into a crack in the boulder—the big people-sized boulder by the side of the road. Two of them. One on top of the other. Preloop the rope on one side—test to see, but the eyebolts are big. It should be able to slide through them even with a knot. Get to the boulder with the rope in your back pocket. String it through the eyebolts. You'll have the food and stuff suspended on the platform. Pull the rope up—it will be the hardest part. Then secure the rope ends and pull the rope through the eyebolts, using the tire as a pulley on this end."

Aaron grunted, seeing it in his mind's eye. The boulder had tumbled down recently—there were cracks in the side, but it was still intact enough to hold the eyebolts once it was screwed in. Still…. "Friction," he murmured. "Burn the rope out."

"Motor oil," Larx supplied. "Two extra quarts next to the eyebolts. There's leather gloves in the center console so you don't get it on your hands."

"How do you *remember* this stuff?" Aaron asked, impressed, as always, by Larx's amazing mind.

"I can just see it behind my eyes," Larx mumbled. "Like the piles of paper on my desk. I can reach into the middle of that pile and pull out a student on request."

"Like Curtis MacDonald," Aaron murmured, not wanting to think about the kid and whether or not he'd survived withdrawal in this heat, tucked almost completely under the giant tree trunk halfway on top of the hill.

"He wasn't doing well?" Larx asked, the sadness apparent in his voice even from under the foil blanket. All Aaron could see of him was his feet. He'd put on cargo shorts the night before, and his ankles looked absurdly fragile poking out between the blanket and his all-purpose cross-training boots.

"Baby, I think his dad and Uncles Percy and Clancy were helping to run the meth business. I don't think he had a choice, really." Aaron sighed and crawled heavily to his feet so he could go back and start rummaging in the Kia's upside-down mess again. His leg was *on fire*. Not figuratively. He could feel the waves of blistering heat coming from under his bandage. "I mean, of course he had a choice, but—"

"Spent his entire life trying to be the man of the family," Larx mumbled, and Aaron was hit, again, by his beloved's compassion. His hand closed around the small box of eyebolts and he almost laughed. Brains, kindness—why weren't they married again?

Oh yeah. Because shit like *this* kept happening to them.

"Yeah. If we can get him out of this damned canyon, maybe he can have a do-over." Aaron set to work, gathering the supplies, determining what he would need to bring with him, what he'd need to do to the rope before he left. He was in the middle of experimenting with the rope to see how he'd make a cradle to hold the wheel cover as a platform when he heard, high overhead, the *whap-whap* of a helicopter's blades.

He turned his face to the sky and tried to get a hold of the wild surge of hope that filled him. Hooray! Grown-ups! Somebody better equipped to help him and Larx get out of this mess and bring their two disabled compatriots with them!

Then Larx spoke. "They're scoping us out," he said softly. "Aaron, they can't land here."

He reminded himself that they knew that. For one thing, there wasn't a flat space big enough for the copter to settle down, but for another, the gravel would become airborne—like shrapnel—in the copter's rotor wash.

"Could they lower a basket?" Aaron asked, but he knew the answer to that.

"The canyon's too small," Larx said. "It's more of a hole in the earth than a canyon. As long as the copter stays far enough away from the gravel not to be a danger—"

"They're too far away to lower the damned basket," Aaron murmured. "But at least they're scoping us out. Hopefully they'll know about the guys in the trees too."

"At least they haven't forgotten us," Larx murmured, and Aaron had to agree.

"They'll work on it," he said, and he felt the weight of being the grown-up thump back on his shoulders again. "In the meantime, let's see if I can't remember some of my old Eagle Scout training."

"Oh you *would* be an Eagle Scout," Larx grumbled.

"Yeah, just like you *would* be a frustrated rock musician," Aaron shot back, but he was smiling when he said it. "We both have our pasts."

"If we ever get out of this damned canyon," Larx muttered, "can we have a future?"

Aaron's spirits, lifted by the whap of the helicopter blades, knowing he and Larx weren't solving this problem alone, lifted a little more.

"You mean am I going to marry you?" he asked, ducking his head under the foil blanket into Larx's cool little tent.

"Yes," Larx muttered, scowling. He was still lying down, somebody's sweater from the back of the Kia under his head and the icepack over his closed eyes. "Yes, I would very much like to marry you."

"Good," Aaron told him before crouching down to take his mouth in a gentle kiss. "You keep focusing on that and we'll get the hell out of here and start planning."

"Yoshi's got it planned," Larx told him crossly. "All we have to do is pick a date."

"Before or after the baby?" Aaron asked.

"First week of August," Larx told him, making him laugh. "So it's a crapshoot. Could be a baby there, could be a very irritated Olivia."

"Either way," Aaron said, "our family."

"Yeah." Larx kept his eyes closed, kept his breathing even. "Keep tying knots, mighty Scout Leader. We've got promises to keep."

"And miles to go before we sleep," Aaron replied, his Robert Frost prodding him gently from long ago. "I hear you. Don't fall asleep."

"Will do."

Aaron backed out of the lean-to like a crab, pulled out the rope, and started playing with it. Much like Larx, Aaron now had ideas.

Damned Kids

OLIVIA WOKE up from a light doze on the hospital bed and glanced around.

Something was wrong.

"Where are they?" she asked, and Rosie Mills glanced up from her phone.

"Where are who, honey?"

"Christiana. The boys. My damned husband. Not one of them is in here with me."

She struggled to sit up from the reclining position, giving thanks for giant T-shirts and leggings because at least her clothing was out of her way. "You—I mean, I love you, Rosie, but the whole reason *we* are *here* is to look after *you.* You should be with Eamon, and one of those damned kids should be with me, and…." Her eyes narrowed. "It's too quiet. It's Christi's-in-my-makeup quiet. It's the-cats-ate-my-goldfish quiet. I know this noise. It's a bad noise."

Rosie's eyes grew wide. "Honey, it's like you got pregnant and woke up with your father's brain. It's terrifying."

Olivia shot her a look. "We don't say the P-word in my house." They didn't, either. They didn't talk about "pregnancy" or "peeing like there's no tomorrow" or "phuck me, why did I do this." And while she and Elton may be making all of the *mechanical* changes to the house that a baby necessitated—room, crib, appropriate furniture, stuffed animals galore—both of them had scrupulously avoided what it was going to be like living with another human being in the house, this one particularly helpless, dependent, autonomous, and terrifying.

There was nothing like denial to keep them both functioning on optimal, right?

But *this* crisis she couldn't avoid. "Where are they?"

Rosie glanced down at her feet, where Cap slept lightly. "I don't know," she said slowly. "Eamon had to go in for more tests, and then

Christi went to find Elton and get a progress report since you were sleeping. I assume they're monopolizing the OR waiting room again?"

With a shove and leading with her stomach, Olivia got to her feet and stood for a moment, waiting for the room to stop wobbling. Ooh, very good. She could stand like a real girl. Great for her!

"I've got to go find them," she muttered and took a step away from the bed. Her head whirled and her vision blackened and she thought, "Fuck me, do I have to eat *again*?" and then Christi rushed inside and grabbed the wheelchair.

"Get in," she ordered. "Elton's got snacks in the waiting room, and the boys have a plan. You've got to catch up."

"Catch up?" Olivia asked, following Christiana's lead anyway. "Whoamygod, *Christi*, we are *not* having a—slow down!"

"You're fine, Princess," Christiana muttered, still keeping up that breakneck pace through the afternoon-quiet hospital corridors. "If you don't get your ass out there, they are going to launch their plan without adult supervision."

"Adult supervision? Where the hell is Elton?"

"Does Wombat Willie count as an adult?" Christi asked, slowing down as she expressed doubt. "Does he *really*? Because I could swear he's encouraging them, and it's weird."

"Encouraging *who*?" Olivia asked. "Christi, slow down and tell me what's going on!"

According to Christi, the whole thing started when she'd left Olivia's room to go see if anybody had heard any news. Lieutenant Johnson's friend was still in surgery, and Elton had heard that SAR were sending a helicopter to scope out the situation. As soon as he'd hung up, Kirby spoke up.

"You know," he'd said, "there's no place in Daffodil Canyon to land."

Then Kellan had said, "Yeah, I've been thinking about that. The rotor wash would turn the canyon into a shooting gallery. How do you think they'll get them out?"

"How would Larx do it?" Kirby had asked.

And that had started the flurry of ideas, of sketches on napkins, and finally, Elton had called Berto and asked him if he could bring Elton's tablet to the hospital because it had physics software on it.

The boys had worked out a couple of scenarios when Johnson got a call—this one saying search and rescue was currently "exploring options" for a rescue from the canyon.

Which was when it had dawned on all of them.

"I'm the one who said it first," Christi muttered. "Because men are all cowards. But I was, like, 'They're doing what we're doing. *Nobody* knows how to get them out.'"

"Oh shit," Olivia muttered as the full import of the situation hit her. "I outed Teddy Goddamned Harris for nothing, and *we're the only adults in the room*!"

Christi grunted. "Well, not the only ones…."

At that point, they were rounding the corner into the OR waiting room, and Olivia saw what she meant.

"Yoshi?" she said, because Yoshi was the figure she recognized besides the boys and her husband, all of whom were bent over a hospital table covered with a large drafting tablet. They were there with two men her father's age she didn't recognize, as well as Jaime's brother, Berto, who was engrossed with whatever was going on with the big piece of paper and was not nearly as anxious as Olivia would have expected. Even Maureen was there, dancing gracefully from person to person to peer over their shoulder.

"Hey, Olivia. You took your dad's AP class, right?" Yoshi asked absently, as though she'd been there the whole time.

"Yeah," she said, "but Elton's the one with the engineering physics classes under his belt. Why? What are you doing?"

Yoshi nodded with his chin to the older of the two men, a man with a dark bronze complexion and raven-wing black hair. "This is Mandeep Singh, he's the county geology specialist, and he teaches classes at the high school and Truckee Junior College. He's the one who helped revamp the elementary school when it was having safety issues because the foundation wouldn't cure. He's got maps of the Dropoff Drive area, as well as Daffodil Canyon. In fact, Larx got a lot of his information about the area from Mr. Singh when he taught classes about man-made disasters. He's here to help."

Olivia held out her hand, feeling like an adulting imposter, and shook Mr. Singh's extended hand. "Nice to meet you, Mr. Singh."

"Nice to meet you," Mandeep said formally. "Your father is one of the bright spots of my job—I hope I can help."

"Me too," she said, while Yoshi introduced the younger of the two men, a sunburned blond man with a widow's peak although he was probably barely in his thirties.

"This is Corbin Baker—your dad hired him as a substitute in math and is talking about training him in AP Physics, which I think is a lie but don't tell Corbin that or he won't help."

Corbin Baker snorted. "Nice to meet you, Olivia. Your dad's one of the best educators I've ever met, and I know that because your brothers here…." He paused and blushed. "They *are* your brothers, right? I… I'm not sure of the family connections."

"Oh, they're mine all right," Olivia said, giving Kirby, Kellan, and Jaime a dire look. The boys returned her glare blandly, and she wondered what horrible thing she could do to them for this—after she hugged them all and wept, which might be horrible enough as it was.

"Glad to hear it," Corbin said with a smile that told her he might speak "family" too. "Because they've come up with some good plans, but since you're the one with the contacts in search and rescue—"

Olivia snorted so hard she started coughing, not sure she could stop. "Did they tell you what my contact *is*, in search and rescue?"

"No," Corbin replied, looking around the table. The wretched boys did everything but stick their hands in their pockets and whistle. Christiana was the one who spoke up.

"She used to date Teddy God— Erm, Harris," she said. "And she seems to be on good terms with his manager. Anyway, tell her what you all came up with."

"You helped, Christi," Kirby said, in the classic "shoving your sibling under the bus" move.

"Whatever," Christi said with a toss of her head that sent her dark hair cascading over her back. "Tell her!"

Yoshi glanced around at the young men as well as his contemporaries and let out a sigh. "Fine," he said and nodded her over to the tablet stretched across a waiting-room table. "Look, see, this is the canyon, and this is the edge."

Someone—probably Elton, who'd had some training—had sketched everything neatly to spec, so it was easy to follow even if you weren't trained. Diagrams always helped. Sitting on top of the diagram was an old road map of Colton, folded so the specific area of Dropoff Drive and Daffodil Canyon were shown.

Olivia stared. "A giant crane?" she asked, staring at the engineer's sketch, because that's what the diagram showed. A crane with the boom projected over the edge of the canyon, the cable lowered to hoist little stick figures out. "That's… all the people in this room and we've got the Hot Wheels solution?"

Christi snickered. "Classy, Livvy. Real classy. But you see the dilemma, right?"

"Yeah," Olivia said, staring at the diagram. "We can't put any pressure on the lip of the canyon or we'll cause more rockslides."

"That's right," said Mandeep Singh. "The edge of the canyon is *very* unstable. But fifty to sixty feet back from the edge is a solid platform of granite—at least according to my surveys. A forty-ton crane would be very stable, and one is being used in the construction of the new grade school, here"—he pointed to the place on the map—"and with some repositioning—"

Olivia grimaced. "The repositioning would be hard," she said and realized she might be the only one who knew this. Yoshi lived on the other end of town, and, well, Livvy and her first boyfriend had been desperate for places to have sex where Aaron or any of the other deputies wouldn't find them, so they'd done quite a bit of backroads exploring in their day. "See here?" She pointed to the network of roads on the map. "These aren't really roads—they're barely cow paths. The only reason they're marked on the map is because people live there and they need a street name to send mail. I get that the crane isn't one of those big ones that could rebuild a ship or something, but it still wouldn't *fit* any way but Dropoff Drive, and from what you're saying, Dropoff Drive is too unstable."

"So we'd be dropping a crane on their heads from Dropoff Drive," Kirby said sourly. "Great. Thank you for waking up, Olivia, to keep us from making a terrible mistake. You can follow our path of crushed hopes back to your room now."

Olivia snickered in spite of the serious situation. God, Kirby and Larx—they were such a pair. No wonder Larx had taken to Aaron's kid so quickly. But she wasn't willing to give up, either, in spite of the blatant invitation to go away.

"But the idea of the winch from the top of the canyon doesn't suck," she said thoughtfully, staring at the plans laid out in front of her.

"Mr. Singh, where's the most stable edge of the canyon in the area they went over?"

"Here," the man said. "It's about a hundred yards away from where Deputy George and Detective Hawkins slid down the embankment."

Olivia grunted. "What about my father? Where'd Larx go over?"

Yoshi grimaced. "With his usual luck, he rolled off the service track almost directly below them. If there's a way to get him up to the service track, we can use the same means to lift him out."

"So," Olivia murmured, now as engrossed as the rest of the room, "we need a stable place to put a winch that won't bring the canyon down on top of their heads. Why won't the flatbed holding the winch do?"

"Because what is that thing where downward force is increased by the length of the vector?" Kellan asked. "Like, you know, a body dangling off the back of the truck might pull the winch off the truck if there's enough yarn to dangle it?"

"I, uh.... God. I forget what it's called," Olivia muttered. "But it works, right, Mr. Baker?"

"Yes," said Corbin Baker dryly. "It's related to tension force."

Olivia sucked in a breath. "Yeah! That's it! Tension force! I remember now—the truck could get pulled back onto the unstable ground, or the winch could get pulled off the truck if we dangled enough line into the canyon and then swung enough weight on the line. We need a pivot or something to distribute the weight." She took a triumphant breath, and Christi and the boys all applauded.

"Go, Livvy," Christiana praised. "Proving that Larx's class is real!"

Olivia shot her a look. "*You* bozos just took the damn class. *Some of us* have been gestating with our brains since Thanksgiving! Anyway—so we need a... a... a...."

"Fulcrum," Kirby supplied dryly, and she blew a raspberry at him.

"Yes! A *fulcrum* to distribute the weight so the truck and the winch don't get pulled into the canyon!"

"Which is where we were going with the forty-ton crane," Yoshi said sourly. "Until somebody told us that we couldn't drag it through backroads without squashing a house or something."

"But the area *around* the canyon is pretty stable," Olivia said. She looked up at Mr. Singh. "That's what you said, right? Once we back far enough away from the lip of the canyon, there's granite underneath the topsoil. There's got to be something around there we can use as a fulcrum, right?"

Singh and Baker looked at each other in surprise. "I don't know…," Corbin Baker said doubtfully, but Olivia felt like she was on to something.

"Well, what's out there? I mean, I know the meth house is here," she said, pointing to a big red X, "but is there a building or anything here?"

"No," Corbin Baker said. "Trees pretty much—giant pine trees."

She frowned and glanced up at all the men from her stupid wheelchair that she was still too woozy to leave. "What about a tree?"

They stared back at her. "But wouldn't a tree like… I dunno, *break*?" Kellan asked, sounding doubtful. "Or bend? Or get ripped out of the earth?"

"No," she said, trying to remember all of the area history Larx had made her and Christi ingest.

"The big trees have taproots," Christi said, excitement building in her voice. "Like, they punch through the granite. They're anchored in there really hard and fast. And pine is *really* sturdy, particularly *live* pine. It's why we use it to build houses. This isn't a couple of dead four-by-fours—this would be a *live* tree, at *least* twelve to eighteen inches in diameter, right? So we find a thick tree, not too far from the edge, and we use it as a, like, fulcrum or pivot or whatever, to keep the cable from the lip of the canyon and to keep the winch from being dragged down!"

"That could just be a really fun way to cut down a tree," Yoshi said doubtfully.

"Not if we affixed a pulley to it," Kirby said, eyes narrow. "Or maybe two, to distribute the weight. Yeah. We could lower the basket without bringing down the canyon, and maybe, if we could find one close enough to the edge, we could have some height to… you know, do the triangle thing. Give us a little more leverage out over the edge."

"So I could climb a tree?" Jaime asked, sounding excited.

"*No*!" every adult in the room said, including the ones who *weren't* family.

Berto shook his head. "My God, Jaime. You're terrifying. I can't believe anybody trusted *me* to take care of you."

Olivia and Elton both snorted. "At least he can feed himself," Elton muttered. "Some idiot decided to put Livvy and me in charge of a fresh, tadpole-looking one in a couple of months. Talk about terrified."

Olivia gazed at her husband, her mouth parted in surprise and an absolute weight of gratitude. "You're scared?" she asked, her eyes burning.

"Duh," Elton told her, and he must have gotten her—he was *so* good at getting her—because his lips curved up a little. "How does a fuckup like me get a pretty wife and one of those tadpole things? It goes against nature."

Olivia sniffled, and then pulled herself together. "Elton, I love you to two orders of magnitude past infinity. Jaime, your brother is right. Stop scaring the shit out of him. Elton and I are attached to both of you." She let out a sigh. "Everybody else, how do we get a winch and a people basket and everything to Dropoff Drive without having the flatbed truck fall of the edge of the canyon?"

There was quiet, and then everybody started talking at once.

Nightlights and Daylight

AARON HAD the rope pulley ready in about two hours, and Larx was ready to sit up and at least direct him by then.

But Aaron was smart—and had apparently done that Eagle Scout thing with the knots—so by the time Larx could lean against the destroyed Kia under the lean-to Aaron had erected and inspect his work, he'd done most of the hard thinking.

"Nice," Larx murmured, pulling one end of the rope, including the handles Aaron had spaced every four feet or so, through the eye of the eyebolt. "Paracord—good shit. It should hold." And it was insanely thin and hopefully easy to use.

"You want to check something out, check my knots here," Aaron told him and then offered the complicated butterfly loops he'd set up for the wheel-well cover to rest on.

Larx gave every direction a tug, and the knots held—and, in fact, got tighter—so he grunted. "It should hold," he said. "The supplies at least." He grimaced. "Don't know about me—"

"I'm not going up there if you can't come with me," Aaron told him grimly. "No leaving Larx here to drink Gatorade and brood." He sighed and cast his thousandth glance up the steep incline of the canyon. "Besides, look at all that loose soil and rock debris. However they decide to get us out of here, we'll all have a better chance of living if we're all in the same spot. And I want you to look over Hawkins's wound and check on MacDonald." He paused and simply looked at Larx, his face softening. "And frankly, Larx, I don't want to go up and get rescued without you, so we're going to make this work."

Larx smiled at him stupidly, pretty sure it wasn't only the head wound that was making him loopy. "I mean, isn't that how we're going to be grandpas?" he said. "Isn't that how we've made this all work until now?"

"Yes," Aaron said, as though Larx had salved a wound. "I'm glad you see it that way. Do you think you could sit on the wheel-well platform? I could pull you up that way—"

Larx grimaced. "Put it in the loops and let me see how high up it will be when the pulley is set up."

Aaron did that, holding the rope up even with the front tire of the Kia, and Larx nodded.

"Maybe," he said. "But you also put handles in the paracord, so maybe you can just pull me up slowly."

Aaron puffed out a breath. "I'd rather *gondola* you up slowly. Larx, concussions—"

"We don't want to screw with them," Larx agreed heavily. "I hear you. So walk me through it again."

"I pack everything on the wheel-well platform," Aaron began, "and set the rope up so it's looped around the tire and the platform is resting on the ground. I've wound the rope and put it in my backpack so it can unspool tightly from the opening as I walk."

"And…," Larx said seriously.

"And I also carry the eyebolts, the star jack, and the Chuckit in the backpack, as well as the extra rope. Oh! And a quart of 30/30 weight."

Because some stuff he would need to set up the pulley and other stuff he simply could not afford to put on the platform in case the platform crumbled while he was pulling the supplies up the mountain.

"And some water for yourself," Larx added primly. "And some protein bars too."

"Of course," Aaron acknowledged. "Thank you for taking care of me."

Larx grimaced and pointed to his already aching head. "It's *literally* the least I could do." He swallowed. "How long, do you think? Before I can take another Tylenol?"

That was a rough question. Time seemed to both fly by and drag as he'd lain under the lean-to and listened to Aaron work, but now that he was sitting up, he could see that the sun had moved considerably. He figured the Kia had gone over the edge of the road at twenty after ten in the morning, but now it was looking definitely afternoonish. Was it two? Three?

"Another hour," Aaron said confidently. "I'll leave you the bottle and lots of water. It will take *at least* that long for me to get up to the service track and then the boulder again."

Larx nodded and leaned his head against the back quarter panel. More time for the swelling in his head to go down, he hoped. He was *really* hoping that the last four or so hours of sitting, icing, and cooling darkness had done its job and that the swelling wasn't *increasing* before it hit his skull. Ugh—the things he used to just power through.

"Okay," he said, and he smiled a little, not wanting Aaron to see him worry, not wanting Aaron to see any doubt. "I'll sit here planning our wedding while you go out and do the heavy lifting."

Aaron gave a choked cackle and sank to a squat in front of him. "Larx?" he said softly.

"Aaron?" For a moment, Aaron just drank him in, like his eyes were thirsty for the sight of him, although Larx was sure he was bruised and exhausted and had blood on his face from where he'd hit himself against the window.

But Aaron—blond, strong, square, solid, beautiful—cupped his chin and gently rubbed their noses together.

"I love you," Aaron whispered. "I want to spend the rest of our lives together. You need to stay awake for me. You need to be ready to sit on that platform when I send it back down. Hell—you'll need to be ready to help place the rope over the tire when I get to the top. There's no guarantee it'll stay put. But mostly, you need to stay awake. I'm pretty sure I can go up there and power through all the stuff I need to do, although"—he grimaced—"using the Chuckit to get rope to Hawkins is going to be a rough gig. But I *think* I can get it done. I… *know* I can't do any of it—or any of the stuff afterward—if I don't have you. I can't be a good father anymore. Not without you by my side."

"That's bullshit," Larx muttered thickly, remembering his heart in his mouth when he'd realized Aaron had gone over the edge of the embankment.

"No, I mean, I *thought* I was being a good father by myself, but that was small potatoes compared to what I can do with you by my side. I can't be a grandfather—not without you. Olivia and Christi think I'm an okay stepdad, but you're *their* dad. And Kirby and Kellan wouldn't be all they could be without the two of us. Don't… don't wander away in your head while I'm gone, okay?" His voice got a little creaky. "Don't… baby, don't fall asleep. It's going to be a long trip up while I wonder if you're still with me."

Larx nodded, and rubbed his lips against Aaron's cheek. "Want me to yell out 'here' every so often?"

"Not if it will hurt you," Aaron said.

Larx grimaced. "It might," he confessed, thinking about the sound of his own voice in his ears or the force he'd have to use to push it out. "But… hey." He reached into his pocket and pulled out his cell phone.

"No service," Aaron said grumpily.

"I know it," Larx murmured, "but…." He found his cache of music downloads and hit Play. The phone blared, Green Day's "Holiday" loud enough for Aaron to recoil and Larx's ears to throb. Larx hit Stop, but he glanced up at Aaron and smiled. "Every ten minutes or so I'll play part of a song. When you hear it, yell back, okay?"

Aaron nodded. It wasn't perfect. It wasn't a guarantee. And it would still play havoc with Larx's oversensitivity to light and sound. But he could see some of Aaron's worry dissipating with Larx's plan. Larx had turned off his internet to save battery power; he had plenty to see them through the next hour.

"Listen for me," Aaron said softly. "If I get nervous, I'm going to call out, okay?"

"Yeah," Larx murmured, and for a moment they rested their foreheads together. They'd tested every knot, they'd gone over the plan relentlessly in the last two hours, and now there was only implementation. "Don't forget to test the rope through the eyebolts before using the motor oil. Paracord is pretty slick. It might not be necessary."

"I hear you," Aaron said. He sighed and then took Larx's mouth tenderly. "Stay awake for me," he whispered.

"Be careful," Larx whispered back. And then Aaron stood, positioned his backpack, and looked resolutely up the scarred portion of the mountain where the car had tumbled down.

Larx said, "Courage is not the absence of fear but the triumph over it."

Aaron gave him a disgruntled look over his shoulder.

"Sue me," Larx said with a smile. "Yoshi has a quote for everything."

"Nelson Mandela. Nice," Aaron told him sourly. "Set your timer, Larx—ten minutes."

"Done."

AARON RESISTED the temptation to look behind him as he climbed. It was hard enough finding footing and then handholds *and* footing as he picked his way through the scarred mass of decomposed granite and shale. The damage left by the small SUV had actually done them a favor—it had knocked away most of the topsoil and loose scree, leaving only the more stable elements of the canyon for Aaron to negotiate, but the going wasn't easy. The best thing about going up was that he was actively *trying* not to succumb to gravity, unlike going down when he was just trying not to fall too fast.

His fingers ached, his knees were scraped through his khakis, and his elbows had been banged and scraped more times than he could count. He was leaning against the side of the mountain, reluctant to look down and see how much progress he *hadn't* made when the first strains of "Holiday" hit his ears.

"On holiday!" he yelled at the top of his lungs, and the music shut off. He smiled. Still didn't look behind him or down, but he smiled.

Larx was okay.

With a grunt he looked up, sighted another handhold, and pushed with his legs, grunting as he went.

By the time he reached the top of the rise, where the road was still firm and not crumbled down into the deeper part of the canyon, he resolved to listen to the whole song, from beginning to end, the minute he had his own phone and some earbuds. The song had—in fits and starts—gotten him up the first part of his climb, and he thought it deserved to be played in its entirety and screamed to at the top of his lungs.

As he scrambled up to the relative comfort of the decomposed granite road, he shouted, "Here!"

In return, the faint sounds of Linkin Park's "Bleed it Out" hit his ears, and he laughed weekly.

"Not bleeding!" he lied, but only a little. Carefully, he turned around and saw Larx, still sitting in position, waving to him. He smiled tiredly and waved back.

"Phase two!" he called, his shoulders aching under the weight of the pack.

Larx held up two fingers in agreement, and Aaron pulled out a Gatorade from the pack and downed half of it. As he turned and made his way to the boulder, he called out, "Hawkins! You still here!"

"Chillin'!" Hawkins replied, his voice rough.

"How's your water?" Aaron called.

"Getting low," Hawkins called back. "Our friend here needs more."

"I hear you. Working on it."

There was a pause.

"You're *what*?"

Aaron glanced up the hill and watched as the small faraway form of Hawkins pushed itself to its feet and stared down to where Aaron was setting up. Aaron waved.

"Be patient!" he called. "And find a good tree to use as a fulcrum!"

"Vertical or horizontal?" Hawkins asked, proving that he was smart even if he couldn't read Aaron's and Larx's minds and see the entire plan.

"Vertical tree," Aaron replied. "Sturdy but not too wide. Easy for you to get to and stand near. Understood?"

"Roger that," Hawkins replied. "Looking forward to seeing what you're up to."

"Just wait," Aaron shouted. "It'll blow your mind." He took another swig of Gatorade then and followed Larx's advice about the power bar before going to the boulder and unloading his backpack. The sun had dipped behind the trees and was casting long shadows over Aaron's side of the canyon. It occurred to him that they'd be lucky to get Larx up to where Hawkins was by the time it was dark. Rescue itself might have to wait until morning.

Good thing they were working on saving themselves.

From down the hill, he heard the next few bars of "Bleed it Out." He pulled out the eyebolts and the star jack and started looking for the cracks in the boulder that would give him the best chance of screwing the eyebolts in.

Out loud, he began to sing.

IT TOOK Aaron about half an hour to prep the eyebolts and start working on the rope. Larx could tell when the rope came into play because down the hill he watched it flutter in determined little jerks, and then Aaron peered over the edge of the canyon.

"It's time! Loop it around the tire and I'll take up the slack."

Whoo boy. After watching Aaron be Captain America for an hour and a half, Larx got to do the ultimate in superhero shit: He got to *stand up*.

He was careful about it; he could use the car for balance, but he couldn't put too much weight on it in case he shoved it out of alignment.

At the moment, the front wheels were pointing up the hill, which was just where they needed them.

Larx stood and leaned over the tire, wrestling the rope into place so the tire could act as a pulley. "Done!" he called, wincing at the echo in his own skull, but it was worth it when he watched, breathlessly, as the rope, which had straggled after Aaron as he'd climbed the wicked slope of the embankment, began to lift up. There was some rubble displacement as it rubbed up against what was left of the edge of the road, but it continued to lift, continued to tauten, until the platform, which had rested on the ground, gave a creak and steadily began to rise up in the air.

"It's working!" he cried and really didn't care what happened to his skull at this point, because *holeee chit*, it was *working*.

"Great!" Aaron ground out. Larx could hear the strain in his voice and squatted to reach under the platform and help it up so Aaron could concentrate on getting the slack out. Carefully, so he didn't tilt it and dump all the supplies, he lifted while Aaron took up the slack. His head ached, and the muscles in his neck and back had frozen up as he'd rested on the ground, but the day was getting away from them, and soon the shadows would make it too dark to see.

Besides needing to see to walk or climb, this was rattlesnake country, and one wrong step could disturb a nest of them, just minding their own business. Daylight mattered, and they were running out of it faster than Larx could have ever imagined.

"Ready, Simon?" Aaron called, and Larx smiled tightly at the *Alvin and the Chipmunks* reference. Besides growing up listening to his late mother play the record of the original recording, he'd taken the girls to see the newer movies when they'd been young.

Larx double-checked the knots, the paracord sturdy and steadfast under his fingers, and also double-checked Aaron's bundled supplies. Yup, the man could tie a knot and organize a package, and it was time to test out this Rube Goldberg machine and see if it could save their asses.

"Ready, Dave!" Larx called, hoping Aaron heard him.

"Okay!" Aaron answered, and the pulley began to move.

Larx pulled up "The Chipmunk Song" by Alvin and the Chipmunks on his phone and watched, anxious and triumphant, as the platform of supplies ascended the steep slope at a stately, measured pace. After the song finished, he turned off his phone and let out a deep breath as the platform disappeared beyond his sight.

"Let me pull it back!" he called, not wanting Aaron to exhaust himself. Pulling Larx up was going to be hard enough.

"Ten-four!" Aaron called. "Give me five to unload."

Soon enough, Aaron reversed the pulley and Larx took over, grateful for the handles Aaron had built into the rope system. The skin under his fingers *still* began to burn and sting, and he ripped off the bottom of his bright yellow Tatooine Desert Vacation T-shirt and wrapped it around his hands, wondering if Aaron was doing the same. The platform was empty and coming downhill, and swinging didn't really matter because it didn't have any cargo to dump, so Larx's job was done a lot more quickly than the first part. Larx watched the repurposed wheel-well cover coast to a stop in front of the Kia wheel, knowing what happened next.

Aaron had lengthened the loops holding the platform when he'd conceived of the next part of the plan, but Larx still didn't know if this was going to work. He understood tension force more than most, and he knew his scrawny ass dangling from the pulley was going to exert a lot more torque on the wrecked automobile down in this part of the canyon and the fragile human up on what was left of the service road than the fifty pounds, maybe, of supplies.

And he knew his head ached, his back and his arms ached, and the thought of climbing on the platform made everything in his body scream in pain—as did the thought of climbing up without help if they broke the pulley by trying too much.

"Well?" Aaron called.

"I'm thinking!" Larx snapped back, playing for time.

"Do you have any better ideas?" Aaron asked, sounding tired and cranky—and Larx couldn't blame him. It's not like they'd had a whole lot of sleep the night before, and their day had been a doozy.

"Sort of!" Larx called. He sighed and took out the last coil of rope Aaron had left him, in case the wheel-well cover broke or something untoward happened. Larx uncoiled a length of it and created a loop that he stepped into. Using a first responder's video that he'd shown his kids about fifty-dozen times, he created a sitting harness for his legs that would support his weight—if painfully—but would also leave his legs free. Then he looped the rope through one of the handles in front of the makeshift platform and adjusted it until he could stand comfortably, but still take the weight off his legs if he needed to.

Carefully, holding his breath, he let the pulley take his weight and was reassured when he only sank a couple of inches—and the Kia didn't automatically start to shift in response to the force. He stood again and grabbed the butterfly-looped handles and locked his wrists in them, relaxing enough to let his back and neck muscles have some ease before he sat up and pulled himself upright, clenching his core and thigh muscles.

"Ready, Simon?" he called, standing up again.

"Ready, Theodore!" Aaron answered back. "Are you sitting on the platform?"

"No!" Larx called. "But if I need to sit down I can. Just pull!"

He felt Aaron's tug on the pulley and, using that force, began to climb the slope.

It worked. It *hurt*, but not his head as much as his hands and his thighs, which didn't take kindly to the rope harness around them. But it worked. Aaron tugged and Larx walked, using the force from the rope to climb the parts of the slope he could manage, and sitting back and letting Aaron do the work when he couldn't. It wasn't perfect—his muscles trembled, and he had to *fight* not to lose his grip, lose his body integrity, and just to dangle from the rope and be hauled to safety. The footing was treacherous, and the rope caught him more times than he wanted to admit, and he knew, without a doubt, that if he hadn't had the help, he would have slid back down the canyon slope more than once, probably until he gave up and curled into a ball and waited for his head to explode. By the time he crested the edge of what was left of the service track, which wasn't wide enough for a golf cart now, much less a rescue vehicle, every bruise, every muscle, every *hair* on his body ached with the knowledge that he'd been in a car wreck and now was doing very unadvised things with his person in the pursuit of not dying in a pile of rubble midway down the canyon.

It was that last thought that kept him clinging to the rope and helping with every ounce of strength his body possessed as he neared the end of the trip.

Aaron gave him a hand up onto solid ground and helped him step out of the harness before disconnecting the harness from the pulley. Then he guided a wobbly legged Larx to the shady side of the boulder, and both of them sank down into the shade and shared a bottle of Gatorade and a protein bar, not a word between them.

"God, I'm glad you did that," Aaron panted eventually.

Larx examined him, his face saturated with sweat, his shoulders still trembling with the strain. "Harder than you thought?" he asked, his own voice thready with pain and exertion.

"You're right. I wouldn't have been able to haul you up on a gondola without your help," Aaron acknowledged, taking the Gatorade and tilting it up to drain it.

"What kind of flunky are you?" Larx chided, leaning back against the boulder in spite of the fact that it radiated heat like that was the thing's *job*.

"Yeah, yeah," Aaron returned. "I hear you. I'm fired as soon as you can find someone with arms as big around as your head."

Larx chuckled. "Not a chance. You can't get away that easy."

"I tried." They panted some more, and finally their breath slowed. Larx was beginning to wonder if they should start again, when he heard a faint voice from above them. He looked up in time to see another helicopter pass and wonder if it was hovering there to assess the situation.

"George?" came a voice.

"Hawkins!" Aaron answered. "Sorry, man. Taking a rest. How you doing?"

"Out of water," Hawkins responded weakly. "Sorry to bother."

Aaron stood painfully, and Larx joined him. "We got a plan," Aaron called up. "Did you find the perfect tree?"

Aaron and Larx were both staring up the hill when they saw a flutter of fabric next to what did look like the best place for the pulley system, phase two.

"Awesome," Aaron called back. "Give me twenty minutes to set up."

"What do I have to do?" Hawkins called back.

"Catch a ball!" Aaron replied. "One attached to a rope."

"Okay…." The doubt in his voice was very apparent.

"Then wrap the rope around the tree and throw the ball back down!" Aaron called. Hopefully gravity would do the rest with the ball.

Hawkins's cracked laugh told Larx everything he needed to know about the young man's resilience. "Sure! Tell me when!"

"Will do!"

Aaron leaned against the boulder to take his next step, and Larx stopped him. “Break over?” he said.

“Break over.” But that didn’t stop them from pausing, just a moment, to rest their sweaty foreheads together and exchange a brief kiss.

Then they went to work detaching the paracord from the boulder and temporarily dismantling the platform so they could pull the rope up the hill in preparation to start the whole process again.

How to Chuck It

IT TOOK Aaron twelve tries—Larx counted them grimly out loud—to get the damned ball up the hill high enough for Hawkins to land it before it rolled awkwardly down the hill. Part of it was the ball was distorted from the hole Larx had bored through it with the corkscrew attachment of his pocketknife, and part of it was that it was carrying the paracord with it, and that slowed its ascent.

And part of it—Aaron knew it, Larx knew it—was that fifty yards was a once in a week throw, even with a Chuckit, and Aaron's back and shoulders were on fire from all the attempts.

It was finally made possible because Hawkins had stripped off his T-shirt and had scooted to the very edge of where the ball was falling. With Aaron's last throw, he used the shirt to foul it up in the paracord, and *that* was how he managed to get hold of the thing.

"God," Aaron muttered, watching the younger man lean heavily on the tree he'd chosen as a wheel for their makeshift pulley. "He's wounded, Larx. I don't even want to know how bad he's hurting right now."

"Well, he's super smart," Larx said. "And super tough. I'd tell you to poach him from SAC PD, but I might be super jealous."

Aaron let out an amused snort. "He's pining for a musician, of all things. But how'd you know he was gay?"

They were leaning against their friend the boulder for a moment, their end of the rope fastened temporarily to one of the eyebolts while Hawkins ripped some of the bark off the tree so it was less likely to rip the paracord to shreds.

"The look on his face when you kissed my cheek in the waiting room," Larx said, tilting his head back and closing his eyes. Aaron had watched him carefully for slurred speech, for sporadic movements, for so much as an eyelid twitch. Aaron had seen him in pain—and actively babying his head and his upper back and shoulders—but he was praying that Larx's concussion hadn't been made worse by any of their activity over the last part of the day.

Aaron didn't even want to address the knots in his stomach, the stealthy inroads that cold fear kept trying to make in his chest. He was almost glad for the pain of strained muscles and the bruises and small abrasions and the *holy God* fire in his leg for distracting him.

"What did he look like?" Aaron wanted to know.

"Bemused," Larx said. "Happy. Relieved. It was like he had permission to be himself here."

Aaron grunted. "Nice. 'Cause, yeah. I'd love to steal him from Sac. He's smart. He's compassionate, and he has some knowledge of addiction and how to deal with addicts, and I gotta tell you, we've shown ourselves to be way short in that area. I'd *so* make him my deputy if we get out of this alive. I'd take his partner in a heartbeat as well." He paused. "If this doesn't scare the crap out of them."

Larx chuckled weakly. "Well, if this little adventure doesn't scare them off, I'd say ask."

"If we live," Aaron warned darkly.

"Yeah, that too."

Larx's eyes were closed, and Aaron had a sudden fear. "You're not falling asleep, are you?"

"I don't know!" Larx scrunched up his face. "Seriously, Aaron, at this point, I don't know what's concussion, what's being hurt and needing to recover, and what's exhaustion from getting three hours of sleep after my busiest week of the year."

"Is it really, though?" Aaron asked suspiciously. "Is it *really* your busiest week of the year?"

Larx let out a chastened grunt. "It's a tie," he admitted reluctantly. "This week, the week before Christmas, and any one of the first six weeks of school."

Aaron let out a humorless chuckle, and in spite of the discomfort, allowed the boulder's heat to seep through the burning muscles of his shoulders, back, and triceps. Heat therapy. It was a thing, wasn't it?

"Hey, it's not all my fault about the busy-ness thing, right?" Aaron said, laughing a little.

Larx grunted, like he was thinking about saying something.

"What?" Aaron glanced up to where Hawkins was scraping away with what looked to be a pocketknife of his own. "And hurry, because he's almost ready."

"I was thinking of…." Larx grunted. "I hate this. Of sharing custody of AP Physics with a new teacher. Not giving it up entirely, you know, just…."

"Sharing custody," Aaron said, laughing softly. "Without a paycheck, I'm sure."

"I don't get extra for teaching it *now*," Larx shot back. "I just… you know…."

"Really love teaching." Aaron leaned against him, just enough to touch, but hopefully not enough to dislodge either of their hurts or discomforts, or even rub their sweaty, salty, stinging skin together.

"Yeah," Larx said, his shoulders sagging. "I really do. And I never thought I'd love being an administrator, but—"

"You're so good at it," Aaron said. "You… you make a difference either way, but you're *so* good at running the school, making sure the kids are safe, making sure your teachers are supported. You…. I *hope* I make a difference, Larx, but you *really* make a difference. It's okay, you know, to set down a little of the old so you can keep improving with the new."

"Heh."

"What?" Aaron eyed him grumpily. He'd poured his heart into that little speech.

"That's almost a marriage vow. It's like I'm taking a marriage vow to principalship, which is only funny because I *want* to make one to *you*."

"Same," Aaron told him. "But see? I get a competent undersheriff, you get someone to take over AP Physics. They're little things, really, but, you know. They give us a little more of ourselves to, you know, be us."

Larx chuckled again. "You're so functional. I mean, you had a *functional* marriage. You know what mine was."

"Shh…." Larx had said once that he wished Caroline was still alive because as much as *Larx* would have missed having an Aaron in his life, Larx loved knowing that Aaron had been happy with her. Aaron's wish was more complicated. Aaron wished that Larx's first wife, the mother to his girls, had been simply not awful. When Alicia had discovered Larx was bisexual, she'd not only divorced him and hadn't let him see his daughters, she'd taken her vitriol out on the girls. Only Larx's friends from work—and a damned good lawyer—had let him get custody of them. For all Aaron admired how much Larx had done with his life, how well he'd raised the girls—how well he dealt with children and teenagers in general—his one real wish for Larx was that Larx could believe in himself, in his ability to have a relationship, as completely as Aaron did.

"Shh, what?" Larx asked now.

"Your first marriage was not your fault, Larx," Aaron murmured. "And even if it was, you're a different person now. You're *my* person. Have some faith, okay? You've already made plans, it sounds like, to make you and me a priority. I've obviously been thinking about it too, because I do *not* like the thought of leaving the department to Warren in case anything goes wampus again. Have some faith in us, okay?"

Before Larx could answer Hawkins called out, "It's as good as it's going to get, but it's not great! We need a lubricant or—"

Larx said, "Send the motor oil up first."

"God, you're smart," Aaron grunted before standing up and getting to work. The sun wasn't just dipping behind the trees, now; it was flashing almost horizontal through them. If Larx and Aaron weren't going to get up that hill in the next hour, Hawkins and MacDonald were on their own through the night, and Aaron didn't want that to happen. It's not that it would get too cold. It was that both men needed tending to, and Hawkins would likely not be in any shape to help in the morning. It had to be done now or not at all.

THE MOTOR oil did the trick, Larx thought tiredly as they watched the platform of supplies swing its way up the hill. Aaron was doing all the pulling for this one, and Larx wondered how long they'd both have to lounge in the pool to work the kinks out of their backs, necks, and arms.

The thought of sitting, clean and fed and headache-free, in the cool lapping water of Aaron's pool, looking up into the filtered light of the trees above, had become Larx's happy place as the shadows closed in and they worked feverishly to get up to the midpoint of the canyon to look after their fellow humans.

"He's got it!" Aaron rasped, and above them, Hawkins gave a ragged whoop. "Now it's your turn."

"Wait," Larx said, abandoning his pretty fantasy and standing up in the still-sweltering, shadowed and gravel-gritted reality. "Neither you *nor* Hawkins is going to make it if we use the pulley to get to him. I say we fix the rope in place and then you use the rope to climb. Then, when you're done, I do the same thing, but you two can help pull me up if I need it."

Aaron grunted. "And once again, I'm leaving you down here, but now it's in the dark. I hate this plan. I hate it with the white-hot passion of a thousand suns."

Larx gave an uneven laugh. "I know you do, baby. But don't worry. Once we get up there, we dish out some first aid, and then we can sit and rest until morning."

"And then what?"

Larx didn't have to imagine the fraught, petulant crack in Aaron's voice—the words had been echoing in Larx's head the same way.

"We think of something else," Larx soothed. "If nothing else, we have the intact portion of the service track. We get Hawkins and MacDonald down to the service track and just walk up. I get that they're not sending rescue vehicles down—it's a mess. I'm lucky I didn't go over *before* somebody shot out my wheel. *We* can walk, but they need help now. They need to be stabilized and treated—at least with supplies—and we've got to be able to make it up to help them, and that's the best way to conserve our strength."

Aaron took a deep breath, and then another, and nodded. "I hear you. Priorities. See? This is why you're a good administrator—leadership, Principal." He took another deep breath, this one shakier. "Larx," he said, his voice sounding lost and a little thin. "I'm really tired."

Larx swallowed. "I know you are, baby," he said, his eyes burning. "But we've got to do this one more thing, and then it'll be easier. That's why we use the rope as a guide wire and pull ourselves up."

"I know. I just… I couldn't do this alone."

Larx let out a broken laugh and leaned his head against Aaron's chest, mindless of the sweat and crusted dirt. "Yeah, you could. And so could I. But I've got a lot more hope with both of us."

"Yeah."

A heartbeat. Then another. Then Aaron straightened and turned and hollered to Hawkins to fix the rope in place, using the extra rope for the platform.

After a few moments, Hawkins called back, "Done. It's solid. Come on up."

"Should we fix it down here for good luck?" Aaron asked, and Larx shook his head.

"If we're coming back down to the road again tomorrow, we're going to need it."

"Good idea."

And still they didn't move.

"You can do this," Larx whispered.

"And we gotta get a move on."

With that, Aaron kissed the top of Larx's head and, grabbing the rope, which sat shoulder high, began to pull himself up the incline.

Magic Humans and Where to Find Them

"COME ON, baby," Aaron gritted out under the pale yellow sky of late sunset. "Come on. We're almost there."

Larx's suggestion to let Aaron go up first and then for Hawkins and Aaron to help pull Larx up had been the right one. Climbing had been a *lot* easier with the rope and the handles to help leverage himself up, and once he'd gotten there, he and Hawkins had made quick work of hauling Larx up after him.

With a grunt and a *heave*, Larx was almost at the crest of the small rise where the tree stood, and Aaron leaned forward to take Larx's hand and *heave* him up.

"Larx?" Hawkins murmured. "Good to see you again."

Larx took a deep breath. "You too, Detective Hawkins."

Hawkins gave a faint smile on a face that even Aaron could see was moon pale. "Call me Tad," he said softly.

Aaron met Larx's eyes and nodded. "All right, Tad, let's get you somewhere you can sit down. Now that we've got some first aid supplies besides torn shirts, I'd really like to clean and disinfect your wound."

Hawkins almost managed a laugh this time. "Can we just… I don't know… shave off that section of my yab? You know, the entire ass-quarter where the bullet went through? 'Cause right now it's on fire, and I'd like that to stop."

Larx snickered. "I can see why Aaron wants to keep you. No, young Tad, we don't perform mountaintop assectomies, but let's see what other services we might have, okay?"

Larx wrapped his arm around Tad's waist from one side, and Aaron took the other, and together they managed the awkward walk-hop of the injured man up to the fallen pine tree with the four-foot base and found a place that was left of a long-ago snapped-off branch where he could sit.

"Aaron," Larx said, "how about you bring the supplies over, and I'm going to go check on MacDonald."

"I brought him some Gatorade while Aaron was climbing up," Hawkins murmured. "I had to keep him from drinking all of it. I didn't want him to make himself sick."

"Good job," Larx said. Aaron watched his expression do two things at once. The first was to soften, probably as he remembered this kid was a student and that he'd had hope for the kid at one point or another as the kid had attended school. The other was harden, as Larx shored himself up for what was sure to be a painful interaction.

As if to confirm everything Aaron knew about the love of his life, Larx met his eyes. "I'd almost rather climb up the damned hill again."

Aaron grimaced and nodded, and then, embarrassingly enough, bent to help Hawkins off with his pants as Tad leaned up against the tree.

"George?" Hawkins muttered as Aaron peeled off the makeshift bandage they'd tied *over* the wound in the back of his upper thigh before peeling off the khakis under that.

"Yeah?" Aaron grimaced and tried to keep his game face on, just as Larx had.

"If I'm going to work for you in the future, you need to make me a promise."

Aaron could still chuckle, even if the sound was hoarse and raspy. "Never speak of this to another soul?"

"I'm serious," Hawkins begged, leaning his head against his clasped hands in front of him. "That musician's skittish enough as it is."

"I promise not to tell him," Aaron said, grabbing a bottle from the flat and running it over the sticky, oozing wound. "But you might want to. 'Cause, you know, you'd be asking him to move up here and be a part of your life, and I wouldn't want it to come up in conversation and freak him out."

Hawkins let out a pained yowl, and Aaron *shh*ed him and dabbed at the wound with some gauze.

"What makes you think it'll get that serious?" he asked, panting a little.

Aaron grimaced. "'Cause you're up on a mountain, in a life-threatening situation with your pants around your ankles for no fun reason, and you're thinking about him." With that he ran some more water on the wound, hoping the conversation was less painful than the gunshot wound. A .22, he figured, a shotgun wound from a distance. The bullet was in there with nothing to do other than generate infection, and his gut clenched. They had to get this kid to a doctor.

"Maybe I'm just hearing him sing," Hawkins breathed, and Aaron broke out the antibiotic cream, thinking that Neosporin at this juncture was like throwing a bottle of water on an inferno. "In my head, I mean."

"Larx can sing," Aaron told him. "I just found out last night. He'll never be famous, but I'll never hear anyone else sing 'Til Kingdom Come' again."

"Mm." Hawkins breathed *again*. "Pretty song."

"Yeah." Aaron pushed on the wound once more to make it bleed a little to keep it from festering before he gave it one final cleanup and applied the Neosporin. "What's your guy sing?"

"That old Linda Ronstadt song," Hawkins confessed, voice breaking as Aaron did the painful thing. "'Long Long Time'."

"Oh God," Aaron laughed. "That'll rip your heart right out of your body." One more swipe of gauze, and then the antibiotic, spread thickly around. "He give it back yet?"

Hawkins was banging his head softly on his clasped hands. "Working on it," he rasped. "Had to bail on him last night, but I was going to find out if I've got… you know. Hope."

Aaron gave a sigh of relief as he folded up a gauze pad and gently stuck it to the wound. "*Almost done* here," he promised softly. "And hope's good. You keep hoping."

Hawkins breathed in, his voice breaking, and Aaron was glad he didn't have to see the young man's face. Aaron would be screaming—*weeping*—and he wouldn't want anybody to see him like that but Larx.

"Will do," Hawkins all but whispered. "Please tell me we're *all* done."

"Gotta put your pants back on," Aaron told him, surveying the filthy, blood-crusted mess with distaste.

"Fuckin' gross," Hawkins said with feeling.

Aaron managed a smile against his own burning eyes. If they could just get this guy to a hospital, Aaron would poach him from his current job in a heartbeat. As he pulled Hawkins's khakis up and left them to Hawkins to fasten, he looked over his shoulder, barely spotting Larx, squatting in the deep twilight as he spoke soothingly to Curtis MacDonald.

As he rinsed his hands in the remains of the water bottle and dried them on one of three beach towels that had been in the back of the Kia, Aaron thought that as hard as it had been to dress poor Tad Hawkins's wound, maybe Larx had the hardest job of the two of them.

LARX'S HEAD ached. Not popping-off-his-shoulders ache like when the car had first rolled, but a steady, nausea-inducing, ear-ringing ache that stretched across the top of his head and to his shoulders and arrowed down the back of his neck to his spine. He wasn't sure if it was a concussion, lack of sleep, exhaustion, or strained muscles—or some demonic combination of all three—but his vision had blurred as he'd neared the top of the hill, and all he'd wanted to do was to sink down on top of one of the blankets or towels and sleep until his head stopped spinning.

But Curtis MacDonald needed someone, and while Larx wasn't on for dragging the poor kid out from under the tree, he was still the kid's best bet.

"Hey, Curtis," Larx murmured, sinking down on his haunches and pulling out his phone for the light. "How you doing, kid?"

He half expected expletives, or "Fuck off, faggot!" which is what he'd gotten a lot of the time when he and Yoshi had been trying to intervene or get his parents in to show some interest. What he got was, "Not so great, Mr. Larkin. I'm… I'm not feeling so great."

A cold shiver rippled up Larx's back, making his shoulders tense to absolute screaming levels, and he tried to calm his breathing.

"Well, kid, I need you to help me out here," Larx murmured. He smelled the old urine—and the old vomit—but maybe it was all the shocks of the day that made the smell not quite so overwhelming. Maybe it was the pine dust and Larx's own BO too. Either way, Larx was grateful. "I need you to wriggle out from under the log so we can take a look at you."

"I'm coated in dirt," Curtis whimpered, as though he'd been reading Larx's mind. "I smell awful."

"Can't argue," Larx told him, because the truth was a good thing, right? "But I'm not a bouquet of roses myself."

Curtis let out a sob or a laugh—his voice was muffled against the ground in the hollow of the tree. "Funny, Mr. L," he muttered. "Always funny. You forget that when you get so mad, you know? Always funny."

Larx felt another frisson of fear rack up his spine. "Curtis, you're being awfully nice for a guy in withdrawal. Is there any way you could, you know, roll out from under the tree so I can see if there's anything but smell left to you, boy? We've gone to an awful lot of trouble to find you. It would be great if we could get you some help, get you some rehab, make a fresh start after all this."

Curtis's shoulders began to shake—but not hard. Like he didn't have a lot of strength left. "Shakes all shaked out, Mr. L," Curtis mumbled. "I'm just so tired… so sad."

Larx reached under the log, heedless of his own fears of crawling things and snakes, and squeezed Curtis's upper arm. "I know you are, son," he said softly. "That's why we were worried. You've been sad for a long, long time."

"Remember when I was on the football team?" Curtis asked plaintively. "I did so good. Then I couldn't keep my stupid mouth shut and you had to bench me?"

"Yeah, I remember," Larx murmured. That had been such a hard decision, but Curtis had been the one to make it. There had been scouts in the audience, some of them looking at Isaiah, some at Kellan, and some, yes, at Curtis. It could have meant a lot to his future if Larx had let him play, but the damage to the team hearing Curtis sound off his racist, bigoted, divisive mouth when he was representing their school—and them—had been incalculable.

"My pa… took a lot of blood from my hide that week. And then he used all those same words about you, about the coach, about the other team."

"Yeah," Larx told him, squeezing his arm with gentle insistence. "It's hard to do good things when you've got a bad example in front of you—I know that."

"I… I was so lost after that. And so sad. And then Uncle Clancy told Uncle Percy to take me on a job. Dad didn't want him to, but Clancy—he's the judge, right? So one day Percy said, 'C'mon, kid, I'll give you something that'll cheer you up.' And it did."

Larx, who had held onto his lunch for so much of the day—or at least held onto his breakfast and a midafternoon protein bar—felt the sudden urge to get sick. Only knowing he'd be adding to the already fragrant bouquet of body fluids drifting from poor Curtis MacDonald kept his control over his own stomach intact.

"That was a shitty thing to do," Larx said softly. "Did your father know? About you taking the taste?"

"He must have." Curtis let out another little sob, and Larx cursed the almost complete lack of light. He couldn't see the boy's face, couldn't see his body, really. Was he hurt? Could he actually move *out* from under the tree? Was he part of the scree and the decomposed granite now? A teenaged troll, forever locked in the most miserable part of his life?

"What makes you say that?" Larx asked.

"He and Percy and Clancy were running the business," Curtis said with another sob. "I told them I had track and tried to stay out of their way, but… but I'd already tasted the candy, right?"

Larx let out a growl. All that stupid wasted time, trying to tell Billy MacDonald they were *worried* about his son, and Billy was the one who had participated in dragging the boy to hell.

"I want some candy," Curtis mewled, his cogency fading in withdrawal psychosis. "I want to die."

Larx's breath caught, and he wondered if maybe Curtis had wedged himself under the tree for a *reason*. "Curtis," he said softly, "why won't you come out from under the tree?"

"Fell off a cliff, Mr. Larkin," Curtis mumbled. "One minute, high as a kite. Dad shows up, drags me out, and there's guns everywhere, and I'm falling. Flying. Felt so good to fly."

Larx remembered those terrifying, tumbling moments in the SUV. "Landing sucks, though," he said with feeling.

"So bad," Curtis agreed. "I don't want to come out. I could land again." He let out a choked little sob. "My shoulder hurts. Why is that?"

"I don't know," Larx said, out of ideas. "You'd have to come out of there so I could see it, right?"

"No," Curtis wept. "No, no, no, no… leave me here to die, okay?"

Larx thought about the last hours, as he and Aaron worked, planned, sweated, and bled to get even halfway up the damned canyon wall to bring this kid some Gatorade.

"Curtis, I haven't given up on you in four goddamned years—do you really think I'm giving up now?"

But all he heard were Curtis MacDonald's soft sobs as the poor kid poured out his heart on the unforgiving rocky earth.

"Here, baby," Aaron murmured. "Sit."

Larx felt himself helped onto the wheel-well cover before Aaron put one of the beach towels over his knees. Hawkins sat next, leaning a little against Larx, and then Aaron passed out more Gatorade and some power bars.

One of the Gatorade bottles he put in front of Curtis's blank hole under the tree. The kid must have wriggled further under, and the darkness was nearly complete now, leaving Larx wondering if the earth really would swallow the kid up. Sadly, he remembered football season, when Curtis carried maybe 250 pounds of pure adolescent muscle. He'd lost so much weight this semester, Larx could almost imagine him sliding under the tree completely, like a worm or a beetle, to become part of the rocky terrain.

Maybe it would be a blessing, but Larx wasn't sure that kind of magic existed. He'd never seen it, so he wasn't going to count on it, right?

His attention was pulled as Aaron, judging where MacDonald's head was (and pointing and shrugging so Larx could tell him yes or no), left a space for Curtis to look out from before sitting down on the other side of that space and taking his own dinner such as it was.

Larx felt the day thud down on him like a wet bag of sand, and he almost whimpered. "Aaron?"

"Yeah?"

"I can't remember if it's time for a Tylenol or not, and my whole body hurts, and my head's going to pop off like a zit."

Aaron let out a humorless chuckle. "Then it's probably time for a Tylenol."

"I don't know. Have we been climbing the damned mountain for six hours?"

Even in the dark, Larx could see Aaron scrubbing his face with his hands. "You know, I have no idea."

They both chuckled then—and so did Hawkins, because Larx was sure those hours weren't a picnic for him, either—and then Aaron's voice sharpened.

"Larx?"

"Yeah?"

"What the fuck is that?"

"I beg your pardon?" Larx asked, squinting in the darkness. All he got for his trouble as he stared toward Aaron's voice was a lot of white spots dancing in front of his eyes and some sort of ambient light from… from….

Slowly, Larx turned his head toward the edge of the canyon that had spilled over that morning, dumping Aaron and Hawkins down when this whole ordeal began.

"No, seriously," Larx muttered. "What the fuck *is* that?"

The question was followed by an electric flickering, like a generator switching on, and then suddenly a giant cage light clicked on, raining daylight on their little portion of the canyon.

They all stared up to the edge, and somebody adjusted the light so it wasn't just in their faces.

Larx saw a pale face peering over the lip of the canyon, and his heart leapt and then plummeted and then raced.

"Christi?" Aaron called, his voice sounding a lot like Larx's heart.

"Christi-lu-lu-belle," Larx yelled, heedless of the sound exploding between his ears, "get the hell away from the edge of that fucking canyon!"

Christi's laugh was sort of a tinkle, even though she was obviously projecting her voice. "Oh, Daddy—don't trip! I'm on a harness attached to a couple of trees. I'm good."

Larx and Aaron stared at each other, at a complete loss.

"She's good?" Aaron said, his voice rising at the end. "I've raised two girls, and I swear, it's not girls—it's *that* one. I'm surprised you're still alive!"

"Yeah, not dead yet," Larx muttered, but then he addressed his daughter, whom, it appeared, was *hovering*, apparently suspended, just like she'd claimed. "Christi, what in the hell!" He'd wanted to say more, but he was shouting, and that hurt his head, and he was too torn between amazement, joy, and fear. Goddammit, what was she doing there?

"We have a plan!" she said excitedly. "A good one! But we had to get equipment, and the right people from search and rescue. It took forever to get organized." She let out a giggle and—although she was lying horizontally, the better to talk to them, Larx assumed—she wiggled her body so she could swing a little on her apparatus.

"Christi!" Kirby's voice came thinly through the dark. "Give it a rest! Olivia's having a heart attack!"

"She's just mad because she's too pregnant to be the one out here!" Christi hollered.

"Why does that matter?" Hawkins asked, and Larx eyed the younger man with amusement.

"Because Christi's harness is attached to trees," Larx said. "More likely tree *limbs*, because a full-grown pine tree is fine with a grown man in the branches. They needed to keep weight off the lip of the canyon so it wouldn't crumble on top of us."

Hawkins grimaced. "Is there any way we could just… I dunno, *fill this place in* or something?"

"With what?" Larx asked, having a sudden doubt for Hawkins's fitness to have Aaron's back.

"Never mind," Hawkins muttered. "Dumb question. Have I mentioned pain and blood loss?"

And like that he was forgiven. "No worries," Larx said. "I mean, that's my *kid* swinging from the branches up there. Obviously my family isn't a brain trust."

"I heard that, Daddy!" Christi chimed, levitating some more, and Larx had to wonder at the acoustics of the canyon. "We *are* a brain trust. Me, Livvy, Mau-Mau, the icky boys—we've got a way to get you out!"

Larx grunted, and stared again at the light. "Right now?" he asked, because he thought that if that had been the case, they'd already be sending people or baskets down.

Christi frowned and looked over her shoulder, then scowled. "Tomorrow!" she called back. "Too dark. Too many variables. Are there any severe injuries?"

"Hawkins was shot!" Aaron called. "It's a flesh wound, but he needs medical attention! MacDonald is in withdrawal, but…." He and Larx looked at each other and Aaron shrugged. "We can't get him out from under the tree," Aaron called, sounding baffled.

"Seriously?" Christi asked.

"He's wrecked, baby," Larx shouted, his head ringing.

"And your father has a concussion!" Aaron added.

Larx was grateful. His throat was raw as it was.

Christi turned and said something to somebody behind her, and Larx recognized his baby when she was turning pit bull on somebody. She turned back around to face them and said, quite succinctly, “Well, shit.”

“Still tomorrow?” Larx prodded gently.

“They can lower a care package!” she shouted back. “Antibiotics?”

“You allergic to anything?” Aaron asked Hawkins.

“Penicillin’s fine,” Hawkins replied.

“Penicillin!” Aaron called. “Clothes for MacDonald.”

“Maybe a sedative for MacDonald,” Tad said, surprising Larx. “The worst thing about meth withdrawal is the psychosis. If we could calm him down, chill him out some, we might get him out from under the tree.”

“Injection,” Larx murmured, thinking about how hard it would be to get Curtis to take medicine in the state he was in now. “We need to get him somewhere safe before we try to get inside his head.”

“Word,” Tad murmured, and Aaron called up the order.

“And wound irrigation for you *and* Tad,” Larx said. “And antibiotics for you too.”

“Oh my God,” Aaron burst out. “This is why I end up going to the grocery store for two things necessary for dinner and getting yelled at because I forgot ballpoint pens.”

“Don’t worry!” Christiana called to them, obviously hearing Aaron but not Larx. “The guys are taking notes.”

Larx elbowed Aaron in the side. “Did you get antibiotics and wound irrigation for two?” Aaron called out.

“Yeah, Aaron—and way to drop the ball about your own ouchie. Kirby’s gonna have words.”

“I look forward to hearing them,” Aaron called, in that tone that said he’d pretty much hit his last nerve on the matter.

Larx shivered and realized they’d better wrap this up. If nothing else, his *daughter* was hovering above this cursed canyon like a *wraith*, and he wanted her back—*way* back—on solid ground.

“Anything else, Dads?” Christi called.

“I could use a sweater,” Larx told him, looking at the ragged bottom of his shirt. The ends were still wrapped around his hands, and Aaron—who had sacrificed his overshirt to bandages and half his undershirt to his own buffers against the paracord—nodded.

"Sweaters and sweats all around!" Aaron called back. And then, as though aware he'd done an awful lot that day on power bars and Gatorade, he added, "And *food*!"

Even from the distance, through the trees, they could see Christi smile. "Burgers all around!" she hollered. She grew sober again. "I'm gonna disappear so they go get you stuff and use the pulleys, but hold on! We haven't forgotten you!"

"Thanks, baby!" Larx called, and waving madly she was tugged back, probably to more solid ground where she could stand up.

"Your kid?" Hawkins asked, sounding bemused.

"Yeah. She's a magic human." Larx's heart swelled in his chest. All of them, he was certain. Christi, Olivia, Maureen—and the "icky boys," he was sure, included Kirby, Kellan, and probably Elton, Jaime, and Berto too. Maybe even Yoshi.

"I've heard of those," Hawkins said. "But she's the first one I've met."

Aaron and Larx both let loose broken chuckles, and although the evening chill blew a cold breath over them, Larx was pretty sure he could survive it. Help. There was help on the way, and their family was leading the charge.

We Are….

THE INDIGNITY of being made to stay in the minivan with her feet up while everybody else ran around and gave directions and suggestions was enough to make Olivia go into labor *right then*, spit out the tiny human inside her, and jump into the family confusion to help get the dads out of trouble.

But her ankles were the size of grapefruits, and the doctor had spoken direly of her getting rest and good food and watching her blood pressure or she'd be going on bedrest for the next four to six weeks.

Fucking. Bogus.

Somebody needed to ride herd on the "icky boys," as Christi had been calling them. Olivia was living in fear that Jaime would find some reason to just fall off the edge of the canyon and roll down the cliff because Larx and Aaron had done it and they could do no wrong. She'd put Elton and Berto in charge of them, but gah! So many teenage boys, so much potential for trouble! And then—oh fuck it all—*Christi* had been the one who'd volunteered for the harness to talk to the people down below.

A thing that was all Larx's fault, whether or not he knew it. Apparently, search and rescue had made a couple of passes over the canyon, unable to land or even get close lest they start a hail of gravel shrapnel with their rotor wash. What had gotten back to the people who had set up their little op center in the OR waiting room was old hat to people who knew Larx and Aaron, but *very* interesting to the rest of the world.

"The fuck is that?" one of the older rangers had asked gruffly, shoving a tablet in front of Olivia.

"It's a pulley," she said, glancing at the picture on it. "And that's—oh! They set up a pulley to move the supplies Dad keeps in the Kia up the hill. See? It looks like—" She paused. "Oh for fuck's sake, Elton, would you believe he found a use for those damned eyebolts we bought for the shit in the garage?"

Elton laughed and looked over her shoulder. "And the five-zillion yards of paracord."

"And the… what is that, do you think?" she asked.

"The flat board thing that… you know, goes over the tire?" Kirby muttered, looking over Elton's shoulder. Their personal boundaries, such as they had never been, had gone completely out the window as the day had progressed. Olivia wasn't sure she could sleep again without a member of what was now her immediate family somewhere on her lap.

"Yeah," Elton said and then looked up, his round face under his perpetual scruff wreathed in a smile. "Babe, your dad, man. Wicked smart."

"And my dad's muscle," Kirby said, backing up enough to flex.

They were laughing because they were *relieved.* Whatever was going on in the canyon, they were doing well enough to make it to what was left of the service track.

As the afternoon progressed and Yoshi, Corbin Baker, Mandeep Singh, and Rodney Smith—the man in charge of Colton's largely volunteer search and rescue—had begun to make calls, their plan inspired by Larx's Rube Goldberg-like pulley systems, Olivia knew she would treasure that image on her phone forever.

Knowing that Larx and Aaron were doing well enough to engineer their own help gave her hope that their little think tank could give them a final hand up the mountain.

But the equipment they needed—from the cage lights to the harness system to the winch and pulley and flatbed truck—all had to come from somewhere, and it had to be transported up the freeway and then along the winding road to Colton.

And then, in the slanting light of the afternoon shadows, it had to be set up.

Search and rescue had been good about consulting Singh and Baker—and even *all* of Larx's physics-savvy kids—about strategy and equipment, but in the end they'd needed somebody light and agile to ride the harness over the edge of the canyon to talk to Larx.

Jaime had wanted to go, but Olivia, through Elton *and* Berto, had put the kibosh on that, because they needed somebody who could communicate in a straight line.

And since—as Christi frequently reminded her—Olivia was bigger than two houses and an elephant right now, that meant Christi.

After helping to direct an electrician in a cherry picker that *barely* reached as far as they needed it to, Olivia had watched her sister step into one of those theater suits that they used to fly Peter Pan across stage and had seen spots in front of her eyes.

Elton, never far from her side, had helped her to the minivan before she'd chivvied him back to the thick of it with all the engineers and search and rescue people to report back what he saw. She hated this. She sat sideways on the middle bench seat, her back against the door, and rubbed her tummy and felt the baby kick—probably in protest of a couple of long-assed days—as she ate an apple and some crackers and wished for news, any news, and something to do.

She was about to get up again, because fuck *this*, when Maureen walked over to sit in the driver's seat and look out into the darkness, where Christi was lit up like a moth.

"She's amazing, your sister," Maureen said softly.

"She's always been like that," Olivia told her, a little jealous but mostly proud. "Christi can make things better. I don't know how she can do that."

Maureen gave a discordant laugh. "Count your blessings," she said. "Remember *my* sister is Tiffany, and we hate her."

Olivia sobered. Aaron's oldest daughter had been the only member of their family who had let prejudice color her reaction to Aaron and Larx's relationship. Olivia had been having her own problems when that situation had fallen out, but she realized now, looking at Christi, how much it must have hurt Aaron and his other children.

"I'm sorry," she said sincerely.

"Don't be," Maureen told her, with a bitter little laugh that didn't sound like Aaron's usually optimistic daughter. "Tiff and I—we were never as close as you and your sister. I… you're both so nice to me. I find myself wishing I'd grown up with you instead."

"You had a mother," Olivia said softly. "A good one." Hers and Christi's mother had *not* been good. Olivia knew now that she'd been mentally ill—and more than a little bit bigoted. When Larx had come out as bisexual, her reaction hadn't just been to leave her husband, but to also neglect his children. He'd fought bitterly for custody, and when he'd gotten it, he hadn't, even once, Olivia knew, taken his daughters' love for granted.

They wouldn't trade Larx for all the mothers in the world, but now, as Olivia approached motherhood herself, she was… well, wistful. Like Mau-Mau had been when talking about their sisterhood.

"We did," Maureen acknowledged quietly. "But that doesn't mean you don't know how to be a good parent."

Olivia gave a short bark of laughter. "With Larx around? No. We've had a good role model. Still… I'm… you know." She shrugged and watched as Christi's animation from 100 yards away lit up the night.

"Apprehensive," Maureen said loftily.

Olivia chuckled. Oh, their family meshed so nicely. There was something to be said for being able to laugh when things got grim. "Look at her," she murmured, and she knew Mau was doing exactly that. "I'm a little freaked-out looking at her. What do you think Larx and Aaron are doing?"

Mau let out a tired cackle. "Oh, they're trying not to lose their shit."

"Yeah," Olivia murmured, rubbing her stomach. The baby kicked back playfully, and she thought about the little human inside her. "That's what parenthood is. For the rest of your life. I don't think apprehensive is a strong enough word."

"Mm." Mau glanced away from Christi to meet Olivia's eyes. "My mother's parents are awful," she said. "And my dad's parents have passed on. You have Larx and Aaron as grandparents, and a whole slew of aunts and uncles who are *dying* to be part of your baby's life. I know nothing can make that—" She waved at Christi without looking at her, which Olivia wished *she* could have done because her maniac sister was bouncing around like she wasn't being suspended by pine boughs and a prayer. "—any easier, but, you know. You'll have help. Our dads didn't. I… I'm sort of impressed by the way they worked to give *us* the young adulthood they never got."

Olivia thought of all of it: The icky boys running around trying to save the dads, Uncle Yoshi rounding up the smartest people he knew, Christi playing the dancing sprite on a jury-rigged pulley system that may or may not send her crashing into the canyon.

"Think they knew what they were doing?" she asked, hysterical laughter bubbling up inside of her.

"Not even a little," Mau cackled.

Olivia liked her new stepsister's laugh. It told her they could be friends now, even though they'd run in different circles in high school.

As they watched, Christi waved madly and got hauled back—and back farther—onto solid ground, and Olivia found herself drawing her first full breath since they'd outfitted Christi to fly. Christi turned and spoke to the group of people gathered around her, and Elton and Berto broke away. Elton was scribbling madly on a pad of yellow paper, and he and Berto were talking in low tones.

As they drew near, Maureen went to hop out of the minivan, and Elton held up his hand, indicating she should stay.

"What's up?" Olivia asked, turning on the bench seat so he could sit next to her. He was wearing a denim jacket over his T-shirt and jeans, and she realized how chilly it had gotten outside the car.

"We need you and Mau to put together a care package," Elton said, after giving her a gentle kiss—not a peck on the cheek but a "speaking kiss" on the lips that said he wanted to touch her. "Yoshi's calling ahead to the hospital. They need some supplies, outlined here, but the hospital will know what to give you. We need sweaters and sweats for everybody, and probably pillows and blankets and sleeping bags too. And food. Christi promised burgers. Kirby's calling the burger place with an order, and I think they're making extra for…." He waved a hand, and Olivia had a burst of pity for the people who had probably been planning to close in an hour or two. "And the animals need looking after." Elton paused and looked at Olivia with too much gentleness in his eyes.

"Don't say it," she warned, but her voice broke fractiously, probably because she was exhausted.

"We're sending Maureen, so after you and Berto round everything up from Larx and Aaron's house, he can go check on our place and you can take your meds and get some rest."

"Elton!" she protested, but her eyes were burning and actual tears were falling and *fuck* this pregnancy shit, and *fuck* her body for not having the resilience it should have and *double fuck* her hormones and her brain chemistry because she *needed* her meds and her sleep, dammit, or she would be one big emo roller-coaster ride without a restraining device, and her family needed her *sane*.

"Berto can go get our dogs and bring them to Larx and Aaron's house, babe," Elton told her. "You can see the dogs, get your meds, rest."

"I should have gotten them this morning—"

"You didn't know this was going to happen," he said, his own voice rising in hysterical laughter. "Babe, this has been a fuckin' *day*. Go home. Take care of yourself. Take care of the squid." He touched her belly lightly because she didn't always appreciate that, and she laced their fingers together and pressed down so he could feel the acrobatics.

"Squidward's been busy," she told him, her voice losing some of the tears.

"Wait until you feed it something besides apples and crackers," Elton said, nodding emphatically. "See?" He sobered. "Go take care of the both of you, and I'll come get you before they go to pull them out. The kids'll probably sleep here. Pick a car, any car, right?" He grimaced. "And can I just say, if your dad wasn't such an awesome guy, I would *really* be pissed about the Kia. Babe. We're still paying it off. Does insurance cover 'father-in-law-falls-into-canyon'?"

She laughed helplessly. "Maybe we can get Aaron's department to replace it," she said with some optimism.

"That's the spirit." He smiled slightly, his round, scruffy face looking adult and in charge when a year ago she could have sworn this sweet young man was neither of those things, as appealing as she'd found him. "So let's get started on the care package, you go rest and get some food and medication, and I'll come get you in the morning, 'kay?"

"Yeah," she conceded, reluctant but, well, following Elton's example. If he could be a grown-up, she could. She kissed him tenderly, ignoring their audience, and then pulled back. "Anything you want me to send?"

"I'll take a sweatshirt," he told her, shivering. "The jacket isn't cutting it. And some camp chairs would be *awesome*."

"Ooh," she said, eyes widening. "We've got a whole bench from when Larx was coaching track. I've got your back, honey."

"Thanks, babe."

She stopped him before he was about to go. "How'd she say they looked?" she asked.

Elton shrugged. "They could see more of her than she could see of them," he said. "The trees were in the way. The detective was in the worst shape. She said the lights showed his pants were soaked with old blood. Aaron has a wound on his leg—his shin, wrapping around his calf and probably up the side or back to his thigh. And Larx has a concussion. He didn't talk to her as much so he wouldn't have to yell. It makes sense. He was depending on the pulleys a *lot* to go up those hills, and you know, that's not your dad."

"But the pulley to help him up is definitely him," she said, determined to hope more than worry. "God, Elton. I will never be that smart."

"He didn't build the pulley by himself, babe. It took two." And with that, Elton kissed her cheek and slid out of the car, and they were on their way.

FOLLOWING ELTON'S texted directions, they pulled up to the main entrance of the hospital and Mau ran inside to get the supplies Yoshi had radioed for.

After about ten minutes, she came out with a small soft-sided cooler and two people Olivia had never seen.

One was a worn, thin woman not much older than Maureen and Olivia, and the other was a man in his late twenties with a heartbreak-handsome face under his scruff and half a blond ponytail pulled behind his head.

"Guys," Mau said, "this is Guthrie and Avril. They have apparently been sent all over the damned town today looking for Detective Hawkins. They're tired, they're hungry, and they need some explanation, but since we're on a time crunch, I figured Olivia could go with Guthrie, and Avril could come with me and Berto, and we could explain and go fetch food at the same time."

"Food," Guthrie said with feeling. "*So* appreciated."

"I'll call the burger place," Mau said.

"How about we go to my place first and start rounding up clothes and stuff. That way, you guys just have to load them in the minivan." Suddenly these strangers seemed more like help, and Olivia was all for that.

"Cool." Maureen blew out a breath, and Olivia could tell *she* was glad not to be doing this alone either. "But Guthrie needs a local to tell him where to go."

Olivia nodded and slid out of the minivan with a yawn. "Lead me to your metal steed, Sir Guthrie," she said, still yawning. "I'll be your guide in this strange and foreign land." She was so tired she was babbling, but when she thought she'd have to tone it down before she scared people, Guthrie, with the grace of a troubadour, bowed and extended his hand.

"Follow me, milady," he said playfully, "and we shall quest for food and shelter."

Olivia laughed, some of her exhaustion lifting. "You guys stop for food," she said. "Guthrie looks healthy and nimble. We can have the shit out of the garage and the clothes ready by the time you get to the house."

"Nimble," Guthrie said, sounding delighted. "Did you hear that, April? I'm *nimble*."

April let out a quiet laugh that sounded a lot like Olivia felt—on her last nerve. Berto, recovering from some severe PTSD, sounded like that when there had been too much stimulation for too long a time. Olivia and Maureen met eyes, and it felt like the sisterhood thing really clicked because Maureen lowered her voice.

"Don't worry, April," she said, correcting the name. "If you're done with talking, you can sit in the minivan, and we'll keep it quiet until you've had some time to decompress."

The relief and gratitude on April's face told Olivia they'd been right.

Olivia followed Guthrie as Maureen situated his friend, and in a moment, Guthrie was helping her into his giant battered Chevy truck.

It occurred to Olivia that she didn't know who the guy was from Adam, but she wasn't afraid in the least.

"I'm sorry," she said, after she'd directed Guthrie toward Larx's home. "I don't know Detective Hawkins. Are you his brother?"

Guthrie let out a sharp bark of laughter. "Uhm, no. I'm a… friend. Just a friend. I don't even know what happened. Can you—how are you and that nice crazy redheaded woman who just ran into the hospital and started buzzing like a bee related. And related to Tad?"

Olivia's bark of laughter was just as sharp. "Okay, so, for starters. Mau and I are, well, stepsisters, sort of. Our dads are a couple. *Her* dad is the local undersheriff. *My* dad is the local high school principal. This whole thing started when they were looking for a kid who didn't graduate… yesterday? Was it only yesterday? Yeah. Yesterday. Go left in a few hundred feet. Watch for it—there's no markers."

"Thanks for that," Guthrie said, following her directions. "Okay, good. So your dads are dating?"

"Living together," Olivia corrected.

"And that's just… that's okay here?"

Olivia grunted. "It's had its moments. But, well, Mau's dad is one of the good guys—and my dad is sort of… well, you'll have to meet him. Once we get them out of the canyon."

Guthrie blew out a breath. "And now you lost me."

Olivia went back and explained the entire thing—including what Detective Hawkins had to do with all of it—and Guthrie's worried expression told her that the young detective meant a whole lot to him.

"They're just… stuck there," he said when she was done. "Like, wounded and hurt and… we can't do *anything*?"

She had to swallow back her defensiveness. "Well we *are* doing something, aren't we?" she told him. "We're getting them supplies tonight so they're in better shape in the morning when we pull them out."

"Why can't we pull them out *now*?" Guthrie asked, his voice cracking a bit, and she knew her voice wasn't far behind.

"Because it's going to be a near thing whether or not we drag the canyon down on top of them, and the rest of my family with it!" she replied. "Do you—you weren't *there*! My little sister jumped in a Peter Pan suit and got suspended by *trees* to talk to them and tell them it was going to be okay. She was just swinging out there in the darkness, and I had to watch that shit because I'm *pregnant* and *fat* and my blood pressure is *stupid*. And we still couldn't pull them up. We just—the dads will take care of your guy, I swear. I…. God, I don't know what'll happen to Curtis because meth is *bad*, and he's under a goddamned *tree*. But… here—pull into the driveway here," she said, and Guthrie almost slid to a halt in the driveway of the house she'd grown up in, the home she refused to relinquish, even if she was building one of her own as unique as Larx's own vision of home.

It was a plain two-story, with a set of soft chairs, a fireplace that cut off part of the back entryway from the tiny dining room for no reason at all, and a kitchen that should have been updated ten years before they moved in. But the outside was covered in regional wildflowers, including giant morning glories that grew on a frieze Larx had installed to shade the walkway, and paving stones he'd probably made Aaron carry for him from the back of the minivan. The lawn was actually lawn, which was rough in this climate and with this soil, and she knew for certain that the garden in the backyard was a wealth of rich imported soil and sturdily constructed planting boxes, the riotous growth contained enough to keep anarchy from becoming entropy. Everything about the place from the outdated brick façade to the new coat of paint on the windowsills and gutters made her heart warm, her body unfurl, her anxiety ease.

Guthrie killed the motor and said, "Nice," into the sudden silence.

"Elton and I live in Aaron's old house," she told him. "It's about two miles away by the service track that runs behind them both. But yeah. After Larx got custody of Christi and me, we moved here." Some of the tension eased out of her face, her back. "Dozer, Aaron's dog, is probably eating the door by now. I need to go let him out the back."

"Does he eat musicians?" Guthrie asked, and she slid out of the truck, laughing shortly.

"Is that what you are? No. Musician is not on the menu. As far as I know he wouldn't even eat intruders, but don't tell anybody that. We like to keep up the pretense."

"Fair," Guthrie said and followed her to the door.

Once inside, she greeted Dozer by "letting" him stand on his hindlegs and give her a full-length hug, pregnancy belly and all, and rubbing his ears and telling him he was a good, handsome boy, and everybody missed him, and they would all be home tomorrow. The day alone must have made him worry, because that hug lasted longer than expected—and she found herself wrapping her arms around his blond, furry retriever body and hugging the dog like she would Larx or Aaron. Dozer whimpered into her shoulder and dropped reluctantly down, following her to the back door so he could go outside and pee.

As he went outside, the cats all slid inside, slithering around her ankles for food. Oh, she missed *her* cat, the battered mostly-Siamese goddess who had kept her calm and sane during her teenaged years. But Delilah was gone, and life kept going, and now there was Dozer and these three idiot cats that Olivia loved as much.

"Nice," Guthrie said, squatting down to pet Trigger, the enormous ginger tom Christi had stolen from a neglectful neighbor near the grade school. (She'd told Larx he'd followed her home, and as far as Olivia knew, he was still buying that.)

"You have a cat?" she asked.

He grunted, and changed his attention to Trixie, the six-pound-wonder calico that Christi had taken from a kitten box in front of the grocery store when Olivia was supposed to be watching her. Olivia had claimed to not have *any idea* how Christi had gotten that kitten, but the truth was, she'd been as helpless as Larx to tell her sister no.

"No," he murmured, letting Trixie sniff his fingers before smoothing back her whiskers. "I got a day job, and I take gigs and sleep on people's couches and shit. It's… it's no damned good for having a cat."

Olivia paused and took a chance. "Or a boyfriend," she added softly.

Guthrie gave her a guilty look. "Or a boyfriend," he murmured.

"But you came," she said.

Toby, a female long-haired torti, started bumping up against his free hand as it dangled by his knee. "I did," he said, mostly to Toby. "He was supposed to show up to my gig last night, but he called to say he couldn't make it. This morning his sister showed up at my work just… freaked the fuck out. Said something about a shooting, and she couldn't get her brother on the phone, and…." He took a deep breath, and she saw that he was wearing a red flannel shirt over some sort of service polo and a pair of jeans, and she knew with a pang what he'd say next. "And I just walked out on the best day job I ever had. Told them I'd be out for a few days, and we drove up here." He scrubbed his face with his hand before dropping back down to pay attention to the damned love sponge who had apparently *never* been loved before, not by the three teenagers and two adults who lived here currently, and obviously not in her five years of existence previous. What a slut.

"Surprised yourself?" she asked, remembering when Elton had shown up that February, and she'd been torn between absolute joy at seeing him and absolute despair because she was a *wreck*.

"Yeah," he said, his voice low. "I… I didn't think I was there yet. Didn't think I'd *ever* be there. And suddenly…."

"Seeing his face was the one thing that was going to keep your world from turning black," she said, and he glanced up at her.

"Yeah," he said again. "I…." He stood, like the sudden movement would hide his heart behind a wall. "Tell me what to get out of the garage. I can throw it in the back of the truck, and we can make them comfy for the night."

"Fair," she said with a sigh. It was a change in plan—a streamlining—and that was good. But she'd felt an affinity for this pretty young man with the guarded heart and wanted to keep talking. "I'll go through their drawers for some old clothes. How big's your guy? Larx is midsized. Aaron's a little bigger."

Guthrie shook his head and shrugged out of the flannel shirt he was wearing, obviously too big for him. It hit Olivia that the shirt wasn't his.

"Put this in the basket," he said, without elaboration.

When she went rooting through drawers, she visited Kirby's room, because the boy was tall but still rangy, a little like Guthrie. Quietly, as he paused in the act of throwing sleeping bags and camp chairs into the back of his truck, she handed him one of Kirby's old sweaters and said, "For you. It'll get cold up there." She'd also packed a knapsack for all the teenagers because nobody had shown up at the hospital that day with the plan of camping out above Daffodil Canyon.

She was hauling a flat of water from the garage to the truck when Guthrie turned to her in exasperation.

"Oh for fuck's sake—go sit down. Go pet the ginormous dog. Order me around, okay? I'd love to do something today besides drive, worry, and convert oxygen into CO2."

She laughed a little and gave him the case. "Fine. When you're done, there's some Gatorade in here, and a lot of sandwich fixins we can put in the bear-proof box to fill in the corners."

Guthrie grunted. "I thought the others were stopping for burgers—"

"Three teenagers, three *teachers*, and a shit-ton of useless search and rescue people who think they're helping. They'll descend like locusts."

"Also, *bear-proof*?"

She laughed. "Welcome to the mountains, Guthrie. I'll be inside with my feet up." She really was exhausted, and her back ached, and her ankles hurt, and *she* was starving. By the time Guthrie was done loading all the rest of the stuff, she was sitting on her father's favorite recliner with Dozer on the love seat next to her, so he could rest his chin in her lap. She held a plasticware container of one of the casseroles from the day before that she was eating cold with a fork, because fuck hamburgers, she was hungry *now*.

When Guthrie came in and shooed away Dozer, she handed him the bowl with a spare plastic fork, which he took gratefully, *taking his own bite*. "This's goo'," he mumbled through a mouthful. "You make it?"

She shook her head. "No. We had a giant graduation party at Aaron's old house yesterday—it's got a pool. Half the town kicked in for food to make sure the kids had a good time. The idea that we don't have to cook for a week has never seemed so heavenly."

"Mm…." He took a few more bites and passed the bowl back to her.

She grinned and scooped more food into her mouth. "Rosie's basic scrap meat and potato chips," she said, like a connoisseur. "You lucked out. I grabbed the good stuff."

He chuckled softly and took the empty bowl from her. "Whole town participated?" he asked.

"High school graduation is a big thing up here," she told him honestly. "There's enough kids who will go on to small jobs in the vicinity that graduation could be their next big milestone until marriage." She grimaced. "Sort of like me."

He gave a slight smile. "No shame in having a little surprise," he said kindly, and her eyes burned.

"There is a *lot* of story to go with the surprise."

At that moment, they heard Maureen's knock on the door.

"That I would love to hear later," Guthrie told her. "Stay there. I'll answer that."

Maureen came in and handed Olivia her own fast-food bag. "Guthrie, yours is still in the minivan. Berto already took off in the Impala for the old house to get the two dogs, and I was going to load up and take off—"

"All the stuff's in the back of the truck," Guthrie said. "Including a bear-proof food chest with extras. If you want to put the takeout in the front seat, you and me can take it to the site and leave the van for—" He glanced up to where April stood in the doorway, looking, Olivia noted, terrified and just beat. "April," he asked softly, "they've got dogs here. And pillows and blankets. Would you like to stay here and rest while I go check on your brother?"

Olivia watched as Tad Hawkins's sister wiped across her eyes with the back of her hand.

"Don't think I can drive much more," she whispered, and Guthrie nodded.

"Oh, honey," Olivia said, keeping her voice gentle. "Come sit with me and keep me company. Berto's going to be most of an hour, and you look worn out. How about—"

Mau had flat-out disappeared, and she came back with some blankets and pillows, and Olivia was warmed to know how comfortable Aaron's daughter was in their fathers' house.

"I'm sorry," April whispered again, and Maureen dumped the blankets and the pillows and came back with some Kleenex.

"No worries," she whispered in April's ear. "You've had a day, and you're worried and scared, and you don't need anything else that will worry or scare you. You came up here, and your brother will be happy to see you when we get him out of this mess, okay?"

"You'll get him out?" April glanced up at Olivia and then at Maureen like they held the keys to the universe.

"As soon as these guys leave, I'll show you what we're dealing with," Olivia said with a little smile. "I took pictures. You'll see."

"Olivia," Guthrie said with a modest incline of his head, "I look forward to seeing you later. April," he intoned, making sure she met his eyes, "don't go anywhere. I'm not leaving you. Tad's not leaving you. We'll both be back, I swear."

She nodded and smiled, seemingly boosted, and this time when Maureen returned, she had a bag of what was probably a burger and fries for April.

"Berto took his to eat on the way," she said. She gave Olivia a quick hug and whispered, "She's fragile," just barely loud enough for Olivia to hear. Unnecessary, probably, but she also probably knew Olivia would get it. Not everybody got to be a superhero; that didn't mean their worry was any less painful.

"You guys, call, text, teleport—as soon as you have word," Olivia told them. "Me, April, and Berto will hold down the fort, okay?"

And they were already out the door.

Olivia turned toward April and pulled out her phone. "Okay," she said softly, turning a little in the chair while April dug into her food. "I'm going to show you some pictures of where they are and what Larx and Aaron were doing to get them out of this jam…."

April leaned over and saw the picture of the first pulley, and of Larx holding on for dear life as Aaron hauled on the rope to help him up the hill. April held her hand over her mouth and laughed in a shocked way, and Olivia saw some of the exhaustion lift.

Nothing like Olivia's father to give people some hope.

When Morning Breaks

GETTING THE care package was harder than it should have been. The first attempt rained scree and gravel down on their heads because the people on top of the canyon tried to lower it *directly to* the stranded people below, instead of taking the whole operation forty feet to their left.

Larx had been exhausted and out of patience by that time, and Aaron was pretty sure the only reason he hadn't actively ripped faces off from a football field away was that even from down in the canyon they could hear Team Larx ripping whole *heads* off search and rescue people for not bloody listening for the sake of the six-headed fucking lizard gods! (That last curse was definitely Kirby, and Aaron had managed a weary blink and a "Wow" in Larx's direction, and Larx had nodded in agreement. Even Kirby's oaths were impressive.)

From a loudspeaker they heard a very apologetic Yoshi saying, "They've fixed it, Larx. They're very sorry. Kellan may not have to filet them open and eat their livers."

"Missed that one," Larx said, his voice rough, and even Tad chuckled.

"Why livers?" Aaron asked. He'd always wondered. Why hadn't Hannibal Lecter eaten kidneys or hearts or pancreases?

"More iron," Larx replied. Aaron wasn't sure what it meant, but he and Tad giggled anyway.

A few moments later they heard the slither and rattle of debris and saw the spotlight shining on a body-basket being lowered down the hill. Yoshi spoke again. "Haul that over to where you are, and we'll let out some slack to hook the basket up to a pulley up here." He paused. "As soon as it's light. Singh and Baker want to be able to check for breakage on the earth and on the trees. Something about not burying your useless asses under half a mountain. I don't know, I teach English."

Larx and Aaron, giggling helplessly because they were obviously punch drunk with exhaustion, both stood and, after stepping carefully over Tad Hawkins, made their way along the tree, guided by the mini-

Maglite Aaron had managed to bring down the mountain in his utility belt, like Batman.

"Larx," he said quietly as they stepped around a rock that protruded for no good reason at all and narrowly avoided a limb that had somehow survived the tree rolling down hill and then lying out in the elements to rot and/or mummify.

"Yeah?" Larx rasped.

"I will never, ever, ever give you shit about overpreparing again. Ever. Your obsession with first-aid kits and rope saved our fucking lives today."

Larx laughed weakly. "And I will never, ever give you shit about trying to keep me out of danger. I was just driving down here, right? To see what I could do? Fuck me, I didn't mean to make things worse."

Aaron tried to wrap his head around that. "You didn't make things worse," he said. "You brought us *water*." Oh Lord, he needed to rest. His leg was still a holocaust of what even he could tell was beginning infection, and the last twenty hours or so had been grueling.

"Aaron," Larx said, his voice letting Aaron know that he was still nearby.

"Yeah?"

"Stop." *That* came out as a bark, and Aaron paused, his foot up, heart thundering in his ears.

"Look in front of you," Larx whispered, and Aaron's vision adjusted. They were both walking next to the fallen tree, which was probably 200 feet long, end to end. Curtis MacDonald had rolled under the thick end, and they were nearing the thinner end, that had been the top in the tree's life, their shins encountering more and more thin branches. This was the same way Aaron and Tad had come earlier, but far more dangerous and difficult to navigate in the dark. They'd had to pick their way through these branches because the tree was held aloft by the thicker ones. The thin ones were like tiny daggers, waiting to catch their skin.

They were perfect cover for the—oh fuck—was that *three* rattlesnakes camped in a coiled, camouflaged ball practically *under Aaron's foot*?

As he watched, his breath coming in sharp pants, three—*four*—corrugated little tails popped up, and four sets of cold, threatened eyes regarded him from what was less than a stride away. The ominous clicking, nervous as coffee, seemed to echo through the canyon.

"Larx," Aaron said softly, trying not to *vomit* at how close he and Tad had been to this exact spot right before Larx had been shot off the road. "I'm excited to hear some suggestions for this situation."

Larx *hmm*ed. "Take a very slow step back."

Aaron did so, and then took another and drew up even with Larx, the snakes still caught in the beam of the light, not at all reassured.

"And this is it?" Aaron asked. "Backing up? Because food and blankets and medicine are completely the other way, remember?"

"I am aware," Larx said softly, and Aaron felt him rustling, doing something with his body, and when he glanced back, he saw two things.

One was that Larx was shirtless—which was normally a good thing, but not now when the wind was picking up and Larx had put the remains of his Tatooine Desert Vacation shirt on a stick and was holding it out to Aaron.

Aaron stared at him. "And with this I'm supposed to…?"

"Drape it over their nest," Larx said patiently.

"It's not like they can't come out from under it," Aaron told him, thinking the *only* reason he hadn't pissed his own pants was because he was probably dehydrated.

"They're snakes, Aaron. They're shy creatures who bite when somebody steps on them. We put this over their heads and they're safe in their den again—"

"But what if they decide to strike?"

"They'll strike the shirt! It's not a bad shirt, but you know… I've got others." Larx shivered, and Aaron thought yearningly of the basket of supplies not twenty feet beyond the damned snakes.

He wasn't proud of what came out of his mouth next. "Can't I just shoot them?"

"No!" Larx said. Then, "Maybe? I mean, if they suddenly decide to go cruising after curling up to go to sleep? I mean… we still have to cross this way in front of them, so I don't know—*no*. No, we are not just shooting a perfectly innocent nest of rattlesnakes for living their lives. Try the shirt. We can skirt around them."

"Oh, I am not going to sleep tonight," Aaron muttered as he slung the shirt as instructed. "No sleep. Zero sleep."

Larx snorted softly, and together they edged, side by side like crabs doing a line dance, around the tree, leaving the snakes alone. Under

Aaron's light, they could see coiling and uncoiling beneath the shirt, but no escaping. Finally they were far enough away to need to turn to see what was in front of them, and Aaron thought the coiling maybe stilled enough for the snakes to go to sleep.

"What was that for?" Aaron asked as they began their trek again. The basket was not far, only a few strides away, and Larx reached it first.

"What was what for?" Larx asked, squatting down gingerly in the flashlight beam and grabbing the two tow ropes the gang up top had attached. He stood and handed one of them to Aaron, who put the flashlight under his arm and worked the loop on the end until he could sling the thing across his chest. Larx saw what he was doing and mimicked him, and together, they turned toward their little makeshift camp and started to slog. They couldn't hug the tree anymore—snakes—and the going was rougher, the gradient more difficult, particularly as they hauled a sled half full of provisions and blankets.

"That little snort when I said I wouldn't sleep!"

Larx let out a breathless chuckle. His head had to be pounding, but a little rest and he was back in the game—Aaron was so proud of him.

And then he said, "You sleep like the dead."

Aaron was stunned. "I've been a father for twenty-four years!" he protested.

"Caroline changed all the diapers," Larx huffed. "C'mon. You can be honest."

"That is not true." Yeah, he said it with authority, but inside he was struggling to remember. He seemed to recall waking up with kids in his *bed*, often sleeping sprawled out and upside down. Kirby had been a master at that. Caro had called it the "fainting starfish." But he couldn't remember a lot of how they *got* there. "What makes you say that?" he asked.

"I don't know—all the times I've had to poke you awake because you were getting a call," Larx said, laughing.

"At least when I wake up, I wake up," Aaron sulked. "Do you have any idea how insane you are? Sure, you pop up like a jack-in-the-box, but then you run into walls!"

Larx gave a rough chuckle. "Yeah, sure, but that's because I sleep in a state of half panic most of the time."

"You're *not* blaming that on my job," Aaron snapped, and Larx's honest surprise shamed him.

"No, no, whoa there, chief. No. That's a leftover from when my girls were babies. Alicia didn't wake up at all, and she didn't nurse. If they were going to get care at night, it had to be me. I was just, you know, tired. I learned to hit the ground with my feet instead of my brains."

Aaron took a couple of deep breaths, the muscles in his chest, back, and legs straining, and wondered how much of his temper tantrum was defensiveness and how much was exhaustion.

"Sorry," he muttered. "I just… I feel bad. You're taking steps to throttle back on your job—"

"Who told!" Larx asked, and Aaron would have chuckled, but he was saving his energy for not falling down and sliding into the tree and another nest of snakes.

"You did!" He said, not sure if Larx remembered. "Baker. Colin Baker. You told me you were going to let him teach the AP class with you. That's… that's a concession, Larx. And I'm pretty sure it's for us."

Larx took his own deep breath, and together they slogged uphill a few more paces, because the damned snakes were *right there*. "It was," he said, letting out a breath.

They trekked in silence for a moment and Aaron said, "My job is only going to get more intense. It's not fair."

"Yeah, but you know, it's like being principal. I took the job because the other guy was a putz. You're the best bet for the town right now. And… and our lives are like that. We work hard so our world is better. I'm not mad, Aaron. I'm not going to stay at home and bake."

"Thank God. You're going to make me fat enough as it is."

"Har har."

Well, Larx was the one who took him running five mornings a week, so that was fair.

"But," Larx managed, and Aaron saw him almost go down on one knee before fighting his way back up, "I *like* being with you. I want *time* with you. If that means I cut back on my paper load, then I'll do that."

For a few moments they both concentrated on pulling the sled, until Aaron's light picked out Tad Hawkins, head back against the tree, apparently talking softly. As they drew near, they heard him singing, his voice rusty and off-key.

Larx must have recognized the song, because he started to sing too. It was a ridiculously sad Linda Ronstadt number, and Aaron wondered why it seemed to give Hawkins comfort, before he had to concentrate on other things.

The next few minutes were a flurry of welcome activity. First, Larx went straight for the medical supplies and worked on wound care, irrigating Hawkins's wound a few feet away from their huddled spot by Curtis MacDonald so the water wouldn't seep underneath them. While he did that, Aaron talked quietly to Curtis, not sure what he'd get. He did notice that the Gatorade had been opened, and his flashlight picked out a little puddle where Curtis had tried to hold the bottle sideways.

Oh, this was bullshit, Aaron thought. He knew in his head all of the terrible things that happened in an addict's mind as they recovered from their addiction, but Curtis could absolutely positively not afford to still be banana crackers the next morning.

"Curtis," Aaron said, "I need you to turn your head to look at me."

Curtis did, and Aaron spotted the pink place around his mouth where the Gatorade had washed away filth and added a layer of dye.

"Kid, your arm and shoulder are right here." Aaron reached down and poked them. "I'm going to rip your flannel shirt and pop this sedative in your arm, and hopefully, you'll sleep for a bit and wake up not quite such a nutcase, do you hear me?"

"Fucking *rude*," Curtis muttered, and his surliness was actually reassuring.

"Curtis, it is late, we're freezing and hungry and damned tired. Tomorrow, we see if maybe we can get out of here without maybe dying. Leaving you here under this goddamned tree is not an option, so I don't care if it's rude. If you want to help me, you can come out of there and I'll give you the sedative voluntarily. If not, hang out where you are and I'll administer it as best I can, but either way, we're working on getting you out."

When Curtis spoke next, his voice sounded almost sane. "I'm so tired, Deputy George," he muttered. "You want to give me something that'll help me sleep, sure. Go ahead. I… my brain is all fuzz. I…." His voice broke. "Man, I'm so messed up."

Aaron sighed and pulled out his pocketknife before reaching down to saw through the boy's soiled shirts. He wiped good and long with the alcohol wipe before popping the pre-prepped hypodermic needle under the skin and depressing the plunger. "Get some sleep, kid," he murmured. "Maybe you can come out tomorrow."

When he glanced up, Larx was waving him over to the same spot Hawkins had vacated, so Aaron could *finally* get some irrigation on the cut on his calf.

Before that happened, though, they pulled out some clean sweats for Hawkins, who was shivering with fever by now, and then went through the shirts.

"Hey," Aaron said, pulling out a red plaid flannel shirt that didn't look familiar at all. Larx had fixed the flashlight in a splintered hollow of the tree, and Aaron used the beam to examine the shirt. "Where'd this come from?"

"Oh!" Hawkins's voice held a note of… joy? Surprise? Pain?

"What?" Aaron asked as he helped Hawkins slip it on over the shredded black T-shirt that had been new that morning.

"It's… it's mine," Hawkins murmured, hugging the shirt around his chest. "I left it at his place."

Aaron and Larx met eyes, and then Aaron helped Hawkins sit back down on his platform.

"Oh," Aaron said softly.

Hawkins buried his nose in the collar and inhaled, then rested his cheek against his shoulder, the better to smell whoever had been wearing the shirt earlier that day.

"He's here," Hawkins whispered. "He's here."

Aaron felt a solid punch of absolute emotion that he'd been trying to repress since he'd watched the damned Kia upend and slide down the hill.

"Good," he said, choked. He felt Larx's hand on his arm, pulling him to lean against the tree, he thought, but that's not where Larx wanted him. For a moment, in the chill of the black night, Larx wrapped his arms around Aaron and rested his face against his chest.

Aaron pulled him tighter, aware that Larx was whispering something into his shirt. Aaron lowered his face to hear what it was, and realized Larx was repeating what Hawkins had said.

"You're here," he whispered. "You're here. You're here."

"You're here," Aaron returned, running his hands up and down Larx's shirtless back and burying his nose against Larx's sweaty, filthy hair. "You're here."

And that's where they were, embracing, trying to push past the weakness of hope, when the faint sound of a guitar drifted over them.

"I know that song," Aaron murmured.

Larx kissed his mouth and then pulled back. "Sit," he said. And then, as he started to unwrap Aaron's dirty bandage, he and Hawkins began to sing to the lovely old Coldplay hit, something about waiting for your love until the world crashed in.

Aaron shuddered as Larx probed the jagged rip in his flesh, and for a moment, all he could concentrate on was Larx's voice, talking about waiting till kingdom come. The cool saline stung but also felt like a blessing on his heated skin, and the wound felt better after Larx scrubbed at it with some honest to God medical supplies and topped that off with a shot of penicillin. The fresh bandage he wrapped around it was not a hot shower—but it did feel like clean clothes after a long day. Afterward, they both dressed, thank God, because Larx was out-and-out shivering by then, and Aaron wanted to chastise the silly man for waiting to put on a shirt, although he knew—*knew*—Larx hadn't wanted to get any saline or blood on the fresh clothes while he was dressing wounds. Then they gave Tad the food so he could start eating and distributed blankets and some rolled egg crate that Larx should have thrown out the year before. Some more shuffling, and the three of them were sitting on the egg crate, insulated from the cold ground, after having packed their worst blanket in over Curtis MacDonald's exposed side. The poor kid was still breathing, but he hadn't moved. He seemed to be sleeping uneasily, finally. They covered up with the sleeping bags that Olivia—Aaron thought it had to be Olivia—had sent and went digging into the food with Tad.

It was delicious, and they devoured it quickly, leaving Tad sighing. "That was great—what's for dinner?"

Larx laughed softly. "Let it digest. There's sandwich fixings in the bear-proof ice chest, so we're not going hungry tonight."

"It had to be Olivia." Aaron chuckled, feeling fed in more than just body now.

"Who?" Tad asked, yawning. He was leaning against Larx, and Larx was leaning against Aaron. Overhead, from out in the trees, the mystery guitar player was playing a Death Cab for Cutie song, and Aaron wondered if he knew anything happy.

"My oldest," Larx murmured. "The one who packed our stuff. So the guitar player in the trees…."

"Mm…." Tad murmured back, as exhausted as Aaron felt. "Probably donated the plaid shirt." They'd long since shut off the flashlight—and Larx and Aaron had positioned the basket, as well as a couple of tattered beach towels, as a barrier to any snakes who felt like exploring in the morning—but Aaron hoped his young friend was smiling.

"So the music is a gift," Larx said, like that made perfect sense.

"Yeah," Tad sighed. "He's here."

The last notes of the song hung in the air over the valley, and Aaron held Larx as close as possible. Those two words thudded with his heartbeat as he slipped into a worried sleep.

He's here, he's here, he's here.

OLIVIA FELL asleep on the recliner, curled sideways but with her feet still up, Christi's fleece couch throw tucked under her chin. April was asleep on the couch, a shameless Dozer spooning her from the back, long doggy limbs draped over April's back and legs.

Olivia, at least, came to when Elton shook her lightly by the arm. "Babe," he murmured. "Get up. I'll make you some coffee. Go pee and wash your face. Daylight's in an hour."

She stared at him groggily, the whump of yesterday's events trying vainly to smack her in the face. "Babe," she muttered. "You look *awful*." His eyes were hollow and red-rimmed from what had probably been a cold, miserable night, and his hair was greasy and long and pointed in six directions.

Elton laughed manically. "You do too!" he said. "Now come *on*, Livvy—they're lowering people into the canyon and sledding the guys up as soon as it's daylight. I know you want to be there."

"Daddy?" she asked, her voice breaking.

"All reports say they cuddled up and slept," Elton told her gently. "It got cold up there last night. I'm sure the sleeping bags and the egg crate and clothes were welcome." He let out a laugh. "We're not sure what happened to your dad's shirt, but Yoshi was watching them with binoculars as they got their care package, and he said Larx was shirtless by the time he and Aaron started hauling it back to the others. Well done."

"Mm…." Olivia wiped her eyes and her brain started to kick in. "Guthrie?"

Elton's face did something complicated then. "He… did you know he's a musician?"

Olivia nodded. "He told me. Why?"

"He got there and helped where he could, and then when it was obvious all there was to do was go sleep in our cars—and thanks for the blankets and egg crate for his truck by the way, that's where me, Guthrie, and Kirby all slept—he pulled out his guitar. Everyone was settling down. There was a trailer for the search and rescue guys, and they had room for Maureen. Christi and Yoshi slept in Yoshi's car, Kellan got the front seat of Guthrie's truck, and we were just lying there, worried as fuck, and he got up, grabbed his guitar, and sat on the tailgate of his truck, playing." Elton swallowed. "All the lights were off, and we just… just stared at the stars and listened. I swear to God, Livvy, it was the most beautiful thing. I… it was so quiet, I bet they heard him in the canyon."

"I hope so," Olivia said, her own eyes blurring. "Tad will know he was there."

"Oh!" Elton said, laughing. "Mau didn't know who he was to Detective Hawkins. She knew his sister was here—but not who Guthrie was."

Olivia gave her husband a fond look. "Babe, remember when you came up to the middle of nowhere and crashed your car into a tree because your stupid girlfriend disa-fuckin'-peared?"

"It was February, Livvy," he said, pulling her against him. "I remember."

She sighed in his arms. "Same thing. But no car crash, no baby, and a guitar."

He laughed softly. "I get it now." He kissed her temple. "Now go pee, freshen up, and get ready."

"Okay," she said. "Let me wake April up. I'll use the dads' bathroom, and she can use downstairs."

"April's up," grumbled Tad Hawkins's sister. "Although somebody needs to tell me the dog is fixed or we might be expecting puppies. My memories of last night are hazy."

Elton and Olivia burst out laughing.

"Dozer is a gentleman," Elton said, and at the sound of his voice the dog rolled clumsily off the couch, landing on his back. "Come on, boy—let's go pee."

"Wait," Olivia said suddenly. "Where's Berto? He didn't come back last night—I thought he was going to."

"Check your text," Elton said. "He tagged us both, said he'd stay at the house and join us in about—" He checked his watch. "—fifteen minutes. Now *move*."

Olivia managed a fast shower in her fifteen minutes, and she raided Aaron's drawer for clothes—she was way bigger than Larx at this point—and her sister's drawer for a bra and a pair of underwear she could wear under her tummy but would still cover her ass. By the time she emerged, still damp but feeling *much* better about herself, with her hair in a wet messy bun, Berto was there with her favorite muffin from their house, Elton had made three travel mugs of coffee, lots of flavored cream, and she thought she could maybe make it to sunrise without sobbing.

After a few moments greeting the babies—Pomeranians were the *best*, with the massive furriness and their little snaky tongues that said, "I love you! Feed me! Pet me! Cherish me!" in one swipe, she stood and went to grab her purse by the couch and the tatty sweater Berto had grabbed from the hook by their door—and then remembered the three coffee cups.

"Not coming with, Berto?" she asked, turning toward the counter where the other three stood, eating their own muffins. Berto swallowed hard. So many scars—his jaw would forever be crooked, and so would his nose. He'd lost forty percent of his vision, and there was a small flap of scar tissue over the corner of his eye.

"I'm afraid," he confessed, his chest heaving. "God, Livvy, your dads. You… you can't know what they mean to me. I-I know I don't say much, but…." His eyes grew shiny. "Me and Jaime have the best home we've ever had, and part of that's the house, but part of it is…." He pulled in a shaky breath. "Dinners here once a week. Your dad making quiet time for me. Aaron dropping by with groceries. I just…."

She and Elton met eyes, and she got it. "Oh, baby," she murmured, moving into his space. She stood for a moment, hands outspread, asking him for a hug. He gave it to her, shaking against her body, and she rubbed his back. "You'll always be our family," she whispered. "There's no getting rid of us. Have a little faith, okay? They were alive and well last night—did Elton tell you that?"

"He did," Berto whispered. "Gave me hope."

"Then have some more hope," she said. "They're like… like a theme park ride away from going to the hospital, getting checked out, and coming home. You don't have to come to see them. So many people, I get that. But don't lose hope."

"Someone needs to look after the dogs," he said gruffly, stepping back and wiping his eyes.

"I'll tell them," she said, and she glanced at Elton, who nodded. "We'll tell them. We'll tell them you were so worried, and you need them to not ever fucking do this again, okay?"

Berto nodded. "Ever," he added for emphasis.

"Good. You stay here and throw the ball for Dozer. You know, we're going to have to get a new Chuckit. I was looking for the damned thing yesterday and—"

Elton snickered.

"What?" she asked.

"Livvy," he said, still laughing, "how do you think they got the rope up the hill? Did you miss the pictures of Aaron using the Chuckit?"

"Oh my God." She buried her face in her hands. "They *have* to get up here, and they *have* to be okay, because the last twenty-four hours are going down in fucking family legend, and there will be *no* living it down. Aaron won't be able to throw the damned ball without one of us asking him if he's building a pulley system. Larx won't be able to put on new jeans without us asking if they fit as good as paracord underwear. Berto, they are going to be okay. I do *not* see another alternative to this scenario. Elton, are we going now?"

"Yes, my liege," he said, grabbing both their coffees. "Miss April, could you get the door?"

April had watched the whole exchange with amazingly wide gray eyes, and now, for the first time, she smiled. "You bet your ass," she said. "My brother couldn't be in better hands."

"LARX!" YOSHI'S voice was ringing in Larx's head like a cathedral bell—distorted and squeaky, but still ringing. "Larx! *Lyman Larkin,* you lazy sonovabitch, get your ass up and help us out. Monday is still piss-on-your-books day, and if I have to pitch half our staff down this mountain, I'll be *damned* if I run that meeting without you!"

"Yoshi," Larx muttered, assaulted by all things—light, sound, heat, and the sudden need to pee. "Yoshi, would you shut up a minute and let me think?"

"Fine. Now wake Aaron up. We need him more than you anyway."

Larx tried not to let his heart thunder in his ears in panic. He'd gone to sleep with a Tylenol and the hope that his brain wasn't bleeding out. Aaron and Tad had gone to sleep a shot of penicillin away from raging with fever! Larx hadn't slept well—his head hurt too bad, even through the Tylenol, but Aaron was hot and restless behind him.

"Aaron?" Larx muttered, turning in his arms. "Aaron, baby, wake up."

"No," Aaron muttered, burying his face in Larx's neck. "Make Yoshi go away."

Larx gave a strangled laugh. "Baby, the sun is up. It's time for them to save us or bury us in the mountain. C'mon, don't you want to see which way that breaks?"

Aaron grunted and then, slowly, muscle group by muscle group, woke up doing a sitting stretch that ended up with his arms fully extended over his head and his mouth open like a lion's, exposing those wonderful teeth again.

"Wow," Larx said when he was done.

"What?"

"Did you live on candy as a teenager? Those are some *serious* repairs on your back molars."

Aaron gave a reluctant chuckle. "How do you know it wasn't a fight?"

"You don't fight," Larx said disdainfully. "By the way—you work in law enforcement. How hard would it be to put a hit out on my best friend?"

Aaron's bleary blue eyes widened. "What'd he do?"

"Told the whole world my first name."

"Kill him!" Aaron said, no hesitation at all. Then, in all seriousness, "How's our young detective?"

And it was time to wake up the other half of his body. "Tad," Larx muttered, concerned. Tad was throwing off heat, which was nice for keeping warm but not so great for the person with the fever. "Tad… Hawkins?"

Tad's reaction was to shiver. "Hey, Larx," he muttered, and then he coughed, long and painfully, the look on his face telling Larx the shot of penicillin wasn't enough by a mile.

"Okay," Larx said. "Tell Yoshi to get a move on. Hawkins here needs all the things, and I'd really like a shower."

Aaron called out, "Okay, Yoshi, what do we need to do!"

"Get your first transport back to where the sled came down!" Yoshi called out. "We used the last hour to lay some heavy plastic down under the path of the cable. It *should* ease the friction enough to not topple the hillside on you."

Tad coughed again, the sound echoing throughout the little canyon.

"Either way," Aaron said, and Larx nodded.

Either way they were out of time.

They put the egg crate in the bottom of the transport basket, mostly for comfort, and covered Tad with the sleeping bag, and then, sherpa-like, they trekked the thing back to the place it had been sent down, steering a *wide* path around Larx's T-shirt, which may or may not have still been used as a snake tent.

Larx's body hurt *everywhere*, and his head was throbbing, and he wasn't sure he had the strength to do this more than one more time.

But then he remembered. He didn't have to. One more time for Curtis MacDonald, and then it was him and Aaron. That gave him strength. They could do this. They *could* do this.

Above them, there was the whirr of a winch, as the cable began to pick up some slack, and Aaron and Larx positioned the sled on the slope, Tad Hawkins belted solidly inside. Larx triple checked the belts, frightened for how pale the young man was, how vulnerable. They had to make sure he made it to the top.

"No flying," Aaron cautioned. "And no leaving town."

"Roger that, Sheriff George," Hawkins murmured.

Larx leaned closer. "Say hi to Mr. Plaid Shirt Guitar, okay? See if you can get him to hang around and say howdy."

Tad closed his eyes. "I can hope," he whispered.

So Larx and Aaron would hope for him.

"So," Aaron said, backing up and waving to the watchers above them to start the winch. "How do we get Curtis MacDonald over here?" Together they watched as the cable grew taut, straight, much like the pulley with the supplies had. The bottom of the basket was a slick piece of metal, and hopefully not much debris would come in through the mesh sides. Slowly, overcoming inertia, the sled began to move.

Larx and Aaron moved quickly away from the original landing place, skirting widely around the snakes again, and then using their fallen-soldier tree as a guide back to MacDonald, the whole time checking the progress of the sled behind them.

Some debris had been dislodged, yes, but they'd covered Tad's face with a light blanket, hopefully keeping it out of his eyes and mouth.

"Oh God," Aaron muttered, watching as the sled reached the edge of the canyon and was pulled slowly completely vertical. "We tightened those belts, right?"

"Yeah, Aaron," Larx muttered. "Shit, I almost can't watch."

But Tad and the blankets stayed strapped in, and Larx wondered if the egg crate didn't help keep him safe.

"All the padding," Aaron said, watching with his hand over his eyes. "I think we need to remember that."

"Will do," Larx murmured.

"That means you have to go up first," Aaron said soberly, and Larx was about to argue when movement caught his eye.

"Oh shit," Larx muttered, seeing a snake sticking its head out from under his T-shirt and a flickering tongue tasting the air. "Hurry, Aaron, I've got an idea."

They got back to where Curtis MacDonald lay, still hidden under the tree.

"Curtis!" Larx barked, and Aaron jerked back in surprise so his parent/principal voice must have been functioning just fine. "Curtis fucking MacDonald, I need you to wake up right now!"

"Principal Larkin?" MacDonald asked, sounding tearful. "Why you yelling at me?"

"Because, no bullshit, there is a nest of rattlesnakes under this fucking tree and it is *heading your way*!"

Larx and Aaron both stumbled back as a thin, ragged adolescent boy came scrambling out from under the tree, releasing the stench of everything he'd been through into the morning air.

"You'd better not be bullshitting me!" Curtis yelled through yellow teeth. Larx wanted to weep—his one-handsome face was tattered with sores, and he must have lost eighty pounds since January. His clothes were stained with all the bad things, and his skin was yellow under the heavy layer of filth.

"Right there," Larx said, pointing toward the nest of snakes now heading out from the shadows into the sunlight in a businesslike slither. "Do you see them?"

"Holy fuck," Curtis whispered. "Holy Jesus, Mr. Larkin, were they there the whole night?"

"Yup," Larx said, and pointed to the wad of tattered clothes and food bags they'd shoved under the far space beneath the tree. "We blocked their passage as best we could." He took a breath and looked at Curtis wearily. "Boy, you're our next person riding the big train out. Would you like to clean off before you get in the basket?"

Curtis swallowed and nodded. "Yeah, Mr. Larkin. Thank you. Give me a rag and some water and some clothes. I… I can be better than this."

Larx nodded. "I know you can," he said softly.

Curtis needed time—his legs were wobbly after the initial burst of adrenaline, and while he was the one who addressed his privates, using lots of water and some of the medical saline to do it, he needed Larx's help getting into sweats and pulling a clean T-shirt over this emaciated frame.

Still, when Larx and Aaron gathered all the dirty clothes and put them into a plastic bag, and then folded the leftover blankets on top of the bear-proof chest, Larx knew this was his last trip walking that crazy incline, using the fallen tree as a guide.

Finally, they were going home.

CURTIS ALLOWED himself to be meekly packed into the basket and securely belted. He balked when Larx tried to cover his face, but Larx murmured, "Curtis, it gets really scary at the end. Are you sure you're ready for an aerial view of the canyon?"

Curtis whimpered. "I don't want to fly anymore," he whispered.

"Then we'll cover your face, and you can pretend you're at an amusement park," Larx said. "Riding the spinning thing."

Curtis laughed a little. "I might scream," he confessed. He closed his eyes. "Not the worst thing I've ever done."

"Go ahead and scream," Larx told him. "And then when it's over, you can heal."

Yoshi had kept the egg crate in the bottom of the transport basket, but Larx was hoping he'd remove it and burn it after they pulled Curtis up. This time as the basket was sledded up the hill, Larx and Aaron saw more dirt, more debris, falling down from under the tarp than with Hawkins, and Larx threaded his fingers through Aaron's as it made that final, vertical ascension before being hooked—was that *hooked*? Like with a pool cleaner? And pulled back behind the edge where they couldn't see it anymore.

"You know," Larx muttered, staring up at the canyon's edge and trying to figure out what the pulleys were doing there, "there has *got* to be a less terrifying way to pull that thing out of here. I have no idea why they'd do that."

From above their heads, they could hear Curtis MacDonald's weak and broken screams echoing through the canyon.

"That is the creepiest thing I've ever heard," Aaron muttered. "I refuse to scream when it's my turn."

Larx laughed softly and pulled Aaron's battered, bandage-wrapped hands to his mouth, where he kissed them, knuckles, dirt, and all.

"You can do whatever your macho heart desires," Larx said. "You literally pulled us out of perdition. You realize that, right?"

Aaron rolled his eyes and wrapped an arm around Larx's shoulders, and for the first time, Larx felt the bump of Aaron's gun belt against his hip. Had Aaron been wearing that the whole time? But then, he must have. Being the protector, the calm head in charge, was so much a part of Aaron's very being that Larx couldn't imagine him without it.

"If you hadn't pulled your soupy brain back in your ears and used it to think, you and I would still be down with the Kia."

Larx laughed a little, his head throbbing dully, and leaned against Aaron's strength. "I would like very much not to slide into a canyon again," he said decisively. "Can we arrange not to do that?"

"Sure," Aaron told him. "But it would be *great* if we could figure out who was shooting at you—and me—in the first place. I mean, me and Tad winged 'em, but they're still out there."

"Wouldn't they have to get treated for a gunshot wound?" Larx asked. "I mean, we were down there, but you know, Tad's detective partner and that nice Lieutenant Johnson—they had to be working with your guys. What… what do you think is waiting for us after we get looked at and… ugh. Bathed." Just *looking* at the state of Curtis MacDonald's skin, and his hair, and the things *living* in his skin and his hair, had been enough to make Larx need a shower. The boy's shoulder had been bloodied to a pulp but not dislocated—Larx wondered if he hadn't landed on it as he'd fallen—but two nights under the tree hadn't done it any favors either.

As they watched the basket get pulled back off the edge of the canyon, Larx realized he could take a deep breath, at least for the moment. It wasn't that he planned to let Curtis MacDonald flail alone—not after the trouble they'd had finding the boy—but for the moment, somebody else was responsible. Larx was not the only one who cared or the only one looking for him.

Although, a little voice in his head murmured, *somebody* must have known where he was.

Somebody sure hadn't wanted Aaron or Larx to find him, had they?

And the question presented itself, now that they weren't worried about life and death for a moment, who *had* shot at them? Who had put this whole thing in motion, and why?

Larx's head began to pound, and he wished fervently for coffee. Or was it sleep? The night before had been a confused blur of Aaron's steady breathing and Tad's weak coughing, punctuated with Curtis MacDonald's occasional helpless moan. His head had hurt even in sleep, and he still felt bleary, tired, and hungry, even though he and Aaron had already done quite a bit before the sun was fully over the edge of the trees above the canyon.

"Baby," Aaron murmured, "the basket is coming back. It's almost your turn."

"I don't want to do that alley-oop thing at the end," Larx said plaintively. "If I scream like MacDonald, the kids will never let me hear the end of it."

Aaron kissed his temple. "Our kids just moved heaven and earth—quite literally—to save our lives. You can put up with a little bit of razzing if we can get out of this fucking gravel pit and into the real world again, okay?"

Larx swallowed, and they both heard the clatter as the sled slid the last few meters to stop in the not-quite-flat spot that had arrested its progress before.

"You'll… you'll follow me, right?" Larx asked, suddenly afraid.

Aaron's arms tightened around his shoulders. "You followed me down here," he said, laughing slightly. "No reason I can't follow you back."

"I'll hold you to that, Undersheriff."

"I won't let you down, Principal," Aaron returned and then kissed him, hard, unyielding, a true promise that sustained Larx for the last trip to the sled spot. Walking to the basket was the same god-awful slog, muscles screaming over the uneven slope, every footfall a perilous choice between skidding gravel and solid ground.

By the time Aaron helped him into the basket, which smelled like wet metal and antiseptic and had different padding than what they'd sent up, Larx was too tired to argue, his head hurt too much to protest, or even to worry. Aaron fastened him in and said, "Towel over the eyes, Larx?"

Larx shook his head. "Just like marriage," he quipped. "Eyes wide open!"

Aaron's throaty laughter was the last thing he heard before the scraping of the bottom of the sled against gravel filled his ears and the shaking of the little life raft in the gravel pit threatened to rattle his teeth from his head.

By the time the sled tilted… tilted… alley—*oop*! Rose vertically, leaving him facing the entire canyon in an unparalleled aerial view—he was numb to fear, numb to danger. All he could think of was a soft bed, clean sheets, relief of pain, and Aaron's hand in his.

The basket was pulled in, tipped up, and then it glided steadily, the trees moving above him until, with a gentle slide, it came to a stop. He lay flat on his back for a moment, looking up at cool, shady pine trees, until an EMT came to unhook his belts.

He was helped to his feet and onto a stretcher, just as an entire battalion of teenagers was loosed upon him.

"Daddy?" Christiana wailed, although her arms were wrapped around his shoulders.

"Dad!" And that was Olivia.

"Larx!" And that was Kirby, Kellan, Maureen, and Jaime, all together, wrapping around the girls.

"Sir," Elton said, somewhere near his ear. He was surrounded, and he was grateful. His eyes watering, his body shaking, he drank in the thought of being out of the damned canyon at last….

"Is Aaron out yet?" he asked.

"Not yet," Kirby murmured. "They're lowering the sled. I-I can't watch.... It was bad enough watching you come up. Jesus. The thing with the pulleys sounded great until we realized what we'd have to do at the end."

Larx laughed, not even able to wrap his brain around "what they'd have to do at the end."

"It's okay, guys," he said, looking around. "You got us out. I mean—*you got us out*. That's amazing!"

"Wasn't just us, Daddy," Christi said seriously. "Uncle Yoshi called in Mr. Singh and Mr. Baker. Mr. Singh saved your lives several times by going, 'No, you can't pull them up here, you'll bring the mountain down on their heads!'"

Larx chuckled weakly and waved to Mandeep, who smiled widely back at him from a few feet away, Colin by his side.

"Uncle Yoshi is the greatest," Larx said gruffly, and Yoshi took his cue.

"Move aside, urchins," he said imperiously, wiggling between the kids. "Bestie coming through!"

Yoshi's embrace was hard and emphatic, and Larx laughed a little.

"Can I stop feeling guilty about you getting shot now?" Yoshi asked, but his eyes were red-rimmed, and Larx cackled.

"Sure. Am I ever going to live this down?" he asked.

"No," Yoshi said. "Not. Ever. Oh my God, the search and rescue people were *losing their minds* when they saw you and Aaron climbing the side of the canyon. And you don't even want to know what your daughter did to get them involved in the first place."

"Olivia?" he asked, and Olivia shrugged, looking suspiciously bland.

"Oh, Daddy," Christi said seriously, "we have *so* much to tell you."

At that moment, somebody gave a whoop! And Larx glanced up in time to see the basket, weighted with Aaron in it, still facing the other way, pulled up until it dangled in the air, and then put on a series of pulleys with makeshift platforms on them, suspended by trees, from the edge of the canyon back to where Larx had been unbelted, about a football field from the alley-oop at the edge.

"Oh my God," he said, staring at the insane collection of cables and pulley wheels and platforms, all connected to a truck with a winch about twenty feet away from where the ambulance was parked. "That's *bananas*. How did this—"

"It was all too dangerous," Yoshi said soberly. "You'd *think* the house would have been built on the granite shelf that holds the rest of the mountain together, but no. Apparently all the hollowing out below it weakened the edge of the canyon. After—"

But Yoshi's next words were drowned out as Aaron was "decanted" and the kids all rushed to embrace *him*. Christi gave Larx one last hug, which he returned, but Olivia lingered.

"Daddy…," she said, her lower lip wobbling.

"Go give Aaron a hero's welcome," he said gently. "He'll… he'll love getting besieged as much as I did."

She wiped her eyes with the back of her hand. "You can't do this again, Daddy," she said seriously. "Elton and I need you. We need you so bad."

She launched herself into his arms, and he held her close, whispering in her hair. He was afraid Elton was going to have to take her, because his head was about to rupture from his shoulders, when the EMT tapped him on the shoulder and she disengaged, Elton at her side.

"Will you and Deputy George be riding in the same unit?" he asked.

Larx closed his eyes. "God yes," he said.

"Good, sir. You're looking really pale. I'd really like you to get checked out at the hospital as soon as possible."

Larx laughed softly, and Yoshi caught his eye. "Do you know," Yoshi said conversationally, "you've got a goose egg on your forehead the size of one of your dog's dumps?"

Larx chuckled weakly, finally feeling like he could close his eyes and lay back against the stretcher pillow. "Yoshi, you little asshole, I will never forgive you."

"But I saved your ass, right?" Yoshi crowed. "Say it, Larx. Say it loud!"

"Not loud!" Larx protested as the EMTs finally belted him in and pulled him up into the bus.

"Oh *now*, when you finally have something good to say about me, you're anti-loud!" Yoshi hollered, and Larx laughed softly.

From far away he could hear Aaron say, "I don't need one of those. Ouch! Okay, fine, you can help me in the—oh. Wow. That's soft. Yeah. Fine. I'll get on the stretcher. Whatever. Where's Larx?"

That last one was plaintive, and Larx closed his eyes against the bright light inside the ambulance.

In a few moments, he heard the thump of the door and the rattle of another stretcher, and then the confined space grew even smaller.

"Larx?" Aaron murmured, and Larx kept his eyes closed, but smiled.

"Right here," he said. "Does this mean we've survived?"

"God, I hope so. I want some goddamned coffee."

"Me too!" Larx murmured, and then he just closed his eyes and floated, content for a little while to let somebody else hold the reins.

White Walls and Clean Sheets

"WHERE'S LARX?" Aaron asked as Maureen popped her head into his room.

"Still getting his head scanned," she replied soberly. "He had a hell of a knock, Dad. They're worried about brain bleeds and the whole nine yards."

Aaron nodded, shaking inside all over again. He'd shoved all that worry behind him when they'd been in the canyon, just like Larx had. It had been absolutely necessary to think of what Larx *could* do as opposed to what might be going on inside him—utilize his function as opposed to stress about potential dysfunction.

But now that Aaron was safe, twenty or so stitches on his leg, wearing a hospital gown over his clean body as they checked his vitals and his bruises—of which there were many from the initial tumble down the hill—as well as administered antibiotics and replenished his fluids with an IV, he could release his full worry about Larx.

"He'll be okay," Maureen murmured, coming to sit next to him and take his hand. She let loose a dry chuckle. "But Olivia made all the teenagers go home and bathe and sleep and eat. She's really something, Dad. That whole 'kid herding' thing that Larx is so good at—he passed that gene down."

Aaron smiled and squeezed the hand in his. "So bright," he said. "Both of them. *All* of you." He shook his head. "I cannot be*lieve* that supercalifragilistic circus ride you put us on to get us the hell out of the canyon."

She shook her head soberly. "Dad, you should hear the city council talking about how to make that safe. They're talking about dynamiting the entire weak ledge, pitching it into the canyon, and setting up a fence. It sounds destructive and awful, but… I mean, I remember Larx talking about long-term eco-damage but I'm starting to think every politician on the planet needs to get stuck in the bottom of that pit for a day before they make policy, you know?"

"I could handle that," Aaron said. "As well as a mandatory day as a substitute teacher in a public-school classroom and a ride-along with a social worker *and* a law enforcement officer." He swallowed, suddenly all of that far, far away. "But that's not what I'm worried about now," he said, shivering a little with fever.

"No," she said. She gave him a broken smile. "And for what it's worth, I'm going to be thinking a little closer to home as well."

He cocked his head. "No Peace Corps?" he said, although he'd suspected. Two days ago—God, was that all?—he'd been thinking that Maureen had the look of someone who needed to talk about something, and he'd worried. She had one more year of education before graduation. It had been going to be the Peace Corps, but now….

"Teaching credential, Dad," she said with a laugh.

He stared at her, thinking about Kirby with his EMT certificate and Kellan joining the police force and… oh my God.

"Have you told Larx?" he asked, his throat aching with laughter and pride.

"I was going to tell him first," she said with a shrug. "He… you know. He inspired me."

Aaron started to laugh softly, squeezing his eyes tight, and that's all he could manage until Chris Castro and Janine Johnson stuck their heads in.

"Sheriff?" Castro said, and Aaron scowled at him.

"You people told me Eamon's okay!" he barked, alarmed, because that had been the *first* thing he'd asked about after they'd been admitted. Well, he may have dozed off in the ambulance a little, because *damn*.

"He is!" Castro said, his hands up.

"And so is Mary Lee," Johnson told him soberly. "And bless you for asking. Larx asked about her too. They're both in the same room right now, because apparently this constitutes a banner fucking day in your tiny hospital and you're running out of room. I understand Eamon's wife and Mary Lee are delighting each other left and right, and may God help us all, so there's that."

Aaron managed a smile. "That's good to know," he said sincerely. "So don't call me Sheriff—"

"Eamon insisted," Detective Castro told him soberly. "Said you were going to take over for him until the election, and as soon as you both had a day or two to sit at a desk, he'd run you through all your paces. But that's not why we're here."

All of the pieces fell into place, or all of the missing pieces showed themselves in minute detail, and Aaron was suddenly all business. It was easier, somehow, to table his worry about Larx and worry about this than it was to think about the terrible, terrible thing his life could be if only the worst ever happened. He glanced at Maureen, who gave a watery smile, then stood and kissed his cheek.

"I'll go see how Larx is doing. And Livvy told me to check on Guthrie and April—"

Aaron frowned at her. "Who?"

"Tad Hawkins's people," she said simply.

Aaron nodded. "That's a good idea," he said. His lips quirked. "Tell him we loved the music, Mau-Mau. It really did help us get through the night."

"Okay, Daddy. Will do."

She left gracefully, and Aaron caught Castro's eye. "Is there an update on Hawkins?" He'd been in surgery getting the bullet removed when Aaron and Larx had been admitted.

Castro sucked air in through his teeth. "He's going into critical care when he gets out of surgery," he said, grimacing. "Infection settled in pretty good there, although they say without you and your principal, he might have been beyond recovery before he came in. But thank you. In fact thank you for taking care of him. I…." Castro grimaced. "He only got his shield last year. I was like, 'Hey, let's go help a friend of mine. It'll be a change of scenery!' And the kid almost got killed on my watch. Not good." He shook his head. "Not good."

"I'm so sorry," Aaron said, remorseful and, worse, angry at himself. "I just wanted to see—"

"About the kid," Castro filled in. "The one who was missing. And you wanted to see the crime scene where Eamon was shot. Good instincts. Both of them. No, don't second-guess yourself. Not your fault someone was hanging out in the trees waiting for his own duck shoot."

And this was the puzzle. "Do we know for *what*?" Aaron asked. "Why would somebody be there? From what Mary Lee said before the shooting started, all the product had been moved already. What were they trying to protect?"

Castro and Johnson looked at each other carefully, and then Johnson said, "Can we pull up a couple of chairs?"

Aaron's eyes widened. "Storytime?"

"Oh yeah," Johnson said. "Storytime."

And what a story it was.

When they were done talking—and Aaron was done asking questions—the pieces fell into place neatly, but the picture they painted was of the ugliest sort.

Billy MacDonald had been the first shooter at the site. Johnson had winged him, and he'd been reported by Auburn Faith for coming in with an untreated gunshot wound to the shoulder. He'd claimed he'd been winged by a hunting buddy—out of season, and far, far away from any good hunting grounds in the first place. Auburn police had him handcuffed to a gurney there, but he wasn't talking, even after Johnson IDed his photo.

Two other people had been wounded when Aaron and Tad had been involved in the shooting in the canyon. Judge Clancy Yarborough had been taken to a hospital after his wife had called an ambulance because her husband had come home bleeding profusely from a wound in his arm. He'd been taken—per his request—to a hospital in Truckee, perhaps because he'd been hoping that nobody would check up on him who would know about the events in Colton. It was as though he didn't know the area *at all*, which was funny because knowing the area and the people who lived there was pretty much what had saved Larx and Aaron's lives.

Percy Hardesty's body had been found dumped on the side of the road by rescue workers heading toward the rescue scene with Larx and Aaron. While half the town and all of their children had been working to pull Larx, Aaron, Curtis, and Tad out of the big gravel pit, not one person—not one—had noticed that Percy Hardesty had been wounded in the shoulder from the front.

And then shot in the head from the back and left to rot in the sun.

"Oh God," Aaron said, feeling a little queasy. "Clancy Yarborough shot Percy in the head?"

Castro nodded slowly. "Well, your forensics team has enlisted El Dorado County's team to help them run ballistics and trace on Clancy's car, but that's our current theory, and Eamon said that was very possible because Percy was tight with your city hall people, and Billy and Percy were related. But he couldn't give us a thing to tie this whole mess together. We, uhm, were hoping you and Larx had some ideas because Colton's DA has disappeared on some sort of unscheduled vacation here, and before Sacramento and Eldorado call in the CBI and the DOJ, we'd really love a few more facts."

Aaron and Larx had spoken softly, as they'd gone about their business, about what Curtis MacDonald had told each of them while underneath that tree.

Aaron took a breath. "What we think—and a lot of this is speculation, mind you, based on what the MacDonald boy told us—is that his father, Billy, had started producing and selling meth. It would be hard for anybody to know this because they live on private property back from the road, with a number of outbuildings. Billy's got a reputation as a hothead with a gun, so it's not like anybody would go looking. We will have to ask Billy MacDonald why he started in the last six months—that we do not know. Percy was in on it."

"You are sure about that?" Castro asked. "I know he's dead, but he's law enforcement, and he's our in to getting Yarborough, so it's important to get this right before we ask another county for a search warrant."

"Curtis told us that he went on Percy's rounds with him, and Percy gave him a taste of 'candy.' Curtis's words because it makes my skin crawl to say it like that. The boy was in a bad place," Aaron admitted. "He'd lost out on a football scholarship that fall because he couldn't stay out of trouble. This is Larx's first year as an administrator. Curtis probably expected a pass because he is"—Aaron remembered the boy's wasted body—"uhm, *was* quite an athlete. So his Uncle Clancy tells him to help his Uncle Percy, and he finds out the hard way that the three of them are dealers, and he gets addicted—and fast."

"I'd want to hide from the world too," Castro admitted.

Aaron sighed. "He idolized his father," he said after a moment. "Every time his father used a bad word—usually a slur—Curtis used it two sentences later. It's a shitty way to abuse your kid, making him grow up into a piece of shit like you are."

Castro grunted. "The kid is still getting treated for whatever he did to his shoulder. It looks like he hit a rock with it as he rolled down the hill."

Aaron nodded. "See, that's what we think this whole thing was about. Clancy Yarborough stalled the search warrant to find Curtis—it's why you all weren't called in until later in the evening two nights ago. I think they were using the extra time not just to find Curtis, but also to move all their product out from under the house."

"In those great tunnels that almost sent the entire road tumbling into the goddamned canyon." Castro shook his head. "My God. I—you wouldn't know this, but Janine and I were both at the canyon site, walking well back from the edge, when search and rescue and your team of geniuses showed up, and all I could think of was, 'Oh shit. I really like these people. My partner's down there, and I'm going to have to live with their skeletons rotting in the sun.'"

Aaron laughed, genuinely tickled. "Obviously our children taught you different."

"Gotta tell you," Castro said, shaking his head in disbelief, "all of Sacramento is *so* impressed."

"I'd be more impressed if we could figure out a way to make it safer," Aaron said. "But right now all I can think of is the controlled avalanche idea. Set some charges, send what's *not* bedrock tumbling into the canyon, and then start to work on the place with edges that won't collapse."

"Better heads than mine to determine," Castro told him, and Aaron found himself yawning. Dammit. "But you're looking tired, and you need to finish this so we can leave you to heal."

"Larx is getting tests done," Aaron said with a sigh.

Castro nodded. "You're worried."

"Yeah." Aaron's smile was brief and taut. "I mean… now that you've seen him in action…."

"I'd be afraid to lose him too," Castro said. He gave a brief glance over his shoulder. "And whatever you said to Hawkins, I need to thank you. He… he refused to talk about his private life. At all. I mean, I *thought* he had a boyfriend, but when Guthrie showed up with Hawkins's sister, he was so panicked. It'll be good for Hawkins to not be afraid of losing his job."

Aaron cleared his throat meaningfully.

Castro narrowed his eyes. "No, you can't have him."

Aaron tilted his head and held up his hands like a begging puppy dog.

"I said no! Now tell us more about MacDonald."

"I'm not going to stop begging," Aaron said, sulking a little.

"Well, that's fine. But right now…."

Aaron sighed and let it slide—for the moment. "So," Aaron continued, "about the night Eamon was shot. I think forensics will find that yes, Percy Hardesty was responsible for *one* of the shots, the one from behind him. As for why Percy didn't *kill* Eamon, I think that was because he knew I'd pull him immediately because I was the undersheriff."

"You did that anyway," Janine said dryly. "It was amazing."

Aaron inclined his head in all modesty. "I was *pissed*. But that was Percy's fault for being an asshole. If he'd just not been an asshole, it would have taken me a whole four or five hours to suspect it was him and not two minutes when I walked into the OR waiting room."

"Don't forget the incompetent part," Johnson told him dryly. "He lucked out because you weren't there the night before. If he'd given you a little bit of respect…." She shook her head, and then they all sobered.

"This might have fallen out very differently. He might not be dead," Aaron murmured. There had been no love lost between Aaron and Percy Hardesty, but the man had been part of his job and his life for six years. Funny how even an enemy could leave a hole. "I'm not going to miss him, but I am going to be wondering who else is gunning for me until I spot the next asshole."

"And that," Castro said, "is what makes a good lawman not dead."

Aaron chuckled dryly and fought against closing his eyes, and Castro cleared his throat.

"So Percy took the first shot—I think you're right, and ballistics will bear that out. Who was the second?"

"Billy MacDonald," Aaron said, feeling certain about this. "He was there to clear out the drug money and the cash, which he did, and I think if we search the tunnels—"

"That's a rough gig," Johnson told him. "They go all over the place, but they're not safe. We may need an ultrasound to map them out."

"Well, use a couple of drug-sniffing dogs," Aaron told her. "But I bet you'll end up at the other meth house. The one closer to town but farther away from the school. I think Billy and Percy had gotten most of the drugs out of there, but Billy saw his son…." Aaron took a deep breath and tried hard not to think about Kirby or Christi or any one of the young people he loved deeply in the kind of shape Curtis must have been that night. "He realized his son was there, and right as the cops were arriving, he hustled Curtis out of the house. And then… I don't know. Something spooked him. Maybe Clancy gave the order to take out Eamon. Something. But Billy pushed Curtis over the edge of the cliff."

"Oh God." Castro looked stunned. "You think… what makes you think that?"

Aaron closed his eyes—but not out of tiredness now. "Because Curtis told us. And then he talked about flying. He was flying, and then he was rolling. Even a junkie knows the difference between flying and falling. When Hawkins and I went over, the lip of the canyon went down under our feet, and the bottom dropped out and we fell. Flying implies somebody pushed him—gave him some air time—and it would be why he landed on his shoulder and not on his ass like the rest of us."

"He tried to kill—"

"No." Aaron shook his head. "If he'd tried to kill him, he would have killed him. I think he was hoping the kid would live. He just wouldn't be *found*, by cops who would listen when he started spouting all this useful information about his father cooking drugs and his Uncle Percy getting him high."

Johnson shuddered. "If my kids went running for the edge of a cliff, I'd throw myself off to keep them from going over," she said. "How could… how could he?"

"Got nothin'," Aaron muttered. "How could he watch his son go south so fast on his own product? I was there at graduation. The man… he was *sure* Curtis was moving on to a future, but… but he'd killed the kid's future pretty much the day he was born."

It was senseless and stupid. Aaron thought about Curtis scrambling up from under that tree, shaking, bloody, wasted away, and his pathetic plea to wash before anybody else saw him. He'd wanted to disappear. His own father had tried to destroy him, and Curtis had wanted to hide under the tree until the darkness took him. Aaron tried to imagine the boy's grief when that didn't happen, and his heart stuttered for a moment. Aaron's whole life had been dedicated to his children, and then to his and Larx's children. He'd needed his kids to grow up *okay*. And even though Tiff was being a flaming bitch, she was smart, career driven, and self-sufficient. She may never come to Christmas again, and that would grieve Aaron sorely, but she was living her life, was healthy and alive, and she was *okay*.

The things Billy MacDonald had done to destroy his son nauseated Aaron, and he forced himself to swallow bile, because if he threw up in the hospital, he'd be stuck here for another day, and the town needed him *now*.

"And Clancy?" Castro said.

Aaron blew out a breath. "Well, the DA disappeared, which means I think we need a forensic accountant to go through his finances—and Clancy's too. I would bet that Percy was paying them both off, but again, the timing…. I don't know for what."

"Oh my God, you're dumb," Eamon said, a nurse with a name tag that read Jed pushing him in a wheelchair, an IV attached. Rosie—and Cap'n—were at his side.

Aaron scowled at him, so relieved his eyes burned. "Aren't I supposed to come visit you?" he asked plaintively.

"I got bored waiting," Eamon said gruffly. "Besides, I figure you're having a confab, and the quicker we get this out, the quicker they can go get IA auditors from the CBI to get in here and clean up our little DA and crooked judge problem."

Aaron grunted. "I'm so not excited about dealing with this, you know."

Eamon shrugged with his uninjured side. "I am on some *amazing* drugs right now, so ask me how much I care."

Castro smirked. "So what did Aaron miss?" he asked soberly. "Why did Percy suddenly need to make money to pay off DAs and judges?"

Eamon met Aaron's eyes grimly. "To keep Aaron from becoming sheriff," he said softly, and Aaron's eyebrows went up.

"You mean… all *this* was to oppose my run for sheriff?"

Eamon nodded, looking unbearably sad. "That good ole straight white penis network," he said, and Aaron remembered their grim laughter about it just two days before. "I think—and again, we'd have to look into everybody's finances—but I can't think of a single thing Percy could get from Clancy or the DA unless it was backing for a bid for sheriff. The White Heterosexuality platform—for your bigots who want *real* change."

Aaron scrubbed his face. "There you go, Castro," he said, looking from Castro to Johnson. "Now you know what to look for. Now we know why it happened." He leaned back and closed his eyes, wondering if Curtis MacDonald's tree was still open. Aaron could hide down there himself, for a damned sight longer than two days. God, he was tired. He needed a nap. He needed the kids. He needed Larx.

What he did *not* need was this bullshit in his life. Not right now.

"I'll go contact the CBI and the DOJ," Castro said grimly. "And you've got two days to get off your ass and come lead your damned town, Undersheriff, so you get ready."

Aaron scowled at him. "For what?"

"For kicking some ass," Castro told him. "This town pulled off a fucking *miracle*, getting you and your husband out of that gravel pit, getting my partner out, saving that kid. I don't care *who* is out there trying to oppose you on the White Bullshit Straight Penis platform. Undersheriff George, *all* of Sac PD will back your run for sheriff because a man who is respected and beloved as much as you are *needs* to be leading and protecting his town."

Castro and Johnson took a few steps for the door, and then Johnson bumped his elbow. Castro looked at her, and she gestured with her chin meaningfully, and Castro nodded.

"One more thing," Johnson said, smiling wickedly. "When we spoke to the press about you and Mr. Larkin, we said you were married. Because Mr. Nakamoto told me you should be, and you would be this August, and we're all too old to say 'boyfriend.' So I suggest when you two are recovered and shit, you work to put a ring on it. We would like to be invited."

And then they walked out, leaving Aaron laughing helplessly into his hand.

Eamon grunted, probably because there wasn't enough pain medicine to make him feel better. "I like that boy. Too bad he's in Sacramento."

"Wait until you meet Hawkins." Aaron let out a breath. "I'm going to try to poach him from Castro. He can be a wedding present."

Eamon let out a weakened cackle. "See? You're made for politics. You'll do fine."

Aaron peered at his old friend and mentor. "You're not throwing me to the wolves early, are you?"

Eamon opened his mouth. It looked like he was going to say, "Of course not!" but Rosie made a… *meaningful* sound in her throat. A sort of "*Aherm*" mixed with "Eamon, you asshole, don't cave," but ladylike.

"Mm…." Eamon hedged. "You know, you're going to be ready for duty *much* earlier than I will. How about I do the paperwork, you do the fieldwork?"

Aaron smiled a little because that was what he'd assumed would happen, but… but this made it real. The one grown-up in the room was leaving, and Aaron would be running the circus alone.

"I *really* need backup," he said nakedly. "Do you think city hall—"

"Will be desperate to keep you now that their judge and DA have proven to be corrupt and facing their own criminal charges?" Eamon said dryly. "Yes. And maybe—*maybe*—if you offer Castro the same package you offer Hawkins, you really can get them both. Castro was my rookie back when I was in SAC PD. His kids are grown. Last one moves on to college this year, I think. I would bet his wife would be happy to relocate if Chris gets fewer hours and a little less danger than he does down in the city."

Aaron stared at him. "We're in the hospital, Eamon. We're living proof of what?"

Eamon cackled again. "Say what you want, George—at least we're alive."

Aaron rolled his eyes, and Rosie nodded to the nurse.

"Aw, Rosie," Eamon complained as Jed started to wheel him back to his own room.

"You said five minutes," she said. "It's been ten. Go rest, Eamon. You and Aaron will have plenty of time to talk later. Besides"—her voice softened—"the boy needs his rest."

Aaron's eyes were closing as she said it, but he wanted to laugh. "The boy." He and Larx would be fifty in what? A year? Two for Larx. But apparently you were *never* the grown-up in the room. The thought was reassuring somehow. *Larx, it's okay if we don't always know what we're doing.*

It allowed him to sleep until Larx's gurney was wheeled in at his side.

THINGS WERE *really* blurry for a while, with too many tests, too many people, and too much noise. When it all cleared, Larx woke up in a darkened room with the feeling that it was somehow the next morning. Olivia was asleep on the gurney next to him, curled into his side like when she'd been a little girl. The baby bump was new, but the exhausted posture was a sad reminder of the year after he'd gotten custody of his kids again and suddenly they could sleep peacefully, without worries of their mother losing her temper in the middle of the night and waking them up to rant at them about their father, who was going to hell.

His head felt better, but he was pretty sure that was the drugs. He vaguely remembered hearing that there had been swelling of the brain, exacerbated by too much activity the day before. So far, it looked like the swelling would be minor—no need to drill a hole in his skull *yet*—but they were keeping him in the quiet and the dark, with very few visitors, for short periods of time only, until the swelling went down.

Larx had begged them for a room with Aaron, and it had been conditional. So he'd expected to find Aaron, still wrestling with the fever of infection, in the bed next to him, but Olivia was a surprise.

"Hey, pumpkin," he mumbled, and she opened her wide dark eyes as she smiled.

"Hey, Daddy," she said softly. "'Bout time."

"Getting lazy," he said. "Whatcha doing?"

"Wanted to update you," she said. "You were out, and they said let you rest, so I copped a nap while you did."

She smiled tiredly, and he smoothed her hair back from her forehead.

"How's the blood pressure?" he asked worriedly.

She grimaced. "Not great," she admitted. "Modified bedrest for a week. Some gentle medication. I may be off my feet until I give birth."

He kissed her forehead. "Enjoy it, honey. You've done a lot of heavy lifting in the last week."

She let out a little laugh that ended on a gasp, and then she was crying against his shoulder. It was a soft cry, not hysterical, but he kissed the top of her head and let her cry. He'd always thought this part of being a woman was not given its due. Women could cry when they were stressed or worried, and usually it left them feeling cleansed and ready to go out and deal with their lives. Men were supposed to suppress that sort of frustration until they hit stuff.

Larx had spent a lot of his adolescence with bruised knuckles and a chip on his shoulder that should have snapped his spine. He wondered sometimes how much sooner he could have cleaned up his act if he'd just curled up in a corner every so often and howled.

The crying jag didn't last long—not like when she'd first come home, her bipolar untreated, her emotions in catastrophic ping-pong—and she breathed out evenly and wiped her eyes on his shoulder.

"Daddy?"

"Yeah?"

"You really need to marry Aaron."

Larx laughed a little. "There's no guarantee weird shit will stop happening to us if I do," he teased.

She gave him a look that said she knew this—she'd accepted it. "No," she agreed. "No guarantees. But that way I can call Aaron my stepdad, and there's no qualifying details. Uncle Yoshi has been talking to reporters left and right, and he keeps saying you're getting married in August. Is he blowing smoke?"

Larx had to chuckle, but softly. He could feel his head straining to ache beyond the painkillers. "No, baby. He and Nancy have been threatening to plan it since February. I just have to give them a green light."

"I'll do leggings and a big gauzy blouse," she decided happily. "That way I can wear it before or after the baby, 'cause I'm supposed to have a dump-truck tummy for a good two months afterward."

"It's not a dump-truck tummy," he chided. "It's a recovery tummy, and you earned it."

"Whatever." She gave a little sigh. "Daddy, I know you need to sleep, but you need to know something."

"Sure, baby."

"Elton and I were *really* worried, you know? 'Cause somehow *we're* going to be in charge of a tiny little person, and what sort of idiot made *that* possible. Not a word," she cautioned, although Larx—who had ended up in the same predicament with Olivia's mother—didn't have a thing to say.

"Go on," he said.

"But these last two days… we… we were a team. Me, Elton, even Maureen and Uncle Yoshi and Berto. And the stupid teenagers too. And I realized that thing you were trying to do when you dragged us up to Colton in the first place, where you wanted to give us safety and a safety net and people to count on. You've done that, Daddy. So… so even if I lose my mind and the meds stop working and you have to lock me in a box and visit me on weekends, my baby is going to be safe. And Elton won't ever be alone raising it. So… so maybe I can worry less about being locked in a box and relax a little about… about being happy." She sniffled, but not from stress. "Elton's a really good man, Daddy."

"I know he is," Larx murmured.

"And he even lets Christi call him Wombat Willie when she's stressed."

"Extra points."

She took a deep breath. "It's not wrong to be happy, right? Because we have people to help, and we're… we're going to have our own little crazy person that we can love and let the family make even weirder than we are. We can be happy, right?"

Larx's eyes filled up, and he wasn't sure if it was the concussion or the pain meds or just the realization that men could *too* cry, and it was fine. "Please do," he whispered. "And honey, if we ever had to lock you in a box, it would be a really *good* box, and *everybody* would visit until you could come out again. And your baby would know you were a good mother, with a slightly crooked brain, and you'd be able to hug them and love them still."

Another deep breath, this one happy. "Thanks, Daddy. Go back to sleep. You sound tired, and when you and Aaron get out of here, you're going to be *so* busy."

"Tell Christi and the boys and Elton I love them, okay?" he mumbled. "And Jaime and Berto too."

"And me," she said softly.

"And *me*!" Aaron rumbled.

Larx turned his head carefully on his *very* stiff neck. "You heard all that?"

Aaron was on his side, staring hungrily at him, his own eyes red-rimmed. "That Olivia and Elton and their little tadpole are going to be happy?" he asked. "Yes. Go to sleep, Larx. Your herd of cats is all safe now. It's fine."

"Love you," Larx mumbled, and he didn't need to specify. It was all true.

OLIVIA CAME out of the hospital room feeling refreshed and grateful, although part of that was that nobody ambushed her with a wheelchair because now that she'd been forced to sleep for nearly twenty-four hours, she was *over* sitting down. She almost ran into Guthrie, who had slept and showered at Larx and Aaron's house and was, in fact, wearing a pair of Kirby's jeans and one of Larx's Killers T-shirt she rather hoped Guthrie stole because it was getting worn.

"Heya," he said, steadying her elbow. "What are you doing not sitting down?"

"Shh," she murmured, holding her finger to her lips. "I'm escaping to the cafeteria. Wanna come?"

He looked both ways, like they were both in covert ops. "Yeah, let's cheese it—nobody will catch us, see?"

She giggled at his Peter Lorre impression and took his offered arm.

"How's Tad?" she asked as they walked.

Guthrie let out a sigh. "Recovering. He's… he might be here a week or so. April needs to go back to her halfway house—they forgave her because things were dire, but, you know, she needs the structure."

She remembered that conversation, right after Tad had gotten out of surgery. After letting the icy side of his temper loose on someone with an apparent stick up her ass over the phone, Guthrie had revealed quietly that April had been in addiction recovery for a year so far, and that she was having a hard time of it. So much of her addiction had been self-medication. Keeping her routine small and safe, keeping her surroundings peaceful—all of these helped her fight the mental illness that had plagued her since late adolescence. Olivia hadn't been diagnosed until the year before, her sophomore year in college, and she understood the need for order, for structure, for the world not to go banana-crackers-batshit on you on a minute-by-minute basis. She'd been kind to April because that's how her father taught her, but her kindness had apparently earned Guthrie's eternal gratitude.

Olivia had sort of adored him from the moment he'd bowed to her and offered her a hand to get out of the minivan. She could live with his rather melancholy company, and his gently wicked sense of humor.

"So you have to get her back?" Olivia asked. She felt a little wobbly and realized that the cafeteria thing, which had started out being a place to talk, might be a necessity. Elton was supposed to come pick her up in an hour, but she didn't think she could wait that long.

"Oop—you got pale." Guthrie spotted a wheelchair in the hallway, and after signaling a nurse to ask if it was okay, he gestured for her to get in. "Got to take care of yourself, darlin'—those little flipper things suck up a lot of juice."

"I called it the parasite in my uterus for the first four months," she confessed, "but now I'm pretty attached to it. It's… it's a *person* in my heart now, so yeah. Sucks up a lot of juice."

Guthrie's hand on her shoulder told her he got it. She thought of all the friends she'd walked away from in college and how they were all too busy—or their lives were too different now—to text, and wondered if maybe Guthrie could be hers, even if he and Hawkins didn't work out.

"So," she asked, "how about you? And, you know, Detective Hawkins. What's the deal?"

"The deal," Guthrie said softly, "is that he's going home to Sacramento in a week for six week's rehabilitation, and my boss just fired me by text. My apartment in San Rafael has been sublet for the summer, although the couch is a go, and I've got gigs two nights a week in the Bay Area, for the next month. My life is a *mess*, and he…." Guthrie let out a sigh. "He wants me to stay with him in Sacramento. Says it'll give me a chance to find a place."

"But?" Olivia asked softly.

"But six weeks is an awful convenient amount of time to fall stupid in love with someone, don't you think?" Guthrie asked unhappily, taking a turn into the cafeteria. "Here, you sit and I'll go get you a burger."

"That's presumptuous," she chided gently.

"And fries," he said, defending himself with his hands up. His voice rose at the end, and she heard the thread of an accent there—something deep south, maybe. Maybe poor. She would ask him about it.

She reached into her purse and pulled out cash. "I'll split them with you," she said, "but I want my own shake."

"My treat," he told her and turned to go buy her food she knew he couldn't afford.

And stiff-necked pride to boot. After he'd turned, she pulled out her phone and texted Elton.

Having lunch with Guthrie in the cafeteria.

Okay—I'll eat casserole here.

Bring me some, okay? Cafeteria isn't great. Then she paused and thought of her husband, who had dropped her off and then gone to spend time with Berto and Jaime and make sure Yoshi and the teenagers were spending the day in their pajamas, binging *Our Flag Means Death* and *What We Do in the Shadows.*

Elton?

Yes?

You're a prize. You're a fucking trophy husband. Every girl or boy in the world should be looking at you and thinking, "I want me one of those when I settle down." Your heart is so good, and you work so hard at making it better. Thank you for not giving up on me.

The phone rang in her hand and she picked up. Elton's voice on the other end was almost tearful.

"Are you dying? Is Larx? Did a bomb go off? Good God, Livvy, the hell—"

She sputtered laughter and then grabbed a Kleenex because she was crying too. "Pregnancy hormones," she apologized with a clogged throat. "But all true. All of it. I just… I'm watching Guthrie be skittish and afraid and thinking he and Tad have the hardest part in front of them and… and I'm glad I have you. That's all."

"Oh," he said, his voice subsiding. "I'm glad you love me, Livvy. I would have loved you regardless, but you can't imagine how excited I am that you feel the same way."

She laughed helplessly and then saw Guthrie pull out his debit card to pay for their food. "I've got to go, hon. I just… I needed to say I loved you."

"Love you back. I'll be there in an hour. With warmed-up casserole."

"God, that's romantic. Bye."

Guthrie came back with a tray on one hand and his battered wallet in the other. He was trying to jam the wallet back in his pocket, but Olivia grabbed it from his hand and shoved her twenty in it.

"Dammit," he muttered.

"My treat," she said firmly. "Now cut up that burger and dish. I get that I'm inundated with friends and family, but that doesn't mean you don't fill a very important niche. Tell me about Tad Hawkins and Guthrie Woodson, and why you're absolutely sure falling in love would be a total disaster."

Guthrie smiled at her a little, and accepted her money with a sigh.

"Honey, I'm a broke musician. Didn't your father warn you about boys like me?"

"Warn me? He wanted to *be* a broke musician. Didn't you know all girls are looking for a guy like her daddy? You're even gay."

That wrecked him, and he set the tray down and laughed—a lot—but his voice cracked a little at the end, and as *she* divvied up the food, because she really did need it, he told her the ballad of Tad and Guthrie.

When he was done, she wasn't sure if he and Tad would make it—although she hoped so—but she was absolutely, positively sure she'd had a Guthrie-shaped hole in her life and was grateful she had her friend Guthrie to fill it. They exchanged phone numbers then, and life stories, and by the time Elton showed up to get her, she was tired all over again.

But she stood up so Guthrie could hug her, and she sensed a sort of need in him—for touch. For love. For caring. She gave Elton a nod, and he hugged the two of them together, hard, until Guthrie said, "Guys, I'm good now. Thank you."

And then they left.

"You okay?" Elton asked, pushing her wheelchair.

"Elton, want to help me and Yoshi and Yoshi's sister-in-law plan Larx and Aaron's wedding?"

"Yeah," he said, sounding excited. "What's the date?"

"First week in August," she said, feeling confident. "Maybe the second."

"But the baby…." He trailed off uncertainly, as a wise man would when faced with a woman who might or might not weigh forty pounds less than she did now.

"Not our wedding, sweetie," she said happily. "Who cares if I'm wearing a big shirt and leggings or a big shirt and leggings and a baby in a Bjorn? What matters is, my dads are awesome, and they're going to be happy, and they hold this town together, and we're going to throw them a party. You game?"

"You bet," he said happily. "Wedding at Larx's house, swimming reception at Aaron's. Maybe sixty people—"

"That sounds like a lot," she said.

"Honey, they're going to have to invite most of SAC PD, as well as the entire high school staff. That's on the small side."

She laughed. "You're good at this. You and Yoshi will have so much fun."

He hit the doors then, leading to the parking lot, and he paused in the alcove and bent to kiss her cheek. "You didn't want a big wedding," he said softly.

"I'm not a leader of my community," she told him, and then her expression grew sober. "Big or small, I think what matters is the person you're marrying is the right one. That's you. Is that okay?"

"Yeah." He kissed her cheek again and went to fetch the car.

Olivia watched him go and imagined wildflower arbors and chair rentals, tulle ribbons and the sun slanting through the trees, and two men she was proud to call her parents pledging their lives together.

She couldn't wait.

Til Kingdom Come

LARX SPENT his first week back from the hospital in the swimming pool at Aaron's old house because he wasn't allowed to go running, for one, and it was hot as balls for another.

And because Aaron had to work super overtime to get the sheriff's department back in order after all the upheaval it had faced after the incident in Daffodil Canyon, and Larx—who had planned to spend *his* summer vacation gardening and wasn't allowed to do that until he was cleared by his doctor, who kept threatening to make his no-working-or-running-in-the-sun sentence a *month* instead of two weeks if he didn't behave—was sad and bored in his house when he wasn't allowed to do things there to make it a home.

He was limited to an hour of swimming in the morning, before the sun got too intense, and washing dishes. Not even "light housework." He couldn't even cook because apparently chopping vegetables and lifting pots and pans might knock his brain out his ears. He could wash dishes, swim in the morning or evening, and spend his day stretched out on a couch or recliner watching television.

And sulking because Aaron wasn't there.

He tried not to let the sulk show. It just seemed the height of unfairness that Aaron, who had done all the heavy lifting in the canyon, had gotten out of the hospital with a course of antibiotics and three sessions of wound care, while Larx, who had spent most of *his* time lying under a piece of foil and trying to count the stars floating in front of his eyes, was stuck doing… nothing.

Nothing but watch Kirby, Kellan, and Christi vie for use of the cars, start their new jobs, and plan dinner.

They were depressingly good at it. Christiana had even given Larx's "kitchen sink spaghetti sauce" a try, and it had been *delicious*, and had used up a good deal of Larx's tomato crop, and many bags now sat in the freezer because he'd taught his girls not only how to cook, but how to cook *leftovers* that could be microwaved at a moment's notice when things got hectic.

Kirby and Kellan, who both had the metabolism of, well, eighteen-year-old boys, were trying to kill both Larx *and* Aaron with fried potatoes.

If only they weren't delicious as well.

The kids had taken on the responsibilities of home for Larx and Aaron in this last week, and while on the one hand, Larx was inexpressibly proud, he was also… obsolete.

And Aaron wasn't there to jolly him out of obsoleteness because Aaron was *not* obsolete; Aaron was saving the world with a course of antibiotics, a slight limp, and a couple of bandage changes.

Larx had just finished his swim—no flipping at the end of the laps, no bobbing, simply dog paddling back and forth and back and forth because, dammit, everything—and was treading water in the shady end of the pool when he heard the gate squeak.

"I just spent two hours arguing with educated people getting paid less than minimum wage to teach the young how to not piss on their books to mark their territory, and you're pouting in the pool?"

Larx grimaced. They'd been able to put off "scheduling day" until midweek, but in the end, Larx finalized the schedule and sent Yoshi to go have the loud icky meeting with all the teachers who thought he was an attention whore because he'd ended up on the news once again.

"Anything interesting I should know about?" he asked. He could almost fake being injured longer if it meant he could avoid this particular discussion.

Almost.

"Yeah," Yoshi said. He was wearing his board shorts, so apparently he'd changed before he came over, and now he stepped into the pool, wincing a little because it was *cold* in the mornings. "You should know that Curtis MacDonald has been in rehab for a week and is asking for you."

Larx blinked. "Really?" he said. He'd planned to visit the boy—he didn't bullshit about that—but he hadn't thought he'd been welcome. In fact he'd assumed that once the withdrawal shakes and the psychosis had faded, Curtis would remember that Larx and Aaron were the enemies again. Curtis had not been arrested for any crimes. He hadn't been part of the weird unholy syndicate his father and Percy Hardesty had invested in—only sad, addicted, and lost. After being treated for the lacerations and strain of his shoulder, he'd been released for a sixty-day stint in rehabilitation, funded by the Colton County City Hall at Aaron's insistence. For his part, Billy MacDonald had confessed to almost everything, including throwing his son off a cliff to protect the whole enterprise. When that confession had added a second attempted murder charge to his docket, in addition to wounding Detective Hawkins and shooting at both Aaron and the detective from the hillside, he'd been stunned.

Aaron had reported he'd turned pale and said, "But I didn't mean to kill the boy!" while the governor-appointed DA pro tem had simply stared.

The woman had still charged him, because by the six-headed lizard god, somebody had to.

But now Yoshi, who was treading desultorily in the chilly water to keep his body temperature up, shook his head. "No, I know you were out of it when he left the hospital, but I told him I'd remind you when you were better. He had the facility call this morning to see if you could visit. They say he'd love to see you."

Larx, who had been working himself into a good pout about how useless he was at the moment, felt a lightness in his chest at the prospect.

"Jaime's at loose ends today," he said. "Maybe we can drag the kid to Auburn, see Curtis, have lunch, do some shopping, and give Olivia and Elton the house alone." Berto worked for a local delivery company, getting artisan works from their studios to their distributors, the boutiques that lined the main drag of the nearby tourist towns. Summer was tourist season—Berto was busy.

"You do that," Yoshi said, doing some Rocky-style water punches. "I'm in for anything that involves food. You owe me sushi after that mishigas this morning."

Larx laughed and pulled his shivering body out of the pool and into the still-mild sun. "You have to drive, but please, let it be the minivan."

"Fine. Whatever. Go dry off and change. You brought clothes, right?"

Larx laughed a little. He had a beach bag there, but apparently half his and Aaron's sweats had been circulated through Olivia's laundry after the "great clothening," as Olivia called it, when they'd been trying to keep the entire family warm and clothed on Dropoff Drive while they'd been focused on rescuing Larx and Aaron. Larx hadn't missed the fact that his favorite Killer's T-shirt had gone missing, and he hoped Detective Hawkins's skittish young beau appreciated the classics.

Aaron's clothes had all come back to *him*, mostly because he was too big for, say, Christiana to claim his best sweatshirt and say, "Oh, but Daddy, it fits so well!"

The fact was, Larx had needed to show up at the house *without* extra clothes in order to raid Elton and Olivia's laundry basket for some of his own stuff. He wondered if Olivia was glad or sorry to see it go. By all reports, Olivia and Elton had been the glue that held the family together—they'd fed, gathered, and soothed everybody involved in the rescue operation, and the more Larx heard about the breadth and scope of that, the prouder he was. His kids had come through. Not only Olivia and Christiana, but *all* his kids, including Mandeep Singh and Colin Baker, both of whom had been his hires at the high school, neither of whom had expected the job. He'd been grateful for both of them—to the point of offering Colin his AP class and contacting Truckee Junior College to see if they wanted to offer Mandeep extra classes since Larx could only offer him a part-time position at Colton High. They'd been awesome teachers—the kids loved them—and solid allies over the turbulent past year, but he never in his wildest dreams had supposed they'd contribute to saving his life.

And they were quick to point out the contributions that *everybody* made, including Olivia, who had apparently brought search and rescue onboard, although nobody wanted to tell him exactly *how* she'd managed to bypass layers of bureaucracy in a single phone call.

But that hadn't stopped her from being a little extra… clingy? No, that implied she needed *him*. This was more like "hovering." She had become, against all odds, a helicopter adult child, making sure Larx didn't go do anything stupid and/or dangerous during his declining years.

It was one of the reasons she'd been so excited about picking up Larx and Dozer every morning for the last week so they could spend their days out in Olivia's backyard. Dozer swam too—as long as Larx was the one who brushed him at night and cleaned the filter—and at present the dog was lying on the concrete apron, in the shade, pointedly pretending Yoshi hadn't snuck up on both of them and he was still a good watch dog.

"Yeah, I brought clothes. And this way, you can drop me off at the house on the way back, and Aaron can pick the dog up during his morning run tomorrow."

"But doesn't that mean I'll have the minivan for a day?" Yoshi asked, surprised.

Larx grinned. "If you'd pulled up to the *front* of the house like a visitor instead of a pool moocher, you would have seen what happens when your stepdad is running for sheriff and the city council feels a deep sense of shame for supporting two meth-selling bigots and a DA who was corrupt enough to be bought out."

Yoshi grinned. "They got the check? They got a new car?"

Larx held his hand out and wobbled it. "They did get the check—but with the price of vehicles right now, they didn't want to go for a brand-new car. They got a gently used Subaru, with a sterling safety report that Olivia claims drives like a dream. So if you take the minivan, they have an excuse to take the Subaru to get groceries."

"And ignore my shitty Toyota in the side lot," Yoshi said wisely.

"Like you're their moochie Uncle Yoshi who was never even here," Larx agreed.

"Good! My goal in life is to be beloved by your children, who laugh at your crappy taste in T-shirts! Go get dressed, oh mighty one, and I'll be out in twenty minutes."

Yoshi grinned and then flipped into the pool like an otter and started doing laps. Larx regarded him for a moment with deep affection as he swam, graceful and fluid, for once not quirky or sarcastic or clever. Yoshi had been an All-State swimming champion in college, missing the Olympics by a hair's breadth, but he never mentioned that part of his life, or the bitter disappointment that must have come with it. Larx had always known Yoshi had the heart of a hero—it had been there in his every interaction with students and with the tenderness with which he accommodated his partner's need for quiet and solitude. He and Nancy Pavelle had been Larx's first friends coming to Colton, and Larx would always claim the two of them had saved his life in those hard years after he'd first regained custody of the girls.

He'd never expected Yoshi's lionhearted friendship to save his life for real—but he thought that, of everybody, Yoshi had surprised him the least. Larx had known his friend had been brave from the very beginning, because he'd always had the ability to be uniquely himself.

Nobody could argue against who Yoshi *was*, so it was impossible to argue with him when he was *right*.

Larx smiled to himself and went to change clothes, suddenly not pouting or irritated at his limitations. Aaron may have been gone for long hours these days, but when he came home, he came home to Larx, and Larx still had plenty to do in the world, even if gardening and running were out for another week.

It would all be good.

OF COURSE, sitting across from Curtis MacDonald, Larx could see that—for Curtis, at least—it would be a *long* time before things would be good again.

Larx had stopped to buy gum by the bucketload, asking Jaime to find the more popular flavors and brands, and knowing that Curtis's mother hadn't come to visit him yet, nor would his father, probably. He'd also stopped for clothes, estimating his current size from those moments on the canyon slope when Curtis was frantically washing before dressing in Larx's sweats (too short) and Aaron's shirt (too wide).

Again he'd asked Jaime for help, and the boy—who was amazingly observant—had been happy to, even though he hadn't wanted to visit Curtis himself.

"There's no guarantees he's not gonna still hate my little brown ass," he'd said, and Larx had to agree. Whether Curtis was going to use this hardship to change, to improve on himself, or simply to be angrier at the world than he'd ever been, remained to be seen.

Still, Larx entered the home-styled institution with hope. Curtis had asked for him, and here Larx was, keeping his promise. Maybe that could start a little trust.

He followed the attendant's directions to the room Curtis shared with another patient and knocked quietly on the open door. He could see Curtis stretched out on his side, a sling and a brace around his outside shoulder, his body shaking. Larx's heart gave a vicious twist.

Please accept help, Curtis. Please. Please. Please.

Curtis startled at his knock and straightened up, wiping his face with his sleeve before remembering the box of Kleenex next to his bed. “Mr. Larkin?” he said, voice clogged, and Larx gave a gentle smile.

“Is it okay if I come in?”

“Yeah,” Curtis said. Then politely to his roommate, a tall, battered Black man who was obviously recovering from being on the streets for a while, he said, “Rodney? This is my school principal, Mr. Larkin.”

“Heard a lot about you,” Rodney said, sitting up from what looked like a doze and reaching out to shake his hand.

Larx accepted it gratefully. “I’m glad you and Curtis are getting along.”

Rodney gave Curtis a dry glance, and Larx could only imagine their conversations over the last week. “He’s still young,” he said softly. “He’s learning. Being on the junk makes you family—you’re no better than anybody else, waiting for your next hit, right?”

Larx nodded. “It’s a hard lesson,” he said.

“I’ll leave you two alone.”

“Sit?” Curtis begged, almost pitifully.

Larx pulled up a beaten-up polyester-covered chair and handed Curtis a *very* full paper bag. “He seems nice,” Larx said, inviting input.

“He didn’t kill me in my sleep after I dropped the N-word on the first day,” Curtis said grimly. “He’s more than nice—he’s a fuckin’ saint.” Some of his grimness faded. “He’s at the end of ninety days,” Curtis added. “I… we talk,” he said simply. “Like he said, I can’t pretend I don’t share the same experience with everybody here. Acting like I’m better than they are isn’t going to get me where I want to go.”

Larx was on the verge of asking him where he wanted to go when Curtis started digging into the bag, as excited as a kid at Christmas.

“Oh my God—clothes!” Curtis gestured to what he was wearing—scrubs, well laundered—and gave a sigh of relief. “And sweats with no cords like the rulebook says. Thanks, Mr. Larkin. Thank you so much. And the T-shirts are great!” He gave Larx a sideways look. “Who picked them out?”

Larx laughed a little. “Jaime Benitez,” he said. “He and Mr. Nakamoto are out going grocery shopping right now so I don’t have to go later.”

“Jaime…,” Curtis murmured thoughtfully. “Little sp—erm, Mexican?”

Larx understood that he was trying. "Mexican is fine because he and his brother are *from* Mexico. If they were from, you know, Ecuador, Colombia, Nicaragua, then Hispanic would be better."

Curtis let out a long breath. "And either way," he said as if by rote, "it's not the only thing that marks him as a person."

"Have you been getting lessons?" he prodded gently.

Curtis shrugged. "I… my father threw me off a cliff, Mr. Larkin. Not to protect me, but so I wouldn't rat on him and his fishing buddy who were selling meth. My first three days in the hospital, when my shoulder hurt so bad and I could only take ibuprofen, I was an absolute whiny bitch. I was mean to everybody, I swore, I yelled, I spit…."

"Sounds like second period," Larx said dryly, and Curtis broke out of his funk and laughed a little.

"Except I was handcuffed to the bed," he said, shuddering. His eyes went far away. "They didn't know what to charge me with, if anything. It turned out the nicest thing my dad ever did was try to kill me. Did you know that in the end, that's how the DA decided not to press charges?"

Larx shook his head. He'd still been in the hospital, getting his head checked every twelve hours at that point. "I did not," he said. "Sorry. I was, uhm—"

"Still lying in a dark room where only one person could come talk to you," Curtis said. "I know. I begged for you then. Finally Deputy George told me he wasn't going to tell you because right then, I was *bad* for you. And that…." He looked at Larx through tired, red-rimmed hazel eyes. "That was a moment," he said. "I was *bad* for you. You'd been the only person to not give up on me, and I was *bad* for you." He shook his head. "I-I remembered that. When the nurse came in after he yelled at me, it was this tiny little woman. She wasn't white, and at first I was going to say something mean about that, but she was… was all stoic. Her face was expressionless. She looked like she'd been thrown into the shark tank, but, you know, that was her job."

Larx felt a pang of pity for the poor nurse, and Curtis nodded soberly, like this revelation was huge.

"Me. *I* was her job. And she hated me—for good reason—but she was going to help me anyway. And I thought, 'What if that's how Mr. Larkin sees me?' And then…." His voice broke a little. "I swear, I heard *my own voice* in my head. I'd never heard my own voice before. I'd only ever heard my dad's. Uncle Percy's. Never my own."

"What did you say?" Larx asked, although he thought he knew.

Curtis hadn't gotten to the bottom of the paper grocery bag yet, and it sat, unnoticed by his side. "I said, 'Can you blame him, dickwad?'"

Larx snickered. He couldn't help it. And Curtis looked up at him with a crooked smile, showing yellowed teeth.

"Yeah," Curtis murmured, nodding. "I… it got really quiet in my head then. The nurse came in, gave me my meds, checked my bandages, and I just let her. Helped her when I could. Didn't say anything. When she was done, she smiled a killer smile. Like I'd made her day just by not being an asshole. She said, 'Thank you, Mr. MacDonald. I'll see you in a couple hours, okay?'"

"And?" Larx prompted.

"I said, 'Yes. Thank you.' And then she left. And I remembered all those talks you used to give me, about… about being my own black hole. About how *I* needed to let the light in. Nobody could force it for me."

"You were in a lot of pain," Larx acknowledged for him.

"I was," Curtis nodded. Then he did the thing—the one thing—that made Larx think he could make this work. "I still am, Mr. Larkin. Thank you for coming to see me. I'd… I'd love it if you came a few more times too." He looked sadly—and covetously—at the paper sack. "You don't have to bring me presents."

"You say that," Larx chided, "but you haven't even gotten to the rest of it."

Curtis gave him a shy smile, like a child's. He pulled out the gum, smiling widely. "All the super sour flavors," he said, nodding like this was the world's greatest. "Jaime help with this again?"

"Yeah," Larx said. "He sends his regards."

Curtis looked at him hungrily. "We can… we can write letters here. And get them. Can I write him letters? You can read them first, if you want. Make sure I don't fuck up."

Larx thought of how much Jaime hungered to be part of the family, how he longed to have his own place in it, to do his own good deeds. "Can I make him in charge of you?" he asked. "Make sure we hear from you every week? Pass on information? That sort of thing?"

Curtis grinned. "Am I his summer project, Mr. Larkin?"

"If you want to be." Larx would read *every* letter first, but yeah.

"That would be cool," Curtis said, nodding. "I… I really need friends."

"Well, me and Jaime can be your friends," Larx said. "Now look to the bottom."

The bottom had been Yoshi's choice—a collection of books by Gary Paulsen, Michael Grant, Carl Hiaasen, and Lois Lowry—young adult adventure novels, a little below grade level reading but fun and engaging and thoughtful.

"Entertainment," Curtis said, smiling.

"Yessir," Larx told him. "See the first one? *Hatchet*?"

"Yeah." Curtis took a moment and read the back. "That's… that's sort of what *you* did, isn't it, Mr. Larkin? I mean, you had more than a hatchet, obviously, but you took what you had and you…." His voice lowered. "You got me water. I remember that. Water. Blankets. You and Deputy George, you thought for yourselves, and you didn't sit around whining, and you got yourselves out."

"Yeah." Larx shrugged. "And you were a part of that adventure."

Curtis gave him an unfriendly look. "I'm the part that shit my pants when that coffin-basket thingy hung me up so I could stare at the whole wide world under my feet."

Larx frowned, and all he could remember was the basket had a sort of antiseptic smell to it.

Oh.

"The more you know about the whole wide world," he said, "the less it will scare you."

Curtis rolled his eyes. "Fine." Then he looked at the clothes and the gum and the books and he frowned. There was one last thing in the bottom of the bag. He reached in and pulled out a tablet of nice cream-colored paper and a package of envelopes.

"We figured pens were supervised," Larx told him. "But see? We were both thinking great thoughts about letters."

Curtis buried his face in his good shoulder and stayed there for a minute. Finally he wiped his eyes one more time and grabbed a Kleenex for his nose.

"Thanks, Mr. Larkin," he said gruffly. "I… I don't feel so alone now. I waited to have them call Mr. Nakamoto to ask for you until I could, you know. Not be bad for you."

"You did good," Larx said. "You did really good, kid. I'm so proud of you right now."

And Curtis broke. "But what if I fuck up?" he asked, and Larx moved, shoving some of the new things aside to sit next to the boy.

"Oh, Curtis, everybody fucks up. They should have told you by now that it's not a one-shot deal. Progress, not perfection, right?"

"But what if it's like the canyon? You fall and fall and fall, and then every step you take slides you farther back?"

"Can I put my arm around your shoulders?" he asked, wary.

"I wish you would, Mr. Larkin." Curtis hiccupped.

"There we go," Larx said, and Curtis sat stiff at first, but then Larx began to talk. "Curtis, everybody's making a big deal out of me and Aaron and what we did *in* the canyon. Do you remember how we got out?"

"No. Well, the coffin-basket thingy and shitting my pants, but I don't know where it came from." Curtis leaned a little closer, like the little boy he probably had to be right now to clean up to be a solid young man.

"My entire family," Larx said, still awed by this. "As well as Mr. Nakamoto and Mr. Baker and Mr. Singh and the entire South Placer County Search and Rescue Department and the ambulance service and a couple of construction sites all got together with equipment and plans and help to *get* us out. It took physics and communication and connections and practical experience and geology and a thousand other things to get us out of that canyon. Did you see me or Deputy George send any of that back because we didn't think of it first?"

"No," Curtis mumbled, sinking a little further into the hug. His shoulder blades felt pitifully thin under Larx's careful hand.

"Because everybody needs help, just like everybody needs a hug."

And Curtis sagged completely, like a nine-year-old boy with a skinned knee. "The hug is awesome, Mr. Larkin," he confessed. "All that mean shit my dad said about fa—gay people, and… and I'd totally be one if I could only get a hug!" The word was wailed, like a terrible admission, and Larx hoped Billy MacDonald was having a *ball* in prison.

"A hug won't make you gay," Larx murmured, keeping the boy close. "A good hug just makes you feel safe."

"You always made us keep school safe," Curtis mumbled, leaning his head on Larx's shoulder.

"I did. It needs to be safe for everybody."

"Thank you," Curtis said. "For making it safe for me too."

"It's my job," Larx said, wondering if Curtis would laugh at him if he fell into this comfort and napped. Not yet. Like in the canyon, miles to go before he slept.

"You're good at it," Curtis admitted.

"Am I good enough to get you a GED packet so you can graduate from high school?"

Curtis's soggy laughter encouraged him. "You never give up, either."

"Nope." Larx thought about being stuck in the canyon, about hoping for the best from this troubled child, about wanting his girls to be happy, and wanting a happy ever after from Aaron George, the kindest, bravest, strongest man he'd ever known. "Not ever."

"I'm glad."

LARX DID *not* get a nap there in Curtis MacDonald's room. In fact an orderly tapped on the door a few moments after the hug and told Larx his time was up. He left, but not before Curtis stood and gave him one of those hugs from an adult child that only felt awkward because they were bigger than the adult they were hugging, and Larx went outside to meet Yoshi and Jaime.

By the time he got home, his head was aching, and he was exhausted, and he had to admit that maybe—just maybe—the enforced time off was *for a reason.* Yoshi helped him inside with groceries and then offered to take Jaime home so he could care for Dozer. By then, all Larx wanted was to go upstairs and nap in his own bed. He would have said yes to anything, even Yoshi's cooking, but thank all the gods, Yoshi didn't offer.

A few hours after he slid into bed in his T-shirt and briefs, he woke up absolutely sure something was different about the day. He peered out the window, trying to orient himself, and realized the shadows were slanting long and cool, which made it probably six in the evening, and then he felt a familiar warmth at his back and a hand around his middle.

Heard Aaron's breath in his ear.

"Hello," Larx mumbled. "Do I know you?"

"I hope so," Aaron replied, sounding as though he'd napped a little too. "I bribed a bunch of people to go sleep at your oldest daughter's house so we could know each other better."

Larx's eyes flew open, and he reached back and stroked his hand along Aaron's *bare* hip.

"Oh my God," he breathed, not sure this was really happening. "We're going to have *sex*!"

He rolled in Aaron's arms, and there it was, the broad chest he hadn't felt up in nearly two weeks, the glorious blue eyes, the sensual mouth tilting at the corners.

"You say that like we're virgins," Aaron murmured, kissing his ear. Larx tilted his head and *let* Aaron kiss his ear.

"I *missed* you," Larx admitted nakedly. "I-I mean I know we're adults and you have responsibilities and…. I *missed* you. I wanted you *here*. I'm *so glad* you're *here*."

"And *that*," Aaron said definitively, "is why I just bought a shit-ton of pizza and told the entire sheriff's department that unless it involves a shooting or a jackknifed semi, we needed Warren to handle it, because I am *so* glad to be here right back!"

Larx didn't want to hear any more about staffing issues or Aaron borrowing staff from Sacramento or the case or the city council or the judge they needed to replace or—*who cared*? Aaron was *here*, and he was *naked*, and he was stripping Larx's T-shirt off his body and making Larx naked *too*.

And in a moment, that's how they were, kissing and writhing, the loveliness of bare skin all Larx needed to amp his arousal. His entire body felt like it hadn't been touched in *years*, not merely the two or so weeks of recovery and cleanup.

Aaron kissed him delicately at first, but then harder as Larx responded more urgently. Finally he pulled back and said, "Me on my back, you straddling me. Go slow."

Larx panted, his cock aching—*dripping* in fact—and his entire body aroused and needy. "Go slow?" he asked, reaching under the pillow for the lube, thrilled when he realized that nobody had moved it since they'd last done this. "I'm *dying* to sit on your cock, and you want me to *go slow*!"

"Go slow," Aaron repeated, pushing up in bed and curling his body so he could taste Larx's dripping erection. He pulled back before Larx could end their entire endeavor early and said, "Please? For me?" He ran a hand down Larx's hip, teasing Larx's cockhead with his thumb. "No banging your tender brain, okay?"

"Fine," Larx huffed, but then Aaron pulled Larx in for a kiss, his big, capable hand spanning the back of Larx's skull, and Larx felt the care, the protection in that gesture, and melted, conceding.

Anything, *anything*, to have Aaron George in his bed. Larx rolled over on top of Aaron, his big, solid body not yielding beneath him. Their kiss went on until Larx did as ordered and straddled his narrow waist, raising himself up on his knees.

"You'd better not—" Aaron gasped as Larx dribbled lube on his cock from behind Larx's back.

"Forget lube?" Larx laughed, oiling Aaron's cock. Aaron grunted and thrust into Larx's fist slowly until Larx's body started to shake from want. He leaned forward and slid a greased finger into his asshole, shivering a little because it was a tease. He sighed, willing his body to go slack, and when Larx felt his rim give, slick and prepared, he fell forward onto his elbows. "No forgetting," he rasped. "Always ready."

Aaron reached under his thigh and positioned himself, right *there*, and then moved his hand, framing Larx's hips. "Your move," he rumbled, but Larx was way ahead of him.

With a sigh he sat, slowly, sliding down, down, down. Every inch, every *millimeter*, rubbing against his sensitive rim, filling him, hitting the tenderest spots inside.

They both let out gasps when he was fully seated, and Larx put his hands flat against Aaron's chest, flexing his fingers and trembling.

"How you doin'?" Aaron asked, laughing shakily.

"You been doing your crunchies, chief?" Larx asked, needing…. *Needing*.

"Oh yeah."

Larx slid his hands to the mattress, rising up, letting Aaron's cock pulse out of him to the head, and then Aaron tightened his grip on Larx's hips.

And thrust up.

"Oh *yes*!"

Larx's thighs and calves were muscled and developed from running, from swimming, from *life*, and he held his position, hovering above Aaron, while Aaron proceeded to fuck him *blind*.

There were no kids in the house, no dog, and the cats weren't telling any tales. Larx cried out with every thrust, begging, urging Aaron to go faster, harder, *oh my God, Aaron, fuck me there! There! Fucking there!*

Aaron wasn't as loud, his brow furrowed in concentration, face contorted in ecstasy, and Larx could watch him forever. *Oh God, Aaron, I'm yours, I'm yours, I'm yours*… until suddenly he couldn't. In one heart-stopping moment, Larx's head tipped back, and he cried out, his muscles spasming tight, tighter, *tightest*, and then going limp with release. Aaron let go of his hip with one hand and grasped Larx's cock, stroking firmly until Larx's entire body convulsed in orgasm and he spattered come across Aaron's chest.

The white strip of ejaculate across Aaron's muscular body made Larx shiver in aftershock, and Aaron thrust one more time before rearing up, wrapping his arms around Larx's middle, and rutting inside his ass as he came.

Larx wrapped his arms around Aaron's head and held on, still trembling, allowing their sex and their climax to wash over him, enjoying the feeling of Aaron's come as it seeped out.

Finally Aaron fell back against the pillows, and Larx sprawled on top of him, both of them covered in spend and exhausted.

"God, that was glorious," Aaron breathed when they were able. "If we could do that every day, I'd live forever."

Larx chuckled weakly, licking the sweat from Aaron's collarbone. "We'd buy a lot of sheets, my friend."

"So worth it."

"Mm." After a few more breaths, Larx slid to the side, mourning the loss of Aaron's cock from his ass. "God, I love you," he said, needing to say it because the last two weeks had been nuts, and they hadn't touched like this in forever.

Aaron nodded, and closed his eyes. "I love you so much," he murmured. "I…. God, Larx. We *have* to get married. Do you see it? It's imperative. Yoshi and Olivia and Nancy have been planning for the last two weeks. It's August sixth. We'll get fitted suits, take the kids shopping one day for their own clothes. Yoshi and Nancy swear all we have to do is write vows." Aaron's breathless rush stopped, and he gazed at Larx with a plea in his eyes. "All I want to do is say the words," he said, every nanojoule of his Boy Scout integrity warming Larx from the inside out. "I want to tell the world I love you. Tell me that's okay."

Larx felt a laugh bubbling up, and he wondered if the day had been sort of a test from Yoshi. If Larx could survive *this* day, he was ready to help plan his own wedding. Knowing Yoshi, that was probably part of it. Larx's best friend didn't *do* stupid.

"It's okay?" Aaron prodded, as though there'd be any doubt.

"I love you," Larx said happily. "I'm stupid with it. Of course it's okay. I'll give up control of my own wedding to have time to marry you." He paused and cupped Aaron's neck. "I'd be so proud to marry you."

"Me too."

Aaron kissed him then, a sort of long, lingering benediction that didn't turn into sex right away. Instead there was more talking and a quick dinner and something fun on television.

Then there was more sex, more touching, soft gasps in the moonlight streaming from the window they'd opened to let the cool mountain night inside.

They weren't live-or-die moments. They weren't "I'll remember that conversation forever" moments. They were quiet moments, companionable in the best ways, savoring moments of being alone, being intimate with each other's favorite person in the entire world. The sex was physical, but it was only a byproduct of that hushed perfection of two souls mingling in the privacy of their own world.

Sort of like the wedding, which they both planned to enjoy with all their hearts.

Who didn't like a garden party in the summer, and a happy ever after to begin the rest of their lives?

August 6th, a randomly picked day for a wedding that the whole town is attending....

"OH GOD, Dad," Christi muttered as they rushed around the house to get ready. "She's going to pop today, I'm not even kidding." Larx stopped her as she went hurtling toward the stairs, for what, Larx had no idea.

"Christi-lu-lu-belle?" he said deliberately.

"What, Daddy? We're running so late, and—"

"Breathe," he commanded.

Christi nodded and let a soft sigh issue out before pulling more air into her lungs.

"And again," he said. "How we doing?"

"Fine," Christi murmured. "I have Olivia's headdress in my room. I told her I'd keep it for her, just in case."

Just in case Olivia decided to pop that day, as Christi so eloquently put it. The girls—Christi, Olivia, Maureen—were all wearing sundresses that they'd chosen for themselves in a pretty morning-glory pale blue. They had baby's breath crowns with tiny buds of lavender and yellow daisies twined in, and in deference to what promised to be a warm day, were wearing their hair up in easy-care do's at their crowns. Olivia's sundress was really a long, gauzy tunic to froth over her baby belly, with pale green capri leggings, so she looked like, in her words, "a big fat flower." There was a special chair reserved just for Livvy so she could sit down pretty much the minute after everybody lined up at the flower arbor that Yoshi and Nancy had ordered set up in Larx's front yard. It stood in the far end, away from the driveway, backed up against the flowered hedges and Larx's garden boxes so the effect was a ship of flowers in a sea of flowers, and Nancy had almost cried it was so pretty.

Yoshi had taken a picture of her crying on his phone and told her that he was showing this to all her students so they knew she wasn't nearly as mean as she claimed to be, and she threatened to replace all his Hello Kitty stickers with Ninja Turtle stickers. Larx wanted to see the whole thing escalate into the next year—but not until after the wedding.

The icky boys—Kellan, Kirby, Jaime, and Elton—were all wearing pale blue dress shirts with yellow suspenders and lavender bow ties. No suit jackets, nothing irreplaceable, everything suited to spill cake on and then wash afterward because Larx and Aaron weren't stupid.

Yoshi and Eamon were *both* officiating, having *both* been ordained by the internet gods, and they were both wearing suits, much like Larx and Aaron, who had splurged a little on fitted suits that they could wear to board meetings and city hall meetings—and for each other, this day, the day they got married.

There were *eighty* people in their front yard, milling about, finding seats, and one of them caught Kirby's eye as he peered out the kitchen window to make sure everybody was behaving.

"Larx!" he said on a panicked squeak. "Larx, c'mere!"

Larx let Christi scurry like a mouse to her room, saying a silent prayer that the cats—who had all been relocated there so there would be no casualties with all of the cars and the new people—would leave her tea-length dress hem alone, before coming to see what was up.

"Oh!" he said happily. "He came!"

Kirby sent Larx an outraged look. "You invited him?"

Larx sent another glance at Isaiah, Kellan's ex-boyfriend, tall and dignified, moving slowly, with… oh. Another young man at his side.

"Plus one?" he said softly.

"Larx, he'll be crushed," Kirby muttered.

Larx sent Kirby a quick glance, wondering if Kirby had committed his "undeclared" heart to the kid he'd lived with like a brother for much of the last year. But Kirby wasn't looking at Larx. He was looking at Isaiah with something like despair.

"He looks good," Kirby muttered. Well, Zay had always looked good—tall with blond/brown hair and brown eyes, Isaiah had been the stabilizing force that had kept Kellan from imploding during his entire high school career—until Zay had gone away to heal, and Kellan had learned to be his own stabilizing force with the help of Larx and his family.

And Kirby.

"So do you," Larx said, straightening the boy's tie. After an active summer getting his EMT certificate and working part-time at the station, Kirby's hair was just a shade darker than Aaron's, and his eyes were a more thoughtful shade of blue, but he was every inch the solid, dependable force that Aaron George was, with a soft touch of whimsy that had probably come from his mother.

Kirby gave him a lopsided smile. "You have to say that. You're my stepdad now."

Larx snorted. "No. No I don't. It's not in the contract."

Kirby's smile firmed up. "Oh, I beg to differ—Kellan, tell him!"

Kellan—who hadn't seen Isaiah or the handsome young man who stood at his side with a… well, a possessive hand on Isaiah's arm—stared at both of them.

"Tell him what?" he asked.

"Tell him that it's in the contract that he thinks we're handsome young men about town." Kirby threw an arm over Kellan's shoulders and mugged for Larx, who laughed.

"See?" he chided. "Why compel what's absolute truth? Hm?" He grunted and checked his watch. "Okay—where's your father, Kirby? It feels like half the town is out there, and I was pretty sure he was going to settle everyone down before you lemurs went out and entertained people."

Kirby pretended to check his watch, and neither of them were looking when Kellan's eyes fell on the people outside.

"Zay!" he said happily, and then, forced but still happy, "And Aubrey."

Kirby glared. "You knew about the plus one?" he demanded.

Kellan shrugged, and while his chin wobbled—once—he took a deep breath and shored himself up. "I did," he said. "I told Zay it would be all right. Friends, right, Kirby? You can't say you'll be friends with somebody and then get mad because they found somebody else. We… we *both* grew this year. And Zay couldn't do what he was doing—healing in a new city, with new friends—all alone. And I was here—with a new family. I… I'll always care for him," he said, patting Kirby's shoulder. "But I'm loved. Right?"

Kirby nodded, his eyes practically limpid. "Right," he said, his voice a little croaky.

"I'm fine," Kellan said and then glanced around wildly. "Okay, so where'd Jaime go?"

"I'm here!" Jaime called out, running down the stairs. "Berto had to lint roll my trousers," he explained anxiously, and Berto followed him down, shaking his head.

"Dog hair?" Larx asked, as if there'd be any doubt.

"So much dog hair," Berto muttered, shuddering. "It was everywhere. I feel like I breathe it in my sleep."

There was a sudden knock at the door, and Larx started to go answer it, but Christiana got it instead. "Daddy!" she protested, and he wondered if she'd *teleported* to and from her room for the extra headdress. "You can't see him this morning. That's the whole reason he spent the night in his old house!"

That and Larx had lost the coin toss, he wanted to tell her bitterly. Aaron had sworn he'd be bright, early, and awake, if only, please God, please, Larx could supervise the freaked-out teenagers, leaving Aaron to have his prenuptial dinner with a quieter, more sedate Olivia, Elton,

Berto, and Maureen. Since Larx's *specialty* was freaked-out teenagers, Aaron had begged, it only seemed fair.

Christi opened the door, and Nancy Pavelle slipped in, looking lovely and matronly in a flowered summer dress with a few sprigs of baby's breath and lavender in her fancy ponytail.

"Aaron's here," she told him. "So's Olivia and Maureen—they're coming in through the back door, so be ready. You've got about five minutes before Aaron has everyone sit down and the processional is played."

Larx narrowed his eyes. "You still haven't told me what the processional is going to *be*," he said. He'd been promised live music to dance to when the pool party started in the late afternoon, but he had no idea who was singing at his own wedding.

"It'll be perfect," she said, her eyes dancing. "You'll love it. Now line up so when the girls get here, you're ready. Next time I open this door, it's showtime!"

At that moment, the door opened and a very pregnant Olivia waddled in, followed by Elton, looking dapper and proud, and Maureen, who, red hair and all, looked so much like her father that Larx wanted to cry. Their children—their gorgeous, brilliant, kind children. There were no words for his pride that this entire circus and all of the beautiful monkeys in it were his and Aaron's. None at all.

Mau had her flower crown with her, but Christiana ran up to her sister and placed it delicately over her updo, pinning it in with gentle little pushes.

Olivia, who was breathing very deliberately, let loose some tension and smiled at her sister. "Thanks, Squirt," she said, and Christi rolled her eyes.

"What's a best bitch gonna do?" she asked, and she might have kissed her sister's cheek, but they both put their hands up in front of their mouths at the same time, probably remembering they were wearing lipstick.

They lined up—the icky boys first, to stand on Aaron's side, the prissy girls next (Kirby's retaliation for "icky boys"), to stand on Larx's. Olivia was walking her father down the aisle, probably because it would be easier for Larx to help her sit down when they got to the end where everybody stood up, but also, Larx liked to think, because she was his oldest daughter and she loved him, and he was so proud of her.

They had barely gotten into their places, lined pretty much from the front door through the living room, when there was a hard knock at the door and Jaime swung it open. And then the music started.

A solid acoustic guitar played into a mic, followed by a sweet, melancholy voice. Larx didn't recognize the voice—but he *did* recognize the song.

It was the same song that had drifted down to him, Aaron, Tad, and Curtis in the dark of night, as they waited to be rescued in the morning.

It was about a lover who promised to wait forever for his love. Even 'til kingdom come.

"Aw…," Larx whispered to Olivia. "Guthrie?"

She turned shining eyes to him. "Yeah. I told him it was a gig and an excuse to see Tad." Her eyes grew bright. "He wouldn't let me pay him, Daddy. He wanted to sing for your wedding to say thank you."

Larx's eyes burned. Livvy had kept them appraised of the tender, painful courtship of Guthrie and Hawkins, and he was proud to play a part. And God, the song was pretty.

He and Livvy advanced up the line, one foot at a time, until they were standing at his doorstep, ready to step over the threshold in front of his friends and family.

For a moment he scanned the crowd, looking for the people he cared about.

He saw Isaiah and his new beau and was happy—and a little sad as well. He and Aaron had fought for Kellan and Isaiah—they'd had such hopes for the young couple, but like all dreams adults held for young people, those hopes had needed to be tempered by the young people themselves and by what life threw at them all.

He saw Rosie Mills, looking done up and beautiful, gazing at her soon-to-be-retired husband with nothing but pride in her eyes. Yoshi's person, his partner and beloved, Nancy's brother, Tane, was sitting near the back, saving a seat for Berto on one side, with Tad Hawkins's sister, April, on the other. Tad sat next to her, but his eyes were on the young man to the side of the arbor, his hair loose around his shoulders, the guitar in his hands so much a part of him he was almost an alien being, made of music, as he built the chords of the song into that fevered promise, to wait for the love of his life until kingdom come.

Curtis MacDonald, tall and not quite as thin, sat next to Tad, looking honored and lonely but happy too. He wasn't done with rehab yet, but

Larx had petitioned for him to come on a day pass, so Curtis could see there could be better times ahead.

Larx's best teacher friends were sitting in a clump to one side, including Colin Baker, Mandeep Singh, and Harvey Hassbender. And Nancy's husband, who was holding a seat for her once the processional was over and she and Berto could finally close the door and sit down. Aaron's law enforcement friends had their own clump, Chris Castro among them—since he and Tad were coming to work for Aaron in September after the special election—as well as Mary Lee and Janine Johnson, and Janine's wife, who were all a little dewy-eyed, and irritated about it.

Warren Coolidge sat with them, and so did others who had proved themselves able officers and loyal friends in a tough situation, and Larx was glad, because they had Aaron's back and everybody there now knew how important that was.

Yoshi and Eamon stood, both of them in their own best suits, grinning at him from the altar, and there, standing in front of them, looking tall and distinguished and handsome and solid and perfect, was the man Lyman Larkin was about to pledge to have for the rest of his life, above all others, to have and to hold, in sickness and in health, 'til death do they part—and even after that they'd wait for the other 'til kingdom come.

It was as though all the other people faded away for a moment. Larx had no room for anybody else's love life or any concerns about work, which started in two weeks. He had no worries about money or his home or what the kids would do with their lives. He didn't, for a breathless moment, even think of his daughters, one of them beside him, clutching his arm a little hard, her fingers squeezing rhythmically.

There was only this one perfect man and how Larx was going to say things in his heart in front of the whole world, and this opportunity to make an ass of himself was the thing he'd been waiting for all his life.

He and Olivia drew near the altar, and he turned for a moment to help her into the specially prepared "comfy" portable chair so she wouldn't be too pained during the wedding. Her fingers had relaxed on his arm, which was good because he could swear she'd left bruises, and her eyes were far away.

And it hit him.

Christi's words before the wedding.

"Livvy," he whispered in her ear, "you're not going to pop right *now*, are you?"

She grimaced. "They're twelve minutes apart, Daddy. We'll make it through the wedding." She let out a breath, as though letting out the last of the contraction. "The reception, maybe not so much."

He could only stare in horror. "Your timing, girl…."

She put her hands out, palms up, as if to say, *Yeah, so it sucks, and I'm sorry, but what're we gonna do?* "I know it," she said. "Now go. I'm not leaving until Aaron makes an honest man out of you. Make it so." She gestured imperiously, and the rest of the attendees must have seen that, even if they hadn't heard the conversation, because they laughed.

Larx went to stand up in front of Aaron, and his eyes probably spoke volumes because Aaron's expression went from complacent happiness to arched eyebrows of *Are you kidding me?*

Larx nodded grimly, and Aaron sent an exasperated look over his shoulder. Larx glanced back to see Olivia's same shrug, and he sighed.

"Let's get this done," Larx said, "so we can be husbands and then grandpas. You ready?"

Suddenly Aaron's attention was completely on him. "To be your husband?" he said softly. "Oh yeah."

"Me too," Larx murmured. And in that moment, that sublime moment, he was. He and Aaron would be ready, a united front. They would hold hands and march into the sunset with the same determination and humor, the same dedication to kindness and order and the future that they'd shown getting out of Daffodil Canyon—or simply raising their own kids.

They both looked up at Eamon, who was taking them both in with raised eyebrows, and Yoshi, who was shaking his head at Olivia with an *I don't* believe *this!* expression, and smiled.

"Ready, guys?" Larx said.

"You ready?" Yoshi demanded.

Aaron chuckled and took Larx's hands in his own. "Not being ready hasn't stopped either of us before," he murmured. "C'mon, Larx, let's pledge our everlasting love—we've got some living to do."

"Amen," Larx said.

"That's my line," Eamon told them primly, and then he raised himself up to his full impressive height and eyed the wedding guests. "Dearly beloved, for reasons we should have all predicted but which caught us by surprise anyway, we're going to hurry this ceremony up a little. But that's okay. The two men in front of me are so perfect for each other, I'm surprised they didn't wake up married the morning after their first date."

Eamon continued to introduce them, and behind him, Larx heard Olivia's breathing catch, growing a little bit faster as she breathed through a contraction.

He looked at Aaron. "Twelve minutes my *ass*," he mouthed.

Aaron glanced at Eamon, who continued with his invocation. "Don't worry," he said. "We've got time."

Larx relaxed a little and listened as his and Aaron's dearest friends told the world about the best parts of him and Aaron and their family.

Aaron was right. They had a little time. They had *years* together, hand in hand, dealing with children and grandchildren, their jobs, their home, their lives. Riding off into the sunset wasn't one day—even a perfect day—of saying vows and dancing by the pool and celebrating with friends.

Riding into the sunset was a busy life, made up of single days and single moments and perfect kisses—and sloppy kisses and drive-by kisses—but always with the promise that the horizon they were riding toward was one they would reach together.

Yoshi began to speak, and Larx fell into Aaron's eyes, and the world fell away again.

Together, into the sunset, one adventure at a time.

For a love and a family like the one gathered around them, Larx would wait 'til kingdom come.

I was in the middle of writing this book when Mate and I saw the commercial on Hulu. First we spit out our drinks, then we laughed in surprise, and then we looked at each other and said, "Old. We are so old." And because I was in a Larx-and-Aaron state of mind, I guess, I thought I'd have our boys react to modern hygiene protocols and a roomful of teenagers who have absolutely not a fuck to give. Enjoy.

Garden of Delights

"DAD," CHRISTI said, "Where's Aaron?"

Larx was in the recliner, trying hard to stay awake for—what was tonight's selection? Oh Lord, not *Breaking Bad* again. *Please, kids, have mercy on an old man who wants a good guy and a bad guy, just once. Uncomplicated.* NCIS. Magnum PI. *Yeah, I know it's stupid but—*

"What?" Larx asked blearily.

"Where's Dad?" Kirby asked, settling in on the couch with Dozer on his lap—a neat trick for an eighty-pound dog, but Dozer was *really* good at it.

"Popcorn!" Kellan said, settling down on the pillows with a giant bowl. Christi was on the other end of the couch, waving Dozer's tail in her cat's face, and Larx had a moment to think *Hey! It's not* Breaking Bad—because Christi *hated* that show—before the question caught up to him.

"He's still at work," Larx yawned. "He and Eamon caught a burglary—they got the bad guys, but, you know, paperwork." That and Eamon had wanted to talk to Aaron after work. Something about a promotion, which Larx thought would probably lead to Aaron running for the office of sheriff that fall.

"Bummer," Christi said. "Daddy, can you believe Kellan and Kirby haven't seen *ParaNorman* yet?"

"Oh!" Larx lowered the foot of the recliner and reached for his insulated cup of iced soda—somehow adding the ice and putting it in its own cup made the soda more of a ritual, so he only needed one. Or maybe two. But definitely not a six-pack before he fell asleep. "That's too bad," he said, meaning it. "Let's watch it."

"He's just glad we're not watching *Breaking Bad* again," Kirby said, talking to Dozer, who grinned at him adoringly. "Kellan, get up here and share the popcorn."

"Are you going to kick the dog off?" Kellan asked peevishly. "If you don't kick the dog off, I'm not going to fit!"

Christi, ever the peacemaker, got off the couch and called to Dozer for his evening snack. Kellan handed Kirby the popcorn and scrambled up on the couch so when Christi got back they could lie on each other like puppies.

Larx's puppy pile of haiku—he'd never regret going from only his Christi-lu-lu-belle to all three kids. If nothing else, they were *endlessly* entertaining.

When everybody was situated, Christi pressed Play, and it wasn't until the first commercial started that Larx wondered which app they were on. Crap. One of the ones with commercials, dammit.

His eyes began to close again—because he was tired, consarn it all!—when suddenly the context of the ad he was watching hit him.

The ad featured a very good-looking young man with his hair pulled back in a man bun as he showered happily. Then he reached for a… well, it looked like a beard trimmer and, eyebrows raised dubiously, pointed that thing *south*.

"Oh dear God!" Larx gasped, sitting up suddenly and putting his hands out to block the image.

"Daddy, the hell?" Christi asked. "What's wrong with you?"

"That's—that's an *ad*?" he asked, scandalized. "For a *cartoon*?"

"It's just a pube trimmer, Larx," Kellan said, nonplussed. "You know, to keep things from… you know, going wild down there."

"Nobody likes to play on the jungle gym if there's a real jungle around it," Kirby added wisely, and Larx stared at them both.

"Nobody's playing on your jungle gyms anyway!" he managed, stunned.

"Well, no," Kirby said, "but it's always nice to prepare."

As far as Larx knew, Kirby hadn't even declared a sexuality, but as he'd always maintained, that was Kirby's business, not his, unless Kirby asked him for advice. "Do we even *have* one of those things?" he asked.

"*I* do," Christi said, shocking him badly—and he thought his hair was standing on end as it was. "Olivia gave it to me as a secret Christmas gift. It's hanging in our shower."

"Which is how Kirby and I got to try it out," Kellan said, like this was common knowledge.

"Oh my God, *ew*!" Christi shrieked, leaping off the couch *sideways*, over the arm. "You two absolute *stinkers*! You've been using my bush trimmers for your jungle? That's *heinous*!"

Larx was well and truly awake now, his heart pounding in his ears and a flop sweat popping up on his forehead. He did *not* know how to moderate this situation, oh no he did *not*, and he wasn't sure how to bring it up to Aaron, and he—

"Oh, cool your jets, Christi," Kirby said. "I'm blond—my jungle's more of a desert. Your little trimmer barely knew it was in the woods. Now *Kellan*, he's got, like, the Belgian Congo in his shorts. I'm surprised it hasn't gone dull!"

"*Daddy*!" Christiana squealed, and Kellan gave her an apologetic look.

"Sorry, Christi," he said, his face swept red with mortification. "I thought you knew."

"Why would I *know* you were using my pube trimmer?" Christi demanded. She was practically dancing in agitation. "Dad—ee! Get it off, get it off, get it off, get it off! Oh my God, get it off!" and Larx decided to make peace.

"Are these things sold on Amazon?" he asked, grateful for Aaron's contribution to the family finances in recent months.

"Yeah. Want me to send you links?" Christi asked, calming down almost immediately.

"Yeah. I'll… uhm, I'll order three. In different…. Do the boys' ones come in different colors?" God, he was boggled.

"I'll take a girls' one," Kirby said. "Like I said—desert jungle."

"Fair," he said and then waved to the television in desperation. "Movie's back on. Watch."

Christi scowled and sent Kellan and Kirby fulminating glances, but she got back into her spot. They must have all enjoyed the movie after that, because when Larx woke up, the television was off, only one light was on, and Dozer was parked on the couch with his head in Larx's lap. As far as Larx knew, they were both drooling.

Aaron stood next to the recliner, and he was shaking Larx's arm gently. "Baby," he rumbled, "it's time to go to bed. I'm sorry I'm so late."

"What was up?" Larx asked, standing and yawning. He greeted Aaron with a kiss on the cheek—after wiping drool, of course, because he was classy like that—and God, the man looked good. Even tired, in a rumpled uniform with some sort of dinner food stain on the front, Aaron looked good.

"Eamon filed the papers now. I'm officially his appointed undersheriff," Aaron replied, not satisfied with a peck on the cheek. He took Larx into a long, satisfying hug, and Larx almost purred.

Then it hit him. "Undersheriff? That means you're—"

"Second-in-command," Aaron said briefly. "After what happened in February, he wanted to make it very clear that I was in charge if anything happened to *him*, you know?"

"God forbid," Larx murmured, enjoying Aaron's chest and arms and warmth immensely. "Is there any more work, or—" He waved his hand, trying to encapsulate all the… the *stuff* that often went with a promotion, and Aaron chuckled.

"Nope. Same amount of work, but now I get to boss more people around."

"You're good at that," Larx said, pulling back to grin. "Want to boss me around?"

Aaron let out a yawn so wide Larx could see where he'd gotten fillings in his back teeth. "Sure," he said when the yawn finally let go, and Larx laughed softly.

"Go get ready for bed, Undersheriff. I'll let the dog out to pee and lock up."

"D'oh!" Aaron muttered. "I never get to have sex when I'm too tired to have sex."

"Yeah, that's a shame. Now scoot, and I may rub your back while you fall asleep."

"Ooh…," Aaron purred. "There's a reason I love you."

Larx chuckled as he went to let the dog out and do his rounds. By the time he got up to brush his teeth and put on his own T-shirt and sleep pants, Aaron was lying on his stomach, shirtless, his head pillowed in his arms—not quite asleep, but not fighting it either.

Larx climbed into bed and straddled his narrow hips, getting more than a tingle in his parts but knowing Aaron was really beat. Well, grown-ups didn't always get sex—sometimes they got to touch each other and know there was tomorrow.

"So," Aaron murmured, "how was your evening?"

"You saw the end of it," Larx laughed. "I fell asleep in front of *ParaNorman*. Kellan and Kirby seemed to like it, so maybe we can watch it again with you."

Aaron chuckled, and Larx, who was almost falling asleep as he kneaded the heavy muscles in Aaron's shoulders, remembered his rather odd purchases from his phone.

"I bought the kids color-coded pube trimmers," he said, a little dazed by the fact himself.

"You *what*?" Aaron was suddenly shoving up on his elbows, almost bucking Larx off.

"It was so weird," Larx said, letting his confusion show. "Baby, when did it become… mandatory for kids to, you know. Trim their junk jungle?"

Aaron gaped at him. "That doesn't make any sense," he said, and Larx nodded.

"I *know*. I mean, isn't the whole point of pubic hair to look grown-up? I… I… I *like* your jungle!" he said. "It's… you know." He gave a lopsided smile. "This most amazing color of gold."

Aaron blinked at him. "I'm flattered?" he said. "But what about the, uhm, trimmers?"

"Well, Olivia got Christi one, and then the icky boys were using it in the shower, and Christi was jumping up and down going, 'Get it off, get it off, get it off!' and now I know *way too much about our kids' pubic areas, and I can't unhear that conversation*!"

"Oh! Baby!" Aaron rumbled, and he rolled over under the covers. This time, when he wrapped his arms around Larx's shoulders and held him, calming him down, they were in the privacy of their own bedroom. Larx wrapped his legs around Aaron's hips as he sat in his lover's lap and allowed himself to be comforted about the awful perils of knowing too much about their teenagers' personal choices.

"It was awful," he whimpered. "*Kirby's is purple*!"

He wasn't sure where that last bit had come from, but somehow the color coding made it worse.

"There, there," Aaron soothed, and if he'd chuckled, Larx would have walked out on him right then and gone to sleep downstairs. But he sounded just as befuddled—and horrified—as Larx had been, so the comfort was genuine, and so was the warmth. And the narrow hips. And the wide chest.

Larx bucked a little and whimpered and raised his face to Aaron's in mute supplication.

This kiss was in private, in their room, and it may have started out as comfort, but it ended desperate, panting, with both of them shoving off their pajamas and sliding back under the covers skin to skin.

Making love was long, glorious, and perfect—and *theirs*. Aaron topped, sliding inside Larx as they were face-to-face, and Larx watched Aaron's head tilt back and bliss cross his handsome features even as Larx's nerve endings—ass, cock, *all his skin*—was tingling with rapture to come.

They took their time, kissed, and rutted until Aaron's body demanded business and Larx's responded. They buried their cries of climax in each other's shoulders, and Aaron's hips stuttered as Larx spread his legs and lifted his hips and spread himself in absolute abandon.

Finally Aaron collapsed against him, and their breathing returned to normal. Aaron slid to the side and pulled Larx into his arms. They'd turned off the lamp somewhere near the beginning, and in the moonlight coming in through their window, highlighting the chill of the April night sky, Larx saw Aaron's eyes close in acceptance.

"Larx?" he asked quietly.

"Yeah?"

"Once those things arrive?"

"Yeah?"

"We're not asking a single fucking question about them."

"Not one."

"I like your… your jungle."

"I'm rather partial to yours," Larx responded, completely truthful.

"We'll just… you know. Grooming. It's a personal thing."

"One hundred percent," Larx agreed.

"I refuse to wear body spray." Aaron nodded sincerely.

"I am *so glad*." Larx nodded in the same way.

"I… I… I *like* not knowing these things!" Aaron told him, burying his face in Larx's neck in shame.

"Let's call it a pact," Larx said. "You and me, we're going to go obsolete with dignity."

Aaron smiled a little and kissed his temple. "Sex," he said, sounding smug and not defensive anymore, "is *never* going to get obsolete."

Larx chuckled, well and truly comforted. "Amen."

"Love you, Larx. Good night."

"Love you too, Aaron. Good night."

Larx fell asleep in the relative hope that when the Amazon package arrived in two or three days, one of the kids would grab it, and he and Aaron could forget they ever ordered it.

Even a fading memory could be a blessing, if an old guy knew how to apply it.

I waffled over putting this fic at the end of the book.

During the pandemic, when we were all looking for comfort, there was a big question in Romancelandia—do we include the pandemic or do we not? Most people wanted us to not*—they needed comfort and normalcy and please, if we were pretending HEAs happened, let's pretend we'd never seen a mask, okay?*

But my FB group is really active, and I would get questions there about, "Hey, how are Jackson and Ellery doing during the pandemic? What about Ace and Sonny? What about...." And so I started the "Stand By Me" fics on Patreon, named after the John Legend/Sam Smith version of the song. (You can find it on YouTube, and it's beautiful.) The idea of this series was for readers to see that some of their favorite characters made it through the bad times. Nobody wanted to see a new *romance with the IRL horror, but they sure wouldn't mind seeing the people they already cared about being okay.*

It was hard to write in the pandemic timeline—some of the fics got really dark, and I've got to admit, my kids were not doing great during what amounted to two years of on-again-off-again distance learning and masking up. So when it was time to write about Larx and Aaron—who had kids about the same age at the time—their story was painful. When I went to write Sunset, *I thought about putting it in the pandemic timeline, but—and this doesn't happen often—after about twenty pages, I just couldn't. Too close to the bone for me, and, I think, too close to the bone for everybody else. We really do need some happy.*

So this story isn't part of the timeline. It's an alternate world for our characters, but we get to see our beloved family hanging in there, and I thought you all might want to see that.

May we all have our happy.

Amy

And the Moon Is the Only Light

A Larx and Aaron Fic

LARX YAWNED and rubbed his eyes, Yoshi's face blurring on the screen in front of him.

"Everybody's got tablets," he said.

"Yes, Larx," Yoshi replied, also yawning.

"We have the deadlines for assignments up on the school website—all the teachers?"

"Yes, Larx." In the background, Larx saw Tane walking by and squeezing Yoshi's shoulder.

"The home ec teacher has distributed all the masks so we can make home visits and leave masks and food to the families in need?"

Tane popped his thin, weathered face into the frame. "Yes, Larx," he said dutifully. "Look, Principal? I'm not questioning your dedication, but don't you have, I dunno, a fiancé or someone who needs you? This shit will be here in the morning."

Larx nodded and waved. "Hi, Tane. Yeah, but Aaron's out doing a final patrol. He was going to help me pick up the masks and the food for the families in need, and I wanted to make sure he got home okay."

Yoshi grimaced. "What you mean is you can't sleep without him home right now."

Well, yeah. Larx wasn't usually this needy—he really wasn't. But Olivia and her husband had declared their household with the Benitez brothers off-limits. Larx was designated shopper, and once a week he left supplies down by their house, waving to his daughter as she stood on the porch looking exhausted and sad—and increasingly pregnant.

Quarantine wasn't doing anybody's depression any good.

Kellan, Christiana, and Kirby were all doing their best to keep up with their assignments. It helped that Larx was their AP science teacher, and he liked to make videos to both entertain his students and have them do small, safe experiments at home. Anything to keep them from losing themselves in their phones, right? But Kirby's birthday had passed in quarantine, and even though all his friends did one of those drive-bys, Larx could tell that all the things the kids had looked forward to—prom, graduation, SAT tests—had left a void when they'd passed with only the family celebration.

Kellan hadn't been able to visit Isaiah in two months, and while he still wrote letters devotedly, his absolute sadness was weighing on everybody's hearts.

And Aaron was on the front lines every day in a town that saw an increase of domestic abuse when the wrong football team won. His job had been grim too.

So Larx couldn't sleep until Aaron got home.

He'd tried. He and Aaron ran longer and longer around the track, and Larx's garden should have won prizes for *Better Homes and Gardens* by now, but it didn't matter how tired he was in body or soul, he couldn't sleep until Aaron got home.

"Go to bed, Yosh," he said. "I'll—"

Christiana leaned over his back and waved. "Hi, Uncle Yoshi! Hi, Tane! How are you guys doing?"

"Just fine, Christi-belle," Tane said, his face growing slack and soft like it always did when he greeted Larx's youngest daughter. Tane was usually so stoic—Larx wondered if he should look up Tane's sister, Nancy's, photos from when she was in high school. Larx had a suspicion that Christiana probably resembled her in some small way. No matter why, though, watching the effect his Christi-lu-lu-belle had on Yoshi's depression-prone boyfriend was totally worth the fact that she was up way past her bedtime.

Of course by now, the kids were all "Bedtime? The hell is a bedtime?"

"You make any good pottery today?" Christi asked, and Larx was about to scold her, but he heard the hunger in her voice to talk to someone, anyone, outside of their little home circle. Yes, all the kids had phones, but skyping or Messenger got old after a while. He remembered being a kid and all the time he'd spent hanging out in his room with his friends. Even if at the time they hadn't been the best influences, they'd at least been human.

"Yeah," Tane said, smiling a quiet, pleased little smile. "You… you, uh, want to see?"

"Yes! Take us on a tour!"

Tane carefully disconnected Yoshi's laptop, and they were treated to a vertiginous journey across Yoshi and Tane's small house to the attached kiln outside. There, stacked neatly on a shelf, were several graceful vases, coated in glazes so brilliant that each color, from the turquoise to the vermillion to the gold, looked like a person could fall into the vase and come out the other side transformed.

"Oh…," Christi murmured. "Oh, Uncle Tane—those are beautiful. They're…." Her voice caught, grew thick. "Aren't they pretty, Daddy?" And Larx heard the edge of someone whose emotions were rubbed raw, frayed beyond endurance by simple beauty.

"They're lovely," he said, holding her on his lap like he'd done when she was a little girl. She laid her head against his chest, her body shaking with suppressed sobs.

"They're so pretty," she choked. "I'm sorry. I get like this. It's so stupid. It's like I've had PMS for two months and I just… I just can't…." She buried her face in Larx's neck and cried softly, and Larx looked at the screen and shrugged, patting her shoulders.

"Sorry, guys," he said, hoping Tane wouldn't take it personally. He was usually so tight, so emotionally closed off. Larx really didn't want him to blame himself for Christi's fragility.

"No worries," Tane said, and he sounded quiet and wise and calm. "Sweetheart, you go ahead and have a good cry. Sometimes the things that make us cry save our lives, okay? No embarrassment, no worries. You be as sad as you want. Ask me any time and I'll show you my art, okay? Yosh, you make sure she has my number."

Yoshi smiled at his lover with such open adoration that Larx looked away, a little embarrassed. People often wondered about the irrepressible Yoshi and his relationship with someone as damaged as Tane, but the truth was, every time Larx got a peek into how deep Tane's heart was, he thought that maybe Tane was the only person good enough for Larx's best friend.

"We will." He looked back at the screen. "Good night, Larx. Get some sleep. Night, Christi. You feel better, okay?"

She sniffled and nodded, and Larx closed the laptop around her grown body and held her a little longer. When her body started weighing down with sleep, just like it had when she was a little kid, he urged her to bed. She kissed his cheek and wandered away, leaving him drained and exhausted. Kirby and Kellan followed, both of them giving him hugs like little kids did, and Larx returned them, not asking any questions.

Everybody was feeling young and uncertain these days, right? Teenagers were no exception. In fact, they were so easy to reassure, compared to adults. The adults watched the news.

Larx got up and tried not to freak out the dog, who was fast asleep in front of the door where he always was when Aaron worked nights. He checked all the doors, opened a few windows to the chill of the late spring night, and then sat down in front of the television to watch an old sitcom that had a million episodes.

Comfort television was a godsend sometimes.

He wasn't aware of falling asleep, but he must have, because when he came to, a freshly showered and shaved Aaron was kneeling next to the couch.

"C'mon, baby. Bedtime."

"You're all showered?" Larx mumbled.

"Yeah, you know. Clothes in the hamper, body all scrubbed."

Larx gave a tired chuckle. "I'm going to pretend that's all for me," he said, because the cleanliness protocols were exhausting.

"It *is* all for you," Aaron said soberly, and Larx didn't even have to try to take that two ways. It just was.

Larx arched up to kiss him, relief and gratitude coloring every touch.

Aaron took his mouth hard, obviously surprised. Between the kids not sleeping until late and Aaron's brutal work schedule, times to make love had been few and far between. It didn't help that neither of them was in the mood after a particularly trying day, but Larx was… was done. His seventeen-year-old daughter had wept in his arms because something pretty had made her heart hurt, and he was exhausted. He needed tonight.

He just needed.

"Bedroom," Aaron rasped. "Now. Before the kids wake up or you pass out again."

Larx managed a chuckle as he let Aaron help him off the couch. "I was not passed out."

"Snoring," Aaron teased, giving Larx a gentle push to keep him going. "So loud. Like sawing wood. Seriously."

"That is a lie," Larx said loftily. "If that had actually happened, you're highly sensitive dog would have woken up, sure those snores were trying to break in."

"Dozer?" Aaron whispered as they tiptoed up the stairs. "I doubt it! That dog's deaf by now, after listening to you."

"Me? Have you even heard yourself snore?"

Aaron choked on a laugh behind him. "Are you serious about that? You do know that violates the laws of physics, right?"

"Wait until I tape you on my phone," Larx mumbled. "*That'll* violate the laws of physics."

"Hush, you, and get in the bedroom so I can jump your bones."

Larx took the left into their bedroom and started stripping down almost immediately. Aaron closed the door softly behind them and left the light off, then did the same. When they met in the middle of the room again, the lightness and teasing melted into the darkness, leaving them two warm bodies, smooth skin, breathless kisses.

Touch.

Ah! Larx needed to touch him *so bad.* Even if there wouldn't be possession, fucking, orgasm, this here, the feel of Aaron's hands on his skin, seemed to ease the eternal rawness of missing people as a whole. Larx missed his students, his friends, his colleagues—all of the activity he surrounded himself with helped him feel vital and useful, and not having it… oh, it hurt. Aaron's touch was a balm to his wounds, a soothing, calming necessity that would help Larx remember who he was without the business he surrounded himself with every day.

But Aaron's kisses were urgent, needy, demanding, and as Larx answered them, their bodies still upright, their bare flesh touching in as many places as possible, Larx wondered at the things that drove him. Larx needed the sex for the touch, but Aaron seemed to need it for the sex—and lucky them that this one thing could answer both their needs.

Aaron backed him to the bed, and Larx arched his hips on the edge, spreading his thighs and propping his feet so his backside was practically hanging off the edge. They'd gotten a new mattress just before quarantine, and after a week of wondering why they seemed to have forgotten how to fuck, they'd figured out that this way… this way right here… as Aaron slid his cock into Larx's waiting body, was their best—oh God! Was their favorite—oh yes! Was their most wonderful thing!

"Good?" Aaron asked, running his hand over Larx's abdomen, teasing the full and weeping head of his cock as Larx bared himself without fear or reserve.

"So… good…," Larx panted. "Fuck now?"

Aaron chuckled gruffly and pulled his hips back and then snapped them forward again. Larx moaned softly, thinking he'd been wrong. The touch had been nice, but this…. Aaron thrust again, harder, and again, and again, his hips a flurry of rutting that pounded Larx's favorite places. Larx raised his hand to his mouth and bit his palm to keep from crying out, keep from getting loud, and in the soft light from the moon outside, Larx could see Aaron biting his lip for the same reason.

Their household was tight, claustrophobic, the kids crowding them physically and emotionally—but the sex was theirs and theirs alone.

"Ah!" Larx gasped, raising his hips off the super squishy mattress as orgasm threatened. "God… oh my—"

"Shh!" Aaron demanded, and Larx bit his palm again and stroked himself with his other hand as Aaron slowed down, catching the head of his cock right… right at that spot, so sensitive it almost hurt, and… oh God!

Aaron groaned, rutting as he spilled inside Larx's body, and the scald of his come pushed Larx over his own peak.

Oh God. Oh wow. Oh damn. Touch was great but this… oh wow. They *needed* this! Larx shook until he thought he'd shatter, and only Aaron's body, coming down and pressing him into the bed, calmed him down.

And then they were kissing again, glutting on each other's bare skin, Aaron's come trickling down his backside, Larx's legs wrapped around Aaron's waist.

Finally the kissing eased up, and Aaron laid his head on Larx's shoulder as Larx shoved himself backward on the mattress so he didn't throw his back out.

They settled, perpendicular to the mattress itself, and Aaron chuckled. "God, I needed that."

"You think? I might live through another month of this yet."

Aaron shoved up on one elbow and peered at him in the moonlight. "You could live through longer," he said, smoothing Larx's hair back from his brow. "You're so tough. Keeping the school together. Keeping the kids together. Keeping everyone on a schedule, and making sure Olivia is okay even when she's not okay."

Larx swallowed. "Baby, I hate to break it to you, but nobody in this house is okay."

Aaron nodded, then swallowed. "Tonight… it was bad."

"That one house?"

"Wife and kids ended up in the hospital tonight," Aaron said, burying his face against Larx's neck. "God, remember, when you think you're losing it, you're not. You're doing good. You may be sad, but you're not losing it. Okay, baby?"

Larx nodded, and swallowed any other complaints he might have had. Aaron knew—but Aaron was working a frontline job, and Larx could fall apart later. As Aaron told the story, fractured words for a darkened room, Larx knew that the best and bravest thing he could do was give Aaron a shoulder to lean on.

The world needed Aaron right now, and Aaron needed Larx, and sometimes that was the job you had to do.

As Larx held his naked lover to his heart, he could think of no job he'd rather do.

Coming Soon
Torch Songs

Bonfires: Book Four

By Amy Lane

Guthrie's a snakebit musician with a runaway heart. Can Tad convince his wandering minstrel to settle down?

Preorder Now

Award winning author AMY LANE lives in a crumbling crapmansion with a couple of teenagers, a passel of furbabies, and a bemused spouse. She has too damned much yarn, a penchant for action-adventure movies, and a need to know that somewhere in all the pain is a story of Wuv, Twu Wuv, which she continues to believe in to this day! She writes contemporary romance, paranormal romance, urban fantasy, and romantic suspense, teaches the occasional writing class, and likes to pretend her very simple life is as exciting as the lives of the people who live in her head. She'll also tell you that sacrifices, large and small, are worth the urge to write.

Website: www.greenshill.com
Blog: www.writerslane.blogspot.com
Email: amylane@greenshill.com
Facebook: www.facebook.com/amy.lane.167
Twitter: @amymaclane

BONFIRES
AMY LANE

Bonfires: Book One

Ten years ago Sheriff's Deputy Aaron George lost his wife and moved to Colton, hoping growing up in a small town would be better for his children. He's gotten to know his community, including Mr. Larkin, the bouncy, funny science teacher. But when Larx is dragged unwillingly into administration, he stops coaching the track team and starts running alone. Aaron—who thought life began and ended with his kids—is distracted by a glistening chest and a principal running on a dangerous road.

Larx has been living for his kids too—and for his students at Colton High. He's not ready to be charmed by Aaron, but when they start running together, he comes to appreciate the deputy's steadiness, humor, and complete understanding of Larx's priorities. Children first, job second, his own interests a sad last.

It only takes one kiss for two men approaching fifty to start acting like teenagers in love, even amid all the responsibilities they shoulder. Then an act of violence puts their burgeoning relationship on hold. The adult responsibilities they've embraced are now instrumental in keeping their town from exploding. When things come to a head, they realize their newly forged family might be what keeps the world from spinning out of control.

CROCUS

AMY LANE

Bonfires: Book Two

Saying “I love you” doesn’t guarantee peace or a happy ending.

High school principal “Larx” Larkin was pretty sure he’d hit the jackpot when Deputy Sheriff Aaron George moved in with him, merging their two families as seamlessly as the chaos around them could possibly allow.

But when Larx’s pregnant daughter comes home unexpectedly and two of Larx’s students are put in danger, their tentative beginning comes crashing down around their ears.

Larx thought he was okay with the dangers of Aaron’s job, and Aaron thought he was okay with Larx’s daughter—who is not okay—but when their worst fears are almost realized, it puts their hearts and their lives to the test. Larx and Aaron have never wanted anything as badly as they want a life together. Will they be able to make it work when the world is working hard to keep them apart?

COVERT ★ BOOK 1

UNDER COVER

AMY LANE

Covert: Book One

For Judson Crosby, the transfer to the elite law enforcement branch of the SCTF is a great escape from the death sentence he earned as a whistle-blowing patrol officer. Calix Garcia, the fierce new guy, makes a perfect partner, catching bad guys while minimizing collateral damage. Crosby loves working with him.

Of course, he'd also love to work him over in a totally different way.

Garcia has waited his whole career for a solid, dependable partner like Crosby. But after six months fighting crime together, he's done fighting their attraction.

Their coming together promises to be everything they need… until a threat from Crosby's past comes back to haunt not just him, but their entire team.

When Crosby goes undercover to keep them safe, Garcia is frantic with worry. One false move could get Crosby killed and Garcia exposed. But they have to fight their way clear, because hiding your lover under the cover of darkness is no way to live. Crosby and Garcia will risk everything for the chance to live their lives in the light.

A LONG CON ADVENTURE

The Mastermind

AMY LANE

"Delicious fun." – *Booklist*

A Long Con Adventure

Once upon a time in Rome, Felix Salinger got caught picking his first pocket and Danny Mitchell saved his bacon. The two of them were inseparable… until they weren't.

Twenty years after that first meeting, Danny returns to Chicago, the city he shared with Felix and their perfect, secret family, to save him again. Felix's news network—the business that broke them apart—is under fire from an unscrupulous employee pointing the finger at Felix. An official investigation could topple their house of cards. The only way to prove Felix is innocent is to pull off their biggest con yet.

But though Felix still has the gift of grift, his reunion with Danny is bittersweet. Their ten-year separation left holes in their hearts that no amount of stolen property can fill. A green crew of young thieves looks to them for guidance as they negotiate old jewels and new threats to pull off the perfect heist—but the hardest job is proving that love is the only thing of value they've ever had.

SHADES of HENRY
AMY LANE

A Flophouse Story

One bootstrap act of integrity cost Henry Worrall everything—military career, family, and the secret boyfriend who kept Henry trapped for eleven years. Desperate, Henry shows up on his brother's doorstep and is offered a place to live and a job as a handyman in a flophouse for young porn stars.

Lance Luna's past gave him reasons for being in porn, but as he continues his residency at a local hospital, they now feel more like excuses. He's got the money to move out of the flophouse and live his own life—but who needs privacy when you're taking care of a bunch of young men who think working penises make them adults?

Lance worries Henry won't fit in, but Henry's got a soft spot for lost young men and a way of helping them. Just as Lance and Henry find a rhythm as den mothers, a murder and the ghosts of Henry's abusive past intrude. Lance knows Henry's not capable of murder, but is he capable of caring for Lance's heart?

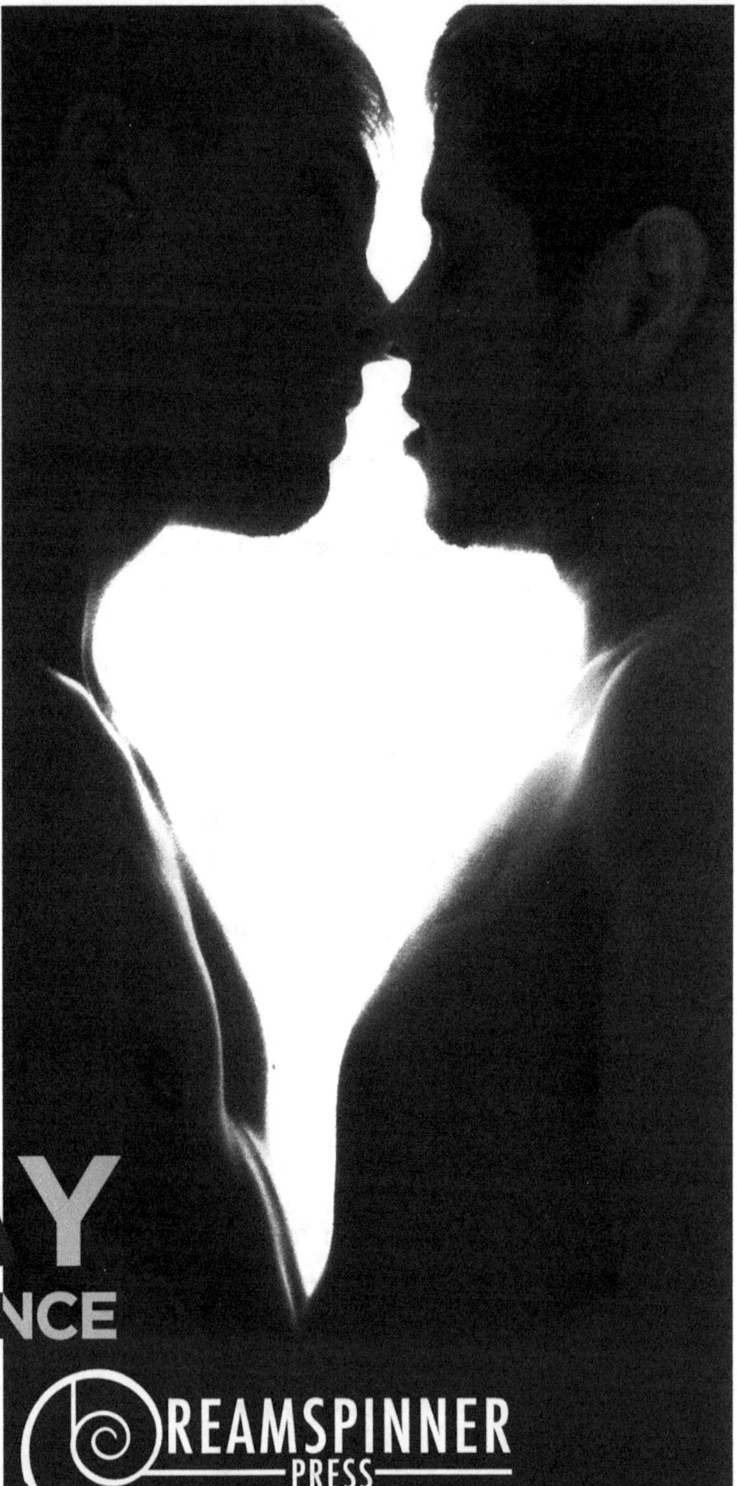

www.ingramcontent.com/pod-product-compliance
Lightning Source LLC
LaVergne TN
LVHW020536100826
845148LV00010B/1493

* 9 7 8 1 6 4 1 0 8 7 2 8 5 *